CURSE & CRAVING

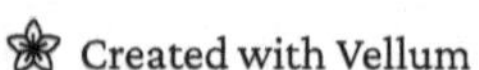

Created with Vellum

<u>BOOKS BY JILL RAMSOWER</u>

THE OF MYTH & MAN SERIES
Curse & Craving
Venom & Vice
Blood & Breath
Siege & Seduction

THE SAVAGE PRIDE DUET
Savage Pride
Silent Prejudice

THE FIVE FAMILIES SERIES
Forever Lies
Never Truth
Blood Always
Where Loyalties Lie
Impossible Odds
Absolute Silence
Perfect Enemies

CURSE & CRAVING

JILL RAMSOWER

To Tyler, Kamryn, and Landon.
You are and always will be my everything.

CHAPTER

ONE

"I've got duct tape, and I'm not afraid to use it. One more word, and you'll be getting on that plane bound and gagged inside a suitcase."

"And if I fight back?"

"I'll *drug* you." The words were drawn out slowly with absolute conviction.

I glared as harshly as I could muster before bursting into a fit of laughter.

My best friend tried to maintain her stern expression but eventually caved with a chuckle. "I'm serious, Becca. No more second-guessing yourself. We are getting on that plane tonight, and you're starting your new life in Ireland."

"Only because you're going with me." I peered at Ashley, sobering. "I'm scared, Ash. This is so far out of my comfort zone."

She joined me on the bed, wrapping her arm around my back and pulling me close. "I know, honey, but you need to do it anyway. This is a once-in-a-lifetime opportunity. Don't let anxiety keep you from achieving your dreams."

I lucked out big time in the best friend department. She drove me a little crazy sometimes, but Ashley Moore was my perfect complement. Where I was timid and conservative, she was bold and dauntless. She kept my life interesting while I kept her out of jail. We were in perfect balance on our friendship seesaw, never allowing one another to hit rock bottom or get thrown off.

"Thanks, Ash. I needed that. I swear I won't freak out once I'm there and settled in."

"Don't make promises you can't keep," she teased with a smirk. "Fortunately, I'll be there with you for the first two weeks, so you have nothing to worry about."

I'd been nervous about telling Ashley about the job offer and certainly hadn't expected her to come with me, but I should have known better. She'd been my biggest cheerleader and insisted I seize the opportunity. Knowing how important this was to me, she planned from day one to use up the last of her vacation days at work to accompany me to Belfast. I was incredibly grateful. Living so far away from her and my parents would be hard, but having her with me while I got adjusted made it all a little less scary. While she would miss me, she wasn't exactly sad to have a reason to travel abroad. It had all worked out perfectly.

So why was a bundle of angry snakes writhing in my belly?

I swallowed and forced a smile. "Absolutely. Nothing to worry about at all."

She laughed and patted my leg. "Exactly. Now help me get this bag packed, or I'll have to wear your clothes on my trip."

Ashley was an expert procrastinator. I'd been packed for a week—created checklists and run through my lists twice over. Ash would be lucky to make it two days in Ireland without needing to shop for something she forgot. Her time management habits, or lack thereof, had been annoying early in our friendship, but I learned to adapt. Knowing my best friend, I'd given her a packing deadline a full hour prior to our true deadline. She was able to do things at her pace, and I didn't have to panic about being late. We packed, got all our luggage checked at the airport, and were crammed into our absurdly uncomfortable airplane seats with time to spare.

Twenty-four hours later, we took our first steps in Ireland.

"I THOUGHT they spoke English here, but I can't understand a word. Is that Gaelic or something?" Ashley grumbled as our cab driver pulled away, leaving us standing outside of my new apartment.

"Gaelic is Scottish. They're speaking English, but I agree, it's hard to understand. Let's hope not everyone has such heavy accents as the cabbie."

"And the customs official," she added. "I had so much trouble understanding the man. I'm a little surprised they let me in the country."

I smirked. "Come on. Let's check out the place I'll be calling home for the foreseeable future."

The line of two-story, attached row houses looked the same as it had in the pictures online, which was a relief. Shopping for a home from an ocean away was not my ideal scenario, but I'd done my research as best I could and was happy with the results. The stretch of red-brick buildings made me think of soldiers standing shoulder-to-shoulder. There were no trees, and the collection of homes had seen their heyday come and gone. However, the neighborhood appeared safe and family-oriented. Best of all, it was only a ten-minute walk to work. It was a great deal at just under six hundred pounds a month compared to the other options I had seen.

The layout was simple. Living and kitchen downstairs with the bedroom and bath above on the second level. The front door opened facing the stairwell, the kitchen to the right, and a furnished living room to the left. A beige loveseat and over-sized chair left just enough room for a two-seater oak kitchenette on white linoleum floors. The large windows and white walls kept the place feeling bright, which was helpful because the only light fixture appeared to be an unadorned light bulb hanging from the ceiling.

"Nice," commented Ashley, when our eyes cast up at the glowing bulb.

"Yeah, well, at least it works." That was more than I could say for some of the stuff in our efficiency back in New York.

"Good point."

The tiny galley kitchen was outfitted with an oven, microwave, and a refrigerator—all of which looked like child-sized replicas of the real things. I was relieved to find that they all seemed to work and reminded myself that this was not supposed to be my dream home. The old wood cabinets were painted a light blue and had seen better days, but they would serve their purpose.

"It'll do. Let's go up and check out the bedroom and bath."

The stairs didn't creak, which was a bonus. The bedroom contained a queen-sized bed with a small particle board chest, and while cramped, it also had two large windows making it feel more spacious. The bathroom was lined in white tiles throughout and had a shower stall, commode, and pedestal sink—not exactly overflowing with storage, but it was decently clean and very doable.

"Oh, Becca. You're going to love it here. I just know it." Her whispered comment was rife with excitement on my behalf.

"I'm not sure about *love*, but I'll definitely manage." I was being a touch difficult. If I was honest, I felt the same bubbling excitement. An electric energy hummed through my body and bolstered my spirits with hope.

I could do this. I could really *do this.*

Deep down, I'd always known I could, or I would never have taken the job, but I was the queen of second-guessing myself. Anxiety and indecision were my constant companions, which was why I clung to feelings of certainty and confidence when they surfaced.

I flashed Ashley a giddy grin. "Let's get unpacked, then we can explore."

"Girl, I'm so glad you're excited, but I'm exhausted. Once we unpack, I'm taking a nap."

"You can't! They say that's the worst thing you can do for jet lag."

"When have I ever listened to what *they* say?" She arched an angular brow.

I rolled my eyes. "Whatever, but don't wake me up when you can't sleep tonight."

"Don't you worry about me. Now let's find the sheets. That bed is calling my name."

ASHLEY FOLLOWED through with her threat and was passed out minutes after the last bag was unpacked. I brought the most I could manage in two giant suitcases and shipped two additional boxes that wouldn't arrive for a few more days. The pull of sleep deprivation tugged at my limbs, but I wanted to get on local time as quickly as possible since I would be starting my job in two short days.

The thought filled me with anticipation.

I'd been out of school for two years waiting tables, unable to snag a job in my desired field until now. That was why I'd been so torn about accepting the position. I didn't want to leave the US, but I desperately wanted the job. Once I could add museum curator to my résumé, finding a job back home would be so much easier. All I had to do was put in my time, perhaps a year or so, and the rest would come.

It's not like Belfast was all that bad. It was just different, and I wasn't much for any kind of change. The sooner this city became my new normal, the better. Seeing as how the museum was a crucial piece of my new life, I decided it would be my first outing. I'd used Google maps street view a dozen times to walk virtually between work and home, but nothing was like seeing the city with my own eyes.

Throwing on a jacket, I left a note for Ashley, then slipped from the apartment. I didn't plan to go into the museum yet. I simply wanted to walk the route and take a quick tour of the neighborhood.

Even though it was still nearly two months from the middle of winter, early November in Belfast meant limited daylight. The sun was already lowering midafternoon and would be fully set around four thirty. There was still plenty of light to see for my afternoon stroll, but my work commute would be in the dark. Fortunately, my time in New York City had helped me overcome that particular fear. If you can't walk city streets at night in New York, you don't get out much. Maybe now that I was out of a large city and making decent money, I could buy a car. Not right off the bat, but sometime in the near future.

A grin lit my face. I bit my bottom lip to contain my excitement and keep from looking like a lunatic smiling at herself.

"Where do you think you're going?" called a deep voice in a slow Irish drawl.

While I might not have been a New Yorker born and bred, I had been there long enough to know that you do not, under any circumstances, talk to or make eye contact with strangers who call out to you. However, this voice was so commanding, so compelling that my steps faltered. Despite my better judgment, I turned to its source.

My lungs forgot how to function as I took in the gorgeous man leaning against a sleek black sports car. I was assaulted by his unexpected perfection. Sculpted athletic frame in a finely tailored suit. Neatly trimmed blond hair mussed in a casual fashion contrary to the extremely intense vibe he gave off. An angular jaw lined with scruff, and eyes so blue the sun could rise in their depths and be perfectly at home. This man was unsettlingly attractive, and every ounce of his attention was focused on me.

"I'm sorry, what?" I asked vacantly, his stunning good looks zapping my brainpower.

"That's an awfully confident smile you were wearing. Think you could just walk past me without me noticing?" He pushed away from the car and stretched to his full height—an impressive stature easily over six feet.

Confident smile? What is he talking about?

I'd have thought he was flirting had his expression not been accusatory. Menacing.

"I'm sorry, you must have me confused with someone else." I tucked my chin and turned to continue my walk, a tendril of unease urging me onward.

"*Stop*," he commanded in a tone that seized my muscles and froze me in place. "You're not from here." Accusation softened into curiosity.

I turned to look back at him over my shoulder. "No, I just arrived today from the US."

He began to approach, and my pulse kicked up a notch with every measured step closer.

"And you truly have no idea who I am?"

I glanced around with wide eyes, wondering if I'd inadvertently stumbled across some modern version of the *Peaky Blinders*. "I'm sorry, but as I said, I'm new here."

"And what is it you think you're doing here?" He was now a few short feet away from me, within lunging reach.

We were on a city street in what was left of daylight. Granted, the street wasn't particularly busy, but I told myself I should be safe. *Should.*

The niggling doubt forced a hesitant retreat. I took a step back toward the vacant storefront, keeping my eyes locked on his—not that it helped me understand his intent. His face was masked in absolute stoicism. With such an attractive face, he didn't seem like he should be dangerous. Or perhaps I just didn't want him to be dangerous. Yet my skin crawled, and adrenaline started coursing through me, making my palms sweat and my head pulse.

"I came to start a new job."

Why am I explaining myself to this crazy man?

I could hear the words of a confident rebuff resounding in my head, but I couldn't force them past my constricted throat. It was no different than any other time I'd been in an uncomfortable situation. I resorted to placating my tormentor. Life was easier that way. Safer.

"Who are you working for?" His eyes narrowed a fraction.

My brows drew together as I glanced toward the stone building behind him. "At the museum. I'm the new assistant curator." Why the hell did it matter to him where I'd be working? "Look, I have somewhere to be. I really need to get going."

I started to turn until a strong hand clamped down around my wrist. Gasping, I spun to find the man inches away, his formidable body towering over me. For several eternal seconds, time stood still. His earthy scent filled the air around me while his penetrating stare held me captive.

Eventually, I pulled in a shaking breath and tried to extract myself from the hold his eyes had over me. "Please, let me go," I whispered.

His hand squeezed tighter.

"If you try to run, I'll find you. It's what I do." His statement was the rumble of distant thunder, threatening a cataclysmic storm.

Suddenly, I was free from his grip, though his body made no move to retreat.

I should have fled the instant he let go, but it took several erratic heartbeats before I forced my body away from his gravitational pull. Securing my coat around my middle, I hurried down the sidewalk with only a quick glance over my shoulder. The man was nowhere to be seen.

CHAPTER
TWO

The next morning, nervous energy had me up early, ironing my best black slacks and cardigan set. I wasn't particularly curvy and never had a flair for girlie outfits, so most of my work attire revolved around slacks and cardigans. While I wasn't blessed with an hourglass figure, I did inherit a generous chest from my mother. That was where the similarities ended.

My parents were both fair with blue and hazel eyes. In contrast, my hair was almost black, and my eyes were a dark brown that suited my olive skin. Growing up, I was sometimes teased about being the milkman's daughter. I had been blond with hazel eyes as a young child, but my coloring gradually darkened until I hardly resembled the blond baby in my mom's photo albums.

Despite the teasing, I liked my dark coloring. I was often asked if I was Native American or something equally exotic. The fact of the matter was, my mom was all Irish/English, and Dad was a mutt with a German predominance.

Mom's Irish ancestry was one of the main reasons I gathered enough courage to take the job in Belfast. When the unexpected email came through from my university's career center stating the Ulster Museum was looking for a curator position, I decided to apply on a whim, but I never thought I'd get an offer. The phone interview had gone beautifully. The next day, I was faced with a life-changing decision. I could accept my dream job in a country I'd always wanted to visit, but that would require moving an ocean away from everyone I knew and loved.

I agonized for two days over the decision.

Eventually, it was my ingrained love of all things Irish that had clinched my fate. Two weeks and three panic attacks later, I was on my way.

The Ulster Museum was an impressive building constructed from smooth white stone. The front half of the building facing the street bore the original turn-of-the-century, multipaned windows with giant stone columns, giving it the appearance of an old courthouse or state building. On the other hand, the back half of the large building, added in recent years, was ultra-modern. The two halves were somehow sewn together seamlessly in a brilliant display of architectural design. Surrounding the property were trees bursting with fall colors and a thick carpet of green grass.

I pulled open the heavy solid-wood door at the front entrance and took in the lobby as I stepped inside. Much like the back half of the building, the interior had been completely updated. Smooth white surfaces adorned much of the entry with occasional rich wood paneling to warm the room. The gift shop was sectioned off by thick plate-glass walls, and through a tall archway, I glimpsed the central atrium of the four-story museum within. Pride and excitement warmed my chest as I took in the beautiful facility where I would be working.

"Rebecca! You look just as lovely as your photo, lass. I'm Fergus Campbell, but you can call me Fergus. It's wonderful to make your acquaintance in person." A middle-aged man in a deep purple suit strode swiftly in my direction.

I was quickly wrapped in a tight hug and kissed on each cheek. That would take me a while to adjust to. I wasn't even a hugger, and I certainly didn't walk around kissing people I hardly knew.

"Thank you so much! I'm thrilled to be here. The museum is absolutely awe-inspiring."

"It's our home away from home. How about I show you the offices, and you can meet the rest of the staff?" he suggested animatedly as he clapped his hands together and turned toward the elevators.

He was exactly as I'd pictured him after our colorful conversation over the phone. At about five-nine, he was not particularly tall but had a proud stature with red hair, a neatly trimmed goatee, and blue eyes. His plum-colored suit was high quality, and the light gray dress shirt and purple striped bow tie polished off his look with sophisticated panache. He even wore shining black patent leather dress shoes that clacked on the floor as he strode to the elevator bank.

"We're up on the fourth floor. I think you'll get along with everyone swimmingly, although there are fewer of us than you might expect. We have a good number of patrons through our doors, but I'm afraid we are still a small-scale museum compared to yours in New York City," he commented as we got on the elevator and headed to the top floor.

His accent, though thick, was refined, and I found it was easier to understand in person than it had been over the phone. I wondered if he had spent some time in England or if it was just schooling that had kept his words discernable through the otherwise thick accent.

"I'd much rather have a hands-on role in a smaller museum than be stuck in an office for a larger one, not that there's anything small about this museum," I assured him as we exited the elevator.

"Excellent, because you will definitely be down in the trenches here. I've needed some help desperately, and finding someone with the proper skills around here has been a bloody nightmare." Lifting his hand, he guided me off the elevator and around to the glass door labeled "Administration."

For the remainder of the morning, Fergus walked me through the office and explained my tasks. He was easy to talk with and even told me all about his background during a sandwich lunch at the coffee shop. We spent the afternoon touring the museum to help acquaint me with the exhibits, roaming the halls as he explained the origins of each display. From the Dale Chihuly glass sculptures to the Takabuti ancient Egyptian Mummy, Fergus was a fountain of information.

A couple of hours into our tour, he paused to glance at his phone. "Ach lass, Claire in the office is texting me, says there's a call I have to take."

"That's no problem. I know I've taken up most of your day getting oriented," I quickly assured him. "There's not much left, and I'm happy to finish on my own. We'll have plenty of time to discuss the remaining exhibits another day."

"Aye, Becca, I'll just be a few moments. Come and find me in the office once you've finished up."

"Will do."

He hurried in the direction of the stairs with what seemed to be his usual high-energy manner. As much as I loved hearing the detailed background on the various works of art and historical artifacts, I also enjoyed having some quiet time to appreciate the pieces in the museum. My love of historical artifacts was the whole reason I'd gone to school to be a curator. Each item told a story if you were patient enough to listen.

I rounded the corner into the next exhibit centered around

a life-sized bronze statue of a stallion reared up on its hind legs. As I approached, I found that I was mesmerized by his captivating eyes.

"Masterful craftsmanship, is it not?"

I started with a gasp at the rich voice coming from behind me. A young man stood not three feet away. At least, I thought he was young at first glance. The longer I looked, the harder it was to tell. His features were not particularly aged, but his eyes had an agelessness to their profound depths. He was trim, just about five or six inches taller than me, and had short hair so light that it was hard to tell if it was blond or white. His pale-blue eyes crinkled at the corners, and his thin lips were curved up in amusement. With his hands clasped behind his back, he gazed at the statue.

"Yes, I'm not sure I've ever seen anything like it." My gaze turned back to the statue. "The expression captured in his eyes is so fierce, you can almost feel the life in him."

"Indeed, as if the very ground quakes from his pounding hooves. All he needs is a commanding rider with a shining sword, and the visage would be complete." His words were spoken precisely, and his voice was soothing, wrapping around me like a warm blanket. His accent was a mystery. It sounded like aristocratic English but colored with something else that I couldn't discern.

"That would make for quite the image," I agreed.

"Have you been in Ireland long?"

My skin warmed with the touch of his assessing gaze. "Brand new, actually. I just got in last week," I responded as I met his eyes.

"And how are you adjusting?" He strolled to a small collection of Pre-Raphaelite paintings. They weren't necessarily my favorite genre, but I had studied the style and was familiar with some of the pieces.

"Very well, although I've hardly had much of a chance to explore the area."

As he listened, he focused his gaze on the paintings. He slowed to a stop as his eyes landed on a piece I had studied in school. He gazed at it for a good while, and I started to think our conversation was over. But just before I began to back away, he spoke again.

"Look at her confidence, her passion. That, at least, Sandys got right. That and the timing, but I'm sure that was more luck than anything else," he said with a glint of amusement in his eyes.

He referred to a work entitled *Morgan le Fay* painted by Frederick Sandys in 1864. The work was not particularly large, about twenty-four by sixteen inches encased in an ornate gold frame. The woman had pale skin, typical of that era, with long curly brown hair. She was draped in leopard skin and silks while in the throes of concocting a spell over a burning fire.

"Are you referring to the Asian silks and symbols? If I recall correctly, the orient was popular at the time Sandys painted the piece. The elements were included in the painting even though they would not have been present during the time the Arthurian legends purportedly occurred."

"Indeed," he said almost as a lament.

His reaction felt odd, engulfing me in a similar unease as my conversation with the man on the street had the night before.

"Well, I'd better get back to work," I said in an attempt to escape my discomfort. "I hope you enjoy the rest of your afternoon."

He eyed me with an intensity that made me pause. "Rebecca, it was very good to see you. Please do be careful while you're here." He gave a slight bow of his head and abruptly walked away.

I floundered in confusion at what had just happened. Had I given him my name? I examined my blouse, wondering if I had worn a name tag and forgotten about it. Perhaps he knew Fergus and was told about my employment.

Yes, that had to be it.

But then, why had he said *good to see you* and not *good to meet you* as if we had met before? I couldn't shake the feeling that I was being pranked, as if men with cameras would jump out at any moment to tell me I was part of an elaborate setup. This country was full of unusual characters, and I begrudgingly admitted that it would at least keep things interesting.

When I finished touring the museum, it was nearly six o'clock. After checking in with Fergus, I wrapped up my first day on the new job and started home. A sense of confidence and rightness put energy in my steps. Until this moment, I hadn't been sure about my decision. Doubts and insecurities had haunted me, but after meeting Fergus and walking the paces, I knew I could do this. Belfast might have been quirky, but it was my new home, and I belonged there.

"HOW WAS YOUR FIRST DAY? Tell me all about it!" Ashley arrived at the apartment an hour after me, throwing down her coat and bags in pursuit of a bottle of wine.

"It was great. Fergus was just as friendly in person as he had been on the phone." I gave Ash a rundown of my day as I continued cooking dinner.

"Bec, I'm so happy for you! I can't believe that just a couple of weeks ago, you were taking orders in a no-name restaurant, and now, look at you. You're a part of a museum and doing work that you love." She pulled over a dining chair and looked up at me with pride on her face, her eyes becoming suspiciously glassy.

"Don't you dare start crying on me. You know I hate that watery stuff. Tell me about your day."

"Yeah, yeah," she said with a laugh. She launched into a detailed description of each attraction she had visited while I set the table and filled our plates.

"I wish I could have gone with you, but I was able to take a tour of the museum, so I got a dose of culture myself."

"Oh, yeah? See anything particularly interesting?" she asked, scooping a large spoonful of rice into her mouth.

"Yes, but it wasn't an exhibit. I had another odd encounter with an eccentric Irishman." I'd told her about the strange hottie who had stopped me in the street the day before as soon as I'd gotten home.

"Maybe the lack of sun does something to the people here. Makes them a bit deranged."

"This one wasn't quite as creepy as yesterday, but still odd. The guy starts talking to me about this statue and then a painting."

"That doesn't sound so odd. I'm pretty sure my gramps talks to everyone he sees," she said matter-of-factly.

"First, he wasn't old. Second, it was more what he said and how he just walked away after." I described the man and recounted our discussion of the artwork and his parting words. "I swear the guy was not in the room when I first walked up to the exhibit, and then just as quickly, he was gone. I have no idea how he knew my name, and I can't tell if I'm reading into his *good to see you,* or if that's just how people talk here."

"Huh. You sure he wasn't hitting on you?"

"I don't think so, but who knows."

"Well, save some of the crazy hotties for me. I didn't get a single suggestive look or anything today."

I snorted a laugh. "You can have them all, promise."

"I still have a couple of weeks. Surely, I can find me a fine young Irishman by the time I go home."

"Undoubtedly," I said wryly.

Ash winked and stood. "I'm going to wash off the grime of the day. You okay getting the dishes? I swear I'll get them next time."

I playfully rolled my eyes. The kitchen was not Ash's favorite place, and it was not the first time I did the cooking *and* the cleanup. "No problem—go ahead and shower. I'll take the next one when I'm done here."

I gathered the dishes and took them to the sink, which was in a dark corner of the room now that the sun had gone down. The single light bulb in the room was not a problem during the day when the windows let in plenty of light, but evenings were another matter.

I was lost in thought and up to my elbows in suds when I registered movement out of the corner of my eye. I turned toward the table where I had seen something move and froze, hands dripping soapy water onto my bare feet.

Crawling around on the table was a tiny man gathering crumbs. He was about six inches tall, had he been standing, and his skin was a leafy green.

I blinked my eyes several times to clear the hallucination, but it remained.

A doll-sized human wearing little scraps of clothing scurried about on the top of the table. Sensing he had an audience, the little man froze. Quick like a bird, his head whipped in my direction. His already large eyes opened even farther as we locked gazes.

Neither of us blinked.

Neither took a single breath.

Shock jumbled my thoughts. Before I could collect myself,

the man vanished like a bubble bursting into thin air. He disappeared. Gone.

I sucked in a lung full of air as I frantically scanned the room for any signs of where he had gone. Panic engulfed me, and I started screaming. All rational thought fled while shrieks and obscenities flew from my mouth in a fiery stream. I ran about the room searching for the man under the couch, in the cabinets, and behind the blinds.

A dripping wet Ashley flew down the stairs wrapped in a towel with a shiny black hair dryer gripped in her fist. "What the hell happened?"

"Ash, I saw a tiny person on the table! He was crawling around getting crumbs, and he was green with big eyes, but then he just disappeared. I saw him, Ash. He was there!" I rambled almost incoherently as my heart rate finally began to slow down, but my hands continued to shake uncontrollably.

Ash set down the dryer and stepped closer to me with her head to the side and an expression on her face as if she was talking to a lost child. "Hey, honey, it's okay. Between the jet lag and drinking wine while talking about all the weird men, I'm sure your mind was just worn out. It was probably a mouse. Nothing to worry about. I'll call the landlord in the morning and have him get an exterminator out immediately."

"Ash—"

"*Hush*. You go up and take a hot shower and then get some rest. I was done anyway. I'll throw on my pajamas and finish up in the kitchen." She gently guided me to the stairs with her hand at my back.

With a resigned sigh, I took one more glance around the empty room and headed upstairs to shower.

Was this why the men here were crazy? Was there something in the water that made people off-balance? Never in my life had I had a breakdown. Panic attacks? Yes, but that had never involved hallucinations.

All the doubt and wariness I'd cast out earlier in the day filled my belly with a sickening dread.

A firm yet nurturing voice filled my mind from years of practice easing myself down off emotional ledges. *Ashley was probably right. The brain does wild things under strain, and you just traveled across the world. You're tired and stressed. Get some rest, and you'll be fine tomorrow.*

Yes. That was it. Just try to calm down and get some sleep.

I did my best to block all thoughts as I cleaned up then snuggled deep under the covers of my bed. I was comfortable but unable to fully relax. There was one thing that was sure to calm my spirit. My mother's voice. I hadn't had a chance to see them before I left the country, and we were incredibly close. My parents and I were a team. We did everything together while I was growing up, and I loved them dearly.

Despite the late hour in Ireland, it was still early evening in Texas. I grabbed my phone off the nightstand and placed the call. The instant her soft voice crossed the line, my chest filled with warmth. She asked about my first day, and though I knew she wished I was closer, she offered a swell of encouragement. Our call was brief but exactly what I needed. With my heart a little lighter and homesickness not weighing quite so heavily on my chest, I slipped into a restless sleep.

CHAPTER

THREE

STILL IN THE CLUTCHES OF SLEEP, MY BLEARY EYES COULD TELL THAT IT wasn't time to get up, but I wasn't sure what had roused my consciousness.

That was when I sensed it—the feeling of a presence behind me.

I wasn't alone. Someone was watching me.

I slowly turned my head and took in the horrifying black form of a man looming over me.

"Jesus Christ! Becca, wake up!"

Heart pounding in my chest, I opened my eyes and realized I'd been dreaming. I was in my room with Ashley, ensconced in darkness and drenched in sweat. The shadow man wasn't real, but he might as well have been. He'd haunted me for years.

My reoccurring nightmare from childhood was back.

"God, Ash, I'm so sorry," I said as I rubbed my eyes, trying to scratch the image of his terrifying presence out of my mind.

"It's okay, but your screaming scared me half to death. That must have been some bad dream."

"Yeah. It's actually a reoccurring dream I used to have as a

21

kid. It's been so many years since I've had it that I figured I had outgrown it."

"You want to tell me about it?"

I sat up in the dark, the room lit only by small slivers of light that crept in around the blinds.

"It's a waking dream. I feel like I'm waking up for real, and this man is standing over me. There's no face or defining feature, just this shadowy man. I used to wake up screaming about once a month like clockwork as a kid. My mom was convinced I was being haunted by a spirit, so she started burning incense in my room at night. It may sound silly, but it was supposed to guard against evil and keep the bad spirits away. After she started using the incense, I didn't have a single nightmare. Even when I slept over with friends, the dreams stayed away. I eventually stopped thinking about him, figuring the spirit had moved on." Looking back on all those nights I had woken in abject terror, my body gave an involuntary shudder.

"That's awful, Bec. I'm so sorry. I could see why you had the dream, though, considering all the big changes in your life. And the odd encounters you've had probably don't help." Ash spoke softly as her hand absently rubbed circles on my back.

I nodded, realizing she was probably right. "It's late. Let's try to get back to sleep, or I'm going to be a zombie at work tomorrow."

I MANAGED to arrive at work the next morning just before the rain began. Knowing moisture was an unavoidable part of the climate, I didn't plan on letting showers stop me from getting around, but my boxes still hadn't arrived, and one of them contained my rain boots. Therefore, when lunchtime rolled around, I headed down to the coffee shop on the first floor rather than venture out onto the wet streets.

"Hot cocoa on a day like this would hit the spot," said a voice beside me. I glanced over to take in the man smiling at me with mischievous brown eyes. He was about five-foot-eleven and trim, judging by his cut jawline. The rest of him was obscured beneath a brown wool coat. Dirty blond hair waved in loose curls every which way, enlivened by the humid weather.

He was an attractive man, but the kicker was his dimples—he had two perfect dimples on either cheek. He was a panty-dropper in a boy-next-door kind of way, and I instantly felt the effect of his good looks. My cheeks heated as a smile crept across my face.

"I was going to grab a sandwich, but a hot chocolate sounds good, too."

"Excellent. You figure out what you want, and I'll start with the order," he said with a wink and walked to the counter.

"What?" I was suddenly confused. Was he planning to eat lunch with me?

"Unless you've got plans already, I'll join you for lunch. Just tell me what you'll have, and I'll get it ordered."

I didn't normally eat with strangers, but his confident, congenial manner swept me away.

"I'm not meeting anyone, but I don't even know your name."

"I'm Ronan, and you are?"

"Rebecca." I wasn't the best at chance encounters and flirting, but I wasn't exactly the Virgin Mary either. Besides, it was time I met one man in this country who wasn't a total fruitcake. Just in case he was yet another Irish nutjob, though, I decided to vet him and make sure I didn't need to go running back to my office.

We put in our order and found a table by the windows. He took off his coat and set it on the back of his chair, giving me an unobstructed view of his physique. He was exceptionally fit but not particularly bulky—more like a swimmer or a runner than a weights kind of guy.

"Were you touring the museum?" I asked after we sat down.

"Something like that, but I seem to have gotten a little sidetracked." He peered at me from under thick, dark lashes, and my chest warmed at his attention. "You as well?" he asked, seeming genuinely interested in learning more about me.

"No, I just started working here. Yesterday was my first day."

"So that would explain the accent. New to Ireland, are you?"

I nodded in response as a server brought our food to the table.

"Ronan, I have to ask because you seem to be decently well-adjusted, and so far, that hasn't been my experience around here. You don't happen to make a habit of chasing girls down the street or have any other stalker-ish tendencies that I should know about, do you?" I asked with one brow raised as I took a bite of my sandwich.

He chuckled before he responded. "Tell me that's not the welcome you've received to our fine country."

"In fact, that and more. It's been an interesting few days."

"Sounds like it. I can easily see what all the fuss is about, but I will endeavor to keep myself well-behaved."

My eyes dropped shyly at his compliment. "Thank you. Should you feel the need to get on the crazy train, at least give me a running head start."

He laughed aloud, and I brought my eyes back to his.

"Well, I assure you that the good doctors who released me

back into society said I was no longer a danger to those around me, so you have nothing to fear from me." He gave me a sly look, and a laugh bubbled up from my chest.

"Tell me, Ronan, what do you do for a living?"

"A little of this, a little of that—I do whatever the boss tells me to. Sometimes, I'm a courier, sometimes, a negotiator, and sometimes, I do research. I'm rather boring, really. I'd much prefer to hear more about you. Did you move to Belfast alone?" He eyed me curiously.

"Yes and no. My best friend, Ashley, came to help get me settled for the first couple of weeks. She heads back to the States soon, and then it's just me."

"That's very kind of her. I take it you two are close?"

"She's like a sister to me. I'm going to miss her when she leaves." My gaze dropped at the sudden feeling of loss.

Not wanting to be a downer, I redirected our conversation and asked about his accent since it sounded like a mix of Irish and Scottish.

"I've traveled around a bit—spent a good deal of time in the Highlands. I'm originally from this area but only came back more recently."

"Did you travel as a child then? You don't seem old enough to have been traveling long on your own."

"Maybe I'm older than I look," he teased with a smirk. "Have you had a chance to tour the sights of our fine city?"

"Not really. I took this job very quickly, so I haven't had any time since arriving to sightsee or learn much about the area. Plus, I'm enjoying my time with Ashley while she's here. I can check out the city more once I'm on my own."

"Well, we can't have a pretty girl like you wandering around all alone. Maybe I can show you some of my favorite places, starting this weekend. I'll be at the Huntsman tomorrow night. Bring your friend and come out for some drinks with the fellas and me." His warm expression and open demeanor were disarming. He seemed relaxed and genuine, although I could feel the bounce of his leg burning off nervous energy under the table. He was probably more nervous than he'd like me to think. It was endearing, and I found myself leaning closer.

A crowded nightclub should be a safe place to meet up. And I'd have Ashley with me. The prospect churned nervous excitement in my belly.

With a small bite at my lower lip, I replied, "I think that could be arranged."

I didn't know who the sex kitten was that had suddenly possessed me, but man was she hot! My cheeks warmed, and my gaze dropped to the remnants of my lunch, which I suddenly felt too anxious to finish. "I should probably get back to my office."

"I suppose I can let you go, so long as I get to see you tomorrow." He rose from his chair and rounded the table, then held out his hand for mine. Once my fingers were in his warm grasp, he brought my knuckles to his mouth for a soft kiss. "It's been an absolute pleasure, Rebecca. I'll see you at the club."

FOUR

BY THE TIME THE MUSEUM CLOSED, THE SKIES HAD LET UP. WHILE THE rain had subsided, the air was infused with a biting chill. My feet had long given up any hope of warmth stuffed in poorly insulated pumps. Despite the freezing, moist air, I was feeling optimistic and looking forward to telling Ashley about the dizzying events of my day.

Reflecting on my lunch with Ronan as I walked down the dark sidewalk, I didn't notice a large crack in the pavers until my heel had lodged itself deep inside the crevice. My ankle rolled to the side, causing me to lunge forward with a squeal. By some small miracle, I managed to catch myself and keep from face planting on the wet ground.

I was fairly certain I hadn't done any damage to my ankle besides some mild discomfort. However, the heel of my shoe had twisted loose. I hobbled over to lean against the nearby wall to assess the black leather heel and determine whether it was salvageable.

The awning above me cast a heavy shadow and made it hard to see, so I moved myself to a better spot. Just as I resituated myself beneath the lamplight, my eyes were drawn to a woman walking toward me. At first glance, I would have said she was heading to an event or a night on the town. Her smooth, flowing blond hair was artfully styled, and she wore a black cocktail dress clinging to her shapely figure. She strode with such a confident air that I couldn't help but gawk at her beauty.

That was when things started to get weird.

When I tried to focus on her facial features, my eyes seemed to play tricks on me. As if she were a holograph, the image of the woman became transparent, and beneath, a much more monstrous figure materialized.

A sickly gray creature with filthy, talon-like fingers. Its bones protruded in a ghastly fashion, and stringy black hair hung limp over small breasts. She was essentially naked, her only covering was the beautiful image projected like a skin to conceal the horror beneath. The most disturbing part of all was her bloodred eyes. They almost glowed as they adeptly scanned her surroundings.

My instant terror was too intense to question. I had the capacity for logic or reason, yet all I knew was fear. Like a rabbit knows to run from a wolf, I knew this creature was deadly.

But there was nowhere to run. It was too late.

Each sultry step she took brought her closer to me until she passed through the same pool of light where I stood transfixed.

To my utter astonishment, she continued as though I wasn't there.

When a swish of air from her passing presence brought a sickly sweet scent to the back of my throat, I sucked in a barely audible gasp. It had been soft but not quiet enough.

Instantly, she whipped her head in my direction, eyes scouring the brick wall for the source of the sound. Evil red eyes skated right over me as if I wasn't there. Or, for some reason, she couldn't see me.

Her nose lifted, and she sniffed the air, searching for a scent.

I kept absolutely silent, even when her mouth opened, allowing the dim light to glint off two sharp fangs. She stood only feet away, so close I could smell her foul breath lingering in the air.

Unable to locate any offending presence, she reluctantly continued on her way, looking back periodically over her shoulder. I watched her retreating form until she was long out of sight. Even then, it took me what seemed like ages before my joints unlocked, and I was able to step away from the wall.

My joints creaked when I finally broke free of my frozen stance. I took one step toward home then stilled when I realized the woman might not have been the only monster out in the night.

Fuck this, I'm out of here.

I dropped my broken shoe to the ground, flung off the other, and sprinted the rest of the way home.

ONCE I FINALLY MADE IT to the apartment, my entire body was a gelatinous mess of post-adrenaline fatigue. I could hardly stand on my shaking legs.

In a stroke of luck, I beat Ashley home for the night. I had no idea what I'd seen or how to feel about it, and I certainly wasn't ready to admit my mounting insanity to anyone else. I went straight upstairs, removed my clothes, and started a hot shower. Only once the scalding water lashed my body was my mind able to start processing what had happened.

What I'd seen had been real.

Logic told me it had to be a delusion—that something so inexplicable had to be a figment of my imagination—but she'd been real. I'd felt her in the air and choked on her horrific scent. She'd been a tangible, living creature, I was certain of it.

But who would ever believe me? If someone else had described these things to me, I would have assumed they were a few crayons short of a whole box.

Maybe I was going crazy. All the other crazies were probably convinced that what they thought they saw was real.

Oh, hell.

How would I know if I was losing my mind?

Maybe I would tell Ashley what had happened. The only reason not to tell her was because she would think I was crazy, and if I was losing my grip on reality, getting help would be a good idea.

The more I thought about it, the more convinced I became that I would end up in a facility with soft padded walls and Nurse Ratchet to keep me company.

What the hell is happening to me?

The water did its best to warm me, but I couldn't seem to clean away the oil residue of fear that clung to me. Whether the woman had been real or not, she was terrifying—either as a sign of mental derailment or as a horrifying alien threat walking the streets.

Giving myself the benefit of the doubt, I decided to consider the facts had she been real. What was she—some kind of vampire? Or demon? An alien sounded more believable, but maybe that was what vampires and demons were.

Okay, now I really sound crazy.

I exited the shower and toweled off, slipping on my heaviest pajamas once I was dry. Clutching a pillow to my chest, I sat on the bed and fended off a panic attack. That was where Ash found me not long after.

"Hey, you." She sat next to me with her body angled in my direction, her voice soft, recognizing that something was wrong. "How was day two of the new job?"

I didn't answer immediately. Fear kept the words I wanted to say trapped in a clump at the back of my throat.

"Ash," I whispered. "I'm worried that I'm going crazy." I met her eyes and let her see the depth of my worry.

"Did you see the little man again?"

"No, this was so much worse. I know you won't believe me, and I understand. If someone told me what I'm about to tell you, I wouldn't believe them either."

"Okay, hit me with it."

I began speaking in a low, steady voice, calmly and rationally explaining the horrifying creature and my miraculous escape. "I know it sounds crazy, but I also know what I saw, and I swear on everything that I love in this world that it happened."

"Um, okay." She nodded once. "You're right. It is hard to believe, but I know you, and I know you aren't lying. I also know you're not crazy, so I guess that means ... I believe you."

"You do?"

"Yes, but at the same time, I'm not sure I can totally believe that these creatures are real without having seen them myself. I believe that you believe. Does that make sense? Hopefully, you understand that it's a pretty huge leap of faith."

I threw myself into her arms. "I know, Ash, and I totally understand. Thank you for not calling me crazy or denying it happened."

We held each other for a long minute before Ash pulled back. "So where does that leave us?"

I shrugged. "I don't know. Maybe I should consider going back home. This place might be dangerous." I didn't want to get hurt, but more than anything, I had to protect my parents. I was everything to them, and if something happened to me, they'd never recover.

"Bec, this is your dream job. You can't quit now," Ashley pleaded, clasping my hands in hers.

"Yeah, but what about the creatures?"

"Well, they haven't hurt you, and I haven't heard of any attacks. Maybe they're harmless." Her brows furrowed as she shrugged. "I'm not sure why you can see them when others can't, but if they aren't harming anyone, is there truly any danger?"

She wasn't entirely wrong.

I hadn't heard of any ghastly murders or vicious attacks either. Usually, word of something violent like that spreads quickly. And hadn't I just been reveling in how optimistic I felt about the new job? If I went back home, how long would I have to wait tables before I got another opportunity like this at a world-class museum?

"I suppose I shouldn't be too hasty," I reluctantly agreed.

"Thatta girl. Now, how about we go downstairs and open a bottle of wine?"

I didn't move. "What do you think they could be, Ash? Could vampires and stuff really be real?"

"Nope." She shook her head adamantly. "We're not doing this. You'll only freak yourself out." With superhuman strength, she yanked me off the bed. "Downstairs. *Now.*"

I couldn't help but smile. Ash knew me almost better than I knew myself.

"Okay, okay. Let me put on a hoodie, and I'll be down in a sec."

"I'll get the charcuterie started," she sang on her way down the stairs.

I grabbed a pink hoodie from the closet, and when I turned off the light, the glowing streetlamp outside caught my attention. I went to close the blinds and saw a figure leaning against the wall not far from the lamppost.

A man in a suit.

A man in a suit with short, ruffled hair and eyes trained on my window.

It was him—the man who had questioned me on the street the day we'd arrived. I wouldn't forget that face so long as I lived.

An ominous chill slithered down my spine.

Had he followed me? His presence couldn't be a coincidence. He'd sought me out, but why? Did he have me confused with someone else? No, he knew that I was new to the country. All I could figure was that he was a stalker. An insanely gorgeous, possibly deranged, Adonis of an Irishman lurking outside my window.

Superb.

And I'd thought things couldn't get any creepier.

CHAPTER
FIVE

After a Xanax and a good night's sleep, I was feeling much better come Friday morning. The prospect of seeing Ronan again also had a lot to do with my bolstered mental state. Ashley and I were equally excited to go out for the night. It was the perfect distraction from my anxious thoughts.

But before I could lose myself in loud music and smiling dimples, I had to get through a full day at the museum. Hopefully, I'd be busy enough to keep any idle thoughts at bay.

"You must be Catronia!" I greeted the young woman behind the visitor desk when I entered the building.

Fergus had told me about the girl who worked at the desk and how she'd been out of town during my first few days at work. She was a few years younger than me and easily identifiable by her shocking red hair curling just past her shoulders, striking green eyes, and loads of freckles scattered across her friendly face.

"Please, call me Cat. You must be Rebecca." She came around the desk to give me an enthusiastic handshake.

"Yes, but please call me Becca. I hope your getaway went well."

Her eyes rolled heavenward. "Had to go with my mam to see her sister on the coast. I tried to get out of it, but Mam's big on family."

"Have you worked at the museum for long?" I asked, wanting to get to know my new coworker.

"For about a year. Fergus … I mean, Mr. Campbell is a friend of the family. Once I got my leaving certificate, that's finishing secondary, I started working here. I was never interested in third-level school, and with my mam's connection at the museum, things just fell into place," she said as she twirled a red curl between her fingers.

"Have you lived here all your life then?"

"All my life, and the same for my parents, and their parents, and so on. You could say we are a pillar in the Belfast community." Her snarky tone hinted at an appreciation for sarcasm, which brought her up a notch in my estimation. "Have you settled in yet? Seen the city and all?"

"Not a ton, but I will. My best friend came with me for a couple of weeks, so I've been spending time with her. Tonight is the first night we're getting to go out and see a bit of the nightlife."

"Oh, yeah? Where to?"

"A club called the Huntsman. Ever heard of it?" I figured she was young and likely had a good grasp on the local scene. Maybe she could tell me about the place. I'd planned to look it up during my lunch break to gauge the dress code, but if Cat knew the place, she could give me the lowdown.

What I didn't expect was the veil that descended over her features.

"You're going to the Huntsman, are you? How did that come about?" she asked with practiced indifference.

Curiosity and a touch of alarm stiffened my spine.

"I met someone the other day, and he suggested my friend and I hang out with him and his friends at the club."

Her hand tapped idly on the vinyl desktop. "It's not the best idea to get mixed up with that crew. Bunch of chancers they are."

"What on earth is a *chancer*?"

"No good, that's what. You take a real chance hanging around them. There's any number of pubs in the city, so I'd suggest you pick another." She shrugged as if it made no difference to her, but I got the sense she cared more than she was letting on.

It was disappointing to know she didn't approve of the place, but she was just one person. Just because she'd had a bad experience didn't mean the entire establishment was bad.

"I'm not sure I could convince Ash to change plans, but I'll definitely mention it." I didn't want to offend my new coworker by disregarding her outright. Her heart was in the right place. "All right, I'm heading upstairs. It was lovely meeting you!"

I was pleased to see her vivacious smile returned, though I didn't miss the glint of wariness still lurking in her eyes.

"Getting dolled up already?" I'd made it through my workday and come home to blaring music and a glammed-out Ashley.

"Yes! You and I are going out to eat. We've been in this country almost an entire week and not gone out once for a proper dinner, so get changed." She went back to applying mascara.

Two dresses were laid out on the bed, which was her

obvious attempt to get me in a dress instead of skinny jeans and a blouse, which was my clubbing outfit of choice.

"It's too cold to wear that dress. I'll freeze to death."

"Beauty is pain, Bec. Put it on."

With a grunt of frustration, I took off my work outfit and held up the offending dress for a second look. At least it had long sleeves, but it was clingy and had a low scoop neck. It also had a low-cut back, which meant no bra.

"I can't wear this. You know my girls are way too big to go braless. This isn't even my dress. How many dresses did you bring?"

"I don't think one can truly ever have too many dresses. Don't make this difficult. I know you have those sticky-front boobie holders, so slap those babies on, and let's get moving," she said as she batted her eyes at me.

I gave her an Oscar-worthy eye roll, but it was undermined when the corners of my mouth lifted grudgingly.

Ashley was similar in size to me, though we were not at all the same shape. She didn't have nearly as much chest as I did, but she did have a small waist and way more junk in the trunk. It meant we could share some of our clothes, depending on the fit, and the stretchy dress worked well on either of us. For herself, she had selected a royal-blue dress that clung to her curves and accentuated her bright-blue eyes. Her straight blond hair had been given some wave, and all together, she was smoking hot.

I applied the boob tape to one side, then the other, ensuring the girls were as well aligned as possible. Giving them a bit of a jiggle, I ensured they were sufficiently secure, then shimmied into the little black dress.

Ash gave me a once-over. "Let's touch up your hair and give those eyes a little sex appeal, then we'll be good to go."

She was much more interested in makeup than I was. The

stuff never interested me much. She pulled me down to sit on the bed and went about finalizing my look for the night. After several agonizing minutes of holding as still as a statue, she stepped back and gave me an appraising look.

"These Irish boys won't know what hit them!" Clapping her hands, she turned to dig in her bag. When she came back around, she had one hand behind her back and the other hand holding up a finger in the universal *one moment* gesture.

"I know you'll probably say no, but I have the most gorgeous necklace that would be *perfect* with that dress."

My head fell back in exasperation. "Ash, how many times do we have to have this conversation?"

"Becca, just think about it. You *always* wear the same necklace. Wouldn't it be okay, just for one night, to wear something different and jazz things up a bit?" She gave me sad puppy dog eyes any golden retriever would have been proud of.

She held out the necklace for me to see, and I had to admit it was beautiful. A collar-type necklace made of shining silver probably would have been more appropriate for a night out than the necklace I was already wearing, but that wasn't going to change my mind.

My necklace had been around my neck as long as I could remember, longer even. I never, ever took it off. My stomach twisted just at the thought of removing it. The silver chain with a stone pendant was a versatile piece of jewelry. The black oval stone was surrounded in feminine silver scrolling, surprisingly detailed for its size—only a tad larger than a quarter. It went with everything, as far as I was concerned, so there wasn't a compelling reason to take it off. It was a part of me, and I'd feel naked without it.

"I know it doesn't make any sense, and I really appreciate you trying to get me to branch out, but I'm not going to change my mind." I cupped the stone in my hand protectively and wondered if she would let the subject go.

"I know, I know. A girl has to try, though." She smirked at me, unfazed by my rejection. "Come on, let's get some dinner. I'm starving."

I breathed out a small sigh of relief as I followed her downstairs and out to catch a cab.

Ashley had chosen a local restaurant suggested on one of her tours, and it was just as delicious as advertised. As the evening progressed, we got a good head start on our night with several glasses of wine.

At close to ten o'clock, we headed to the Huntsman.

Our cab pulled up in front of a four-story building thrumming with activity. I learned with a quick internet search that the Huntsman was a full-fledged nightclub rather than a pub. It was located on the top floor of the building, boasting floor-to-ceiling windows overlooking the city. The building itself was decently modern, and with its location in the heart of Belfast, it had either been a full remodel job or the prior occupant had been torn down to make room for the large modern structure that was now standing.

Just inside the entrance of the building was a bank of elevators with two enormous men standing guard over a line of approximately thirty people.

I felt a surge of disappointment, unsure if we would be able to make it upstairs to the club with so many people waiting. We weren't the type to attempt to cut in line, so we started for the back, but before we went far, I heard my name.

"Rebecca Peterson?" one of the bouncers called out in a strong voice that carried above the noise of the music and chattering crowd.

"Ah, yes?"

"You can go on up. Ronan is expecting you." He eyed me

curiously as he pressed the call button on the elevator, and the doors opened.

How the hell did they know it was me? Aside from the fact that I hadn't given Ronan my last name, he didn't have a picture of me, as far as I knew.

While I stumbled to register my confusion and unease, Ashley took the lead, more than happy to accept their invitation.

"Perfect! Thanks, guys!" She grabbed my arm and tugged me into the open elevator.

Before I could argue, we were on our way upstairs. The elevators had a retro style with decorative wrought-iron caging on the inside for aesthetic purposes rather than functionality. Dim lighting from antique fixtures, rich wood paneling, and burgundy carpet set the tone for a trip into the 1920s. The Huntsman club was a perfect replica of a 1920s speakeasy.

Detailed mural wallpaper covered the portions of the walls that weren't lined with intricately carved wood booths, each in a circular shape and enclosed just enough for a private conversation but still remaining part of the room. Softening the ambiance were enormous red velour draperies that hung in various locations around the perimeter. The bar itself was a work of art running nearly the room's length. The marble bar top was inlaid into a wood frame with evenly spaced brass and carved wood ornamentation. Bar-height wood tables lined the periphery of the room, and in the middle of the club was a dance floor packed with people. While the ambiance was retro, the patrons and music were definitely modern-day. The whole setup was amazing, and we helplessly gawked as we entered the giant room. It was so unlike anything I had ever seen, and I had to take a minute to appreciate all the artistic touches.

"Rebecca, you came!" Ronan approached with a grin, dimples on display, and gave me a small kiss on the cheek.

Seeing his smiling face and feeling the swell of life all around me helped me discard the worries that had tried to poison my night on the way upstairs. Everything about this place was fantastic, and we were going to have a perfect night.

I grinned broadly. "We just got carried away talking at dinner. Ronan, this is Ashley."

She put her hand forward, and he lifted it to his lips for a kiss.

"It's lovely to meet you, and I'm so glad both of you could make it. I've got a table for us over here." He ushered us toward a booth labeled VIP, perfectly situated near the dance floor but just removed enough to have a bit of privacy. "What would you like to drink?"

A server scurried over to take our orders, and Ronan joined us on the curved bench seats. Wanting to embrace my carefree night, I ordered a lemon drop shot, and Ash followed suit.

"Do you work here?" Leave it to Ash to come right out with the questions. She was never afraid to talk to anyone or ask questions.

"My boss owns the place, so I'm here most days. You ladies look stunning tonight, by the way." Although he addressed both of us, his eyes held mine while he spoke.

I dropped my gaze but quickly peered back up through my lashes. I wasn't sure if it was the alcohol affecting me or Ronan's attention, but I was feeling good. I knew my cheeks were growing more flushed, and I couldn't seem to wipe the silly grin from my face.

Ronan waved over someone from the bar and sat tall as they approached. "Rebecca and Ashley, these are my friends, Liam and Michael."

"Evenin', ladies," said Liam, who was a lanky strawberry-blond with laugh lines creasing the corners of his eyes. The other man was solid, not quite as tall, and had deep green eyes. He was considerably more stoic than his friend and merely nodded in our direction. The guys stepped aside to allow the server to serve our drinks, and Ronan lifted his glass in a toast.

"For every wound, a balm. For every sorrow, cheer. For every storm, a calm. For every thirst, a beer."

We all threw back our shots with a laugh, and Ronan extracted himself from the booth. He turned back to where I sat, holding out his hand. "Dance with me."

I glanced back at Ashley in question, not wanting to leave her alone if she wanted me to stay, but her eyes were glued to Liam. He flashed her a mischievous grin and held out his hand on the other side of the booth to help her out.

The four of us danced for some time among the throng of gyrating bodies. Every couple of songs, we'd head back to the booth to have a drink and cool down. We had such a great time that I was able to completely relax and just enjoy the night out. Liam was hilarious, regaling us with embarrassing stories about his friends, including Ronan. He was also particularly well-versed at dirty jokes, so I laughed more than I had in weeks.

As the night progressed, the DJ began to play more sultry, languorous songs. I found myself pressed against Ronan, his arms wrapped securely around me. I had acquired a perfect buzz from the alcohol. My inhibitions had taken a hike, but I wasn't so trashed that I wasn't aware when Ronan's hands slid from my lower back down to my ass. Before I could even decide if I was comfortable with his hand placement, he squeezed and pulled me forward, pressing his erection against my lower belly.

I wasn't a prude, but he was making me uncomfortable. I tried to gently pull away from him, not wanting to make a scene, but he held me firmly in place.

"What's wrong?" he called over the music close to my ear. "We can go somewhere more private if you prefer."

The alcohol swirling in my stomach soured. Was that why he'd invited me here tonight? For a quick fuck? Maybe I'd totally misunderstood. I'd thought Ronan was interested in me. That he might be a new relationship in the making.

Apparently, I'd been wrong.

"I need to use the restroom." I shook my head and pulled away more sharply, freeing myself and fleeing from the dance floor toward the back hallway. Before I made it to the restroom door, someone took hold of my hand and stopped me mid-stride.

"Wait, please." Ronan's brows knitted together. "Don't be upset. You're just too gorgeous, and I got carried away. I guess I misread things." His words sounded genuine, but I was off-kilter and wasn't sure I was comfortable in a dark hallway alone with him.

"Um, I've had a great time tonight, and I appreciate you inviting us out." I stepped back a bit and tried to pull my hand free, but he held tight.

"But..." he started for me.

"But we just met, and I've had more to drink than I probably should have, so I think this might be a good time for me to call it a night."

"I'm not going to force you into anything, Rebecca. I didn't mean to make you uncomfortable. Give me another chance—give me your number before you disappear tonight."

I searched his chestnut eyes and wondered if I'd overreacted. He hadn't given me any real reason not to trust him, aside from getting a little handsy. We'd both been drinking. I wouldn't want someone to write me off because of my drunken actions, so I shouldn't do that to him. But then again, being cautious had always served me well.

"You know where you can find me. Let's just keep it at that for now." I offered a small smile, hoping to soften the blow.

A flash of emotion flitted across his eyes. "Of course. I'll stop by for lunch again sometime soon." He placed a small kiss on the back of my hand. "Good night, Rebecca." His warm eyes held mine intently before he turned to walk back into the club.

I took in a lungful of air, not realizing I had been holding my breath, and continued to the restroom to collect myself.

Consistent with the rest of the club, the restroom was decked out like a retro-Hollywood dressing room with feather boas and bare-bulb vanity lighting. I felt like I should be wearing a feather boa and garters holding up silken hose. Whoever had designed the place had done an outstanding job transporting visitors to another age.

Once I finished my business, I exited the restroom with the intent to round up Ashley, but I slammed into a hard body just beyond the doorway. Before I could fall on my ass, large hands grasped my arms and pulled me forward to press firmly against a hard chest.

"I'm so sorry," I blurted. "I didn't see ... it's *you!*" My words faded to a whisper when I looked up into the eyes of my stalker. The man who had been lingering outside my window the night before.

Had he followed me? Did he plan to hurt me? If I didn't know better, the parting of his lips and raised brow would indicate he was just as surprised to run into me as I was him, but the coincidence would be too great. He had to have known I was here.

"What do you want with me? Why are you following me?" Frustration and alcohol blended to form a powerful cocktail in my veins. One that successfully diluted the fear that would have otherwise had me quivering and speechless. Instead, my words grew forceful and accusatory. Sober me might even have been a little proud.

The man grabbed my hand and yanked me into a room. Slamming the door behind us, he pressed me up against the back of it with my hands firmly pinned beside my head. Our chests touched, both rising and falling with heavy breaths as we held each other's eyes. Turbulent cerulean eyes almost too bright for the dimly lit room.

Dear God, who was this man?

I knew I should run screaming and get the hell out of there, but his actions had stunned my already dulled senses. All I could muster was a fiery indignation and enough morbid curiosity to keep me from thrashing against him.

As with our previous encounter, his face was expressionless except for the slightest tick in his jaw. Up close and in better light, I could see that his right eyebrow had a scar running through it, and his lips were full, though currently pressed firmly together.

Oh God, I'm staring at his lips.

This is bad.

"Following you? That's rich, considering you're the one in *my* club." His deep timbre resonated through my body and stoked an unwelcome ache deep in my center.

I shook off the feeling and concentrated on his words. *His club?*

"You own the Huntsman?" I blurted, confused.

"I do, along with several others."

"I didn't know. If I had…" My eyes fell to his lips again.

His eyes narrowed. "If you had…? You wouldn't have come?"

My lips clamped shut, not sure I wanted to know my own answer to that question. "I saw you outside my window." My words were nothing but a whisper as a tendril of fear finally made itself known.

As if sensing my growing unease, his grip on my wrists softened. "I don't know why you're here, but you don't belong. Surely, you must know that much."

Despite the calm presentation of his words, they packed a devastating blow. This man should have meant nothing to me. I shouldn't have cared if he wanted me around or not, yet his condemning words twisted a knife deep in my chest.

"*Fuck you,*" I hissed, displaying more hurt than I would have liked.

He allowed me to wriggle free of him, watching my every move with a predatory eye.

I rubbed my wrists and glared at him. "No need to worry. I won't be back here again." I reached for the doorknob when he spoke again.

"Did Ronan invite you?"

I paused, recalling that Ronan had said his boss owned the place. Was this man his boss?

"Yes, he did." I peered over my shoulder curiously.

"You'd be wise to stay away from him."

"Doesn't he work for you?"

"He does, but that doesn't make us friends."

The softly spoken words of warning hung in the air, the hum of pulsing bass vibrating around us. Once my heart rate matched the frantic beat, I opened the door and fled the room.

"Where the hell have you been?" Ashley rushed to my side as I crossed the dance floor. "I was looking everywhere for you!"

"It doesn't matter. Let's get out of here," I muttered as we neared the elevator.

She pressed the button for the ground floor, and I leaned back against the elevator wall, eyes cast upward unseeing.

"I thought we were having fun. What happened?"

I could see the concern in her eyes, but I was too worn down to detail all the events with Ronan and my stalker.

"Just these stupid Irish men—I think I may have to become a nun while I'm here. I'd say a lesbian, but I just don't think I can swing that way."

We both burst out laughing, and Ash put her arm around me. She was more buzzed than me, but I could still feel the dizzying effects of the alcohol pulsing through my system now that the confrontation was over. The world seemed to lag when my gaze moved from one direction to another. It was definitely time to go home.

Once outside, we set off in the direction of a busy cross-street where we could see cabs lined up in the distance. The side street we were on wasn't totally abandoned, but most of the bustling activity of the Belfast nightlife kept to the main thoroughfares.

I told Ashley about Ronan. She offered to knee him in the groin for me. I assured her that wasn't necessary but giggled at the thought. Before I had a chance to tell her about seeing my stalker again, something grabbed my arm and yanked me into the shadows of an alley. Ashley called out my name and came running to my side as we both stared in horror at the hideous creature with my arm in its grasp.

In a hissing voice, the hunched creature as tall as my waist glared up at me with glistening saliva dripping from its jagged, sharp teeth. "*Give it to me, girrrrrrl.*" It drew out the last word on a long breath, almost a growl. "*It's not yourssss. It belongs to usss. Give it to usss.*"

The filthy creature covered in grime reached its obscenely long fingers toward my chest, grabbing my necklace and yanking so hard that I knew the chain would break. Instead, my head was pulled viciously down into the creature's face, but the chain didn't give.

Eyes narrowed, and a snarl on his face, he prepared to yank even harder.

Ashley jumped between us, slapping the creature's hand away from my neck. Startled, it released the necklace. Ashley hauled us backward into the alley, keeping herself between me and the creature. "Get away from her!" she screamed fiercely.

I wanted to fight him off for myself, but I was rendered helpless with shock and fear.

The best I could do was cling to Ashley as we both looked desperately toward the main road, which was out of our reach, blocked by the creature standing in front of us. Behind us, at the other end of the alley, was a tall chain-link fence preventing us from an alternate escape.

Our panting breaths puffed out in clouds of steam in the cold night air.

The creature made a rumbling sound in its chest that was so horrifying, I could feel myself start to hyperventilate. It lunged forward and grabbed Ashley by the arm, throwing her several feet into the air and against the alley wall. Her head slammed into the brick with a sickening thud, and she fell to the ground in a limp heap.

"*Ashley!*" I darted toward her, but the creature lunged into my path.

"*Give it, or I takesss it.*" Snarling and hissing, it stepped closer. It lifted its hand to attack but then froze briefly before grabbing my arm and flinging its back against the wall with me held tightly in front of it like a shield.

Emerging from the shadows, my mysterious stalker stepped slowly in our direction.

"Please, help us!" I begged hoarsely but stopped on a cry

when my arm was squeezed so hard, I was afraid it would break at any moment.

The creature made a frustrated whining sound followed by a growled, "*Hunterrrr.*"

"Unless you want me involved, I suggest you disappear," he warned in a menacing tone.

My heartbeat pounded in my ears as I waited to see what the creature would do. I didn't have to wonder for long. Seconds later, his touch disappeared, and the air behind me cooled with a phantom chill. Suddenly off balance, I fell back into the wall, scanning the dark alley to see where the creature had gone. All I saw was a cloud of smoky shadow melt into the surrounding darkness.

For a second, I was too stunned to move. I wasn't sure if I was more concerned about the creature's disappearance or the fact that it had run in fear of our rescuer.

Who is this guy?

I shook myself out of my dazed state and jumped up.

"*Ash!* Oh God, Ash, please wake up!" I hurried to where my friend lay on the damp alley ground. She was breathing but unconscious, and her arm beneath her laid at an odd angle.

"We need to get out of here, now." The man bent down and scooped up Ashley like she weighed nothing.

I grabbed our purses and ran after him, not about to argue.

"Where's the closest hospital?" I asked when I reached his side.

"We can't go to a hospital. We can take her back to the club."

"What?" My steps faltered. "She needs a doctor. If you don't want to take her, then put her down, and I'll call an ambulance," I demanded with enough conviction that he stopped and turned.

After our eyes had been locked long enough for me to

notice that tic in his jaw, he dropped his chin and acquiesced. "My car is on the street."

He headed toward a black sports car parked in front of the Huntsman building. I crawled into the back seat, and he placed Ashley next to me. Cradling my best friend's bleeding head in my lap, I softly stroked her hair as tears ran down my cheeks.

"It's going to be okay, Ash," I whispered, my throat seizing tight with fear as the reality of our night began to sink in.

We'd been attacked by a monster. No ... *I'd* been attacked. It had come after me, demanding my necklace. Why? What the hell was happening?

Another stream of tears trailed down my flushed cheeks as I looked toward the silent man in the driver's seat. "What's your name?"

His eyes flicked to mine in the rearview mirror. "Lochlan."

"You see them too then?" He hadn't been surprised by the creature's existence. Whoever he was, this man was linked to the chaos occurring in Belfast.

"We can discuss that after we get your friend some medical attention."

Not the answer I was hoping for, but I wasn't up for a fight. Not at the moment. Ashley was hurt, and we both could have died. I hated to even consider what would have happened had Lochlan not arrived at that moment.

"Thank you for saving us." It was the least I could offer.

He pressed the accelerator and kept his eyes on the road.

SIX

A TEAM OF DOCTORS TOOK ASHLEY AWAY ON A GURNEY WHILE A NURSE questioned me. After I told her we were mugged on the way home from a club, she directed me to a small waiting room. Without anyone else around to distract me, my thoughts drifted back to images of the alley.

To the horrifying creature.

I wasn't even sure how to describe it—like a small human man had been dehydrated to a hunched bony thing. His skull was overly large, seeming to balance precariously above his skeletal frame. Boring out from that skull were two giant black eyes. His skin had been tough, almost leathery, and he wore a tattered, sleeveless tunic that appeared to be made of animal hide. He was so bony that it made him appear fragile, but his strength had astounded me. How could something that thin and seemingly frail fling Ashley up in the air as if she had been a doll rather than a full-grown woman? It was incomprehensible.

Just as baffling was his interest in my necklace. Did he simply like to collect any type of shiny treasure, or did something draw him to my particular necklace? If so, I couldn't imagine what. The piece wasn't flashy or expensive.

Something odd had been going on ever since I stepped foot in Belfast. It felt as though I had a doppelganger and had fumbled my way into her life by mistake. Could that be the case? Would that explain the odd encounters?

I tried to analyze the possibilities, but the waning adrenaline and alcohol made my thoughts fuzzy.

I felt Lochlan enter the room before I saw him as if my body was tuned to his frequency. He folded his large frame into a chair across from where I sat, leaning forward with his elbows on his knees. I hadn't been one-hundred-percent certain he would come in or if I even wanted him here, but now that he was across from me, I realized I was relieved to see him.

"How's your friend?" he asked, breaking the silence.

"Don't know. They haven't come out to tell me yet."

"What did the Draug want with you?"

I sat up taller at his unexpected offering of information. I glanced around, seeing that we were still alone in the small waiting area with a television playing a late-night talk show softly in the background.

"What's a Draug?" I whispered.

"I'll tell you about the Draug after you tell me what it wanted," he said with a raised brow, clearly implying that he was the one running the show.

"What makes you think it wanted something?"

"There's no way a Draug would make a scene so close to the Huntsman unless it had a very good reason."

The club? What did it have to do with anything?

"Why would he avoid the Huntsman?"

"Woman, just answer my question." His exasperation was evident, and I didn't want to piss him off. He had information that I desperately wanted, and the Draug had been scared of him—both good reasons not to make him angry. However, I didn't know what Lochlan's role was in all of this, and if the Draug was willing to kill me for my necklace, that could mean Lochlan might be similarly motivated. I wanted more information, but I wasn't going to hold out at the cost of my life.

With a sigh, I offered him some of what I knew. "The creature said something about give it to him and that it wasn't mine to have. I think he was just trying to rob me. What was that thing? Please, tell me what's going on."

He sat motionless, arms crossed in a stance that I was beginning to associate with his interrogation mode. "Draugs are extremely dangerous, and it should not have been here. It's not the first creature to find its way into Belfast, and we are investigating how they are getting here."

His statement generated so many questions, it was hard to know what to ask first.

"We?" I blurted, letting my mouth think for me.

"Me and my colleagues."

Apparently, I wasn't the only one answering questions with vague generalities. I grunted in frustration and stood with my hands on my hips, pacing in front of the chairs. "What is going on? Why are you being so cryptic? I want to know exactly what that thing was. Some kind of mutant? An alien? I want some answers, or I'm going to go crazier than I already am!" I threw my arms in the air, my voice rising the longer I spoke. By the end of my rant, I was breathing heavily and had stopped in front of Lochlan's chair.

He stood, forcing me to take a step back. He placed his hands on his hips and mirrored my stance. "What I can tell you is that you aren't crazy, and the world is not as simple as you may have once believed. For most people, the unseen ... *complexities* of this world aren't an issue, but you're not most people. I would demand an explanation, but I'm starting to realize that you're somehow clueless about your role in this mess, so I doubt I'll get any answers."

"Well, you certainly aren't a wealth of information either," I snapped back.

Instantly, his face was inches from mine, his eyes blazing. "Was saving your life not enough?"

Recognizing that I sounded ungrateful, I calmed my voice and spoke softly. "Maybe if I knew more about what was going on, I wouldn't have needed saving."

Our eyes were locked on one another, mine pleading and his fathomless. Suddenly, I was achingly aware of just how close our chests were from touching, and I could feel the air around us shift. Ignite. Electric anticipation snapped and crackled around us.

But the moment was cut short when a man in scrubs entered the room. "Family of Ashley Moore?"

All arguments fled from my mind as I rushed toward the doctor. "Yes! Well, I'm her best friend, but she has no family here. She's visiting me from the States." Hope and anxiety both swelled in my chest, battling for dominance. "Is she okay?" My voice cracked on the words.

"She's good. She has a concussion that we'll need to monitor for a day or so, and her humerus bone in her right arm is fractured. The orthopedist is currently setting it, but other than that, she just has some minor scrapes and bruises."

"Can I see her?"

"The others are still working on her arm, and she's on some heavy pain medicine. My suggestion for you is to go get some rest and come back to see her in the morning."

My lungs deflated with relief that she was okay and frustration that I wouldn't see her tonight. Something about seeing her awake with my own eyes would have gone a long way to reassure me that she was alive and well.

Resigned, I nodded and told the doctor how much I appreciated his help. As the man left the room, I turned back to Lochlan, who was still standing in the same spot with his head tilted down in contemplation.

"Come on, I'll take you home," he offered.

I was too tired to argue, so I fell into step behind him as he made his way to the hospital parking garage.

I didn't give him my address. We both were aware he knew exactly where I lived. The drive wasn't long, and while I still needed so many answers, I couldn't seem to form a single question. I was pretty sure shock had set in and shut down my brain because not only were my thoughts suspiciously quiet, but I couldn't seem to summon any emotion either. Instead, a peaceful numbness enveloped me as the city lights flew past my window.

When I opened the door to exit his car, he spoke softly. "Try to keep yourself out of trouble, Rebecca." He held my eyes for a couple of beats longer than necessary, igniting a sudden surge of feelings in me more intense than I cared to recognize.

Once I was safely inside, his black car sped off into the night. In a zombie-like state, I dragged myself upstairs, then removed my makeup and put on pajamas. My brain had blown a circuit, leaving my mind mercifully blank. I fell into a blissfully dreamless sleep.

I woke with the dawning awareness that my face was resting in a puddle of drool. I'd slept for over ten hours. Grogginess clung to my eyelids until a freight train of memories from the night before slammed into me, rocketing me upright.

Ashley was in the hospital.

I glanced around and confirmed that she wasn't in bed

with me. The black dress I had worn last night was wadded up on the floor, and a glance down at my arm where the Draug had held me revealed a large fading bruise. I was surprised at its blue and green coloring as if it were already several days old. My dark complexion had never bruised easily, and I healed faster than most of my friends, so I wasn't terribly unsettled, but it was odd enough to catch my notice.

Add it to the ever-growing list.

What was it about this place? If I were to leave Belfast, would the craziness follow me? Had it always existed, and I'd simply been too oblivious to see it?

I desperately wanted to run back home and pretend this had all been a horrible dream, but a sinking feeling inside me felt more and more adamant these things were happening to me for a reason. I couldn't simply ignore the facts without getting some answers first.

That was what I would do. I would get some answers, then pack up and leave. Maybe if I discovered that my necklace was at the bottom of these crazy events, I could get rid of it and go back to my normal, boring life.

A surge of hope fluttered in my chest.

My fingers clasped the pendant on my chest, and I held the stone that had basically been a part of me for as long as I could remember. My mom had always been more about the earth and transcendence than personal possessions like jewelry. Because of that, I had assumed that growing up under her influence was why I had never wanted to change out the necklace with something new and shiny. Thinking back on my conversation with Ashley, I couldn't help but wonder if my attachment to the necklace had been more abnormal than I wanted to admit.

Slipping off the bed, I went to the cheap mirror hung on the back of the bedroom door and studied the necklace intently. Inch by inch, my arms lifted toward the back of my neck, and my skin broke out in goose bumps even though the room was plenty warm. My stomach roiled as I forced my fingers to the clasp. I stood there, hands behind my neck, and held my own eyes in the reflection as a nauseating revelation hit me.

I couldn't make myself take it off.

My fingers worked, in theory, but I couldn't seem to carry out the command. Like the signal was being sent from my brain, but there was interference in the synapses on the way to my fingers, and the message was lost.

Take off the necklace. You can do it. Just open the clasp.

My body stood perfectly motionless. Not a muscle moved.

Finally, I let my arms fall to my sides with a defeated sigh. As much as I wanted to believe that this was all some kind of mix-up, I would be lying to myself. Something about my necklace was special.

I hadn't fallen into a mess.

I was at the center of it.

I stepped closer to the mirror, just inches away, and turned my body to the side in an attempt to see the back of my neck. Worse than I had suspected, there wasn't a single mark from the Draug's brutal yank on the chain—not a cut, not any scabbing, not even a bruise or a welt.

My necklace was magic. How else did I explain it?

That was why the Draug had targeted me. How the hell had I acquired a magic necklace? How had I gone this long without knowing?

I thought back at how I had obtained the piece of jewelry and drew a blank. It had been some time in my early childhood on one of our family vacations, but other than that, I had no idea. I was going to have to give my mom a call and see what I could learn.

The necklace had always just been there—when I slept, when I swam, on my first date, and even at prom—like a friendship bracelet that you tie on and don't remove until it falls off with wear. The piece became a part of me. Except this wasn't a simple friendship bracelet, and it was evidently not going to come off anytime soon.

CHAPTER
SEVEN

The nurses' station gave me the number of Ashley's recovery room and pointed me in the right direction. When I entered her room, she was mindlessly staring out the window.

"Hey, Ash! How are you feeling?" Relief flooded me at seeing my best friend, and I began to choke up. Knowing she wasn't crazy about tears, I stifled the emotion as I bent over and gave my girl a hug.

"Oh, thank *God*! They won't let me watch television or anything—something about a concussion and letting my brain heal. I'm bored out of my mind already, and they want to keep me another whole day. Then there's the fact that I have to wear this damn cast for a *month*." She pouted the last part as we both glanced down at the shoulder-to-wrist white plaster. "They didn't even give me a choice of colors."

I grinned, knowing that a sassy Ashley was a great sign. "Well, at least you're left-handed." I shrugged.

"That's got to be a first. It usually sucks being left-handed."

I scooted myself up onto her bed and trailed my fingers

gently down her cast. "I'm so glad you're feeling better. You scared me last night."

"I was pretty scared myself," she said quietly. "What happened after I got KO-ed?"

In a hushed whisper, I told her about Lochlan's appearance and how he scared off the creature.

She listened intently, her forehead crinkled in concentration before she spoke. "Bec, not to say I didn't believe you before, but now, I *really* believe. That thing was not human, or animal for that matter. I don't know what it was, but man, was it strong." Her eyes lifted to mine. "It wanted your necklace."

I nodded warily.

"We need to find out why."

I'd come to the same conclusion, except I hadn't counted on Ashely jumping into the mix. She'd already nearly been killed. I couldn't risk her life again when she had nothing to do with my troubles. In fact, I was hoping she'd consider going home early to heal.

"Ash, you don't understand. I'd never forgive myself if ... if something worse happened to you." Emotions clamped tight around my throat.

She placed her hand over mine. "Bec, I know you desperately want to protect the people around you. I understand why. But accidents happen—things like what happened to Callum." She hurried on, knowing I usually stopped her whenever she tried to bring him up. "You aren't responsible when tragedy strikes. It's not your job to protect your parents or me or anyone else."

You're wrong. It was my fault, and because of that, I owe it to my parents to save them from ever feeling that kind of pain again.

"Whether it's my responsibility or not, we can both agree that it's safer back home. You have a concussion and a broken arm—neither of which makes you a prime candidate for protecting yourself. You can either let me do the job while you're here or go on back home early."

Ashley dug her heels in with a haughty glare. "Don't even think about sending me home. I see it on your face, but there's no way I'm bailing on you. Not until I absolutely have to."

She was only in the country for another week, and she'd be restricted with her broken arm. Surely, I could humor her until she left, then pursue my answers once she was safely back in the US.

I nodded. "Okay, I'll tell you what I know, but it's not much." My hand lifted to my necklace. "You know how I'm so picky about my necklace? I started thinking about why I never take it off. I realized that my attachment was a bit ... unusual, so I tried to take the necklace off." My voice lowered to a whisper. "I couldn't do it."

"Like you couldn't get the clasp to work?" she asked.

I shook my head slowly. "I brought my hands up, and I tried so hard to make them do it, but they wouldn't move. Ash, there's something special about this necklace. I think it's the reason all this weird stuff is happening."

"Are you saying you have a magic necklace?" Her eyes rounded with something strangely akin to delight.

"I know it sounds absurd, but I guess I am."

"Come here and let me try."

"Ash, you only have one functional hand."

"The break is way up on my arm. If you just lay your head down here by my hand, I can totally do it." She gestured with her good hand for me to lay my head on her lap.

"I can't believe I'm doing this. If your arm hurts, you better stop."

I bent over the bed with my neck positioned right next to the hand of her injured arm. My hands began to sweat profusely, and my breathing increased as I squeezed my eyes shut. My skin positively crawled with the need to pull away.

Thirty seconds.

A minute.

Two minutes.

"I can't make it budge," she conceded softly, meeting my gaze as I sat up. "But I'm not willing to admit that it means anything. You've worn it for so long, it's probably just rusted shut. Have you asked your mom where you got it?"

"Not yet. What I do know is that the creature was ready to chop my head off to get his hands on my necklace. He yanked on the chain so hard that I thought my head was going to come off, but you just saw my neck. It's not even bruised."

Her determined stare bore into mine. "We definitely need more information."

"Agreed, but I'm not sure how. Lochlan doesn't know that the creature was after my necklace, and I don't want to tell him. Maybe he'd come after it as well if he knew. I have no reason to trust him. If this thing isn't coming off my neck, I think it's best to keep its potential magical properties to myself."

"Absolutely." Her face split in a wide grin. "Holy shit, can you believe this is happening?"

The few crackers I'd forced down before leaving the apartment threatened to make a reappearance.

"Ugh, don't remind me. I know I need answers, but I'd also like to pretend this isn't happening and just go back home. This is so much more than I bargained for."

"It's *magic*, Bec. Who doesn't dream of having magical powers?"

"They're not so fabulous when people want to kill you for them," I shot back dryly.

Her lips pursed as if to concede my point. "Okay, what else do we know? Knowledge is power."

"Lochlan told me the creature that attacked us is called a Draug. I haven't had a chance to Google it yet. The only other thing he told me was that they aren't normally here in Belfast, and he and his 'associates' are trying to figure out how the creature got here."

"A Draug? I think I've heard of that!"

I was so startled that I stood off the bed. "Are you kidding?"

"No, but I'm having trouble pinpointing where I remember it from." She squeezed her eyes shut and scrunched up her nose. "Give me my e-reader," she demanded, reaching for the bag I'd brought her.

Ash was a voracious reader with her face in a book every chance she got. It was no wonder she had pursued a career in publishing.

She turned on the reader and began searching frantically through her library while I waited anxiously.

"A-ha! I knew that I had heard the term. This book I read not too long ago had a Draug in it. It's a type of Fae or Faery." She handed me the device, and I skimmed the pages.

In the book, the Draug was a Faerie that used people's deepest desires to lure its victims to remote locations and kill them. That was not what had happened in this instance, but it wasn't entirely off base. It was at least somewhere to start.

"All the creatures you have seen could definitely be categorized as Fae. I've read a ton of books about them, so that should help. So how does this Lochlan know about the creature?"

"He didn't exactly say."

"Well, we're going to need to make him unless we find another source."

I chewed on my lower lip, wondering how on earth I could

possibly coerce information out of the domineering nightclub owner.

~

"You shouldn't be here."

I let out a startled gasp at the unexpected voice.

Seated in shadow against a far wall of the empty club was Ronan's quiet friend, Michael. Although he had been present most of the night while we all danced and laughed, he had been more of an observer rather than a participant. He seemed more at home here in the dark by himself than in the middle of the crowded dance floor. He wore jeans and a T-shirt and sat back in an assessing manner. Strewn before him were stacks of papers on the table, and a trail of smoke wafted into the air from his glowing cigarette.

"So I've been told, but I'm here anyway. I'd like to talk to Lochlan."

"How's your friend?" he asked, his words barely audible.

"She's going to be okay, but if we're going to avoid something like that happening again, we need some answers."

"You sure about that?" His eyes traveled slowly down the length of me before returning to my face. "I think you're in way over your head."

My jaw clenched tight because I knew he was right.

"Do I really have a choice?" I ground out in frustration. "It's not like I wanted these Faerie creatures to come after me."

As soon as I said the word Faerie, his body went inhumanly still. All nonchalance evaporated from his features, leaving in its place menacing intensity. "Be very careful, Rebecca. The creature in that alley is not even remotely the most dangerous thing out there." If I hadn't known better, I'd have thought he might have been referencing himself.

Well, shit.

Now I was really freaked out.

His hand slowly lifted to point toward the back hallway. "He's in the office."

Just get your answers. Figure out how to take off the damn necklace and get the hell out of Dodge.

Yes. I could do that.

I sucked in a deep breath of stale, smoke-laced air and forced my feet to walk farther into the lion's den. The office door was open, enabling me to stand in the doorway and study the contrary club owner before clearing my throat to gain his attention. "I need to talk to you."

Lochlan's eyes flitted briefly to mine before dropping back to his computer screen as if I wasn't there. "About what?" he finally murmured.

I took his words as an invitation and helped myself to one of the chairs across from his desk. "I need information."

"Don't we all."

"I'm pretty sure you know a hell of a lot more about what's going on than I do." I was usually very even-tempered, but Lochlan had a way of lighting a fire under me.

He finally sat back and wove his fingers together in front of him. "Fine, what would you like to know?"

"The Draug, is it a Faerie?"

"It is, but that doesn't do us any good unless we know why it came after you. I don't suppose you've had any revelations in that department?"

"No, I haven't," I shot back.

Lochlan grinned with more canine visible than would be considered polite. "Now who's keeping secrets?"

I wasn't willing to go there, so I ignored his jab. "The Draug called you 'hunter.' What did he mean by that?"

Leaning forward, he considered me, resting his elbows on

the desk and steepling his fingers. He was quiet for so long that I was just about to get up and leave when his rumbling voice filled the room.

"My organization keeps tabs on Fae activity. Ireland and sometimes Scotland happen to be the only places on earth with the ability to support portals from Faery. While those portals should be closed, every now and then, one is opened and something comes through. In this case, the Draug is an exceptionally dangerous Faery and cannot roam free. We will hunt him down. That is what we do. We are hunters." His eyes studied my face, gauging my reaction.

"Like some kind of secret border patrol agency? Do you work for the government?"

I had a bad habit of asking more than one question at once. My mom used to chastise me to slow down and let a person answer before I peppered them with another question. But when I was emotional, it was hard to remember.

"We have ties to the government, but we're an independently run organization. That's as much as I'm willing to tell you about us." His brow arched decisively.

"It seems odd to have a law enforcement agency running a bar."

"Normally, things are quiet. The club affords a level of entertainment. Plus, the Fae are drawn to human emotion and sexual energy. A gathering of drunk, horny humans is the perfect environment for keeping a pulse on Fae activity."

"What do you mean they're drawn to human emotion and sexual energy?"

"They feed off it."

"What does that even mean? Like when little kids get hyper and feed off each other, making each other even more hyper?"

"No. It's a complicated answer. There are different kinds of

Fae with different forms of magic. All magic must be fueled by energy, but the source of that energy varies depending on the type of magic."

"If they feed off sexual energy, does that mean they have sex with humans to feed from them?"

His eyes flashed, and he went eerily still. "Some do, yes."

An image of the vampire woman's beautiful projection came to mind. Did she trick unsuspecting men into having sex with her in order to feed? Why did she have fangs? How exactly did the feeding take place?

The foreign concept left me overwhelmed with questions.

"Until you're willing to explore why the creature sought you out, I'd suggest you stay indoors at night. It's not fool-proof, but it'll help."

"That would be convenient if you were wanting to keep tabs on me."

The hair on my arms stood on end as the temperature in the room seemed to plummet.

"I suppose I should encourage you to go out dancing and fuck around as if your life wasn't in danger." The words were spit out harshly, and I had no doubt as to their intent.

"What is your problem with Ronan?" It wasn't like Ronan had known I'd be attacked. At least, I didn't think so. Surely not.

"I don't need to give you an explanation. You can take my warning or leave it, your choice."

Not particularly helpful, but he has a point.

"If you don't like him, why do you still work with him?"

He stood and peered down at me, a clear power move. "It's my turn to ask questions. Have you ever seen any Fae before coming to Ireland?"

If I was going to get answers from him, it would probably

be wise to offer him something in return. So long as he didn't ask about the necklace, I'd indulge his inquiry.

"Not that I remember. I'm not sure if I ever came across any, or if I'm just now able to see them."

His chin dropped in acknowledgment. "Aside from the Draug, what else have you encountered?"

"The first thing was this little greenish man on my kitchen table."

"Sounds like a Brownie, harmless. They aren't technically supposed to be here, but they're not necessarily uncommon. Were there more?"

I explained my incident with the vampire creature. Just thinking about her made me want to crawl into bed and never come out. My legs bounced anxiously as I described the incident.

"You encountered her out on the street by yourself?" he asked skeptically.

"Well, there were other people farther down the street, but where we were, it was just us."

"You observed her openly, and she made no attempt to harm you?"

"I told you, I was standing against the wall, and she didn't see me. Maybe she was like a T-Rex and could only see movement. I have no idea."

"I seriously doubt that, Rebecca. The creature you have described is absolutely ruthless. Had she known that she was being watched, especially by someone as defenseless as yourself, you would have been dead in seconds. What aren't you telling me? Or do you even know?" His arms crossed in his interrogation pose, and his insinuation had me rising to my feet in self-defense.

"I don't know what you're implying. She. Didn't. See. Me. That's all there is to it."

The air once again charged with intensity as he came around the desk to stand before me. "Don't get your hackles raised with me. I might push back," he growled in my face.

I threw my hands up in the air, eyes turning skyward in a plea for patience. "I'm not keeping anything from you! I have no idea why she didn't kill me!" I yelled in his face.

Before I knew what happened, he had grabbed my hands and spun me around, pulling my back to his chest with my hands held tightly between us. And then, as if everything wasn't weird enough, he smelled me.

Not like a small, discreet sniff, but a full-blown scenting of my hair and neck.

It was unexpected and foreign but somehow also erotic and possessive. Despite knowing I should have been appalled, my breath hitched and then released on a ragged sigh.

"Well then, Rebecca, I hope you survive until you figure it out because until then, you're a dead woman walking." The velvet caress of his voice did nothing to soften the harsh slap of his insult.

When his hands released me, I whipped around but stopped myself before I could strike him. It was a terrible idea, but his jab had been horribly cruel. I resented his implication that I was bringing this on myself. I was doing everything I could to keep myself and my loved ones safe.

He could shove his opinions up his tight, perfectly sculpted ass.

I forced my face to soften with indifference, lifted my chin, and walked confidently away.

CHAPTER

EIGHT

After stress-eating enough carbs to feed a small village, I called my mom about the necklace.

"Hey, Becca, baby! It's so good to hear your voice. How have you been?"

"I'm doing really well." I infused as much sincerity into my voice as I could, knowing Mom had likely been anxious since my last call.

"Better? That's so wonderful to hear. I've been so worried about you."

"I figured you might be. But there's no need. Everything here is going beautifully. The museum is perfect—everything I could have hoped. And I've even made a new friend, I think, with the girl who works at the visitor's desk. She's really sweet. How are you guys doing?"

"That's such a relief! It's all good here. Dad has been buried in his latest book. You know how he gets. I make him come up for air and maybe a sandwich every few hours." Dad was a writer and immersed himself when inspiration hit. From what I understand, he'd always had a propensity to lose himself in his writing, but it had become an escape of sorts over the years. Dad preferred to live in his imagination rather than face reality.

I couldn't say I blamed him, but it hurt my heart for him to be so distant.

"That sounds about right. Hey, Mom, I was wondering about something. You know my necklace?"

"You mean the only one you've ever worn?" Her question was dripping with sarcasm.

"You make it sound like I refused to take it off."

"Honey, I did try, but you would have none of it."

"You tried to get me to take it off? When? Why?" I was floored. I had no memory of ever discussing the necklace with my mom.

"Not for a long time now, but when you were younger, I tried. One time, I remember you receiving another necklace as a gift. I can't remember who it was from, but I tried to get you to wear it. No way, no how, you were not taking yours off for any reason whatsoever. After seeing how much it upset you, I let it go. It wasn't worth fighting over."

"Really?" I exhaled in surprise. "I don't remember that at all. I was just thinking about the necklace and wondered where I got it. I was hoping you remembered."

She made a humming noise while she dug into her memory. "It's been so long. I know it was on one of our trips, but I can't honestly say which one. I'm sorry."

"It's not a big deal, Mom. I was just curious."

"Okay, baby. I was thinking, maybe Dad and I should start making plans to come see you. International travel takes some planning, and we haven't seen you in ages."

My pulse began to pound against my eardrums.

I didn't want my parents anywhere near this place, not when monsters lurked in the streets. Mom and Dad were the only family I had left, so I wasn't about to risk losing them. I felt bad enough about Ashley's injuries. If that had been my mom in the alley, I never would have forgiven myself.

"I'm still getting situated. I think it might be best to wait. Maybe I'll just come home for a quick visit at Christmas instead."

Questions raced through my head the second the words were out. Would these creatures follow me home? Could they already be finding their way out of Ireland?

The enormity of my problems suddenly seemed overwhelming, sitting on my chest like a giant Irish blarney stone until I couldn't properly breathe.

"All right, sweetie," she said with a note of sadness. "You just let me know. I'll talk to you soon. Love you."

"Love you, too," I wheezed from constricted lungs.

How had I not considered the impact of what was happening? I'd been scared for myself and Ashley, but what about others? Would the other people I loved be at risk if this problem worsened? The deeper entrenched I became, the more likely I would be to drag others into this mess. I wanted answers, but maybe the safest answer was to run like hell.

Yes, I ended up with the necklace, but that didn't mean the monsters were *my* problem to solve. My only real problem was getting myself out of danger, which needed to be my primary focus.

Get the necklace off.

Stay safe.

Protect the people I loved.

That was all that truly mattered.

～

THAT EVENING, I sat at my computer searching for anything I could uncover about my necklace. I figured the majority of information I would find about magic jewelry would be *Dungeons and Dragons*–type lore that wouldn't mean crap for me, but there might be a nugget of truth to be uncovered. I had no idea how I would identify that nugget, but I certainly wouldn't find it if I didn't try.

I used a hand mirror to examine the pendant. I wanted to see if I might have overlooked any defining characteristics that would help me research the piece. The chain was thin but not overly delicate. I had always assumed it was silver, but it never tarnished, so perhaps it was white gold or platinum. The stone itself was black with tiny glittering specs throughout. The surface was smooth, but there was a small carving that I had forgotten about on the back. As a child, I used to absently rub my thumb up and down across the indentations of the carving. I had assumed the artist had made the etching as a type of signature. Now that I was analyzing the necklace, I realized that it was odd that the carving didn't seem the least bit worn down after all these years. It was a tribal-like design with three crescent moons back-to-back and a solid circle in the middle between them. Three shaft designs also protruded outward between each moon.

Turning back to my computer, I searched for black stones with carvings. No matter what I searched, the results were never quite right. The stones too shiny or opaque. The carvings too Indian or Asian. None of the information seemed connected to the pendant around my neck.

When I exhausted my search options, I decided to look at what the internet could tell me about Draugs and the Fae. Information would be my best weapon until I could get myself out from under this mess.

An abundance of information came up, but I had no way to

verify what parts might be accurate and what was a fabrication. As best as I could tell, the Draug was linked to Norse mythology and sounded like a kind of zombie creature with a thing for treasure, which would explain his need to have my necklace. They were noted for rising from graves as wisps of smoke and having super strength—both of those facts were consistent with what I had witnessed. However, I also read that they stank badly, and I hadn't noticed any particular stench aside from his rancid breath. None of the articles tied the Draug to the Fae, but otherwise, the descriptions seemed consistent.

Turning to the Fae, I realized the name alone had a variety of spellings, and the etymology was diverse. I noted all the historical references, associated charms, and legends before I got to a section on the Tuatha De Dannan and the Aos sí. I took particular interest in the groups as they were both legends of Faeries originating from Ireland. I wasn't sure how much of the legends pertaining to each were true, but surely, some of the stories had been founded in truth.

After a while, I started to feel like a dog chasing its tail.

Sitting back, I processed what I'd learned and attempted to apply the information to my new reality. If the legends were right, the Fae had been around for eons. Lochlan had indicated he and his men acted as gatekeepers. When had their organization taken on that role? How had the Fae remained secret before that point? How had the group originated?

So many questions circulated my mind that I decided to make one last inquiry to see what I could uncover about Lochlan and the men of the Huntsman. At first, all that came up were pictures of the club and articles I had seen previously. But when I entered Huntsman Fae, what came up made my palms tingle and my heart race in my chest.

The Wild Huntsman Legends—the ruthless warriors of The Wild Hunt.

Why hadn't it occurred to me before? I felt like an idiot. I might not have been as well-versed as Ashley, but it wasn't like I hadn't read books about Fae and heard of The Wild Hunt. I had studied at a liberal arts school and read a handful of books about the Fae, including a *Midsummer Night's Dream,* which I had studied extensively. I was generally familiar with fairy tales and legends, but I had never entertained the possibility that they had any truth to them.

Words escaped me.

If Lochlan and Ronan and the other men who ran the Huntsman were actually members of The Wild Hunt, that meant they were Fae. They had to be if the two were truly one and the same.

I lowered my head into my hands.

Of course, they are. How naïve can you be?

The Draug had called him hunter and had fled in fear. That wasn't something that would have happened if Lochlan had been a human. Looking back now with a clear head, I knew the truth deep in my bones. I'd been surrounded by Fae and never had a clue.

What was it Lochlan had said? *We have ties to the government.* I had assumed he meant our human government, but I doubted that was his intent. Just like in the myths, the Fae were master manipulators. He'd wanted me to believe he was human, and I'd gladly taken the bait.

I was going to have to be more critical of everything from now on.

At least my instincts to keep my necklace a secret from them had been accurate. If they decided to come after me, I didn't know what I'd do. I wanted to run long and far, but they were my only source of information, and until I could get the necklace off, I needed them. I needed to maintain the ruse of friendship, no matter how terrifying the prospect.

"God, it's good to be out of the hospital. Irish food isn't my normal palate, but Irish hospital food is plain torture." Ashley eased herself onto the loveseat the following morning after I retrieved her from her sterile prison.

"No hospital food. In fact, I picked up some scones yesterday. Cranberry. You want one?" I brought her a blanket and a glass of water.

"You bet I do. A scone and some mindless movies sound perfect, but first, I want to know if you've learned anything else while I was gone."

"After I visited you yesterday, I went to the Huntsman to talk to Lochlan."

Ash's eyes got big, and she leaned forward. "And?"

"Annnd, he and his *associates* are like a police force for the Fae."

"He confirmed that the creatures are Fae?"

"He did, but what he didn't tell me was that he and the others are Fae as well."

Her jaw dropped. "Get out," she breathed.

"I'm not one-hundred-percent certain, but I'm pretty darn sure that he and his men are actually The Wild Hunt."

She smacked her forehead with the palm of her good hand. "How did I not make the connection? Fae. The Huntsman. It's so *obvious*! It's like they didn't even try to disguise themselves."

"Well, it clearly hasn't been an issue."

"True. Okay, let's see where this puts us. If we know we're dealing with Fae, I'm a veritable encyclopedia. I can give you a rundown of the basics. First, you can't eat or drink anything from Faery because it will *mess you up*." She began to tick off all of her acquired knowledge of Fae lore on her fingers. "They can't lie, but they can be super tricky when you talk to them."

"Yeah, I got a taste of that one already," I grumbled and received a raised brow in response before she continued.

"There's the gentry—they are the sophisticated, more people-like Faeries, but there are loads of other kinds, too. The scary part about the gentry is they tend to be the ones who go after sex. Some books say it's because they're extremely sexual, and others because they feed off humans' sexual energy."

"Lochlan mentioned something about feeding on sexual energy, but I'm not sure what that means."

"I'm not certain how it works, but it means they sometimes ensnare humans to feed from them. The Fae use their power to make you so turned on that you don't know which way is up or down, and you basically become a sex slave."

"Are you serious?"

"Yeah, it's all you can think about. Sex becomes your world, and you lose yourself."

I thought back to the times I'd been near Lochlan and how I'd been so drawn to him. How hard it was to think around him and how my body responded to him.

Embarrassment and shame blazed across my cheeks.

Had he used his magic on me? Had he been toying with me from the beginning? I was horrified, which inevitably stoked my anger. How dare he manipulate me like that! How dare he abuse someone weaker than himself just because he can.

A part of me wanted to go knee him in the crotch, but I'd just last night impressed upon myself how important it was to maintain the illusion of friendship with them. I'd have to bite back my anger. Lives were at stake, and I couldn't afford to lose myself in emotion.

Unaware of my internal revelations, Ashley continued.

"Most books say there's a Seelie Court and an Unseelie Court, but sometimes they call them Day Court and Night Court, or Summer and Winter Courts. It seems like each book has the courts set up differently, so I'm not sure on that one. The Unseelie are nasty, but the Seelie aren't much better because they all like to screw with humans. One book that I read had some kind of water horse that dragged people into lakes and ate them, but I'm not sure if that was Seelie or Unseelie. Let's see ... they usually can't use technology because of their Fae energy, or something like that."

"I think that one must not be true. When I got to Lochlan's office, he was working on a laptop."

"Okay, we can take that off the list. Across the board, though, every book has some variation that the Fae cannot tolerate iron. That *has* to be true."

"How on earth do you remember all this?" My head was starting to spin at all the information and the rate she was throwing it at me.

"You know fantasy is my thing. Most books follow the same general principles, depending upon the creatures involved. Read enough of them, and these fantasy worlds become familiar."

"I've always stuck to classics or mysteries," I said with a bit of a frown, wishing I had branched out more in my reading selections.

"No worries, that's what I'm here for. What else can I drudge up ... Hmm, some of the Fae can trace or fade or sift— whatever you want to call it—when they teleport from one place to another. Oh! And time spent in Faery is almost never the same as Earth time."

"What is Faery? Like a whole other planet?"

"That's another one of those things that change based on what you read, so I'm not sure. Sometimes it's a whole other planet, and sometimes a whole different realm or dimension." She paused, casting unseeing eyes at the ceiling. "Most of the Fae use glamour to hide what they are. I'm sure that's what that vampire girl was using, but I'm not sure how you were able to see past it. My understanding is that us normal humans shouldn't be able to see past a glamour."

"I'm telling you, it's the necklace. I think it's magical. The little green man seemed surprised I could see him. Maybe he had a glamour on too."

"Man, you're so lucky. What I wouldn't give to have a magic necklace."

My teeth ground together. "It's not some joyride, Ash. Look at your arm. This damn necklace did that. I could be in a ton of danger, not to mention you, my parents, and anyone else I know—all because of this silly thing around my neck. All I want to do is get it off and go back to the way things were."

Ashley peered at me gently. "I know you like to keep things safe, but I'm not sure this is something you can just ignore, honey. There may not be any going back from here."

I gave her the scone I'd been holding hostage during our discussion and curled up in the oversized chair across from her. "Of course, things can go back to normal. If needed, I'll just quit my job at the museum and go home. All I need to do is get this necklace off, and that will take care of everything." I turned my eyes to the television and turned on a movie, effectively ending our discussion. It wasn't my proudest moment, but I'd had all I could take.

Magic powers might have been her dream, but it wasn't mine. I liked a simple life with the people I loved. I found comfort in normal and reassurance in routine. This necklace threatened to take all of that from me, and I wanted no part of it.

CHAPTER

NINE

Sleep was a welcome escape from my worries, but it wasn't the reprieve I'd hoped for. Sensing a familiar presence, I rolled over in bed and took in the ominous shadow man looming over me in the darkness.

I didn't scream like I usually did when he appeared. This time, I lay still and studied the menacing form. It had no discernable facial features, only the swirling of dense smoke-like particles that made up his shape. Technically, I wasn't even sure if it was male or female. Just that it exuded a malicious energy.

His gaseous arms slowly lifted toward me.

My heart rate skyrocketed, and I reminded myself that this was just a dream.

The edges of his form began to blur until I could no longer recognize the shape of a man. The inky mass in front of me seemed to vibrate with energy, and in a sudden rush, the thick cloud shot toward my face and funneled into my mouth and nose.

I was paralyzed.

Not just with fear. This was something different. A violent outside force held me completely immobile while my body was seized.

My lungs screamed for air as I helplessly watched the darkness fill me.

A fullness pressed against the walls of my chest, like a balloon filled just shy of bursting. He was there, inside me, taking my body for his own, and I couldn't do anything to stop him.

Not one second felt like a dream. Every ounce of terror was real, and the threat was imminent.

But before the blackness could swallow me whole, I bolted upright in bed, wrenching myself from the clutches of sleep. I attempted to inhale ragged breaths in a futile struggle for more oxygen. My lungs were frozen tight in a painful contraction, and not until I sat on the edge of the bed, dropping my head between my knees, was I able to get a taste of air. I did my best to exhale slowly and entice my lungs to relax. My hands began to shake, and my body broke out in a fine sweat as the adrenaline drained from my system.

I had thought facing the shadow man might help me overcome my fear of him, but it had backfired. His presence now terrified me more than ever. Considering how real it had felt and everything I'd recently learned, was there a chance the dream was more than a figment of my subconscious?

In the past, the dream had always been exactly the same each time it occurred. Not once had there been a single variation.

Without the past week's events, I would have dismissed the mutation of the dream as a product of watching too many horror movies and gone back to bed. This change had me worried.

I ran my hands over my face, quickly jerking upright when I

felt moisture trickle from my nose. I held out my hand to examine my fingers, and even in the darkened room, I could see that they were now smeared in blood.

My head swam with dizziness, and my already knotted stomach threatened to revolt. I stumbled to the bathroom and stood for some time over the toilet. Once the nausea settled, I splashed my face with water and stared into my reflection in the mirror. Aside from the unnatural paleness of my features, nothing about my appearance was any different than it had been before the dream. I wasn't sure what I was searching for, but I needed reassurance that the shadow man was only a dream.

He had to be.

Monsters and Fae and magic necklaces were a stretch. I couldn't tackle dream demons, too. A girl could only take so much.

I retreated to my bed and snuggled under the covers. Ashley had fallen asleep on the couch during the movie, so I had the room to myself, for better or worse. Having her close would have been comforting, but even her bravery wouldn't ward off a bad dream. The shadow man was yet another demon I'd have to fight on my own.

THROUGHOUT THE DAY THAT FOLLOWED, I couldn't shake the melancholy that had come over me after the dream. I went through the motions at work but was lost in my head, attempting to sort out how I'd overcome my mounting problems.

At noon, I took my packed lunch to the small break room. I had only taken a couple of bites when Cat came in with her sack lunch and asked to join me at the table.

"Of course, have a seat," I said with less enthusiasm than I meant.

"Are you sure? I can just head to the café if you'd prefer to be on your own." She started to turn away.

"No, please sit. I just had a rough night's sleep, and I'm dragging today. I'd love for you to join me."

She offered a timid smile and sat. "Did you make it to the Huntsman on Friday?" she asked, shooting me a curious glance.

"Yeah, we did, but you were right. We should have listened to you and found somewhere else to go that night." She'd warned me about shady guys, but she had no idea how right she'd been. That place was every kind of trouble.

"What happened? I hope nothing too bad."

You wouldn't believe me if I told you.

"We just happened on bad luck after we left. Ash and I were pulled into a nearby alley and mugged. She ended up with a broken arm, but otherwise, we're okay."

"Oh, shite, Rebecca. I'm so sorry! I hope Ashley's okay."

I could tell she was genuinely upset. Her concern made me feel bad that I couldn't tell her the truth, and at the same time, pleased that I had a friend here when Ash headed home. It was good to know that not everyone in Belfast was out to intimidate or harm me.

"Thanks. I'm sure in the future I'll be much more careful."

"Actually, that reminds me." She dug in the bag that she had carried in with her. "I dabble in making jewelry, and this was a little something I made. It's yours if you want it."

She slid her hand across the table and revealed a soft, light-brown leather bracelet with ties on either end. The band was about half an inch wide and decorated with a repeating design of lines and dots that had been artfully burned into the leather.

"This is gorgeous! You made it?" Fingering the delicate

markings, I wasn't sure I had ever seen something so simple yet so beautifully crafted.

She nodded and offered hesitantly, "Would you like some help getting it on?"

"Definitely." I extended my left wrist, and with deft fingers, she tied the strings into an intricate knot before using a small pocketknife to cut off the excess.

"Thank you, Cat. I was thinking that we ought to get some coffee or have a drink after work sometime. I want to hear more about your jewelry and any other hidden talents you might have."

"I'd like that. Maybe once Ashley's gone home, and you have more time. Anyway, I'd better hurry up and finish, or Fergus will have my hide."

"I don't think Fergus could harm a fly if his life depended on it. He certainly wouldn't get upset with you. You're like family to him."

"*You've* never been on his bad side. It doesn't happen often, but when it does, look out!" She shook her finger at me, and I couldn't help but laugh at her and the image of Fergus on the rampage. He was firm and had high expectations, but he was all marshmallow on the inside.

NOT LONG AFTER LUNCH, Fergus offered to finish my tour of the exhibits that had been cut short on my first day. I jumped at the chance to learn what he knew about the remaining artwork in the museum. We picked up at the bronze stallion sculpture that I had found so captivating. Fergus explained that it was a permanent piece in the museum created in the Japanese Meiji Period in the late 1800s. From there, we made our way to a temporary exhibit on loan from the National Galleries of Scotland as part of an Artists of the UK Exhibit.

"This first piece is *The Quarrel of Oberon and Titania* painted by one of my Scottish kinsmen, artist Joseph Noel Paton in 1849."

"I remember this one from my studies. It's a depiction of the argument between the king and queen of the Faeries from Shakespeare's *A Midsummer Night's Dream*." I had not paid particular attention to the painting on my first trip through the museum, but in light of recent events, I was much more intrigued this time around. I quieted the questions bouncing around in my head to pay attention to what Fergus had to say.

"Indeed, the couple fought over the custody of a child. Each wanted to keep him for their own reasons. Oberon, doubting the veracity of Titania's reason for wanting the child, tricked her into thinking she was in love with a man with a donkey's head to punish and distract her. You can see the child, who was rumored to be an Indian king's son, hiding behind Titania. Eventually, the two reconcile and forgive one another, but only after Oberon has taken the child."

"To be his henchman, or knight, I believe." I tried to recall the story's details, but I had studied the literary elements more than the mythical legend and would have to review the writing again to refresh my memory.

"Correct. The piece was painted around 300 years after Shakespeare wrote the play in the 1500s, so the imagery was impacted by the techniques and customs popular during Paton's era. Nudity on a canvas would not have been tolerated in decent society, which meant his Faeries had to have wings to differentiate them from humans. Naked men and women would have been risqué, but if they were Faeries, the rules didn't apply." Fergus raised his brows conspiratorially. "You can see by the Faeries swarming the owl at the top of the painting and in the more grotesque appearances of some of the characters in his depiction that the Faeries were not entirely benevolent. This was thought to be representative of the violence occurring at the time in the Scottish Highlands." As his summary came to a close, we both stood deep in concentration, taking in the many details of the painting.

My mind raced with questions. Were Titania and Oberon truly king and queen of Faery? Was there any truth to the Shakespearean tale, or was it merely fanciful imaginings? If it had been real, how would Shakespeare have known about the Fae?

I made plans to see what I could dig up on Titania and Oberon when I got home, adding the names to my mental list of possible characters in this new world I was discovering.

BEFORE BED THAT NIGHT, I called my mother. I had a question for her, but I also wanted to hear her voice before surrendering myself to my dreams. Even my sleep no longer felt safe.

"Hey, Mom!"

"Hey, sweetie! I'm surprised to hear from you again so quickly. Is everything okay?"

"Yeah, just had something kind of odd happen. I've started having that dream again about the shadow man. I was wondering what was in the incense you used to burn in my room as a kid. I'm hoping I can locate some here, and it'll help me sleep better."

"Oh, honey. I hate that you're having to deal with that. It always made you so upset."

"Yeah, but I was a kid then. It's just an annoyance now."

"I wonder why it resurfaced?" she mused.

Could be the supernatural mugging or the creepy vampire lady, but who knows.

"Probably just my brain out of sorts after the move. I'll bet it was a fluke and won't even happen again." *I wish.*

"I hope so. If not, my offer to come out there stands."

I smiled sadly. "I know, Momma. Thank you. I'm sure the incense will be plenty to restore my balance." I didn't want Mom to worry and wouldn't have asked about the incense if I wasn't in desperate need of help. I never wanted to face whatever I experienced the night before again.

"I don't know everything that was in it, but the two key ingredients were frankincense and myrrh."

"Like the gifts the wise men brought when Jesus was born?" I asked, surprised.

"Yes, they are supposed to have protective qualities to ward off evil. A hippie friend of mine had suggested we give it a try. It all seemed like a bunch of malarkey to me, but when your nightmares stopped, I didn't question it."

"Perfect. I'll see if I can track some down when I get a chance. It'll remind me of home anyway."

"My sweet girl always was a homebody, at least until college. You've really spread your wings since then." Her voice held pride tinged with a sadness she couldn't hide.

"I won't be here forever, Momma," I said softly.

"I know, baby girl. And even if you were, it's okay. I'll just move to Ireland," she teased, lightening the mood. "Night, Becca baby. You try to get some sleep."

"Night, Mom. Love you."

"Love you more."

Armed with Mom's love, I went to bed with a full heart and enjoyed a dreamless night's sleep.

CHAPTER
TEN

I started my Tuesday with a bit more energy and optimism than I had the day before. I tend to wear my feelings—dark colors on rough days and bright colors when I'm feeling cheerful. Confidence and optimism meant a red sheath dress that hugged my frame perfectly and black patent peep-toe heels. It was one of the few dresses that fit my figure and was professional enough to wear to work. The bold outfit bolstered my psyche even further, and I felt ready to deal with whatever came my way.

A couple of hours into my workday, I got a call from Cat informing me that I had a visitor in the lobby. When I exited the elevator, Ronan was waiting for me just a few feet away.

"Rebecca, you look amazing." He flashed his charming smile, and I patted myself on the back for the choice of outfit.

He was looking particularly sharp as well—his long wool coat hung open to reveal a light gray suit with a white dress shirt. His wavy hair was plastered back in an attempt to tame the curl, but he lost the battle with a wayward strand or two. His stiff gelled hair was not my favorite hairstyle, and I wondered how it would lighten his appearance if he let his hair flow more naturally.

"Hey, Ronan, what can I do for you?"

He might have been easy on the eyes, but he wasn't *human*. That changed everything.

His face grew more serious as he came to stand directly in front of me and reached out to take hold of my hands. "We need to talk. I know you have a lot of questions, and Lochlan thinks it's better to keep you in the dark, but I think you deserve more information. I was hoping we could meet after you're done with work this evening—have some coffee and talk. I want you to get to know me. Maybe even learn to trust me."

His expression was hopeful, and a small voice inside me pointed out that I shouldn't condemn an entire race of people just because some are dangerous. Being cautious was one thing, but I hadn't been given any reason to truly fear any of the Huntsmen. I wasn't going to forget anytime soon that they were Fae, but I didn't have to assume the worst either. This would be a great opportunity to get information and maybe even form an alliance.

"Yeah, I can do that."

"Thank you, Rebecca. There's a coffee shop down the road called Common Grounds. Meet me there when you get off work. Six o'clock, right?"

I nodded. "I'll see you there."

I ENTERED the coffee shop and immediately spotted Ronan sitting at a table. He rose at my approach and helped me remove my coat, making every effort to be a gentleman.

"Hot chocolate again, or something different this time?"

"I think some tea would be good for now, thank you."

He gave a lighthearted bow and headed to the counter to order our drinks. When he returned, he placed two steaming teacups on our table. "I want more than anything to earn your trust, Rebecca. Tell me what I need to do."

My gaze drifted uncomfortably around the room. "I'm not sure, Ronan. Right now, honesty is all I'm asking for, but trust will be difficult when I feel like my whole world has been undone. Nothing is what I thought. How do I trust anything anymore?"

He leaned forward and placed his hand over mine, drawing my gaze back to him. "I can understand that, and I'm here to help you in any way that I can. Tell me, what questions do you have?"

"You're Fae, aren't you? You and Lochlan and the men of the Huntsman." It wasn't so much a question as a statement I needed to confirm.

Pride brightened his eyes. He was pleased that I had figured it out. "Yes, we are."

I had expected his answer, but it still blew me away to think that these men were not human. "Are you immortal then?"

"That is one of those subjects we are not supposed to discuss. However, because of ... extenuating circumstances, the rules don't exactly apply. We are immortal, but probably not as indestructible as your myths would have you believe. We stop aging around thirty, and then we are very long lived, although not totally invincible." He peered at me coyly. "If you were to cut off my head, it wouldn't grow back. We are quick to heal, but there are limits to the damage we can sustain. Our healing abilities also keep us from getting sick, which means we can potentially live for thousands of years unless we meet an *untimely* end."

"Am I allowed to ask how old you are?"

His lips quirked in a wry smile. "I suppose you just did."

I returned his smile and arched my brow to indicate that I was still waiting for an answer.

"Let's just say I have the benefit of centuries of experience in life."

I sat back in awe of his answer. "And Lochlan, too?"

The moment Lochlan's name left my lips, Ronan stiffened before he caught himself and regained an air of perfect ease. "Yes, he's quite old."

I got the sense Lochlan's distaste for Ronan was mutual. "Can you tell me about Lochlan?" I asked cautiously. "Why is there so much animosity between you two?"

He breathed deeply. "Of all the questions you might have, I cannot fathom why you would want to waste one on him." He paused for a moment, his brown eyes distant. "But I promised honesty, and it's probably best you know the truth about him anyway. He tried to take everything from me. At every opportunity, he has plotted against me, and after we had been in the Hunt for some time together, he even tried to take my life. He set an intricate plot to make others think I had orchestrated a bloodbath, but in reality, he had engineered the entire scene to give him an excuse to kill me. I would have died, too, if the others hadn't intervened."

"Why do you stay in the Hunt if you hate him so much?"

"Not just any Fae can be in the Hunt. We're like your American Navy SEALs. A limited number of men are accepted in our ranks, and the standards are rigorous. Many freedoms and privileges also come with my station. I wasn't about to let that piece of shite drive me from what I had earned. I may not have the option to avoid him, but you do, and you would be wise to stay far away from him."

I nodded, noting his palpable distress, and navigated our

discussion to safer waters. "Tell me about the portals and why Fae aren't allowed to be here."

"Nearly a thousand years ago, Guin, the Seelie queen, made the decision that man was becoming too territorial and power-hungry to coexist peacefully with the Fae. Not to say that we were living entirely out in the open, but the Seelie came and went basically without restriction, and it was not uncommon that magic was performed on Earth. However, the human populations began to unite under sovereign rulers, and campaigns such as the crusades spread out to conquer surrounding lands. With the end of the Middle Ages and the spread of the Renaissance and enlightened thinking, it became clear that the Fae would no longer be able to live outside of the rule of man. Nor was the queen interested in waging war against mankind to rule Earth.

"As there was no other acceptable option, Guin summoned the Seelie back to Faery and sealed the portals. She prevented all but a select few, such as the members of the Hunt, from crossing between worlds. The Unseelie had long been prohibited from entering Earth by the queen's magic, and once the Seelie no longer inhabited Earth, our existence dissolved into rumor." He took a sip while I processed his words.

If I understood him correctly, some Seelie were allowed on Earth, and I wondered just how many that meant and how scattered they were. Guin must be remarkably powerful. The queen of the Fae.

"I know it might sound silly, but stories tell of Titania and Oberon as the king and queen of Faery. Are either of them real?"

"There is no Titania that I am aware of. However, Oberon is real."

"Is he the Fae king?"

"No, that and many other facts about the Fae have been

lost or warped through the years. Fae magic is matriarchal and prefers women, so the strongest of our kind are almost always female. There are no kings. Oberon does exist, but he is nothing like a king." His eyes dropped to his hand, and his words bore a note of distaste.

I wanted to know more, but I knew I'd already pushed my luck asking about Lochlan, so I let my questions about Oberon go unanswered. "Lochlan said that the creature that attacked us was a Draug. Can you tell me about it?"

"Aside from the Seelie and Unseelie, on the fringes of Faery live the savage Fae of the Shadow Lands. Unlike the Seelie and Unseelie, their magic is dark and malevolent. They are ruled by an ancient creature named Lolth and usually keep to the darkness of the Shadow Lands. That's why it was so unusual that the Draug attacked you."

"Would the light harm it?"

"The brightness of day is excruciatingly painful to any Shadow Fae. However, I can't say how they would be affected by artificial light. Encounters with them are rare and often lethal."

My entire body shook with a violent shiver, but I pressed on. "After the Draug attacked us, it seemed to dissipate into smoke when Lochlan showed up. Can all Fae disappear or trace?"

One of his eyebrows rose in superiority. "What you describe is not the same as tracing. Certain Fae can manipulate shadow to disappear, and others that can trace, or what you might call teleport. Tracing is primarily a gift of the gentry, and only a few lower castes of Fae have the ability."

"If portals are needed to transport between the worlds, does that mean Fae can't simply trace or transport between them?"

"Correct. Tracing is only performed in relatively short distances, making tracing between worlds impossible."

Short distances—that was vague but promising. Anything limiting their power was a good thing. My eyes looked off into the distance as I pondered my next question.

"Are there any other types of Fae besides Seelie, Unseelie, and the Shadow Fae?"

"No, just those."

"What is the difference between Seelie and Unseelie?"

"They aren't all that different, per se. Both use light magic, but the Unseelie choose to live isolated lives and reject a sovereign ruler. Most of them are less sophisticated than the gentry. They choose savagery over community and focus only on self-interest."

"If they don't obey Guin, do they escape to Earth very often?"

"The Unseelie and Shadow Fae are not burdened by rules, and periodically a resourceful one can find a way between the worlds. Over the past few months, there has been an increase in this activity. Someone has figured out a way to open portals and has been sneaking Fae onto Earth."

His words made my stomach turn. "What does that mean?" I asked quietly.

"We aren't sure. We've been tracking the portals and attempting to locate the responsible party, but they're powerful and have managed to stay well hidden."

"Is there anyone who can contain the Unseelie and put a stop to it?"

"Several millennia ago, the Unseelie were ruled by Queen Mab. She was a malevolent and vindictive queen and one of the only Fae in our history powerful enough to bend the Unseelie to her will. The best that Guin could do was ward the Seelie realm and keep the Unseelie contained to the Wilds of

Faery. Since they are by nature solitary creatures not found in groups nor apt to unite in any great numbers, they haven't posed a threat of escape. Should they ever have the opportunity to make their way onto Earth in any great numbers, the havoc and destruction they would wreak would be unending." He paused, eyes distant.

"What happened to Queen Mab?" If she was so powerful, why wasn't she still around?

"She had a fatal weakness that ended in her downfall. Her love for her twin brother was her Achilles' heel, and that love got her killed. You will likely be familiar with her brother—his name was Merlin Ambrosius."

"Merlin, as in the legendary sorcerer in King Arthur's Court? Of course! He was rumored to be half-Fae—the son of a Faery woman." I gasped, eyes wide in total astonishment.

"I'm not sure where the half came from. He is full-blooded Fae. As far as I know, conception between the races is not possible."

I ignored his musing as my mind threatened to explode. "Are you going to tell me the Arthurian legends were *real* as well? Guin ... is that short for Guinevere?"

His lips quirked in amusement. "Sometimes, there is a seed of truth in fairy tales. Yes, your fabled Guinevere is the Seelie queen. The Fae have a long and complicated history. Although many Arthurian legends are fictional, the people—Arthur, Morgan, and many others—were very much real."

I was blown away, though I shouldn't have been. At some point, I would need to start expecting the unexpected. Question my beliefs and assume nothing.

I wanted to ask more about what he'd unveiled, but my entire fact-finding mission was aimed at gaining information about my necklace. I needed to stay focused.

"I was reading on the internet that the Fae often have

objects of power like a cauldron or a spear ... or an amulet. Does that kind of stuff exist?"

"Yes, there are any number of Fae objects imbued with power."

"Could something like that be destroyed?"

His head tilted just a fraction, and I was hoping he was contemplating his answer rather than becoming suspicious of my question. "I suppose nothing is indestructible, though the magic used on the object would likely create a challenge."

As he spoke, my eyes were drawn out the window behind him. That tingly sense of being watched clawed at my skin.

The reflection on the glass made it hard to see, but my eyes zeroed in on a puddle of shadow containing the outline of a man. As I stared, the form clarified, revealing that Lochlan had returned to his stalkerish habits.

He was suspicious of me, and though I wasn't sure why, his scrutiny pissed me off. How dare he question me when he's the mystical magic man masquerading as a human. He was the one who was a member of a mythical band of savage warriors. I was just a simple girl trying to make sense of what was happening around me.

Outrage simmered in my veins, spurring me to action.

"Hey, Ronan? I just remembered that I never told Ashley that I'd be coming here after work. Let me give her a quick call before she thinks I've been kidnapped. I'll be right back." Before I could overthink it, I slipped from my seat, phone in hand, and escaped to the back door.

I stepped into the cold, realizing too late that I had left my coat inside. Hurrying around to the side of the building where I couldn't be seen through the window, I called out in a whisper-yell, "Why are you following me again?"

His body slowly shifted from the shadows, then prowled in

my direction. He was a hunter in every sense of the word, and I hated how my body responded to his. I could understand if my legs itched with the need to run. That would make sense. It was the warmth that pooled deep in my belly that I found unsettling. It had to be of his making. How could I possibly still react to him on such a visceral level when I knew the truth about him?

He didn't stop until we were toe-to-toe. His frigid azure eyes assessed me. "Why don't you ever listen?" he asked with subtle accusation.

"I'll listen when I've been given reason to trust the person speaking."

His massive body maneuvered me against the frozen brick wall, and he spoke so close to my face that I could feel his warm breath ghost against my skin. "When I saved your life, was that not reason enough?"

My lips parted in preparation for a quick reply, but the resounding truth of his statement stole my thunder. He was right. Actions speak louder than words, and Lochlan *had* saved our lives.

Well, shit.

"You didn't tell me you were Fae," I said softly.

His hands came up to rest on either side of my head, caging me against the wall. "You weren't ready to hear it." His voice was as coarse as the brick at my back, grating along my skin like a tangible caress.

"I'm ready now."

"You think you are, but you're not." His eyes drifted ever so briefly to my lips. "You're still clinging to a reality that doesn't exist. Tell me, Rebecca, are you looking for answers or an escape?"

Both, is that so shameful? Who wouldn't want to escape such a dangerous situation?

"I'm keeping myself alive," I quip, irritated at his insinuation.

"If that's the case, you're not doing a very good job." His eyes lifted to indicate my presence out on the dark street.

"Are you saying you're a threat to my safety?"

"That's what you want to believe, isn't it?"

"It's not a matter of want. I'm trying to be cautious, but obviously, I trusted you enough to come out here." My voice trailed off with the reluctant admission.

Lochlan slowly pulled back, and my body shuddered at the loss. "If you're being cautious, then you won't pretend Ronan is something he's not. His past is far uglier than you could imagine." He turned to start walking away when I called after him.

"Funny, he gave me the same warning about you."

He glanced over his shoulder with a look as sharp as a razor's edge. "For once, he isn't wrong." As his figure retreated, his booted feet didn't make a single sound on the glistening pavement.

What the hell was I supposed to do with that?

Lochlan was an enigma, buried in a maze—all locked inside an impenetrable vault.

My shaky legs managed to carry me back inside, though just barely. As hard as it was to end the Q&A session, regardless of Lochlan's warning, I truly needed to get back to Ashley. The reality was, she couldn't cook or do much of anything one-handed. I'd told her I would be late, but it was time to get home.

"Ronan, I really appreciate you sharing all of this with me today, but I've got to get back to my place and help Ashley."

He held perfectly still and watched me closely. "What did Lochlan have to say?" His tone was flat and cold compared to his casual demeanor just minutes before.

I wasn't sure how he knew I had spoken with Lochlan, and

at that point, I didn't want to know. "Nothing of any relevance. I think he was keeping tabs on me, though I don't understand why."

He gave a curt nod. "I have my car here. Let me give you a ride home."

"That would be great. Thank you."

We gathered our things and walked to where he had parked his candy-apple red Audi.

"What is it with you Fae men and fancy sports cars?" I asked teasingly.

He gave me a sly grin. "I'm pretty sure every man, Fae or human, gets a hard-on for a fast car. The difference is, we can afford them."

"I see. That brings up another question. I heard somewhere that Fae can't use technology. That obviously isn't true, but is there a reason behind the myth?"

As I asked my question, he glided the car away from the curb and headed in the direction of my apartment.

"We were slow to adapt to technology. In Faery, the natural energy on the planet causes periodic electromagnetic pulses as magic ebbs and flows, making human technology useless. Plus, there is little justification to use technology. Why use a tool when you can use magic? But with Guin demanding our existence remain a secret, using cars and other technology is imperative to blending with society."

We finished the short drive in silence. Not until I had walked inside my apartment did I register that I had never given him my address.

Damn Fae men needed to learn some boundaries.

ELEVEN

"Quitting time," I sang out to Cat as I neared the visitor's desk. "Time to go home and relax."

She stood with her bag and scoffed. "Not for me. Not with my mam. Think I'm going to pop into the pub across the way for a pint first."

"By yourself?"

"It's better than going home," she muttered.

I hated that for her. Being with my parents was my favorite place to be. I couldn't imagine not having that. "Well, Ash is still laid up at the apartment, but I could probably stay for one drink if you'd like some company."

Her emerald eyes beamed. "You bet I would. Come on, I'll lead the way."

The pub was the epitome of what I would expect an Irish pub to look like. The narrow room was somewhat dark, giving it a cozy, if not cramped feeling, considering the large number of people gathered for happy hour. Cat led the way through the packed room to one of two unoccupied wood tables and selected a chair with her back to the wall. I sat opposite her, facing the wall filled with sports pictures and memorabilia. We both ordered beers and took in the varied crowd that conversed animatedly with each other.

"This place is great," I said over the din of chatter.

"Yeah, I stop over sometimes when I'd rather not go straight home."

"You live with your parents?"

"With my mom, and she drives me up a wall. I love her, but there comes a time when a child should leave the nest, and that time has come."

I shrugged with an embarrassed smile. "I can't really relate. I'm one of those crazy kids who did everything with her parents." I paused as the server dropped off our drinks before asking, "Do you have plans to move out?"

"I've got a cousin of sorts who graduates this year. Once she's out of school, we're hoping to get a flat together."

"That sounds awesome. I'm going to miss living with Ashley."

"My family is pretty traditional, and I can't live with just anyone. Aileen is on the list of approved roommates. She's not exactly a good friend, but at least I'll be out from under my mom's watchful eye."

"She a helicopter mom?"

"What on earth does that mean?"

I laughed a bit at her confused expression before I explained. "It means she hovers over you, overprotective or controlling."

"Oh, Rebecca, you've no idea. Her hover is more like a crow perched on my shoulder."

We both giggled, and I started to relax from my day as the beer worked its way into my system. I scanned the wall littered with pictures, scarves, and flags for a soccer club called Linfield. I could imagine game day here would be a memorable experience and decided that I would have to come back for a game.

Out of the corner of my eye, I noticed that Cat, who had been relaxed moments ago, suddenly sat up stiffly. Her face drained of all color, and her eyes rounded. She murmured something under her breath as her eyes quickly dropped to her hands, and I leaned toward her in concern.

"Cat, what is it? Are you okay?"

Her eyes darted around and eventually came back to me as she forced a smile on her face. "Yes, I'm sorry, just remembered I needed to let the dog out to wee, but it's no problem." Her blatant attempt to cover her fear did nothing to shake me, and I pulled my chair around to sit next to her.

"If you think I believe that, you're absurd. You looked like you saw a ghost. Tell me what happened?"

Her eyes grew hard, and her mouth set in determination. "I'm telling you, it's nothing. Let it go."

I sat back in my chair at her reproach and wondered what had gotten into her. Being at a bar, it was entirely possible that she had seen a boyfriend or an ex out with someone else. It made me realize that I had never asked about a significant other.

My eyes subtly scanned the animated crowd for any young men around Cat's age but instead, they landed on a shapely blonde who I knew all too well. As I watched her, just like the last time I had seen her, my vision blurred, and her image morphed into that of the vampire woman.

I released an audible gasp as the woman openly flirted with an attractive man at the bar. Her clawed fingers seductively caressed his upper arm, and she leaned her chest into him as she laughed. Before I could see more, Cat's hand grabbed my arm and wrenched me around.

"Don't look at it! Never let them know that you can see

them. We will sit here with smiles on our faces, drinking our pints like everyone else in the pub." All shock had gone from her face, and she now wore a fierce expression.

"You see them too! How ... are you Fae?" In my surprise, I spoke a bit louder than I had intended. I was stunned and elated to discover I wasn't alone. I'd thought it was me up against the Huntsmen, but if others like me existed, that changed everything.

"Quiet, you *eejit*! Of course, I'm not one of them."

"How can you see them?"

"I have the same question for you." Her brow raised expectantly.

"I don't really know. I just started seeing them when I got to Belfast, and I wasn't sure if I couldn't see them before or if there weren't any for me to see where I lived." I wasn't ready to tell her about my necklace.

After considering my answer, she lowered her chin in acceptance. "This is not the first time you've seen them here?"

I shook my head solemnly.

"And you didn't seem surprised to see this one. Have you seen her before?"

"I've seen her once before. What did you say when you saw her? Something about LeeAnn?"

She leaned in so that her lips were almost touching my ear. "Leannan Sidhe." The words sounded like *lee-anan shee* and were completely foreign to me. She pulled away but still spoke softly. "I've never seen one before, but I'm pretty sure that's what she is. They appear to be gorgeous women who lure men with their beauty and then feed from the men. It's probably where the idea of a vampire comes from. While she has fangs and will drink blood, that's just the means by which she takes the man's energy. Drains him until he's either dead or wishes he were." She paused, almost lost in her own words. "More have appeared lately, and I've no idea why."

"How is it you know about them?" I asked softly.

"My people have known about them for centuries, but I can't tell you any more than that. I'll have to tell the elders about you, and they can decide what you can be told. It would help if you'd tell me more about yourself and how you can see the Fae."

Of course. Yet another person who knew what was going on but couldn't give me any information. I fought off a surge of frustration. "There isn't anything else to tell you. I'm totally in the dark."

Intelligence sparked behind her narrowed eyes. "The other night when you were mugged, was it a human who attacked you?"

I slowly shook my head. "No, it was a Draug. I'm pretty sure it would have killed us if Lochlan hadn't shown up. I assume that's why you told me not to go there. You knew they were Fae."

Her brows came together in confusion. "Did they tell you about the Fae then, or did you know already?"

"I've gotten a small amount of information from them. They don't share easily."

"Lochlan knows that you are aware of the Fae, and he didn't have a problem with that?" She leaned back, crossing her arms over her chest.

"Yes, but he doesn't seem thrilled that I showed up here."

She paused, eyes tight as if trying hard to put together the pieces of a puzzle. "It's my understanding they keep to themselves and are not usually open to humans knowing about them. But for *some* reason ... they have accepted you. I'm not sure if I'm more intrigued or terrified by you."

"Please don't be scared of me. Everything about this move

so far has been traumatizing. You and the museum are the only normal, comforting parts of my life here. Although I suppose you aren't entirely normal since you see the Fae, too. I could really use your friendship, though. I swear there's nothing dangerous about me."

She glanced down at her hands. "Lucky for you, I take more risks than I should—or so my mam says." Her eyes peered up at me through her lashes, and a corner of her mouth curved up. "I'm not sure who you are or what's going on here lately, but I suppose we'll figure it out. Don't you worry. I'm not going anywhere."

"Thank you, Cat. You don't know how much that means to me. Can I ask why you seem so surprised that Lochlan and Ronan talk to me?"

"I can't tell you much, but they're predators, Rebecca. Those men are frighteningly powerful and dangerous. I've seen what they're capable of, and you don't want anything to do with them."

Somewhere in her warning lay a history of events, but she wouldn't tell me more. She honestly believed in her warning, and I wouldn't dismiss it, but I had only seen Ronan and Lochlan behave like typical human men. It was hard to condemn them when I hadn't witnessed them do anything wrong. In fact, each had helped me in their own ways.

"I know you can't tell me more. I'm just glad to know someone else out there knows." I met her eyes and hoped mine conveyed my sincerity.

"I'll see what I can do, but my family is exceptionally private."

I gave her a thumbs-up and finished the last of my beer as I watched the Leannan Sidhe walk hand in hand out of the bar with the unsuspecting man. She would kill him, and I couldn't do a thing about it. My internal struggle must have been evident on my face because Cat placed her hand on my arm and shook her head.

"You can't interfere. It's too dangerous." Her voice was soft but firm, and while I understood, it still pained me to watch the man walk willingly to his death.

"How can creatures like that kill humans willy-nilly? Wouldn't people start to figure out a predator is loose?"

"I've no idea how often she feeds or if she always kills. She may know to cover her tracks to keep from alerting the Hunt. They'll find her, though. Most likely, she hasn't been here long, and that's the only reason she's still alive."

"I've told them about her. I guess that means they're already hunting her."

Regret bubbled up inside me. If I'd had Ronan's number like he had offered, I could have called to tell them that the Leannan Sidhe was here. I realized that there was still hope and grabbed my purse, whipping out my phone and googling the Huntsman. Cat watched in confusion as I listened to the phone ring time after time, but no one answered. The regret blossomed into a full-blown case of guilt, knowing that my decision not to exchange numbers would most likely cost the man his life.

"I thought maybe I could tell them she was here, and they would come help, but no luck," I explained to Cat, eyes cast down to my hands in my lap.

We sat quietly for a while longer to ensure the Fae was long gone before we made our way outside and said our goodbyes. I was hypervigilant on the way home after the all-too-real reminder of what could be lurking in the dark.

CHAPTER

TWELVE

THE FOLLOWING DAY WAS A THURSDAY, AND IT WAS ASHLEY'S LAST full day in Belfast. I scooted toward her in bed and watched her steady breaths as she slept. Soon, she'd be safely back in New York, and I could at least check one worry off my list.

Her eyes fluttered open, and her face screwed up in a cringe as she met my eyes. "Hey creeper, you watching me sleep?" she asked in a hoarse, sleep-filled groan.

I couldn't help but giggle. "You know it. It's my last day with you here. I'm going to stare at you as much as I can."

Ashley rolled onto her back, gazing thoughtfully up at the ceiling before she asked, "You think there's Fae back in New York?"

"From what I've learned, there aren't many Fae on Earth, so I doubt it. But I suppose it wouldn't be surprising if the few here were drawn to big cities. They apparently like debauchery and mayhem."

Her eyes slid over to mine as a grin spread across her face. "Debauchery and mayhem? What are you, Jane Eyre?"

"Shut it, woman." I gave her a playful glare. "Why are you asking about Fae in New York?"

She shrugged. "I feel like going back to my job, and *normal* life seems odd. Like I'm pretending the giant elephant in the room doesn't exist. It's just a lot to wrap my brain around."

"That makes sense." We sat quietly for a moment before I spoke again. "I don't think you'll be missing anything of consequence if that helps. The guys at the Huntsman keep the Fae out, and life will go on as it always has." Ashley was too brash for me to tell her the truth. That the influx in creatures wasn't normal, and nothing was certain.

She didn't look convinced.

"I tell you what," I continued, "if it makes you feel better, I'll make you pancakes before I head to work."

She playfully rolled her eyes toward me. "What, am I five now?"

"You don't want pancakes?"

"Hell yes, I want pancakes! Get cooking, woman." She tossed her pillow at me, and I ran from the room laughing.

WHEN I WALKED into the museum later that morning, a stranger sat behind the visitor's desk. I was informed that she was the weekend worker filling in for Cat, who had called in with a family emergency. I hoped that Cat was meeting with the elders she had referenced and would be allowed to tell me about her secret society when she returned.

I spent a good portion of my morning on a conference call with a museum in Greece, discussing the possibility of a temporary exhibit arrangement. I wasn't ready to take the lead on negotiations, but Fergus was great about including me in the discussions and paperwork so I could learn what was involved in acquiring an exhibit. It was common for museums to swap pieces periodically to drum up interest and provide new displays for visitors. The terms of the arrangement were generally standard, but sometimes, pieces required increased security or other special accommodations that had to be ironed out early on.

When I hung up from the call, my office phone buzzed, and the girl at the front desk let me know I had a visitor. I made my way to the lobby and found Ronan standing by the front windows, staring out the rain-streaked panes.

"I hope you didn't have to wait long," I said when I joined him at the window.

"It's my fault for showing up unannounced. I wanted to see how you were doing. All of this is a lot to take in."

His eyes were warm, and I appreciated that he had stopped by to check on me. I walked toward the arched doorway, leading us into the heart of the museum where we couldn't be overheard.

"I saw a Leannan Sidhe last night. It was the second time I've seen her," I whispered.

"How do you know what this creature was?" His studious eyes assessed me, brow pinched.

Shit. Didn't think that one through, did you, Becca?

"Research," I shot back cryptically.

Rather than question the source of my information, Ronan assumed my secrecy was founded in my own reservations. "Rebecca, I want to earn your trust. That was actually the other reason I came by this morning. Come with me after work, *please*. There's something I need to show you." His features were set with determination.

"I don't know, Ronan. This is Ashley's last night here. I need to be with her."

"It won't take long. You want answers, and what I will show you will reveal more than any words I could give you."

Well, damn. How was I supposed to say no to that?

"Okay, but I can't be out long."

His eyes lit with relief and excitement. "I'll pick you up just after six here at the museum."

I nodded, then called out as he started to leave. "Oh! I nearly forgot. I realized last night that I should have had your number so I could have alerted you." My gaze dropped to my hands. "I think she killed a man last night, and I had no way to call for help. I won't let that happen again." I held out my phone for him to put his number in my contacts.

"Of course." He accepted the phone and entered his information, then texted himself so he would have my number as well. "I'm sorry you had to witness that last night, and I hope you realize you couldn't have done anything."

I gave a small nod. He leaned in to place a chaste kiss on my temple. I wasn't sure how to receive the gesture, so I simply offered a small smile.

"I'll pick you up out front after work."

As I watched his lean figure walk toward the front of the museum, I wondered what he would take me to see. I also thought about his kiss. My heart had raced when his lips grazed my temple, but more from surprise than desire. Nothing like the way I felt when Lochlan was near. Was that evidence of Lochlan manipulating me? If I found one human man more desirable than another, I wouldn't have to question the reasons, but my thoughts were riddled with doubt when it came to the Fae.

Why are you even thinking about this? They're Fae, Becca. *Would you really consider a relationship with a Fae man?*

I was surprisingly unable to formulate an answer.

Was it smart to reject them because of their magic? Or was

that the fear talking? Surely, I wouldn't reject any form of friendship merely because a person was Fae. That seemed narrow-minded and ignorant—two things I refused to be.

None of it would be an issue if I wasn't in the middle of some twisted game of tug-of-war between Lochlan and Ronan. Hormones were confusing enough. Throw in magic and their warnings about one another, and I had no idea who to believe.

RONAN WAS WAITING NEXT to his car outside the museum when I left work for the day. The rain had let up, but ominous clouds still shrouded the evening sky in a heavy darkness. Ronan held open the passenger door for me, then hurried around to the driver's seat.

"You going to tell me where we're going?" I asked, using a teasing tone to keep the mood light.

"To a warehouse over by the docks."

"Um ... should I be worried? You're not going to hack me into pieces and feed me to the fish, right?" I gave a nervous laugh.

He glanced over at me out of the corner of his eye and spoke with a sly smile. "Rebecca, I doubt cutting you into pieces would further my goal of winning you over." His continued pursuit was flattering, but it put me in an awkward position. I could sense he wanted more than just my trust.

"You don't have to win me over. Just be yourself."

He didn't respond, and we spent the remainder of the short trip in silence. We were both somewhat on edge, each for our own reasons, and it made the atmosphere in the car thick with anticipation.

We pulled up to a large metal building set back a good distance from the waterline. The parking lot had deteriorated to gravel and weeds, and the building hadn't fared much better. After we exited the car, Ronan led the way to a side door that opened into the main room of the warehouse. The first thing I noticed was the rancid odor permeating the cool air. I covered my nose and mouth with my hand in a pointless attempt to escape the awful stench. I scanned the area but saw no hint at the odor's source. Empty pallets were stacked in various locations throughout the room, and at the far end of the building, a staircase led to a set of offices upstairs.

Ronan continued to lead us to the back corner of the building behind a large pile of pallets. The farther we went, the more overwhelming the smell and my fear of what lay hidden.

"Holy crap, it stinks," I groaned as I lifted the collar of my blouse to cover my nose.

When we rounded the pallets, I witnessed something that would have turned my stomach even without the awful stench. As it was, my already rebelling gut couldn't handle the additional strain. I leaned over the pile of wood and retched. Ronan hurried to my side and helped with my hair as I wiped off my mouth and tried to regain control of myself.

"What happened to him?" I asked, referring to the corpse sprawled on the ground. He was coated in dry blood from a number of open wounds across his body. His wrists, neck, and belly were all slashed with deep cuts, and the escaping blood had formed a dark, sticky pool beneath him.

"He was a sacrifice. We don't fully understand how these portals are being opened, but we know they're using dark magic, which requires a high price. You can see the remnants of the markings beneath him that were used as part of the spell. We discovered it early this morning, though the ritual was performed during the night. We don't know what came through, but we were able to capture the Fae man working on this end of the portal."

"Does this mean that every time a portal is opened, someone has to be sacrificed?" The nightmare was even more horrific than I could have imagined.

"Unfortunately, yes. Has Lochlan told you anything about the portals?"

I shook my head absently, unable to draw my eyes from the gore in front of me.

"He and I have never been particularly close, as you know, but lately, he's been even more erratic and short-tempered than usual. I've been keeping an eye on him. The Hunt can't afford to question the loyalty of one of its highest-ranking members."

"You think he had something to do with this?"

Conflict and uncertainty aged his boyish features. "I don't know what to think. We were able to capture the individual working on this side of the portal and were hoping to get more information from him. Not only will Lochlan not allow anyone near the prisoner for questioning, but I have no idea where Lochlan was last night when the portal was opened."

"I don't know how the Hunt works. Is it normal for you to work independently, or do you usually work together?"

"There are no secrets within the Hunt." His voice dropped, and his eyes shone with intensity. "Has Lochlan given you any information about his whereabouts or what he may be up to?"

"No, he hasn't told me anything."

"I have a bad feeling about all of this. Each portal seems to allow more Unseelie through, and we are no closer to finding the source."

"Could you tell how many came through this one?"

"We're estimating about a dozen."

My mind flashed to all the people who would be totally unsuspecting and defenseless. How much worse would the nightmare get? How many would have to die before it was over? Saying I was in over my head was a monumental under-statement.

"Will the Hunt be able to stop it?"

"I'm afraid that if someone inside the Hunt is allowing this to happen, there will be no end in sight. The culprit will always be one step ahead."

It couldn't be. I couldn't imagine Lochlan behind this. This was a senseless slaughter—something performed by a monster.

"I wanted you to know the danger, Rebecca." He stood in front of me and lifted my hands to hold them between us. "I want you to be safe."

My tear-filled eyes met Ronan's, overwhelmed with every-thing he had revealed. "I think I want to go home now."

He pulled me into his arms, and I was so confused and upset from what he had shown me that I clung to him. Ques-tions about friendships and feelings were irrelevant. I desper-ately needed his strength and support.

The gory vision of the dead man would be forever seared in my mind.

"Come on, sweet Rebecca. Let's get you home." With his hand around mine, he led us away.

"What will happen to the dead man? Why was he just left there?"

"We aren't totally unlike your police or crime scene investi-gators. Aside from attempting to use magic to identify a culprit, we take fingerprints and analyze the scene. At some point, we will remove the body, but for now, the building has been spelled to keep unsuspecting humans out."

"What about his family?"

"I think you know the answer to that. They can't know. There is no way we could involve the human authorities. They cannot begin to dig into what caused this or why it was done."

As much as I hated his answer, I knew it was the truth.

Ronan drove me home in silence, allowing me to keep my turbulent thoughts to myself. Exiting his car, I turned back to thank him, my tone solemn and resigned. "I hated seeing that, but I appreciate you showing me."

"Thank you for coming with me. I'm sorry it upset you, but you need to know what we're up against."

"I understand. I'll see you soon."

"Sleep well, Rebecca."

CHAPTER

THIRTEEN

WHEN I WALKED INTO THE APARTMENT, A HAZY SMOKE FILLED THE room as Ashley frantically flew around the kitchen.

"Oh honey, you tried to cook for me." I rushed to grab a hot pad and pulled the charred meat from the oven.

"I thought I could do it, but man, it's hard to cook with one arm."

Her excuse made me laugh. She might have wanted to blame the broken arm, but I knew better. The result would have been the same whether she had one arm or three. Ashley's antics in the kitchen were the life vest that I needed to save me from drowning in my own emotions.

"I love you, Ash, but please stay out of the kitchen."

She stuck out her tongue and jumped out of the way as I swatted at her with a wooden spoon.

"Okay, okay! I'm out. Stop chasing me, crazy woman. While you fix my mess, tell me about your day."

I forced strength into my voice and willed myself to sound upbeat. "It was great. Sorry I had to work late. I needed to help Fergus get some paperwork ready for a meeting tomorrow." In

116

less than twenty-four hours, Ashley would be getting on a plane. I wasn't risking her changing her mind by unveiling the truth about Belfast.

"No problem," she said almost wistfully, her voice trailing off as she slumped into a dining chair.

"You okay, Ash?"

"Not really. My plane leaves tomorrow, but I don't know how I'm supposed to leave you here. I keep wondering if I should stay."

"What? Why would you need to stay?"

"It's not so much a *need* as a *want*. You've uncovered a magical new world. It's not fair for you to have all the fun."

My reactions warred with one another. After seeing that poor man in the warehouse, I wanted to lash out and chide her for assuming any of this was fun. But at the same time, a maniacal laugh teased the back of my throat at the knowledge that Ash *would* see the danger as a great adventure. I adored my best friend, but she was sort of a lunatic.

I took a deep breath. "You just have a bad case of FOMO—fear of missing out. Nothing wild is going to happen here while you're gone. And if you don't go home, you'll break your lease, possibly lose your job, and discover the only thing you would have missed was 360 days of rain."

She didn't look convinced but agreed reluctantly. "I suppose you're right. And I could always fly back over if things change."

Which, they won't, because I'm not going to tell you if they do. In fact, I'll be on a plane back home as well, just as soon as I can get this necklace off.

"Absolutely."

Ash gave me a sheepish smile, and knowing neither of us was the sentimental type, I stuck my tongue out and crossed my eyes to lighten the mood. We both laughed until one of us snorted. And then we laughed some more.

THE NEXT MORNING, by the grace of God, we somehow managed to get all of Ashley's new purchases to fit in her bulging suitcase and summoned a cab. We kept our conversation light, despite the obvious weight of our impending separation. After I helped get her suitcase checked, and we had said a teary goodbye, I was on my own in Belfast.

ONCE I WAS ALONE in the cab headed to the museum, I considered Ronan's suspicions about Lochlan. What he'd implied was so much more alarming than a simple rivalry. Granted, Lochlan seemed to think Ronan was equally as devious. Their animosity made it hard to judge how much weight I should lend each of their accusations.

The one thing I could say on Ronan's behalf was that he'd been very specific in naming his concerns. He believed Lochlan was behind the portals. While I didn't want to believe it was true, at least it was something tangible to analyze. I could investigate and determine for myself if the accusation bore any validity.

As for Lochlan's disdain of Ronan, that was a mystery. It was hard to weigh the evidence of an undisclosed crime. And in that case, I would have to give Ronan the benefit of the doubt. I wasn't going to condemn him for vague, unidentified offenses.

My primary objective was still gaining information about my necklace, but in the meantime, it would help me to learn who I could trust, starting with whether Lochlan was behind the portals.

How could I gather more information about him?

I could go to the club tonight among the Friday night party scene and sneak off to snoop in his office. I seriously doubted he would keep anything important out in the open, but I wouldn't know unless I looked. He was too secretive to leave private matters lying about.

If there was any truth to be uncovered, I had a feeling it would be found in the basement of the Huntsman. Ronan said that was where Lochlan was keeping the Fae man they'd captured. While it was a safe bet I'd get my information, it was also the most dangerous option. I had no desire to get caught by a bunch of Fae Huntsmen while breaking into their building.

I hadn't wanted to admit it, but the most practical tactic would be to put on my big girl panties and simply ask Lochlan directly.

So why did that sound like such a terrifying prospect?

I wasn't a fan of confrontation, but it was more than that. For some reason, I felt like giving credence to Ronan's claims would be letting Lochlan down. Why? I didn't owe him any allegiance. Yes, he'd helped me, but so had Ronan. We were two grown adults who could have a difficult conversation without getting insulted.

Right.

Because exchanges between Lochlan and I had always proven so civil and rational.

I sighed loudly in the back of the cab and tried not to question my decision. The conversation would be hard enough, so dwelling on it all day wouldn't help.

I procrastinated that night until ten, when I forced myself to put on a warm hoodie and caught a cab to the club. When I arrived, the lobby was full of Friday night clubgoers, and two men stood guard at the elevators. I squared my shoulders and tried to project confidence as I approached them.

"Hey, guys, I need to go up and speak with Lochlan."

"He's busy," the taller of the two drawled indifferently.

Not letting him sway my resolve, I tried another tack. "It's important. I need to talk to him about the *stuff* in the basement."

The stockier man glared at me with disgust. "You don't need to talk about shit. What you need to do is turn that pretty ass around and leave because no one here has anything to say to you."

My ears flamed at his rude brush-off.

Hoping for more luck with the other guy, I glanced at him, but he refused to acknowledge me. His eyes casually moved over the crowd as one corner of his mouth lifted in a smirk. I spun around indignantly and stormed into the crisp night air.

What assholes!

Here I was trying to do the right thing, and they were taking that from me. What was I supposed to do now? I didn't have Lochlan's phone number or email. I could come back tomorrow in the hopes that Lochlan was at the club and that these two dildos weren't there to keep me out. That would be the logical next move, but that was not what happened. In an incredibly uncharacteristic dismissal of rational thought, I stalked around to the back of the building. I normally avoided risk at all costs. But that was normal Rebecca. This was stuck in a nightmare, overwhelmed, and endangered Rebecca, who was sick of feeling out of control. This Rebecca had read from Ashley's playbook and was hell-bent on getting some damn answers.

Entirely focused on my task, I strode determinedly past dumpsters and piles of trash to the rear of the building. Ronan had said they were keeping the Fae man in the basement for questioning—if he was still alive. Merely verifying his existence and the level of security around him would help me determine how much of Ronan's suspicions were true and how much was unfounded speculation.

Something was better than nothing, and I was tired of being in the dark.

A single light on the backside of the building illuminated an old metal door. My heart pounded as I took hold of the door handle, praying it was unlocked. As I turned the handle, initial resistance had me cursing my luck. But before I had even finished the thought, a faint clicking sound signaled the lock giving way, and the door pulled open. It seemed odd that the men left their headquarters unprotected. Though it wouldn't surprise me if their sense of superiority made them overconfident. Who knew? I wasn't going to look a gift horse in the mouth.

Inside was a dark hallway, and I could hear the music and chatter from the front lobby carry through the empty halls. Stepping through the doorway, I sensed an odd sort of shock. My head swung around, searching for the source of the sting, but I was alone and could find no evidence of a threat.

I regained my bearings, pulse pounding in my ears, and quietly searched for a stairwell to the basement. Once I located it, I made my way down the stairs to the landing, which was a well-lit space around ten feet by six feet. Before I could open the door, I heard masculine voices approaching.

I would never make it to the main floor in time, and there was no place to hide.

With no other options, I backed into the stairwell corner next to the door. It would hide me when the door opened, but once it closed, there would be no chance of concealing myself. I would have to hope they were too preoccupied to notice me.

When the door opened, I stayed perfectly still, not even taking a breath as two men entered the stairwell. Liam and another man walked casually up the stairs, absorbed in conversation. The men reached the landing and stopped as Liam finished something he was saying.

I couldn't even process his words over my disbelief that they hadn't noticed me. I was right there, plain to see. The other guy's eyes even fell briefly to where I stood, then drifted on. I'd been invisible to them, and the only explanation I could fathom was the necklace. It had kept me hidden. Protected me.

I stopped my thoughts from reeling over the implications and forced myself to focus. I was in the Huntsman basement and needed to pay attention, or I could end up in danger. I had no clue if the necklace would continue to keep me hidden, or if that was even what had happened. I needed to get my information and get out.

I pressed open the basement door just enough to peek into the hallway. Seeing it unoccupied, I stepped inside and quietly closed the door. Almost immediately, I heard a low keening, like the whine of an injured dog. Keeping close to the wall, I cautiously continued toward the sound but froze when I heard a low voice rumble in the same direction. After a moment of silence, I resumed walking and finally neared the room from which the sounds had come.

The door was closed enough to prevent me from seeing within. I strained my ears to hear what might be happening, only to cringe when an ear-piercing shriek blasted from the room. I clapped my hands over my ears just as the cry abruptly stopped. The poignant silence was broken only by the sickening thud of a body hitting the ground.

My hands left my ears and slammed over my mouth to keep from gasping.

"He had no loyalty, just a paid grunt." The callous voice

sounded like it belonged to Michael. Definitely not Lochlan, which gave me hope. Perhaps Ronan's claims that Lochlan wouldn't allow anyone access to the prisoner were inaccurate, and if that was the case, his entire argument could be flawed.

"He still had to die. We can't have him out running his mouth." Lochlan's words soured my stomach.

Not only was he present but his comment also sounded horribly damning. Why would he need to keep the Fae man from talking? My eyes drifted shut at the implication.

"The portal will be open tomorrow, and our timing will be crucial," Michael commented after a brief pause.

They knew when the next portal would be open. Who would know that besides someone working with the other side? And now they'd killed the only person who could point the finger at them.

Shit.

Shitshitshitshit.

I needed to get out of there and fast.

"I'll take care of it. This time, it'll work," Lochlan said in a low, determined voice.

I needed to leave, but I told myself that I had to take a peek in the room—to be absolutely certain. I was invisible, after all, wasn't I?

Ever so gently, I pulled the door open just enough to see into the room and was miraculously able to do so without a sound. It was small and appeared to be an interrogation room of sorts with concrete floors and bare white walls. Lochlan and Michael stood in the room, and at their feet were the remains of a man who lay in a pool of blood, his body mutilated.

Air left my lungs with a whoosh, and both men whipped around in my direction. Falling on my butt, I scuttled backward in a crab walk. I only managed to get a few feet away when the door flew open, and Lochlan's hard eyes seized mine. Invisibility had failed me and left me dangerously exposed.

"You're the one bringing them in!" I breathed out with shock and horror.

His face contorted angrily as he yanked me to my feet.

"*Let me go*! Get away from me, you fucking monster!" I struggled for everything I was worth, kicking and hitting anything I could reach in an attempt to free myself of his grasp.

Barely fazed by my struggles, he threw me over his shoulder and carried me into a room next to the one containing the dead Fae. Slamming the door shut, he set me down and blocked the door, face cool and detached. He stood inhumanly still as I frantically scanned the small, empty room.

"You listen in on two minutes of a conversation, and you think you know anything?" His voice was a blade gliding effortlessly through expensive silk.

"Ronan showed me the sacrifice, cut open just like the Fae in that room. I know someone on this end has been helping the Unseelie escape. You said you know when the next portal is opening and that you had to silence the man. How else am I supposed to reconcile all of those circumstances? You haven't given me any explanations, so what else am I supposed to believe?" Though I was backed into a corner like an injured animal, my self-defense instincts gave me the confidence I needed to confront him, though that wasn't the way I'd hoped to have the conversation.

He stalked toward me, eyes blazing. "It seems you know everything then, don't you?" His hands reached behind his back and pulled out a gun from the waist of his pants.

My legs quaked beneath me.

How had this night gone so terribly wrong? This was what came of being brash. This was the consequence of losing my temper and acting on emotion.

I had no doubt Lochlan was going to kill me, the same as he'd killed the man one room over, but instead of pointing the gun in my direction, he offered me the handle.

"If you're so confident I'm the culprit, here's a gun. Shoot me," he commanded harshly.

My fingers grasped the warm metal while confusion and fear clouded my thoughts.

Why is he doing this?

I didn't want to kill him. I didn't want to kill anyone. I'd only wanted answers so that I could escape the horror-filled ride I'd been stuck on for weeks.

Lochlan stepped closer, pressing his chest to the barrel of the gun.

"Why are you doing this?" My question was hardly a whisper.

He leaned in and spoke with a deadly calm. "I don't know what you thought you heard in there, but you are gravely mistaken. We did what we could to get information out of that piece of shit about who was opening the portals. No, it's not a pretty job. It was poetic justice—he died in the same way that he killed the man in the warehouse. It was a fitting end. But even if we hadn't killed him, we couldn't let him go and risk him warning whoever is behind all this that he'd leaked the details of the next portal opening. We would miss our opportunity to trace the magic. It's crucial we get to this one before it closes so that we can trace the source." He stepped back and turned toward the door as my arm holding the gun dropped to my side.

His explanation made sense, but so had my own deductions.

"It's not my fault everything Ronan said lined up with what I witnessed. Maybe if you shared with me, I wouldn't have to question your motives."

Before I knew it, he had whipped around and was back in front of me. "What do you think this is? Some kind of partnership? You think we should meet over coffee and discuss the investigation?" he bellowed in my direction. "We are the Wild Hunt! It's our *job* to hunt down those responsible, not yours."

"That's not what I—" I paused, my voice dropping to a hush. "I was only trying to figure out who I'm supposed to trust in all this."

"Ronan tells you I'm a monster, and you were all too ready to believe it."

"If I'd believed him, I never would have come down here searching for answers." The truth of my statement struck me. I hadn't realized until now that my gut hadn't bought into Ronan's claims. I hadn't gone to the basement looking for evidence of Lochlan's wrongdoings. I'd gone in search of validation that my instincts were right. That Lochlan wasn't evil.

"You want information? I'll give you some. Ronan spent a decade planting the seeds to end almost a hundred years of peace in Ireland. Whispering tales and twisting men's minds to set Protestants against Catholics, Irish against British, men against women, and fathers against sons. So many factions that after his machinations, the place was a war zone for centuries. When I discovered what he was doing, I confronted him, and he gave me this." He brought his hand up to indicate the scar on his eyebrow. Now that he pointed it out, I realized how odd it was to have a scar when the Fae had healing powers. "It was a blade laced with a liquid lead polymer. The skin couldn't fully heal. Had his aim been true, I wouldn't be here today."

"How did the fight end?" I asked in a whisper.

"The Erlking, our leader, broke us apart, but only after we had beaten each other to near death. I will never forgive him, and I will never forget."

"Why couldn't you tell me that from the beginning? It would have been so much easier to understand. To trust you."

His head cocked to the side, and his arms crossed in front of his chest. Instead of answering my question, he posed one of his own slowly and deliberately. "Tell me, Rebecca, how did you get down here without my men stopping you or setting off our wards?"

I had no answer to offer him.

"Exactly. You've chosen to withhold information, just as much as I have." He backed away again as the door opened.

Michael, Liam, and the man who had been with Liam on the stairs came to stand just outside the doorway, their posture stiff and faces hard.

Lochlan left the room, keeping his back toward me. "Get her out of here."

Michael stripped the gun from my hand, and the other two took hold of my arms. The execution of my sentence was doled out in silence. I was not worth their effort, and I had nothing to say in my defense.

I was unceremoniously tossed onto the alley pavement. I couldn't say I blamed them. I probably would have done the same had the roles been reversed.

Accepting defeat, I tucked my chin and started toward the main road in search of a cab ride home. When I entered my quiet apartment, I didn't turn on any lights. I went straight upstairs to my bed, where I curled up in the darkness. My actions weren't unreasonable, yet I felt disappointed in myself.

If Ronan was as devious as Lochlan claimed, could he have set up this entire sequence of events just to toy with me? Or perhaps he wanted to drive a wedge between Lochlan and me? Whatever his reasons, Ronan's intent hadn't been innocent. He knew he'd been misleading.

Lochlan, on the other hand, had yet to do anything to

cause me harm, and I had taken his help and thrown it back in his face. I could only hope that I hadn't lost Lochlan's favor permanently.

I had to try to repair the damage that I'd done, but I also needed to give him time to calm down. Tomorrow, once we'd both slept on the matter, I'd go back and apologize. He might not accept my apology, but I wouldn't know unless I tried.

FOURTEEN

I waited until midafternoon the next day to trek back to the Huntsman. I didn't know Lochlan's schedule, but it seemed likely that mornings for a nightclub owner wouldn't be the best time to reach him.

I was relieved to find the main club empty. I'd stressed all day about being turned away. Passing silently across the empty dance floor, I wound my way to the back hall and knocked softly on the closed office door.

My heart mimicked the pounding bass that would be thundering through the club a few hours from now.

"Come in." His exasperated command resonated through the door.

A trickle of relief helped dilute the potent anxiety coursing through my veins.

I opened the door to find Lochlan at his desk. His penetrating azure eyes tracked my every movement, wary and frigid as a Belfast night.

I felt too self-conscious to sit, so I remained on my feet and jumped in headfirst.

"I'm sorry, Lochlan. I shouldn't have spied on you, and I want you to know that I tried to come talk to you face-to-face, but the guys wouldn't let me up. I let my frustrations get the better of me. The past two weeks have been difficult, to say the least."

He lifted his chin, and the harsh angle of his jaw softened. "What is it that you want from me, Rebecca?"

"Answers. Honesty."

"I can only give what you're willing to hear." He stood and strolled to the window.

"What does that mean?"

"It means you won't hear the truth until you're willing to accept it. Instead, you'll find reasons to be suspicious or skeptical. You'll raise your defenses and fight me, and there's no point in going down that road."

"I told you that I realized I'd been wrong. What more do you want from me?"

His eyes locked with mine again, this time with a hint of challenge. "If you truly want answers, as you say, then come with me tonight to the portal opening."

I was stunned. Why would he ask such a thing? I could only imagine I'd be in the way.

"Won't it be dangerous?" I chewed at the inside of my cheek, wondering what I'd gotten myself into.

"There's always a degree of danger in everything. Tonight, I'll hide away until the portal is opened, then use a spell to trace its source. I'll need to deal with whatever Unseelie comes through to this side, but it shouldn't be a problem. You will remain hidden throughout."

Then why go? Did he still feel the need to prove that he wasn't the problem? Or was this his way of luring me into a trap?

Are you seriously going down that road again? You're here to apologize for not trusting him, not dream up new imaginary grievances.

I grimaced on the inside.

"Just you? Won't you need others there just in case?" Everything about this venture sounded ridiculously dangerous. I couldn't fathom why I should go.

"The more men present, the more easily we'd be detected."

Lochlan took one step closer, then two, until I had to lift my chin to hold his gaze.

His hand lifted to trace a large finger along the edge of my jaw. "Have I ever let anyone or anything hurt you?" The question ghosted across my skin, then settled in a deeply vulnerable part of my soul.

Words escaped me.

When his hand slid down to cup my throat, I swallowed but didn't pull away.

"I think you're more deeply ingrained in this than you want to admit. None of it will make sense unless you can find the courage to face that truth." His thumb caressed a path up to my chin, then back down. "The courage to trust me."

How can I trust blindly? There are so many ways a man can hurt a woman.

"I'm trying," I breathed.

"Then come with me." He leaned in, bringing his cheek close to mine, and inhaled deeply against my hair.

Arousal like I'd never experienced liquified my bones and pooled into a molten mass in my belly. My lips parted on short, shallow breaths.

When Lochlan pulled back to meet my eyes again, his were glowing bright blue like glittering shards of sapphire. Something about my expression pleased him, his eyes widening a fraction and lips drifting apart.

"*There* she is," he murmured.

I couldn't help but relish his praise. I didn't know what was happening between us, but it was the most wanted and safe I'd felt in two weeks. I didn't even care if it was all a ruse constructed of magic and manipulation.

"Come by the club tonight at ten, and we'll go in search of your answers." His hand fell away, leaving me bereft and cold.

I couldn't bear to question my reaction to the loss of his touch. Instead, I wrapped the memory of him around me like a cloak to provide comfort and warmth. That way, I felt his strength there with me when I stepped onto the sidewalk outside the building and nearly collided with Ronan.

"Rebecca, what are you doing here?"

"Why? Worried I'll find out you lied to me? Too late. I talked to Lochlan about the portal and the Fae he had captured. You purposely twisted the facts to make it sound like he'd been at fault."

"You've spoken with Lochlan and suddenly decided that everything I shared was all a lie?" His anger was evident, but he reined it in and studied me imploringly. "He's manipulating you, Becca. Don't you see that? Everyone here is under his spell, except for me. I'd hoped you at least would see through his games." He cupped my cheeks. "I've only ever been open with you. Kind and thoughtful. Doesn't that count for anything? Don't you see how good we'd be together?"

His words unnerved me. I pulled my face away from his hands. "Together? This isn't about a relationship or choosing sides; it's about stopping the Unseelie from getting on Earth and hurting people." I stepped back and glanced away as he slowly lowered his hands to his sides. "I don't want to hurt you, Ronan, but I can't be the rope in your tug-of-war. It's not helping anyone. We need to work together."

"I see. You've made your choice." Jaw clenched, he lifted his chin. "Though I must say, you've chosen poorly." Before I could respond, he stalked into the building.

FIFTEEN

I WORE ALL BLACK FOR MY STAKEOUT AT THE PORTAL OPENING, WHICH would be helpful when I ended up dead—I'd already be dressed for my own funeral.

All day, I'd argued with myself about backing out. It was too dangerous. I convinced myself that I needed to find another way to get back in Lochlan's good graces. He would understand. He would have to. Why did it even matter what he thought? I didn't *need* him. What I needed was to get this damn necklace off and go home. I spent the next half hour with every tool I could round up, trying desperately to cut, bend, and wrench the necklace from my body. I didn't so much as make a scratch on its perfect silver links.

That was when I came back around to admitting I needed help.

I needed Lochlan. And if I wanted his help, and he wanted me to go to some damn portal opening, I was screwed. I needed to at least make an effort to be receptive to his brand of help. Therefore, I dressed to stay hidden, and in the alternative, I'd be casket ready.

Just like the first time I saw him, Lochlan was leaning against his car when I arrived at the Huntsman building. He wore jeans and a black long-sleeve Henley that clung to his broad frame, outlining his sculpted shoulders and arms. His black biker boots were a stark contrast to his usual business attire, though I had to admit they suited him. Together with his blond hair and blue eyes, he was the vision of an avenging angel. A vision that muddled my thoughts and made my mouth water.

"I wasn't sure you'd come." He pushed away from the car and opened the passenger door.

"I wasn't either," I muttered as I slid onto the soft leather seat.

The remainder of the trip was taken in silence. Lochlan felt no need to fill empty air while I was busy fretting over the fact that I'd neglected to bring a weapon. I'd been too distracted about whether I *should* go to think about what I should take with me if I did.

We pulled into an industrial park lined with warehouses and commercial buildings. He directed the car down a row of rentable garage shops, some with signage advertising their business, and others were vacant. Lochlan parked next to Rupert's Auto Repairs, among several other parked vehicles. Once he was out of the car, he came around to my side and tapped his knuckles on the passenger window, motioning for me to get out. Instead, I rolled down the glass.

"I think I'd be safest here," I informed him. "Maybe you should just leave the keys with me as well."

"Get out of the car, Becca," he drawled slowly.

My nickname on his tongue for the first time distracted me from my argument. I liked the way he said my name, all soft and familiar. I liked it entirely too much.

Lost in a haze of warm fuzzies, I did as he asked. The

second I was out of the car, a chilly gust of reality refocused my thoughts. The night air was freezing, and the clear, moonless sky was endlessly dark.

"This way." He led me down the row of shops and stopped in front of the long-abandoned auto garage at the end.

Brown paper covered the interior of the glass door to block the view inside, but the thick grime on the glass performed the same job admirably. As one of the larger locations, its storefront was twice the size of the shops we had walked past.

Lochlan grabbed the door handle, and I could see the knob catch as if it had been locked but then click open—strikingly similar to my experience opening the back door of the Huntsman building. I wondered if the necklace had somehow helped me break into the building. I hadn't even considered what other powers it might possess. An interesting question to file away for another time.

"Whoever's in Faery opening portals needs someone here to set up the spell requirements on this end. We'll go in and wait for that individual to arrive, and only once the portal has been opened will I attempt to trace its source." His eyes were hard, voice quiet. He dug a hand into his pocket and handed me the car remote. "If anything goes wrong, or I need to go through the portal, go to the club and get help."

We took our first steps inside the building, silently assessing our surroundings. The space held four garage bays, though it appeared to be abandoned. Large lift equipment remained in the middle of the space with a heavy coating of dirt and grime. It was nearly pitch black inside, yet I was surprisingly able to make out stacks of tires and equipment nearby.

When Lochlan started to press forward, I threw up my arm in front of his chest to stop him. In the corners of the room, totally shrouded in darkness, I could feel the presence of at least a dozen creatures. I wasn't sure how I knew. It was as if the dark had whispered to me. As if I was a part of that darkness and knew its secrets like they were my own.

Before I could tell Lochlan to run, his body jerked back as two arrows lodged deep in his chest.

Horror gripped me. Seized my lungs and stole my capacity to think.

Thank God for Lochlan. He managed to stay on his feet and maneuvered himself in front of me while throwing his arm up to cast a magical light above us.

We were instantly surrounded by what looked like gaunt old men, larger than the Draug, but somewhat similar. Baring their sharp fangs and claws, they wore rags draped on their thin bodies, and beneath the tattered red beanies on their heads, wicked black eyes speared us in place. One of them threw a stack of tires out of his way as if they had been inflatable pool toys rather than heavy rubber. Bloodthirsty and powerful, the creatures far outnumbered us.

"Look, boys, it seems the hunter is now the hunted." The one that spoke was off to our right and stood several inches taller than the others. His too-wide mouth curved up at the ends in a grotesque attempt at a smile, and his cloying voice made goose bumps rise across my skin.

"Who sent you here?" Lochlan spoke with menace, and I realized I was seeing a dangerous side to him that I had not yet witnessed.

"You are in no position to be asking questions." The creature's comment incited the others as they shook their fists and inched forward aggressively.

"You'll be hunted for defying the queen."

"Not if there is no queen." The creature's face lit with perverted glee.

Lochlan broke off the shafts of the arrows with a curse and

yanked me behind him, handing me a knife he pulled from his boot. "Stay at my back. Cut anything that gets near you."

"Can't you trace us out of here?" I hissed.

"I can only trace myself but not others along with me. Plus, these arrows are iron, and it's limiting my magic."

His words nearly stopped my heart as I gaped at the horrifying creatures, realizing that Lochlan might not be able to fight them off. It was also entirely possible that he could pull out the arrows and trace away, leaving me there to die.

As if he knew exactly where my mind had gone, without his eyes leaving the swarming Fae, he grabbed my arm firmly. "I'm not going anywhere. Now stop panicking and pay attention."

"*Enough!*" shouted the creature, who seemed to be their leader. "*Kill them.*"

My eyes scanned the snarling Fae as they held their clawed hands out, ready to tear through our flesh if given the opportunity. The majority were arced around Lochlan, who had faced the middle of the room, leaving me with the few who had squeezed in along the wall.

Lochlan lunged forward on the offensive, and as I sensed him move, I stepped back to keep as little space between us as possible. He was shooting some kind of energy blast at them and would conduct a brutal assault with his fists and the occasional well-placed kick between blasts.

I wasn't able to watch him as I would have liked, too busy fending off the few creatures who had me in their sights, jabbing and swiping at me. I stabbed at them with the knife as best as I could, but their claws caught my skin on multiple occasions, blood staining the sleeves of my shirt.

A growl came from Lochlan just as a head from one of the creatures plunked on the concrete floor and rolled in front of me. I wasn't sure how he had done it, nor did I want to know.

It hit me in a moment of clarity amid my panic that I had assumed the magic from my necklace would somehow keep me protected. That was the only reason I'd taken the risk of showing up to this massacre. It had kept me hidden and safe when I'd needed it most, and I'd subconsciously relied on that fact. I'd counted on its help to bring me home safely. But as I slashed at the Fae closing in on me, it was clear that my assumption had been a grave mistake. If I didn't find a way out of here soon, my parents would have to bury another child. It would break them. I couldn't let that happen. I *had* to survive this.

How the fuck does this thing work?

I tried to mentally summon the necklace's powers without any luck. With each second that ticked by, the vicious creatures surrounding me were inches away from ending my life.

Taking a particularly large lunge forward on an attack, Lochlan separated from my back just long enough that a creature reached in from beside me in an attempt to grab my left arm. I slashed with the knife in my right hand without making contact. My miscalculation allowed him enough time to grab my downcast arm and yank me away from Lochlan. The creature threw me back against the wall, my back slamming so hard that the air squeezed from my lungs, and I gasped for breath.

Approaching me with wicked delight, the creature raised its clawed hand and viciously slashed at me just as I lifted my arm in a feeble attempt to protect myself. Instead of the searing pain I had expected, there was a loud pop and an intense pressure on my wrist. I watched in astonishment as the Unseelie was thrown backward several feet, and Cat's bracelet slid from my wrist, dropping to the floor. The bracelet had contained some sort of protective ability.

I was stunned but had no time to dwell. Before I could

make a move to grab the bracelet or get back to Lochlan, a second creature yanked me away from the wall and landed a brutal blow to my face that threw me headfirst into the wall.

Lochlan bellowed out in fury, calling my name, but I couldn't respond. I was too disoriented and writhing in pain on the floor. Knowing I needed to get up, I dazedly pulled myself back to my feet. Scanning the floor, I searched frantically for the knife I had dropped when I was punched.

"Looking for this?" The raspy voice chilled my bones.

I lifted my gaze to see the creature who had thrown me into the wall. The perverse expression on his wrinkled face was evidence that he delighted in toying with his prey.

With a surge of adrenaline, I launched myself toward Lochlan but was quickly grabbed from behind and tackled to the floor. I managed to twist onto my back as we fell and land with the Unseelie above me. His spindly fingers plunged the knife toward my chest, and my hands shot up to grab his wrists. While I slowed the knife's progress, it wasn't enough to stop the blade from sinking into my chest just below my right shoulder.

White-hot pain seared through me, and I cried out in agony while I pushed with all my might at his arms to keep the knife from sinking farther. His saliva dripped between jagged teeth and fell in long strands onto my face and neck.

Panic coursed through my body as I grappled with the creature.

There was no way I could win this fight.

I was going to die.

In desperation, I removed one hand from his arm and pressed it against the side of his face to push him away. A tingling warmth radiated across the palm of my hand to the tips of my fingers just as small black tendrils branched out beneath his skin like inky veins consuming his face.

Instantly, the pressure on the knife relented as he grabbed my forearm. I slammed my other hand against his other cheek, and he screamed in horror and rage.

Attempting to get away from me, he pulled backward, but I kept my hands fastened against him. When he flung his body back, I surged forward until we switched places with him on his back and me towering over him.

I watched in a delighted fascination as the veining darkness emanating from beneath my hand spread down his neck and beneath his tattered shirt. I had no clue what I was doing. That didn't matter. All that *did* matter was that this awful creature was dying, and I would survive.

My movements had jarred loose the knife, and it fell to the floor beside his head, but neither of us paid it any attention. The creature's eyes cast unseeing to the ceiling, clouded over from a shiny black to a milky gray.

An intoxicating feeling of power coursed through me, and I rejoiced in watching as his body stilled and the life drained from his eyes.

I had done this.

I had saved myself.

He'd only been one creature out of a dozen, but I'd killed him all on my own. For once, I hadn't felt helpless. I was the one in control. I was the one with the power.

Eventually, the sound of others grappling drew me back to reality. I looked around to discover that Ronan had joined us and was finishing off the last of the Unseelie while Lochlan stood with his eyes glued to me.

Between the two of them, they had made relatively short work of the dozen Unseelie that now lay dead, strewn about the room.

I attempted to stand, but an intense dizzy spell took me to

my knees. One glance down at my chest confirmed that I was bleeding profusely. Blackness threatened my vision.

Before I could hit the ground, strong arms gently swept me up. While I'd expected Lochlan, it was Ronan's stubbled jawline that came into focus when I opened my eyes.

"Look at what you've done," Ronan snarled at Lochlan. "What the fuck were you thinking bringing her here?"

Two broken arrow shafts still protruded from Lochlan's chest, blood staining the length of his shirt. "We need to get out of here, *now*. We can have this discussion at the club."

Ronan sneered but followed Lochlan out of the building to the car. Once I was securely in my seat, my eyes drifted out the window to a figure leaning on a wall not far from the car. My addled brain took a moment to recognize him, but it was clearly the man from the museum. He stood casually with his hands in his coat pockets as if simply enjoying an evening stroll.

I wondered if my head injury had me hallucinating and gave a silent thanks that if my head was going to mess with me, it was the museum man I saw and not the shadow man.

He tipped his head in my direction and then vanished. At the same time, the blackness that had been dancing at the edges of my vision consumed me, and I slumped onto the seat in oblivion.

CHAPTER

SIXTEEN

I woke in Ronan's arms as he carried me inside the Huntsman to a conference room with a large oval table and thirteen chairs. He gently set me down on a black leather sofa along the back wall. The cool leather was a shocking contrast to my heated skin, stirring up goose bumps on my arms and legs.

Shortly after, Lochlan joined us with a large first-aid kit. "Rebecca, we need to cut away your shirt so that we can treat the wound." He pulled out a pair of bent scissors with rounded ends.

I nodded my consent, and he cut from the neckline of my shirt down the length of my arm so that he could peel the entire top right portion of my shirt away.

"I really liked that shirt," I murmured dazedly.

Lochlan cut through my bra strap, and our eyes connected. Adrenaline brought me fully awake.

"I can get you one of mine," he offered quietly, his eyes returning to my wound. Tension marred his features.

"Is something wrong?" I peered down at my chest and discovered that what I had thought was a serious stab wound looked more like a bad cut, about an inch long and not terribly deep. I was relieved, especially since they hadn't taken me to a hospital, but confused because I had watched just inches from my face as the knife had sunk excruciatingly slowly into my chest.

The necklace had helped me heal. That was the only explanation.

Lochlan had to be aware that my body had repaired itself at an unnaturally fast pace, and I wondered if he was going to say something. Instead, he carried on cleaning the wound, which hurt like a bitch, and bandaged it with butterfly strips and a gauze pad.

"This should take care of it." He pulled a blanket off the back of the couch and wrapped it around my shoulders, wincing as he moved.

"You need to treat your wounds. I can't believe I let you work on me when you have two arrows in your chest," I fussed to no avail.

"I'm fine. One of the guys will clean me up after our meeting." His voice was haggard. I wished I could do something to help him, but I wouldn't get anywhere arguing with him. We had been alone in the room, and I wasn't sure where Ronan had gone, but I was glad for the bit of privacy his absence had allowed. However, the reprieve was short-lived as Ronan reappeared with bottles of water, crackers, and an extra blanket. "You need to drink some water and have a couple of crackers. The sugars in your system will help with the shock."

I reached for a bottle with trembling fingers. "I'm feeling better, but this will help. Thank you."

He was still visibly upset, shooting a harsh glare at Lochlan. "Your recklessness nearly got her killed."

Lochlan ignored the accusation. "Why exactly *were* you there, Ronan? I believe the plan was for the rest of you to stay here tonight on call." His words were deceptively calm, but the gleam in his eyes was lethal.

"I was worried about Rebecca. When I heard from Liam that she had gone with you, I rushed over to make sure nothing went wrong, and I'm glad I did. If I hadn't shown up, you would have been sorely outnumbered." The snarl of disgust on his face soured his features.

Lochlan grabbed Ronan and slammed his back against the wall. "And why was that, Ronan? Why the fuck did I walk into what looked like a well-laid trap?"

The room sparked with energy.

"I don't know, Lochlan. What the fuck are you accusing me of?"

Lochlan swung a fist into Ronan's face with a sickening crunch. The hair on my arms stood on end in anticipation of Ronan's retaliation. Instead, he slowly turned back to Lochlan with blood dripping off his chin and a bone-chilling smile.

"That's right, you always did want to take my head off. Going to see if you can finish the job this time?"

Lochlan grabbed him by the shirt, but before he could make another move, Ronan landed a vicious uppercut to his gut.

Liam, Michael, and the others filtered into the room at that moment, pulling the two enemies apart with no small show of force.

"What the fuck is going on here?" barked Michael. He got in Lochlan's face, shoving him to get his attention.

"Same shit as always," muttered one of the others.

"Shut the fuck up, Sean." Lochlan yanked out of Michael's grasp. "Everyone *sit*. There's a lot to discuss."

Ronan walked with an impassive expression to the opposite end of the table as Lochlan.

As the room filled, murmurs and shared looks set me on

edge. A few men sat at the oval table while others remained standing and grumbled in my direction.

The man who had refused me access to the club the night before addressed Lochlan sharply. "She can't stay here while we discuss business."

The room quieted.

"She was there tonight and has information to offer. She stays." Lochlan's commanding tone brooked no argument. After a heartbeat, the men who remained standing went warily to their chairs and sat at the table.

The importance of this moment wasn't lost on me. Had these men ever allowed an outsider to witness their inner workings, let alone a human woman? My seat, though not technically at the table, was a statement both to the other men and me.

After everyone settled, Lochlan addressed the group in a grave tone. "Tonight, I went to the site of a suspected portal opening, like we have on many occasions recently. However, this time, I was met with a dozen Red Caps."

The room came alive with the low hum of men's voices.

"Had they just come through the portal?" one of the men asked.

"No, they were hidden in shadow, awaiting my arrival. Without question, this was a setup."

Michael spoke up, addressing the group. "I agree. A group of Red Caps that large had to have been assembled. They're too self-serving to remain in numbers for long. Not without the command of someone as powerful as Mab."

Various heads nodded, and the room buzzed with murmurs of agreement.

"Everyone here understands the implications. Those of us in the room were the only ones who knew I was going to the garage tonight. Yet somehow, I was set up. That means information was somehow leaked from our group—unintentionally or otherwise." Lochlan's stare rounded the room poignantly.

"If they figured out that we'd taken the Fae traitor, they might have assumed he'd squeal," someone offered.

"The last portal was closed when we entered the building. There's no way they could have known that we showed up just after," responded Michael.

"What about the girl? How are we to know she isn't involved?" asked the same one who had suggested that the timing had been merely coincidental.

Ronan spoke rapidly in my defense. "She almost *died*. Why would a defenseless woman knowingly walk into a trap full of Red Caps?"

Defenseless.

The word brought back the memory of those inky veins spreading throughout the Red Cap's body, strangling the life from him. I'd been anything but defenseless.

How could I possibly escape all this when I was drowning in magic?

I'd wanted to think that my life could go back to normal without the necklace. That all of my problems centered around the damn necklace. But that wasn't the case. I could now sense with an unsettling certainty that I was a central part of whatever was going on.

Not my necklace.

Me.

And if that was the case, I couldn't go back home. Not now. Maybe not ever. I couldn't risk this magical world following me and harming my family.

Of course, getting the necklace off would be the one true test. And if anyone could do it, wouldn't the men of the Hunt be my best chance?

"My necklace has powers," I blurted over the murmur of the men's voices.

The room grew eerily silent, and all eyes turned to me.

"I know many of you are wary of me, and I can understand. I've been secretive, but only because I've been scared. I didn't know what was happening or who to trust. All of this is new to me." My hand absently lifted to finger the pendant on my chest. "I've had the necklace as long as I can remember, but it never showed signs of being anything other than an ordinary necklace. The first time I had any hint that it might be otherwise was when the Draug came after me. He wanted the necklace and tried to yank it from my neck, but it wouldn't come off. I've tried to remove it myself, and it won't budge. Yes, I'm involved in this. However, I don't know how or why, and I certainly had nothing to do with setting up the trap in the garage." My hands fidgeted nervously under the heavy weight of their stares.

"What powers does the necklace have?" asked Ronan.

"It kept me hidden when I was in danger and revealed the Red Caps to me when they were hidden in the shadows. I think it might have helped me heal as well."

Several of the men whispered to those around them. My eyes met Lochlan's apologetically. He'd asked over and over what I was hiding, but I'd been too scared to tell him. I was worried he'd resent me for lying, but instead, he gave a small tilt of his chin in approval.

Bolstered by his encouragement, I continued. "At one point in the warehouse, a Red Cap had me pinned, and I thought he was going to kill me. I put my hands on his face, and it seemed to put a darkness into him. It spread like roots through his skin until it killed him." I said the last part quietly, almost afraid to acknowledge it myself.

"I've never heard of such a thing," said a man at the other

end of the table, voicing the thoughts that were so clearly written on all their faces.

Lochlan moved to sit next to me on the sofa, his eyes fixed on my necklace. His fingers raised to touch the pendant, lifting it off my skin without incident. His eyes began to glow, and a pulse of energy buzzed across my skin right before his hand ricocheted back away from the necklace.

"What happened?" I breathed.

He shook his head, face scrunched in frustration. "I tried to use magic to break the chain. The protections placed on the amulet are impressive. While I'm still limited by the iron arrows, I doubt I'd be able to break the chain even at full power."

Hopelessness hollowed out my chest.

This was what I'd feared most. I was trapped.

Unaware of my horror, Lochlan returned to the table and addressed his men. "We all have many questions and even fewer answers, but tonight is not the time to search them out. My purpose in calling you here was to make sure we all know what we're up against." His eyes found mine. "Rebecca, do you have anything else you want to share?"

I cleared my throat again, and the number of soft whispers that had started throughout the room stopped abruptly. "There is one more thing. I don't know if it means anything at all—I may have just imagined it—but I saw a man as we were leaving the industrial park. I recognized him as a man I spoke with once before on my first day at the museum. Nothing of consequence, just admiring some of the artwork. I know that I hit my head during the fight, but I'd swear he was outside the garage by the car, and he gave me a nod as we were leaving. I passed out just afterward, so it may have been my eyes playing tricks on me, but I thought it was worth mentioning."

"Can you describe the man?" Lochlan asked warily.

"He seemed young, but it was hard to tell. His skin was youthful, no wrinkles or anything, except a few laugh lines around his eyes. Those eyes were what confused me—they felt ancient. He was close to six feet tall and had light blond hair, almost white, and his eyes were an ice blue. When he began to talk to me, I could have sworn the room had been empty. It was like he just appeared behind me. Now, I can't help but wonder if he had traced into the room."

"Was his accent like the rest of ours?" Lochlan asked.

"No, he wasn't Irish. More like British with a hint of something else. Maybe Scandinavian?"

"Is there anything else you can recall about him? Something he said or a mannerism?"

I waded through my memory of the conversation and attempted to recall if anything he had said would now have significance. "The only things that stuck with me were that he knew my name and commented that it was good to see me. I remember thinking it was odd to say *good to see you* instead of *good to meet you*, but I figured it was just a difference in colloquial language. I had no reason to suspect him of anything more than a friendly gentleman."

Michael stood quickly and spoke to Lochlan in an alarmed tone. "Why would he be here?"

"Does that description mean something to you? You know who he is?" I asked with astonishment. I couldn't imagine that I had given them enough information to go off, but they all had the same man in mind by the concerned expressions on their faces.

"We can't know for sure yet, but your description sounds like Merlin." The name spoken aloud created a frenzy of chatter in the room, but Lochlan continued. "Did he give you any hint as to his purpose?"

"No. I don't know anything else. What does this mean?" I looked at Lochlan for answers.

"Merlin keeps to himself. He's an ancient Fae of great power and would not involve himself in a trivial matter. His presence indicates that there is a greater danger than we originally suspected."

The room was quiet as everyone considered the implications of Merlin's appearance.

Lochlan continued, this time addressing his men. "As for your concerns that Rebecca was involved in setting up the trap, I'll vouch for her innocence in this plot. It is evident to me that we have a traitor somewhere at this table, and that is where our focus should lie." When he spoke, the room stayed chillingly silent. No one moved or spoke. "Throughout my years in the Hunt, nor in any times in its history, have I ever heard of treachery from within. But I know of no other way this could have transpired." He took a brief pause as he met the hard stares of the men at the table. "With our protections in place, there was no way information could have left these grounds without it coming from one of us. No one here would have dropped that kind of information accidentally."

Several men grunted in agreement.

"We cannot afford the weakness of a traitor among us. We must discover the source, and I know of no other foolproof way to test each man's allegiance than the Sword of Light."

I scanned the room in a futile attempt to read the men for any signs of fear or derision. If there was a traitor in the group, he must have had nerves of steel to sit among such dangerous men and boldly lie to their faces. Despite my efforts, I could not read a single defensive posture or possible sign of guilt.

"Lochlan, no one has seen the sword for a millennium. How will we get it?" asked Michael.

"We'll do whatever we must to uncover and retrieve it. I'll

speak with my sources to start the search, and in the meantime, we must all be on our guard. There's no telling what other information has been leaked from behind these walls." Suspicious eyes scanned the room as he spoke. "Does anyone else have anything further for the group?"

There were murmurs throughout the room, but no one offered anything aloud.

"Get back to your duties. Once I know more, we'll meet again."

The men stood and disbursed. When the room was empty, Lochlan approached me. "If you'll wait a moment, I'll get these arrows out and take you home."

I should have been more adamant that he needed rest after getting his wounds treated, but I was too tired and defeated to argue. Instead, I plopped back down on the couch with a wince, momentarily forgetting my healing wound. I lay my head on the arm of the sofa, and visions of Lochlan's hand being zapped off the necklace played in my head.

I was bound to this reality with little hope of escape.

The fantasy of magic may be alluring for some, but the feeling that had overcome me when I was killing that creature was terrifying. If I didn't know better, I'd say there was a darkness to this magic. Under its influence, I reveled in that creature's death.

That wasn't a gift. It was a curse.

As I lamented my situation, my eyelids grew heavy. Before I knew it, Lochlan was murmuring for me to wake up, his warm hand lightly touching my arm. He had changed into a clean shirt, and I couldn't see any evidence of his wounds.

"Sorry, I guess I was more tired than I realized." I stood on legs that were thankfully steadier after my power nap. "Is your chest okay?" I asked groggily.

"It's fine. Now that the iron has been removed, it won't

take long to heal. I grabbed this for you." He held out a T-shirt, soft and faded.

"You didn't have to do that, but thanks." I faced the wall and put on the clean shirt. His smell enveloped me, and my eyes slowly shut while I soaked in his woodsy scent.

"Iron prevents you from using your magic?" I asked on our way downstairs.

"For the most part. It makes it difficult to trace, heal, or do any magic that requires substantial power."

"Was that the extent of the Hunt, the twelve of you?"

"There are thirteen here in Ireland when our leader is among us. He's in Faery at the moment. We have a good number more men back in Faery, so he has to split his time between the two realms."

I was ridiculously curious about the Hunt and figured I'd ask questions while he was in an accommodating mood. "He's the Erlking, right? Does that mean he's the king of the Hunt?"

"That's his title, but he's not exactly a king. It means he's the leader of the Hunt, but we aren't bound to any particular lands as a kingdom would entail."

"A while back, you said the Hunt had government ties. Do you follow Queen Guin?"

"No, the Hunt isn't ruled by the Seelie queen. Although, we often ally with her when it suits our purpose. We have no desire to wage a war against her, but we have no true allegiance to anyone but our own. That's why it's such a grave insult to have one among us turn into a traitor."

"The queen didn't command the Hunt to stay here and keep Fae out?"

"No, it was more like a good fit to our natural proclivities. The Hunt seeks those who would run, which tends to be the guilty and scared. Prior to the Fae returning to Faery, the Hunt roamed both Faery and Earth, tracking prey wherever the trail led."

"Do you hunt humans?" I asked cautiously.

His eyes cut over to mine, and I could see a feral glint in them. "At times, but they aren't the challenge that Fae present."

It was clear that he liked the chase. The exhilaration of the hunt. I wondered if the men became a part of the Hunt because that drive was already a part of them or if being a part of the Hunt fostered that need. "How do you end up in the Hunt? Are you forced into it, or is it something you choose?"

"We have no desire to have a fellow hunter as a brother if he doesn't want to hunt. In my case, I was raised by our leader, so I was practically born into the Hunt. It's in my blood."

I took in what he had said, and when I compared the Hunt to a military organization, it didn't sound nearly as horrifying as it had been depicted in legend. Granted, they didn't have to report back to the Pentagon or some other governing body, but I had never suffered the delusion that the US Army Rangers or the Navy SEALs were exactly Boy Scouts.

Before long, we arrived at my apartment, and Lochlan turned off the car. There was only a twinge of pain in my chest as I stood, and I wondered when I took off the bandage just how much of the wound would remain.

Lochlan walked me to the door and followed me inside, scanning my small home. "Pack your things. You're moving in with us at the Huntsman."

For a moment, I was too stunned to respond. "What?"

"There's more going on here than we know. You'll be safer staying with us."

"But you just said there's a traitor among you."

"You're *still* safer with us."

I shook my head and tried to push past him for the stairs. "That doesn't make any sense."

Lochlan swung me around until my backside was pressed against the back of the loveseat. One of his thick thighs pressed between mine with his body molded against me. I could feel every hard inch of him.

His hands cupped my face, assertive warmth searing my skin. "You can't run from this, Rebecca. I know it frightens you, but there's only one way forward." His velvet words caressed my ragged soul with assurance.

I wanted nothing more than to melt into him. To fuse myself to his strength and allow him to carry me through whatever storm awaited.

"I am scared, but it's more than that," I whispered. "Losing me would kill my parents, and I can't ... I can't do that to them. I owe them—"

His mouth slanted over mine, silencing me with a kiss that coerced and seduced. His lips and tongue laid siege to the darkest parts of my soul. His touch shattered me into a thousand pieces, then built me back stronger than before.

If the reward at the end of my fight was half as sweet, I'd face an entire army without hesitation.

Pleasure didn't just coil in my belly. It crawled through my veins and turned me inside out with need. With craving and addiction. I needed this man more than I needed life itself. I clung to him, desperate for more.

And then it hit me.

This wasn't right. It wasn't normal to feel so overwhelmed with desire. He was Fae, after all—not even human. Had I forgotten?

What if he was using his Fae powers to manipulate me? Stirring up my hormones until I couldn't think beyond my intense desire for him. I'd suspected it before, but this time it was too much. I'd already had to embrace magic, save myself from being killed, and accept that I likely wouldn't get to see my parents again for the foreseeable future. I wasn't being forced into one more goddamn decision.

I tore myself away, stumbling to the side. "Don't you *dare* use that Fae shit on me!" I seethed.

He recoiled as if I'd slapped him. "What are you talking about?"

"Making me sex crazy so you can use me and get what you want. I know you were doing it, so just *stop*." My voice was pure venom. I poured all my strength into my assault, unleashing every helpless frustration I'd been suffering.

Lochlan's face blanked of emotion. "You assume because you get wet for me that I must be manipulating you? You think you couldn't possibly want a Fae monster? Maybe you need a taste of what I can really do. Then you'll know the difference."

As he spoke, an intense aching pleasure spread through my body. A perfect storm of chaos that promised to end all my suffering with a single touch.

I fell to my knees and gaped up at my tormentor.

My savior.

My everything.

A guttural moan ripped from my throat as my hands kneaded my engorged breasts.

It wasn't enough. Only his touch would do.

"*Please*," I whimpered.

"Please what, Rebecca?" he asked icily.

Fill me, touch me, taste me. End this delicious torture.

It was agony and bliss, all at once.

I rolled my hips and mewled as I imagined my mouth on his cock. The taste of his salty essence and the rewarding groan I would wrench from him as I sucked him dry.

Saliva pooled on my tongue.

"Please ... *stop*." The one single word took all my mental fortitude.

I desperately wanted to beg him to take me, touch me, fuck me. But somewhere down deep, I knew I couldn't let that need win out.

I couldn't lose this battle.

And as soon as the whispered word passed my lips, the painful need vanished, leaving me panting and my clit pulsing. My body was mine again, but just barely.

"*Get out*." A breathless whisper and broken accusation of betrayal.

He must have realized that arguing would be futile. Heeding my command, he left my apartment without a word. Seconds later, the shattering glass of a car window broke the heavy silence, followed by the whooping call of a car alarm.

Good. I was glad he was upset. I shouldn't be the only one.

What he'd done had been inexcusable. It had never occurred to me that a person could be assaulted without ever being touched, but that was what his magic had felt like. He'd taken control of my body and used it against me. I felt violated and betrayed. And the worst part was, the remnants of that need still hummed in my veins. My engorged clit knew no right or wrong, only that it was swollen and desperate for relief.

My eyes fell shut with embarrassment as I reached down to cup myself and soothe the ache. All it took was the single touch, and my body exploded in the most intense orgasm I had ever experienced.

CHAPTER

SEVENTEEN

THE NEXT MORNING, I LAY IN BED FOR HOURS AS THE SUN ROSE HIGHER and higher in the sky. Having a night for my body to recover, my chest showed no evidence of a wound, and the scratches and black eye were gone. There was no denying that I was healing inhumanly fast.

Oddly enough, that didn't seem to weigh on me as much as the lesson Lochlan had instilled the night before. I had been so sure that his powers were to blame for my intense lust whenever I was near him. As angry as I was at him for his teaching method, I also recognized his message. He had never used his magic to manufacture my feelings.

The attraction between us was entirely natural and utterly undeniable.

There was no confusing my natural arousal to the blinding, all-consuming lust his power had provoked. How was I to know he hadn't been using his powers on me until I experienced the difference for myself? I understood why he'd done it, but his vindictive use of the power had been inexcusable. I'd lashed out verbally, and he'd followed suit with his

158

magic. We'd both been wrong, but his offense had been egregious.

He'd used desire as a weapon, and the result was terrifying.

It would be easy for someone to lose themselves completely when subjected to that Fae desire. Reduced to a mindless body, living for one thing and one thing alone.

Sex.

Fucking—raw and carnal, and as crucial as oxygen.

When I was lost in that sexual haze, I knew for a certainty that if I wasn't touched, stroked, filled … I would die.

Living at the Huntsman might keep me safer from the Unseelie, but it would increase my risk in other ways. Plenty of those men sitting around Lochlan's table had glared at me like I was the source of all evil. Staying under their roof would give any of them easy access to me. What if one of them thought it was wise to send me a message like Lochlan had?

I shivered at the mere thought.

No, thank you. I might have been convinced to make the move had I not been treated to that little display. Foolish or not, I felt safer in my own tiny apartment, so that was where I'd stay.

It was Sunday, and my plans consisted of laundry and taking a personal day, meaning no bra, no pants, and binge-watching Netflix. I forced myself from bed and got the first load of laundry going when Ashley texted.

Ash: Made it home and slept all day yesterday—how's it going there?

Me: Great, been nice and quiet, watching Versailles today.

Ash: U sure? No new sightings or information?

Me: Nope, like I said, things have settled down.

Ash: K, tell me if that changes.
Me: Will do!

I hated lying, but sometimes, it was necessary.

Other than my brief chat with Ashley, I spent the day entirely alone, and it was glorious. I had desperately needed the time to regroup and felt decently refreshed by the time I strolled into work the next day.

I found Cat sitting at the front desk when I entered, returned from her unexplained absence.

"Where the hell have you been?" I whispered conspiratorially.

She came around the desk and spoke softly. "Come on, let's visit in the coatroom."

I followed her lead into the small, empty room, and she closed the door.

"I told my family about the Unseelie, and the elders called a meeting out of town. It can take a while for everyone to gather and settle on a course of action."

"What did they decide? Are they going to help?"

She frowned. "They want to see how things unfold before taking any action."

I was more disappointed than I had expected. I knew the chances for help had been slim, but I'd managed to raise my hopes high enough that her news was upsetting.

"I don't suppose you're going to tell me about this group or how they know about the Fae?"

"I don't suppose you're going to tell me how you see the Fae?"

We held each other's eyes, clearly at a stalemate.

"That's what I thought," she said with a brow raised.

I rolled my eyes and relayed what had happened at the

garage, keeping my newfound abilities to myself. If her people were wary of the Fae, I didn't want to be marked an enemy just because I'd wielded powers.

Cat was shocked to hear about the Red Caps. "They're supposedly exceptionally vicious, cannibalistic even. The legends say that they get their name from a time when they served as Queen Mab's guard. Similar to human cultures that took scalps or ears as trophies of their kills, the Red Caps used to mop up the blood of their slain enemies with their hats and wear the soiled cloth as a badge of honor. At least, that's the rumor. I've certainly never seen one to confirm."

I recalled their crusty red hats and shivered. "That sounds insane. Every new thing I learn about the Fae is more twisted and messed up than the last. And on top of it all, after everything that had happened Saturday night, I fought with Lochlan. He wanted me to move into the Huntsman."

"You didn't agree, did you?" she blurted in horror.

"No, of course not!" I held off telling her why. I knew she already feared them, and I didn't want to give her more reason to hate them. I disagreed with what he'd done, but I didn't think he was innately bad. We all make poor decisions at some point.

"Thank the Lord."

"Cat, I need to know why you're so afraid of them. I'm sinking into this world more and more every day, and I need to know why you think they're so dangerous."

Cat's eyes flitted to the door, and I could plainly see on her face that she was torn. Just as I resigned myself to her refusal, she spoke softly. "I can't tell you everything, but I will say that my ancestors were killed by the Wild Hunt to keep the Fae secret. They slaughtered many innocent people until few were left, and those who survived went into hiding. The Hunt cannot know of our existence. We don't know if they would still try to eliminate us, and we can't risk it."

I was heartbroken for Cat's family, and I hated to know that Lochlan could have been involved in murdering innocent people.

"I won't say a word; I swear to you." I gripped her hand in mine, trying to assure her that I understood the importance of her secret.

Our eyes locked in understanding. With no small amount of trust, our budding friendship was quickly forming a solid bond. I was grateful for that because the value of a genuine friendship was priceless.

LEAVING WORK LATER THAT DAY, I exited the museum to find Lochlan waiting for me outside. He was back to wearing an expensive suit, swathed in effortless power.

Just the sight of him was intoxicating.

A flood of embarrassment and anger froze me in place. "What do you want?"

"You can lower your shields. I'm not here to fight."

I hadn't truly expected him to attack me, but I'd definitely tensed into a defensive stance. Taking a deep breath, I relaxed my shoulders and walked to where he stood on the marble steps.

"I fucked up. It won't happen again." He handed me a small rectangular box. "There's a holster inside. I would strongly suggest wearing it at all times."

Inside lay a black blade similar to the one he had given me during the fight with the Red Caps. The blade was sleek with a solid handle, and though I wasn't an expert by any means, I could tell it was a beautiful weapon made for precision.

I hadn't expected an apology. The Fae warrior didn't strike me as the type to easily give that sort of admission, which made his contrition all the more meaningful.

"Thank you, Lochlan."

His jaw flexed. "Walk with me. We need to talk."

I wasn't sure a single bit of good news had ever started with that sentence in all of history. "We need to talk" might as well show up in *Webster's Dictionary* under the synonym "We've got a problem."

Anxiety was an insidious weed taking root deep in my gut, but I fell into step with him, ready to confront whatever he had to say.

"I've sensed your reluctance to be involved in our world from the moment we met. Somehow, you've lived completely in the dark up until recently, and you've clung to that life in the face of all the evidence to the contrary. I've refrained from forcing the issue, but you need to accept some truths after all that's happened. The first time I spoke with you, I did so because I sensed that you weren't fully human."

I stumbled, then gawked up at him, thinking surely, he was joking, but his stoic features held no humor.

"I have human parents, baby pictures, and I know I'm not adopted. Mom has pictures of my birth!" It was absurd. Inconceivable. He had to be wrong.

"At first, I thought perhaps you were the offspring of Fae and human. I've never heard of such a thing happening, but I knew of no other way that I would sense both human and Fae from you."

"I'm human. If you sense Fae, it's because you sense the necklace," I stated firmly.

"Your powers, Rebecca—" He started before I cut him off.

"*It's the necklace,*" I insisted. "That's the Fae power you're sensing."

"I wish it were that simple, but I'm a hunter, and I can sense these things. You are Fae, at least, in part. Maybe you were once fully human, but you aren't entirely human anymore." He stepped closer. "I forbid any of my men to speak of my discovery to you or anyone else. If the knowledge of your existence got out, you could be in even more danger."

My breathing was labored, making it hard to get enough air. "How could that have happened? Is it even possible?" I began to walk again, wanting to get to the safety of my home and away from Lochlan's terrifying words.

"I'm not aware of this happening before although that's not my area of expertise. After learning about the necklace, my best theory is that your body has been absorbing its power over the years. Now that you're that much closer to Faery here in Ireland, where the veil between worlds is the thinnest, the process has sped up. The energy in the necklace has transformed your body and changed its molecular structure."

What was this, some deranged version of Spider-Man? People didn't just mutate.

Every time I thought I was starting to get my footing, some new bit of information knocked me on my ass. This more than any. Being stuck with a magic necklace was one thing, but becoming Fae was another.

My lungs struggled to get enough air.

"The necklace only came to life just recently, like it didn't even have power until I came to Belfast. How could this all have happened so quickly?"

"That doesn't mean it wasn't always powerful. You were just unaware." He effectively shot down my argument. "Your healing abilities are examples of your new Fae nature. I don't believe the necklace was imbued with healing powers. As Fae, we don't need to put such magic in a talisman as we already possess those powers on our own."

I was quiet again, raw with emotion and unsure what to say or what to think.

"There is one more thing."

"*Seriously*?" I balked.

He grimaced. "The powers you've exhibited ... they're unknown to me."

"Unknown? As in you've never seen them before?"

"Precisely."

"When I put darkness into the Red Cap?" I recalled the way he'd watched me. There'd been a severity to his features that had worried me.

His chin dipped in confirmation. "And how you knew the Red Caps were hiding in the shadows. These are not normal gifts for Seelie or Unseelie. We use light magic. What you exhibited was more in line with the Shadow Fae and dark magic. If that amulet is, in fact, the source of your powers, I'd say it was forged somewhere in the Shadow Lands. How it ended up around your neck is another matter entirely, but with Merlin's appearance, I'd say he likely played a role."

I nodded absently, but I struggled to keep up.

I was becoming Fae. And not just any Fae, I was going dark. Gaining the power of something grotesque like the Draug, lurking in shadows and hunting to kill.

My despair was crippling.

I was a hornet's nest of fear, and frustration, and frantic desperation. Emotions so intense and overwhelming that my brain packaged them up neatly into a box and buried it deep inside me, leaving me blessedly numb and safe.

I didn't say a word until we reached my apartment. Turning, I spoke in a hollow voice, unable to meet Lochlan's eyes. "Thank you for being patient with me and for explaining this. I think I'd like to have some time alone to process it all."

He pulled me into his arms, pressing his lips against my

temple. "Don't be afraid of the unknown merely because it's unknown. Your strengths will see you through this."

I nodded and pulled away, needing to be alone. The silent darkness of my apartment was a welcome reprieve. I didn't want to see or hear or think.

As I stepped toward the stairs, thick arms wrapped around me from behind, one giant hand firmly covering my mouth. I wrenched forward violently, panic ripping me from my protective cocoon of numbness. I fought fiercely but was no match for my assailant's vise-like grip. The element of surprise had tipped the scales vastly in his favor.

He released one of his hands, but before I could try to pull free, that hand came to rest on my forehead, and my body went limp. Everything faded to black.

CHAPTER

EIGHTEEN

I was too groggy to comprehend what they said. My addled brain simply listened to the melodic back and forth of conversation like a boat swaying on the ocean. Eventually, I roused enough to identify two voices—a man and woman—talking in hushed tones. They sounded like British aristocracy. Aloof and slightly bored.

"I've tried to take it off, both with magic and force. It will not budge. I don't think it can be done, at least not by us," said the man from my left.

The woman responded coolly. "I would have been surprised if you could. He would not be so careless as to allow its removal." Her voice was confident, firm, and a bit frightening.

Where was I?

Who were these people?

My heart rate increased as I recalled being attacked in my apartment. The floral scent around me wasn't familiar. I was no longer at home. My head ached somewhat, but I was other-

167

wise uninjured and seemed to be comfortably resting on a bed, clothes still intact.

"We could always kill her," the man said flatly. "Removing her head should do the trick."

I could only assume they were talking about me, making fear and adrenaline rouse me fully.

"That is not an option. I do not need to make an enemy of him. We all know what he did to his own sister. We shall have to leave him to his schemes."

The room was silent for a moment, and I wondered if they had quietly left.

"I know you are awake, Rebecca. Open your eyes, and we shall talk."

Shit. Here goes nothing.

I opened my eyes to a softly lit room. The man and woman studied me. As my eyes focused, my body tensed at the recognition of the man who had abducted me from my apartment.

"You kidnapped me," I rasped, moving to sit on the edge of the bed. Pain shot through my skull, but I attempted to ignore it as I took in my surroundings.

"You were not so much kidnapped as summoned," countered the woman.

She was tall, around five-eight, with long red hair flowing in smooth waves nearly down to her waist. Her porcelain skin was dotted with freckles, and her eyes were almost too green to be real, like freshly sprouted spring grass or a field of summer clover. She wore a diaphanous long-sleeve gown of dark green silk that hugged her lithe frame. Her body might have been willowy, but her regal stature spoke to her strength and confidence. Like seeing a striking work of art for the first time, I stared unabashedly at her perfection.

Eventually, my eyes slid to the bedroom around me, which was lavishly decorated in soft shades of blue. A painted vanity with a tall mirror sat on the same wall as the door while an ornate fireplace warmed the room from across the bed. Two large multipaned windows were framed by sheer white drapes cascading the length of the exceptionally tall walls and highlighting a comfortable sitting area. Beneath me, luxurious velour bedding felt softer to the touch than the most opulent of fabrics. The place was absolutely stunning, decorated with such luxury that I was totally overwhelmed. Every tiny detail of the room was crafted to perfection and designed to proclaim enviable wealth.

"Where am I?" I couldn't keep the awe from my voice.

"You are in Faery—in Avalon to be precise," spoke the woman, drawing my attention back to her.

"And who are you?" My eyes flickered back and forth between them, unable to read anything of their intentions.

"I am Queen Guinevere of the Seelie Court, and this is Durin. He assists me in ... sensitive matters." She gestured at the man standing next to her before continuing. "What you *should* be asking is why you have been brought here." Her aristocratic brow arched as if she were painfully aware of my inferiority.

My breaths grew shallow as her question sank in. "Why *have* I been brought here?" I asked, fighting my growing hysteria.

"I wanted to see the half-human, half-Fae girl for myself. So here you are," she offered smugly.

My eyes jumped back to Durin. His hair was buzzed close to his scalp, and though he was short, his muscular frame was intimidating. I imagined he would pulverize anyone who challenged him in a fight, and I desperately hoped my situation didn't come to that.

Guin drew my eyes back to her as she continued in a disinterested tone. "Merlin seems to think a war is approaching."

"A war?" I asked in confusion. Someone was opening portals, but no one had said anything about a war—not that I was going to say anything about any of it to Guin. Considering my luck, she'd probably blame the whole thing on me.

"I disagree with him. My spies have been sent to the far reaches of my kingdom and beyond, and they have found no evidence of an uprising. Aside from my interest in your Fae abilities, the other reason I had you brought here was because Merlin also seems to think you have a role to play in this alleged war. I wanted to see who he was relying upon. While I have not found evidence of an amassing army or insurgence, I have not held the throne for over a thousand years by ignoring possible threats."

Her eyes gradually made their way down my frame and back up, clearly unimpressed. Dismissing me, she turned to Durin. "Merlin had better hope he is wrong. If there is a war coming, there is nothing this child could do about it."

Both of them turned for the door.

"*Wait!*" I cried after them. "How long are you keeping me here?"

"You will have dinner with us when the bell tolls, then you will be returned to your home," Guin called from the doorway without turning back.

Dinner. Okay, I can do dinner.

I tried to relax and assure myself that I'd be back on Earth in no time. To keep my mind from panic, I examined the artwork and priceless objects casually placed throughout the room. A seemingly priceless silver-handled hairbrush inlaid with intricate scrollwork sat on the vanity. Every detail of the room was extraordinary, lest anyone forget they were in the queen's palace.

The light coming through the windows indicated it was midafternoon if Faery daylight was comparable to Earth's. It had been nearly seven in the evening when I was taken, and I wondered if that meant I had been unconscious all night and morning. I started to panic until I remembered Ashley saying something about time not working the same in Faery as it did on Earth. I could have been gone from Belfast for days and not just a single night, or it could have been only hours. There was no way to know for sure.

My room appeared to be on the second floor, with an amazing view of the vast gardens. Lush flowering plants and fruit trees dotted the landscape in intricate patterns. If I hadn't known better, I would have said that I was in France gazing out on the infamous gardens at the Palace of Versailles. I was clearly far from wintery Belfast.

What was this place? A separate planet? Or perhaps a different dimension? It appeared unsettlingly similar to Earth. The building and décor, while fitting of a different era, were nonetheless familiar. If I hadn't met the austere queen myself, I would have said this was some kind of lavish joke at my expense.

A soft knock sounded at my door, and after a quick debate, I opened it to peek at who had come calling. The woman on the other side offered a soft smile with warm eyes, but it was her greenish skin that took me by surprise. Not the green of an olive complexion or the pallor of illness—her skin was literally green, like a human-sized version of the little man in my apartment. She didn't appear threatening, so I smiled in return and pulled back the door.

"Good afternoon to you, ma'am. I brought you some food and thought I could help you freshen up for dinner tonight." She spoke timidly, her hands hefting a tray filled with fruit and cheeses.

"Oh, thank you. That's very kind. I suppose you can set the tray anywhere."

She set the tray on the vanity, then looked at me expectantly. She wore a plain servant's dress that would have been commonplace back in the early 1900s on Earth.

"My name is Cyrene. I'm here to help you in any way I can." Her shy smile was so endearing that I liked her instantly.

"I'm Rebecca." I reached out to shake her hand, and she regarded me curiously. After a moment, she touched my hand awkwardly, unsure of my intent. I clasped her hand slowly and shook it.

Her eyes met mine, face lit with fascination.

"It's a handshake. That's how we say hello on Earth."

"This is how the Fae greet an acquaintance." She bowed her head with eyes lowered.

I repeated the gesture, and we both grinned.

"Can you tell me what's going on? Why am I being kept here for dinner?"

"It's customary for guests of the palace to stay for dinner, if not stay the night. Dinner is always a formal affair, so I am here to prepare you. It would be an affront to her majesty if you were not adequately attired." She walked to a large basin across the room. "I'll prepare a bath for you. While you soak, I'll fetch a gown for the evening." She touched the basin, and steaming water magically appeared inside.

"You can control water?" I asked, watching as she poured bath salts in the tub and gathered towels.

"Yes, I'm a forest nymph—a type of elemental. No great magic, but I can do enough with water and earth to be of help here in the palace," she said proudly, then stepped back to examine me. "Do you need help getting out of your clothes?"

A surprised bubble of laughter escaped me. The entire scenario was so foreign, so unexpected. "No, thank you. I'll get in the bath by myself."

She gave a slight bow and slipped from the room, leaving me alone to bathe.

The water maintained a perfect temperature. I hadn't realized how much I needed a good soak, but after all that had transpired in a single day's time, my body was riddled with tension. There was nothing for me to do but try to relax. I had no clue how to get back home, which made escape practically impossible. I would hold myself together, get through dinner, then have my mental breakdown once I was somewhat safely back home.

It was decided.

I closed my eyes and tried not to think until Cyrene returned.

"It's time to wash your hair. We don't want you to be late."

I wasn't accustomed to strange women bathing me, but I didn't want to be rude either. It would be wise to follow the lead of those around me in the unknown landscape.

I swallowed my protest and leaned my head back. The soaps she used had a refreshing scent, and by the time she was done, my hair was silky smooth and clean. I rose from the soapy water, and she wrapped a towel around me.

"Look what I found! I think it's going to be just beautiful on you." She held up a royal purple gown made of ethereal fabric that hung in the air for my inspection. The dress was not particularly intricate, which suited me well. The combined effect of the color, fabric, and design was stunning. It was absolutely perfect.

"Cyrene, I love it. Thank you!"

She beamed in response and laid the dress on the bed before heading to the vanity. "Come put on this robe and have a seat. We'll see what I can do with that beautiful hair of yours."

"It takes forever to dry."

"Trust me." Creases formed at the corners of her large eyes as she grinned with amusement.

She held her hands over my head and swept them slowly down my back to the ends of my hair. When she was done, my hair was completely dry.

"Do you have any idea how amazing you are? I would do my hair all the time if I didn't have to dry it!"

She giggled at my outburst, delighted that I was overwhelmed with something considered trivial in the Fae world.

We chatted for the next hour while she combed, brushed, curled, and braided my hair. The final product was worthy of the front page of *Time* magazine. The top portion of my hair was pulled back with curls and a couple of intricate braids adorning my head, while the back portion fell in perfectly formed waves.

I had never felt more beautiful.

Once I completed the look with the purple gown, I stood dumbstruck in front of the mirror. I never thought much of my figure, but the fabric draping my body hugged me in all the right places, displaying my body to its fullest potential.

I turned to Cyrene and took her hands. "Thank you so much."

"It's my pleasure, Rebecca. But please be careful." Her face fell, and her eyes pleaded with me. "The Faery Court is a dangerous place, and the Queen can be a jealous ruler," she whispered the last part as she took her hands back and nervously clenched her skirt.

"Thank you for the warning. I have no intention of angering anyone tonight. I'm just trying to get myself back home." I gave her a tight smile.

"The bell tower tolls when it is time for the evening meal. Once you hear it, you will go down the hallway to the right, and it will take you to the main stairwell. At the bottom of the stairs, you should see the gathering of people entering the dining hall."

"You aren't staying with me until then?"

"No, I'm sorry. I need to go help in the kitchens."

Reaching out, I gave the Fae woman a warm hug. After her initial surprise, she returned the gesture. Pulling back, I realized that her oversized eyes brought none of the horror that I had felt when encountering the other Fae creatures. She was kind and sincere, but most importantly, she was a wonderful reminder that not all Fae were hunters or criminals.

"I'm so glad I met you, Cyrene. Thank you for all your help."

"Be well, Rebecca. I hope you return home safely." With a soft smile, she slipped from the room, closing the door behind her.

I walked to the small bookcase in the bedroom and scanned the titles. Most were in English, some in what I assumed to be an Elvin language. I examined the books for only a few minutes when a gong resonated throughout the room.

That was my cue to perform.

I had no doubt that every moment of my stay was part of an intricate test. I was not naïve enough to believe that I was safe, despite the absence of visible dangers. Power emanated from the Faery Queen like waves of radiant heat off the scorching pavement. If I was not careful, I would end up badly burned.

NINETEEN

Between the elegant ball gown and the enormous stairwell, I felt like Scarlett O'Hara descending the grand staircase at Tara.

Dozens of people stood in formal attire at the landing below. Sipping from crystal glasses while they mingled, the crowd slowly moved toward the double doors off the main room. Had I not known they were Fae, I would never have suspected the guests were anything but human—aristocratic humans at a fancy retro costume party—but humans, nonetheless.

Several sets of eyes were drawn my way as I approached the last few steps. Could these people tell I was different? Had they been informed of my presence? Would they care?

Does it matter? You're stuck with them regardless.

I sucked in a deep lungful of air and merged with the crowd. We wound our way through a large set of double doors into an enormous dining room. Elegantly crafted crystal chandeliers hung from soaring paneled ceilings with matching crystal sconces lining the walls. Still-life paintings, portraits, landscapes, and any number of other subjects adorned the walls in the hundreds. A single long table that seated what had to be nearly one hundred people filled the middle of the room. Pristine silverware sets were arranged around sparkling white dinner plates. Down the center of the table, among dozens of silver serving dishes, were grand candelabras and opulent bouquets of fragrant flowers.

Without realizing, I had stopped in the middle of the entrance to take in the room's grandeur. I was not brought back to the present until a man spoke softly near my ear.

"Let me escort you to your seat." The man extended his elbow. He was about six feet tall with light-brown hair swept to the side and dark copper-colored eyes.

Relief brought an easy smile to my face. I would have had no idea where to sit with so many options. I gladly placed my hand on his forearm, and he led me to the far end of the room where an opulent gold armchair presided over the table.

I should have known I'd be stuck sitting with the queen.

Holding back a grimace, I followed the man to the chair just left of the queen's. I gave him a quiet thanks for his help before he took a seat several places down on the opposite side.

All at once, the crowd stood. The room instantly grew hushed as the queen approached, her head held high and shoulders back in a statement of supreme authority. Once she rounded the table to her chair, she gracefully bowed her head. Her subjects took their seats, resuming conversations as if they had never been interrupted.

I bowed my head to the queen as she sat in her demi-throne, unsure what else to do. It was clear she wanted no question as to who was in charge, so any sign of deference seemed a safe bet.

As soon as she was seated, hordes of servers appeared, placing small plates of food with a savory aroma on top of the charger plates in front of each guest. Those around me took their utensils and began to eat with relish. However, Ashley had told me that under no circumstances was I to eat Fae food. But refusing dinner with the queen seemed a grave insult.

Indecision held me motionless.

"Go ahead, girl. There is nothing to fear in eating the food at my table," the queen said as she raised her glass of wine to her dainty pink lips.

My chin dropped in acknowledgment, but my eyes again wandered until they met with the eyes of the man who had walked me to my seat. He held his fork out meaningfully and placed a bite of food in his mouth, keeping his eyes fixed on mine the entire time.

I took a deep breath and picked up my fork to place a bite in my mouth. Rich flavors that I had never experienced burst across my tongue, and my eyes fell shut in pure delight. When they reopened, the man still watched, but this time the corners of his mouth hooked upward in a smile.

The food was indescribable. Course after course, I gorged myself until I could not eat another bite. I hadn't touched the food Cyrene had brought, so I'd entered the dining hall starved.

Throughout the meal, the man glanced in my direction periodically. I rarely caught him engaging with anyone around him. Near the end of the meal, my curiosity got the better of me, and I turned to the queen.

"Who is the man in the gray jacket just down there?" I motioned with my fork down the table.

"We do not discuss any matters of politics at dinner," she said with a dismissive tone before continuing. "You and I shall walk the gardens after the meal is done. We will talk then."

I hadn't considered my question to be particularly probing, but I wasn't going to argue with the queen.

Fortunately, I didn't have to wait long before the queen

rose. On her mark, the rest of the guests stood. She motioned for me to join her, and with all eyes on us, we strolled the length of the room and beyond to the formal entry.

The gardens were lit with an ethereal light emanating from Faery lanterns. They hung throughout the area, casting a soft blanketed glow on the landscape. Every now and then, I caught a glimpse of what I initially thought were humming-birds flitting about but quickly realized were tiny Faeries tending to the plants. They moved too quickly to get a good look at them, but I could tell they had gossamer wings the full length of their bodies.

"Are they pixies?" I found myself asking.

"Yes. They are useful in the gardens but can also be quite an annoyance. They do not let their small stature hinder their demands and expectations." Her wry sense of amusement intrigued me. The Faery queen maintained a seamless image of power, but she was a woman just like any other beneath it all. She was more than just her station in life, and I was curious about that side of her.

"I have to say, I can hardly wrap my mind around the fact that I'm walking in a garden with Queen Guinevere. That you're real—you, and Arthur, and Merlin, and the rest. I could never have imagined that there was truth in the old stories."

"Some truth, but few of the stories are all that accurate anymore. The brevity of human existence is vastly limiting; knowledge is lost, priorities skewed. The urgency of time warps rational thinking—such strange creatures," she mused. "Makes them unpredictable."

"We do the best we can," I said wryly.

"There is no 'we' anymore, Rebecca. You had better start getting used to that."

"I haven't had time to get used to it. It's just been a handful of hours since I found out." I tried not to sound antagonistic, but it was difficult. My own demons got in the way of decorum.

"It always comes back to time. Stop thinking like a human. You are Fae. There is no getting used to it. You simply are. Accept it and move on."

She did have a point, but the newness of the subject made it a sensitive matter. Despite her insistence, I knew it would take time to accept my new circumstances. "Can you tell me about the war you mentioned? Did Merlin say what my role would be?"

"If there is a war brewing, it is likely Merlin's own doing. He tinkers in matters best left alone." She spoke of him like an annoying younger brother, and I supposed such a familiarity might evolve after so many years of acquaintance. After a brief pause, she turned her assessing eyes back to me. "How long have you been Fae?" She arched her brow in expectation of my answer.

Her sudden change of subject caught me off guard, and I stuttered for a moment. "I'm not sure. I've never shown any sign of power until I moved to Ireland a couple of weeks ago. That's all I know."

"What powers have you exhibited thus far?"

Dammit, I was a terrible liar. I had no desire to answer her question, but the thought of being caught in a lie made my heart leap in my throat. "Nothing major—unlocking a door, seeing through glamour, and healing quickly." Relieved my words came out steadily, I calmed my breathing and tried to project an image of innocence. If my powers were unique like Lochlan had suggested, there was no way I was telling her about them.

She stopped beneath the swaying branches of a flowering tree and turned in my direction. Her cool green eyes bore into me before she spoke. "No doubt your powers shall be revealed in time. What you need to know is that once your transformation is complete, you will be under my rule. I have mandated that the Seelie remain in Faery. Outside of my personal guard and the Wild Hunt, there are no exceptions. My man will be watching, and once you fully transition, you will return to Faery." She looked down her nose at me, asserting her dominance in anticipation of my challenge, but I was too dumbstruck to mount a defense.

I hadn't even had a chance to process Lochlan's claims that I was becoming Fae, let alone make the connection that I might have to live in Faery. My already aching head began to pound as helplessness and despair settled heavily in my chest.

"Durin," said the queen before large hands reached around to my forehead, just as they had done in my apartment, and my world went black.

I CAME AWAKE FASTER this time, my eyes flying open to discover I was back in my own bed. I checked my phone and was stunned to discover it was 11 p.m. on the same day I was abducted, merely a few hours later. It felt like a full day had passed, but in reality, it had been a fraction of that.

I sat up abruptly. The movement was too fast, and my stomach lurched. I rushed to the bathroom and stood vigil over the toilet, expecting to return my dinner at any moment.

Head still aching, my stomach settled enough that I stepped over to the sink and splashed my face with water. My reflection caught me off guard, and I froze to take in the stunning woman in the mirror. The beautiful hairstyle Cyrene had created was a bit worse for wear, but the effect was still there —I looked like royalty. I still wore the purple gown, leaving no room for argument that it had all been a dream.

All of it had been real.

I'd been to Faery.

I gathered the silk skirt and walked to the bedroom mirror for the full effect. Once I turned on the light and located my phone, I snapped a couple of selfies. It might have been crazy, but I felt like I had to keep a record of what had happened. As though the dress might disintegrate like Cinderella's night at the ball, and I'd have nothing to show for my visit with the queen.

For a second, I considered sending the picture to Ashley. The thought had hardly formed before I remembered that I couldn't tell her about any of it. She'd be on a plane and back in Belfast in a heartbeat. I needed to keep her safely in New York.

But if I continued to keep these increasingly monumental secrets from her, would I still be able to call her my best friend?

I was becoming Fae.

My life was already unrecognizable. Between the secrets and geographic distance, the foundations of our friendship would dissolve. Even if I found a way to stay on earth, Ashley would be lost to me.

The realization snatched the warmth from my mood and left me chilly instead. Turning the light off, I carefully removed the dress and hung it in my armoire before pulling on my pajamas. I crawled into bed and tried to comprehend the enormity of what was happening.

I was becoming Fae.

I pictured the dining room full of beautiful faces all frozen at the age of thirty. Would I stop aging as well? A surge of panic raced through my body, sending an arctic chill deep into my bones.

My parents would notice eventually. Could I risk telling them what was happening to me? If not, I would have to let them think I was dead because I couldn't continue to show my youthful face without explanation.

No, faking my death wasn't an option. I couldn't knowingly hurt them like that if it was in my power to avoid. In that case, it might be better to tell them now before I'm taken to Faery forever. I had to make sure they knew I was safely alive if I ever disappeared, but I didn't want them to worry unnecessarily. Maybe I could find a way to stay and glamour myself to have wrinkles so they didn't suspect. They could live out their lives as they should have if I'd never come across this damn necklace.

I was becoming Fae.

And it was all the necklace's fault. Without its magical influence, I could remain human. I would live a normal mortal existence with my family and friends. Monsters wouldn't be after me, and I wouldn't have a Faery queen threatening to keep me a prisoner in a distant land.

To think, I'd argued with Mom and Ashley to keep the damn thing around my neck.

Now, I could only summon feelings of hate for the collar leashing me to a life I didn't want.

CHAPTER

TWENTY

I woke the following morning in a desolate mood. Feelings of hopelessness had haunted my dreams, and while I hadn't had to face the shadow man, my current reality was a nightmare in itself.

After I had showered, dressed, and eaten breakfast, I grabbed the knife Lochlan had given me and dropped it in my purse. When I set my dishes in the sink, it stirred the memory of the little Fae man I had seen on my table and how much his green skin had reminded me of Cyrene. She'd been kind and gentle. Was the little man the same sort of creature? Had I been unforgivably rude in my shock?

Instead of rinsing the uneaten bits of egg from my plate, I set it on the counter and added some cheese and a couple of crackers. I had no idea if the little man would come back or what he liked to eat, but if he did return, I figured an apology by way of food wouldn't hurt.

I mostly hid away all morning at work. I wasn't fit company for anyone. By the time lunch rolled around, I felt somewhat less nihilistic and went in search of Cat to see how she was doing. Having her didn't totally make up for the potential loss of my parents and Ashley, but it was something. My friendship with Cat meant I wasn't totally alone.

"How have things been here on the ground level?" I asked when I saw her, forcing a small smile.

"Quiet. I've already breezed through the gossip rag I brought to read. What about you? Have a good weekend?"

I shrugged. "I was kidnapped and taken to Faery, so it had its ups and downs."

Her eyes opened so wide that I was mildly concerned her eyeballs were going to pop right out of her head. "You're joking," she breathed.

"I wish I was. Queen Guinevere had her man kidnap me. I spent the day there, had dinner with her Court, talked to her in the gardens, and then they deposited me back home."

"She knows that you know about the Fae, and she didn't kill you?"

I suppose I hadn't thought of it like that. It's a small silver lining.

"No. She just wanted to ask me questions." I suddenly realized telling Cat what had happened would churn up some awkward questions I wasn't willing to answer. Cat was terrified of the Fae. I couldn't possibly tell her I was becoming one of them.

Great. There goes the last of my friends.

"What did she ask? What was it like there?"

I outlined the events of my trip to Faery in detail, only skirting the issue of my Fae transformation. Cat listened raptly to every word.

"She said there's a war coming?" Cat asked. "The elders are worried about that, too. That's why they want to meet you, Rebecca. I'm not sure when yet, but they said it was time. After I told them about the Red Caps, everyone's been on edge."

They might not want to meet with me if they knew I was part Fae. Maybe if I formed a relationship now, they might make an exception for me. See me as more than my genetics.

"I'd love to meet with them. The more allies and information, the better. You just tell me when and where, and I'll be there."

She quietly clapped her hands in excitement. I wasn't sure how things would turn out with Cat, but I'd do my best to keep her as a friend. "Oh! That reminds me. When I told you about the Red Cap attack, I forgot to mention that your bracelet saved me!"

"You're joking." Her eyes grew round again, and I laughed.

"Is that all you can say today? No, I'm not joking. One of those nasty creatures went to slash me with his razor-sharp claws, and when I put my arm up to defend myself, the charm on the bracelet threw him back and left me unharmed. Unfortunately, the bracelet was damaged by the hit and fell off, but before that, it was a lifesaver."

"I've never seen the spell work." She spoke in awe of the magic and studied a similar bracelet on her wrist. "I've drawn out the protection rune a million times, thinking it was more like a lucky charm. My mom swore the runes work, but I've never had any tangible proof."

"I'd love for you to make me another one if you wouldn't mind."

"I'll work on it tonight."

"Perfect! Thanks, Cat. I better get back upstairs before the others wonder where I've run off to."

She saluted me with a goofy grin, and I headed back to the fourth-floor offices feeling a tiny bit more optimistic.

～

I was exhausted by closing time. I gathered my things and headed home in the crisp evening air, which was refreshing and helped reinvigorate me. Even in the dark, the trees that hadn't already dropped their leaves still boasted beautiful fall colors.

I wondered whether the food scraps I had left out would be gone when I got home. And if they were, did the Brownie take them, or did I have mice? How would I be able to tell the difference unless I witnessed him retrieve my offerings?

When I opened the door into my dark apartment, my gaze went straight to the small plate I had left on the counter. Only crumbs remained.

He'd taken my offering!

I stepped through the threshold of the entry but froze when I sensed a presence in my living room. A hulking figure sat at the far end of my loveseat, causing me to drop my bags and stumble backward with a screech.

"It's me, Becca. Calm down," said a familiar deep voice.

Lochlan.

"Were you trying to scare me to death?" I picked up my purse and work tote, gathering the items scattered on the floor. "What are you doing here? You can't just go letting yourself into people's homes. Not only is it breaking and entering, it's *rude.*"

He seemed enormous in my tiny apartment. His domineering presence filled any room, but cramped into tight quarters, there was no escaping him.

"I heard you took a trip to Faery. Want to tell me how that happened?" His gravelly voice in the quiet room sent a tingling awareness through my body, and I was suddenly too hot in my own skin. This was the first time I had seen him in a T-shirt, and it was stretched perfectly over his muscular frame. I could see the bulges of his sinewy muscles, and a nagging voice insisted I trace them with my tongue. His shirt was untucked over faded denim jeans, and he wore his black boots beneath. Casual Lochlan felt a hair less intimidating but just as devastatingly dangerous to my libido.

"How did you know I was there?" My words came out breathy, and my eyes dropped to his full lips.

God, what I wouldn't give to suck on those lips.

Those tasty lips curved up in the corners, and I realized I must have telegraphed my thoughts.

"Does it matter how I know?"

"I was kidnapped by a man named Durin. He took me to the queen. We had dinner."

He slowly prowled closer. "That's a very concise explanation."

I nodded, my body heating as he approached. My thoughts were choppy and disconnected amid an ocean of sexual tension.

Lochlan erased the distance between us and leaned down until his lips were close to my ear. "Are we going to play this game again?"

I would love to accuse him of manipulating me—to find some other reason to explain this insistent desire that overcame me around him—but it would be a lie. The cravings I felt were my own. A biological response I couldn't deny.

I slowly shook my head left to right.

A feral growl rumbled from his chest as his arms came around me. He lifted me against his hard body, and I wrapped my legs around his waist. I moaned with yearning when our lips finally collided. The relief set off an avalanche of frenzied need. My hands pulled at his short blond hair, and I rolled my hips to press my center against the hard ridge of his cock. My lust was a dragon raging inside me, threatening to singe me from the inside out if I didn't meet its heady demands.

Lochlan walked us to the wall, pressing my back against it. One hand fisted in my hair while the other held me securely in place.

Nothing about our kiss was delicate or romantic. It was primal and erotic, and I couldn't get enough of his masculine taste. Seizing my chance to bite his bottom lip, I nibbled and sucked, drawing a groan from deep in his chest. The vibrations made my nipples pebble so hard it was almost painful.

I gasped, giving us both a second apart to catch our breath.

Lochlan's forehead rested against mine. "When you get riled up, your eyes go the most amazing shade of black."

His words were a bucket of freezing water dousing my fiery lust.

"*What?*"

I struggled to set my legs down and wiggled out of his grasp.

"Becca, don't..."

"Let me down," I urged. "I need to see."

Eventually, he relented with a grimace. I ran to the bathroom, flipping on the light and freezing at the sight in the mirror. My cheeks were flushed, lips swollen, and my hair was ratted from where his hand had clutched my dark waves. None of that stuff registered, though, because all I could see was black.

Like the Draug, I had no irises. No whites. Just solid black orbs staring back at me.

"*I'm a monster,*" I breathed.

Lochlan pulled my back flush against him, his arms wrapping around me. "They're beautiful, Rebecca. Remember what I said. Don't be afraid just because they're different." He met my black eyes in the mirror. "I have never met a Fae whose eyes switched back and forth like yours. Most Seelie and Unseelie have irises and whites. Only the Shadow Fae have solid black eyes, but theirs don't change. It seems that yours can switch between the two. It's incredible."

Hearing his perspective helped, but it was hard to overcome my panic.

"What happens if they go black at work or around my parents or something? I can't let people see me with black eyes," I stuttered anxiously, turning my face back to peer up at him.

"You'll have to keep yourself calm and be aware that if you do get worked up, you need to excuse yourself somewhere private until you're under control."

It sounded simple, but how did he know that my eyes would continue to return to normal? Maybe once my transformation was complete, my obsidian eyes would be permanent.

I looked back at the mirror, where I watched myself blink several times. As my heart rate started to normalize, the black shrunk back down to my normal human pupil.

The weight of my relief bowed my head.

"Come here. I've got something for you." Lochlan led me downstairs to the sofa where he had left his jacket. Reaching inside, he pulled out a small flip phone and held it out.

I took it and looked at him questioningly. I already had a phone, and he knew it.

"This one's safer."

"Is it spelled or something? Like a magic phone?"

"No, Rebecca. It's just a burner. I like to stay off the grid as much as possible. If you need to contact me, use that. I've got my number programmed in it. You can text on it, but it's a pain in the ass, and I probably won't text you back."

"Thanks for the warning," I quipped playfully, hoping to avoid the awkwardness of addressing our heated moment earlier. There was only so much emotional gymnastics I could handle.

But Lochlan didn't smile in return. Instead, he sighed and picked up his jacket.

"I'll be in touch," he murmured, then let himself out.

I stared at the closed door for long minutes after he was gone. Was he disappointed we didn't have sex? I definitely sensed a note of discontent, but what was the reason? Surely, he couldn't expect me not to be upset at learning my eyes look reptilian. What did he want from me? I was doing the best I could, given the circumstances.

I stretched my neck, rolling my head from one side to the other.

I could guess at his thoughts all night and still be wrong. There was no point. I was tired and hungry and not entirely human anymore. I deserved some grace from Lochlan and myself.

Setting aside my worries, I made myself some pasta and happily ate my troubles instead.

CHAPTER
TWENTY-ONE

THE NEXT EVENING, I OPENED UP MY LAPTOP TO CHECK MY PERSONAL email and discovered a message from my mom. She generally stuck to phone conversations, which made me curious about what she might have sent.

HEY BEC,

HOW HAVE YOU BEEN SLEEPING? My friend said she could make some of that incense if you want, and I can get it shipped to you. Just let me know. After we talked about your necklace, I went through all of our old pictures. I should do that more often. It was wonderful pulling up so many happy memories. Anyway, I found a picture of you with the lovely man who sold us the necklace! With you in Ireland, I should have remembered that you got the necklace on our trip to the UK. The old memory isn't what it used to be. Dad helped me scan and attach the picture. You know how bad I am with technology. 😊

. . .

Love you lots,
    Mom

I DOUBLE-CLICKED on the attachment and enlarged the photo taken at some kind of outdoor market. It was me around three or four years old—back when I'd still had blond hair, held up in pigtails. I was talking to a man. He was smiling, squatting down low in a friendly manner.

Recognition soured the food in my stomach into a heavy lump.

Merlin gave me the necklace.

He looked no different than when I'd seen him at the museum. It was unsettling. As though the photo had been doctored, but I knew it hadn't. The man in the photo didn't age because he wasn't human.

Merlin gave me the necklace.

I hadn't stumbled upon some cursed talisman as a child. This whole thing had been engineered. He'd intentionally given me a Fae object of power, knowing it would change my life forever.

Merlin thinks there's a war coming, and he gave me the necklace.

What exactly were his plans for me? Had he known I would become Fae? If he'd done this on purpose and knew I was here, why hadn't he come to me and explained himself?

As my questions grew, so did my outrage.

This was never my fight. My life was derailed as a child before I ever had any say in the matter. And now, I was expected to stop a war I knew nothing about.

Bullshit!

Merlin had no right to drag me into his fight and force these changes in my life. I stared helplessly at the little girl and wondered what my life would have been like had he not intervened. I thought of my black eyes and the dark magic I'd been subjected to.

The glass of wine I'd been holding slid from my fingers and shattered on the floor.

A blond little girl with light-complected parents.

A necklace from the Shadow Lands.

"She must be the milkman's daughter!"

"Look at how dark her hair's gotten."

"Are you of Native American descent?"

Years of teasing and wondering why I looked so different from my parents smacked me in the face. The changes didn't start when I'd arrived in Belfast. They'd begun the moment Merlin locked that clasp around my neck.

That son of a bitch.

What other fundamental changes had the magic caused? Had it changed who I was as a person?

I dropped to my knees and gathered the shards of glass as tears streamed down my heated cheeks. I wasn't sure if I was angrier at my helplessness or sad for the child who had her choices stripped away from her.

Before I knew what I was doing, I walked numbly upstairs and pulled out a small photo album. It didn't look like much, but it was my most prized possession. I sank to the floor and flipped open the cover. Each page was a single four-by-six photo behind clear plastic. The first showed a screaming newborn, still covered in blond fuzz.

More tears blurred my vision as my fingers reached longingly for the image.

I hadn't opened the album in years. When I was younger, I used to flip through the pages daily. I would talk to my little brother, tell him how sorry I was, and do everything I could to keep his memory alive. The pain lessened as the years went on, but I never forgot.

I flipped to the next page. A photo of me, the proud big sister, holding my newborn brother. I'd been five when he was born. Old enough to be gentle and understand the importance of protecting the newest member of our family. I only suffered minor bouts of jealousy. For the most part, I adored my little brother. Callum became the center of my world. I lived to make him giggle and talked to him endlessly, though he couldn't talk back.

Every photo in the album was another frozen moment in time when life was simple and full and effervescent. A year's worth of love chronicled in smiles and silly faces.

But a year was all we had with Callum, and it was all my fault.

I'd only ever wanted to make him happy. My job as his big sister was to help, especially after I started school and was officially a big girl. One evening, he and I sat at the kitchen table together while Mom got dinner ready. She'd given us grapes as a snack to tide us over. I colored in a coloring book, and Callum watched. He was still at the age when he tried to eat crayons, so he didn't get to color unless Mom was helping him.

He put everything in his mouth. Rocks and sticks and anything he could get his hands on. We had to be very careful to watch him. I'd always tried to be so cautious.

After only a few minutes, he'd either eaten or thrown all his grapes on the floor and began to fuss. Mom had gone out front to talk to a neighbor, so I decided to give Callum a few from my bowl until she got back. I placed three purple grapes on his tray and went back to coloring.

It worked. He was instantly quieted by my offering, allowing me to focus on making sure not to scribble outside the lines of the crown I was coloring. I didn't notice how much time had passed. All I knew was that when Mom came back into the kitchen, she started shrieking. She snatched Callum out of his high chair and began to smack his back and shake him about.

I'd never seen her so terrified.

She demanded to know what had happened. I told her what I'd done, and she lay Callum on the counter and tried to free his airway. She worked frantically, becoming more and more hysterical with each second that passed.

I retreated in fear until I'd backed myself into the far corner, horrified at what I'd done. I hadn't known babies could choke on whole grapes. I hadn't realized the importance of Mom always quartering his grapes when she left mine whole. But that didn't change the fact that I'd been the one to give him the grapes. My brother would still be alive if I hadn't done that.

Mom was never the same after that day.

She never blamed me. In fact, she insisted it was her own fault, but I knew better. I'd stolen the light in her eyes. I'd forced Dad to hide in his books, too hurt to face reality. I'd broken my family irrevocably, and there was nothing I could do about it. Nothing except ensure my parents never faced that kind of heartbreak again.

My chest ached with a hollowness that could never be filled. Not fully. There would always be an abscess where Callum should have been. A gaping reminder of how badly I'd hurt the most important people in my life. Keeping their lives as happy and painless as possible had been my one goal ever since, and now I'd be forced to hurt them all over again. All because of Merlin and the damn chain around my neck.

Anger helped soothe the heartbreak, calming my shuddering breaths. As my thoughts quieted, I noticed a faint whispering in my mind. It wasn't as pronounced as when I sensed the Red Caps in the shadows, but a similar awareness told me I wasn't alone.

I peered around, my gaze snagging on the darkness under my bed. There in the shadow, the Brownie stood watching me. Remembering what Cyrene had taught me, I bowed my head slowly as I lowered my eyes. He seemed immobilized at first, then dropped his head a fraction.

Warmth filled my chest. The ocean of heartbreak that lived inside me hadn't been forgotten, but for the moment, I was able to keep my head above its icy depths.

I offered the little man a small smile before asking, "Do you live here?" I wasn't sure if he spoke English, or if he spoke at all, but talking to him seemed the next logical step in making friends.

Seconds after I spoke, he disappeared.

I sighed, replacing the photo album back on the shelf and going back downstairs to clean the mess I'd made. In my continuing efforts of friendship, I left out a small plate of food before I grabbed my new bag of incense and headed upstairs. Mom's message had reminded me that I'd stopped on my lunch break at a tea shop that sold incense and had been able to buy something I hoped would work. After I lit one end, the familiar smoke filled my bedroom and wrapped me in the comforts of home.

Despite our grief and sorrow, my family had persevered, and I could only hope the same would be true when I looked back on these dark days in Belfast.

THE FEATHER-SOFT TOUCH of words buzzing in my mind stirred my conscience.

I wasn't alone.

He was there. The shadow man.

I opened my eyes, and despite the darkness, I could clearly make out his ominous form standing over me. Without warning, he flew at me like he'd done in recent weeks. He entered my body, filling my lungs and mouth, seeping into my very pores.

I didn't fight him this time. I was all out of fight.

I lay still and found that when I relaxed, I didn't need to breathe. I didn't need to panic.

Once the rush subsided, I opened my eyes to the dark, empty room. A chilling calm took hold of me as I walked to the bathroom. I didn't turn on the lights. I had no need for them.

Creatures of the shadows were not handicapped by a need for light.

Our eyes observed everything.

Glorious black eyes stared back at me from the mirror, and I reveled at the wicked intent hidden in their depths. Raising my hand, I licked at the blood coating my fingers. Still warm and sticky. My eyes glided shut as I savored the rich flavor. The coppery liquid served as a delicious reminder of how each of them screamed when I took their lives.

Flashes of the ones called Mom and Dad.

How they'd begged. Pathetic.

Fool humans never even tried to save themselves. Better to have ended their miserable existence.

I opened my eyes again.

My dark reflection leered back at me, red-stained teeth bared in a beguilingly vicious grin.

I am the darkness.

I am silent death.

I bolted upright in bed, gasping for breath. My eyes immediately fell to my trembling hands, desperately searching for confirmation that it had been a dream. No blood. No sticky evidence of the hideous crimes I'd seen except for visions planted deep into the recesses of my mind.

They'd been so real. I could still hear my parents' horrified cries, begging me to stop.

Why, Rebecca? Why are you doing this? My dad wept as we both stood over my mother's mutilated body.

A sob wrenched from my chest, and another, and another, until I could hardly breathe.

Fear struck so deep in my heart that I could no longer feel it beating.

What was I becoming? Was the vision a sign of things to come? What more could this dark power do to drain my humanity from me? What small vestiges of me would remain?

Fear devoured me, leaving a weeping pool of snot and tears. A pathetic heap of pain, powerless to change anything.

I hated feeling powerless.

I hated the incense for not keeping the dreams at bay.

I hated Merlin for changing me.

I hated Guin for her threats.

I hated the secret enemy threatening us with war.

But most of all, I *hated* what I'd become—a woman swathed in fear, shackled to fate.

I was a pawn—a tool to be used and disposed of without care—because I had no purpose of my own.

My fists pounded the bed. I screamed, rage bursting from my throat in a wailing howl. I vented all my frustration and fury, but no amount of crying would change anything. It didn't matter how much I pled or raged or schemed—my life was on a collision course with disaster unless I found a way to stop it. No one else was going to help me. My life and the lives of those I loved were in my hands.

I jumped from my bed and stumbled over to my bedroom

mirror. Ignoring my snotty, tearstained face, I stared at my brown-eyed reflection and reached back for the necklace clasp. I tried to remove the offending chain until my shoulders ached, and I whimpered in frustration.

Getitoffgetitoffgetitoffgetitoff.

I chanted in my head as panic swelled to a breaking point. Slamming my fists on the floor, I screamed at my reflection.

My eyes shifted to black, and the mirror splintered.

I stilled at the evidence of my power. I'd done that. I'd broken the glass just like I'd turned invisible and killed that Red Cap. I have powers that I could use to break free of my Fae prison. If I could turn Fae, then surely, I could return to being human. I could use my magic to get the necklace off, and all my problems would be solved. I'd be free.

Power surged in my chest and into the air around me, making the hair on my arms and legs stand on end. My long dark curls around my face flutter in an unnatural breeze. I embraced the magical charge, wrapped its tendrils around me, and beckoned it to grow.

My eyes still fixed on my reflection in the fractured mirror, I reached up again to the necklace clasp, continuing the chant. Sweat beaded on my forehead, and heat bloomed around my neck until it was almost unbearable. Just as the pain became too much and I considered giving up, the clasp gave, and the necklace slipped from my hands into my lap.

I did it.

Holy shit, *I did it!*

With trembling fingers, I lifted the necklace and examined the object that had derailed my life. It looked so innocuous. So ordinary. A hysterical laugh bubbled up from deep in my belly, and tears of relief filled my eyes.

It was done. I was free.

But what now? Did I jump on a plane back home? No, I

needed to make sure danger didn't follow me, and I needed to get rid of the damn necklace.

I surged to my feet before crippling pain shot through my head. My hands clamped down over my temples, and I bent at the waist as a wave of devastating nausea caused me to dry heave without warning.

Stumbling to the bathroom, I curled up around the toilet and vomited repeatedly. Black dots floated in my vision.

Was this a result of removing the necklace? I couldn't imagine what else would have caused such a violent reaction. I'd been so confident I could return to being human, but what if I couldn't? I'd failed to even consider that removing the chain might have a deadly effect.

Even if it did, you're still better off.

I wasn't sure I agreed with that particularly dismal thought.

Eventually, my stomach calmed enough that I was able to sit back against the bathroom wall. The necklace was still clutched in my hand. I lifted it, staring at it again for long seconds before getting on my knees and removing the lid on the back of the toilet. I tied the necklace to the flushing mechanism, then replaced the lid. The object was too powerful to risk it falling into the wrong hands. Until I could figure out what to do with it, the toilet was its new home.

Sinking back against the wall, I rolled my head to the side. The Brownie man stood not far away with one of my kitchen cups half-full of water and his eyes fixed on me unwaveringly. He tipped his head in my direction, then toward the cup of water, before stepping back from the glass.

Slowly, so as not to scare him, I reached for the glass and brought it to my lips. A part of me worried that perhaps drinking the contents wouldn't be wise, but a larger part was thirsty and exhausted and tired of questioning things. The water was heaven going down my ravaged throat.

When I placed the empty glass on the floor, I was alone again.

I dragged myself to my feet, and using the wall as support, I fumbled my way to the comfort of my bed. Shock settled over me like a dense fog, dulling my emotions and leaving me incapable of holding a thought. The dream images, the raging emotions, the suffocating magic, removing the necklace, the headache and sickness—it was all more than my body and mind could take. I let the fog wrap me in its cocoon and drifted to a place where there was no time or space.

CHAPTER

TWENTY-TWO

My alarm going off the following morning felt like a drill burrowing a hole into my skull. After turning it off, I lay on my back staring at the ceiling and contemplated calling in sick. A girl could only take so much. However, my heavily engrained work ethic was already gearing up for a guilt trip about calling in sick when I hadn't even worked at the museum for three weeks. Until I was certain I would quit and move back home, I needed to refrain from getting fired. Besides, the headache made me miserable either way. Might as well be miserable at work.

I rolled myself out of bed and into the shower. After fifteen minutes of scalding water, I was starting to feel alive again. I dressed in a scoop-neck sweater blouse with slacks and real-ized that my years of unwavering commitment to the necklace meant I didn't have a single replacement piece. I wasn't all that particular about fashion, so instead, I put on some large dangly earrings and called it an outfit.

After breakfast, I gathered my things and noticed Lochlan's phone in my purse. Scrolling to the contacts, Lochlan and

203

Michael were the only two listed. Lochlan hated texting, but I wasn't up for phone calls. He'd have to manage.

I clicked on his contact and typed out a message informing him that the necklace had originated from Merlin. Lochlan needed to know about the necklace because the most logical course of action was for me to entrust him with the magical object. I wasn't making any hasty decisions, but that was my number one plan at the moment.

Not waiting for a reply, I threw the phone in my purse, put on a coat, and left for work. It was a gorgeous morning—crisp but not bitingly cold, and no wind or mist for a change. I walked with a new energy in my step. Not even a pulsing headache could slow me down when I'd achieved such a victory as gaining my freedom.

I was almost to the museum when I noticed Ronan on the sidewalk ahead of me. His eyes were trained on me, giving me the impression that it was no coincidence I was bumping into him. He wasn't my favorite person at the moment, but I was feeling generous. I flashed a small smile and slowed when I approached.

"Hey, Ronan. What are you doing out here?" I stopped a few feet away and peered at him cautiously.

"I wanted to see you." Lifting himself away from the wall, he emitted an unsettling vibe, and his stare was frighteningly intense.

"Care if we walk and talk? I'm pretty chilly out here." Anything I could do to get us closer to the museum and safety.

"I don't want to talk around others. I just want you." His voice was a desperate growl.

"Ronan, I don't want a relationship right now. Plus, you lied to me. You implied things that weren't true about Lochlan, and that's not okay."

He snarled at Lochlan's name, making me flinch. Was this

the same man who'd been so funny and thoughtful during our time together? How had he hidden his true nature so thoroughly?

"You know you mean nothing to him, right?" His lips lifted in a sneer. "He's only using you for information. I'm the one who's tried to help you. I'm the one who's tried to be your friend. And what do I get? The grand brush-off? Maybe you're one of those girls who likes to be treated like shit. Is that what gets you off?"

His words were a blow to the gut, and I gasped for air.

How dare he talk to me like that!

I reared back and slapped him as hard as I could. Hands trembling with rage, I stood my ground and said what would hurt him the most. "You're just scared Lochlan is better than you, and you know what? *He is*," I hissed.

Fury sparked in his copper eyes.

He grabbed my arm in a painful grip and yanked me close, but before he could spew a vicious reply, he froze. Instead, his brow furrowed, and his gaze traveled back and forth in shock from my left eye to my right and back.

Had my eyes gone black?

Shit. Shit. Shit.

I didn't know what had happened, but I needed to get out of there.

I yanked my wrist from his grip and tore off toward the museum. By some small miracle, he didn't chase after me.

As if my headache hadn't been bad enough before, the incident with Ronan and the run into work had my head pulsing angrily. Cat wasn't in yet, and it was just as well—I was not fit company for anyone. I trudged to my office, hoping I could make it through the morning without vomiting.

When lunchtime neared, and some pain relievers had helped rein in my headache, I went downstairs to talk to Cat. In my search to determine if I was safe to leave Ireland, I felt it imperative to learn more about the man who had started me down this path.

"How's it going, Cat?"

"Hey, Becca! Whoa, what in the name of Mary and Joseph happened to you?" she asked, wide-eyed.

"That bad?"

"You look like my aunt Moira after she gets herself langered on the black stuff."

"I have no idea what you just said."

"Drunk on Guinness. My aunt's got a nasty problem. After a particularly long night out, she looks a bit like death the next day," she explained, not holding any punches.

"Super. Thanks for that," I responded dryly.

"Oh, don't be cranky. You're not as bad as her. I'm just saying I can tell you aren't well."

"I'm sorry, you're right. I've got a headache from hell, but I didn't want to miss work. And I wanted to ask you something."

She leaned in with interest. "What's your question?"

"What do you know about Merlin?"

She sat back, lips pursed in thought. "He's very old and powerful."

"I gathered that much."

"Give me a second, will you? He had a twin sister, Queen Mab. When he fell in love, Mab became insanely jealous of his lover. She kidnapped the Fae woman, and it took him years to figure out who had done it. He had to kill Mab to get his lover back, but by then, it was too late for the woman."

"That sounds like something you'd hear on a soap opera. I

wonder what kind of weird relationship he and his sister had for her to be jealous of his lover."

"No idea, that's just the legend I was taught as a child. I would assume they were close since they were twins. The Fae don't have many children, and I've never heard of another set of twins. Though our knowledge is limited."

"I suppose if you live forever, it's better not to have many children. Otherwise, the Fae population would be staggering. Do you know anything else about him?"

"Our stories say that he's a bit of a hermit, but that's about it."

"I was told Mab was extremely powerful and that she ruled the Unseelie. I'm guessing he must be unbelievably strong to have killed her."

"I thought we established you already knew how powerful he was," she poked teasingly.

"Yes, but there's a difference between powerful and god-like."

"Don't be daft. They're all too powerful for their own good. We're but gnats to them. Does it matter to a gnat if it's a car or a truck that runs over it? No, it's just dead. Powerful or god-like, either way, they can kill us just as easily."

I smirked wryly at the young woman. "All right, I get your point."

She arched a brow.

Pulling back from the counter, I sighed with a glance toward the stairs. "Well, if you think of anything else about Merlin, let me know."

"Happy to."

In the elevator, I thought about the mysterious Merlin and his purpose for giving me the necklace. Would he be angry that I had removed it? If he was so powerful, why didn't he end the war himself?

I exited the elevator to the fourth floor and found Lochlan standing against the opposite wall.

"Oh, hey. What are you doing here? Did you get my text?"

His lips curved up in an uncharacteristic smile as he pulled away from the wall. "I wanted to check on you. Is that a problem?"

"Uh, no. Just wasn't expecting you. I ran into Ronan this morning. You were right. Something's not right about him. He scared me."

"He's a member of the Hunt. He won't hurt you," he offered absently, eyes drifting down the length of my body.

Not the response I expected.

"Thanks for your concern," I muttered. "Look, I have to get back to work."

He clasped my forearms gently and drew my eyes to his. "I'm sorry. You're just so distracting. I'll make sure everything is okay, all right? You have nothing to worry about."

I nodded, reminding myself to trust him. Lochlan had been unerringly supportive in his own mercurial, brutish way. I sent him away with a smile, only realizing after the doors had closed that I'd completely forgotten to tell him about removing the necklace.

Clearly, I hadn't reverted to fully human, or he would have noticed himself. I wasn't exactly disappointed. I'd known that would likely be the case, but I'd held out a small degree of hope. It had taken years to enact the transformation. It only made sense it would take years to reverse.

FOR THE SECOND time that week, I came home to find Lochlan waiting for me in my apartment.

"You're back." I set down my bags and closed the front

door. "I didn't expect to see you again so soon." When I turned back around to face him, he'd closed the distance between us in the blink of an eye. I found myself toe-to-toe with every hard inch of his six-foot frame. My eyes slowly rose to meet his, and my breath hitched at the raw hunger in his eyes.

"I needed to see you. All of you." His mouth slammed down on mine, tongue plunging deep between my lips.

I opened to him, relishing his branding touch.

His kiss was even more demanding than it had been before, surprising me with its urgency. His hand left my back and snaked around to knead my breast. His touch was possessive. Ravenous. He took, and I gladly gave.

He lifted me, guiding my legs around his waist, then started for the stairs.

Apparently, it was time to finish what we'd started.

Neither of us spoke, but no words were needed. We were starving for one another. Weeks of pent-up desire had boiled over and ignited a chain reaction of uncontrollable lust.

I couldn't speak for him, but for me, I was finally able to drop my guard because I knew I was free. I could be with him and not worry about alliances or consequences or motives. This was simply two people sharing in their mutual desire. That, and in a way, it was a goodbye.

It wouldn't be long, and I'd be going home, but this wasn't the time to tell him. This was about us, and I wanted it to be as perfect as I knew it could be.

I kissed and sucked on his neck, absently noting that he'd worn cologne for a change over his normal woodsy scent. It smelled good on him, though I liked his natural scent as well. Something about his pheromones spoke to the chemicals in my body on a primal level. I could almost feel the endorphins release at the slightest trace of his masculine scent. Cologne was good, but endorphins were better.

When we reached my room, he set me on my feet and began to strip off my clothes between kisses. That morning, I'd been feeling powerful and had chosen a black lace bra and underwear set. Now, I was especially grateful for the decision.

His hungry eyes roved over every inch of me. I had hoped to have the pleasure of watching him undress—to see each inch of him revealed one savory muscle at a time. However, the second the last scrap of my clothes fell to the floor, his clothes disappeared from his body as though he'd never been wearing any. We were too close for me to get a good look, but I assured myself there'd be time later.

He lowered us onto the bed, his body towering over mine. His head lowered, and he took one of my hard peaks into his warm mouth, rolling his tongue around and around the pebbled nipple until I was writhing in pleasure.

"This is all I ever wanted. To have you mindless beneath me." His guttural tone resonated in my core, and my hips flexed, helplessly trying to soothe the ache.

"I need more," I murmured.

A wolfish grin split his face, and he lowered himself down my body, burying his face in my folds, lapping at my clit. I screamed out in pleasure, the sensations overwhelming me each time his rough tongue licked across my swollen flesh. My head fell back into the pillow, my fingers gripping his thick curly hair. It had been so long since I had been with a man that I raced toward my release.

Once my legs began to quiver and shake, Lochlan stopped, rising back up to align our bodies again. His scalding erection pressed against my belly, and my legs fell open in invitation.

"Is this what you want? Tell me you want my cock."

"I do. I want to feel you inside me."

He didn't delay a second longer, thrusting into me in one swift motion. My body tensed at the sudden intrusion but quickly stretched to accommodate his size. His breaths were stuttered, equally as affected by our connection as I was.

Once we had both recovered, he slowly pulled out almost all the way before slamming back inside, burying himself all the way to my womb. A wanton moan escaped my throat as he rocked faster and faster into my body, his hand snaking around to rub my clit in rhythmic circles.

"Oh God, Lochlan. It feels *so* good."

His pace picked up even more to an almost punishing rhythm, and his head lowered to my neck, where he licked and sucked. My muscles started to contract, already primed from his earlier attention. Just as my body exploded in orgasm, his teeth clenched the base of my neck. He thrust his release deep inside me, unleashing a victorious roar at the same time. The pain of his bite added to the pleasure of the moment, and I rode wave after wave of bliss as he languidly slowed his pace.

As the last shudders ghosted through me, he rolled himself onto his side, pulling my back against his chest.

"I knew we'd be incredible together," Lochlan murmured behind me.

I smiled. "Well, if it weren't for my eyes..." I trailed off, thinking we would have already discovered how good we'd be together had I not panicked.

"What about your eyes?" he asked sleepily.

Surely, he hadn't forgotten. Maybe he was just so sex drunk he didn't understand that I was referencing our discussion about my one-of-a-kind black eyes that had stopped us from having sex a few days earlier.

That would make him awfully sex drunk. I didn't imagine Lochlan would brush aside such a pivotal conversation.

"Yeah, if I hadn't freaked out, we'd already have slept together," I reminded him.

"Ah, yeah. I'm glad we waited. This was so much better."

Huh. I'm not sure I understand, but okay.

I pulled his arm snug against my chest. "I didn't get a chance to tell you earlier today at the museum, and I suppose you were too preoccupied to notice this evening, but I got the necklace off." Now that the words were out, I did find it odd that he hadn't commented on its absence. As observant as he was, he surely had to have noticed.

Confusion and unease pricked at my insides.

"How did you accomplish that?" He lifted onto his elbow and looked down at me, his hand tracing a line where the necklace had been.

"I used magic, but I'm not really sure how I did it."

"I'm happy for you. I know you never asked to be sucked into our world." He smiled and lay back down, pulling me close. "You'll be safer this way."

Again, his reaction surprised me. I hadn't expected him to be so laissez-faire about what I'd done. Something was off, but I wasn't sure what.

"Did you check the message I texted you earlier? I thought we could go to the French restaurant that's down the street from the club." I wasn't sure why I was testing him, but something in my gut told me to.

"Yeah, I saw that. We can definitely grab dinner."

Don't panic. Do. Not. Panic.

He'll know. He'll sense the racing of your heart.

I didn't know what was going on, but Lochlan wouldn't lie about checking the message, and I certainly didn't text about dinner. Either Lochlan's memories had been tampered with or ... the man I was lying with wasn't Lochlan.

An image flashed in my mind of Ronan's eyes incredulously narrowed as he studied me this morning. He'd noticed the necklace was gone.

"You've figured it out, haven't you?" he mused condescendingly. "Ah, well. It was good while it lasted. I had hoped we'd get a couple of rounds in before you caught on, but this saves me the trouble of pretending." He rolled to the edge of the bed and stood, allowing his glamour to fall away like water down a window. When he came back into focus, Ronan stood before me, now fully dressed.

"What did you do?" A whisper was all I could manage. I was horrified. Shocked. Disgusted.

"You sure didn't look disappointed ten minutes ago when my cock was making you come," he said snidely as he began to riffle through my things. "Tell me where you've stashed the necklace."

Self-righteous fury engulfed me.

He'd used me. Tricked me in the most unforgivable way imaginable. He was a soulless monster of a man, and I wanted him to die. I wanted to scratch his eyes out and make him suffer.

How could he do something so callous? So vile and deceptive?

The flames of hatred turned my body to ash.

I would kill him.

I would make him suffer.

I tore from the bed and threw myself at his back, wrapping my arms around his neck and squeezing with all my might. I placed a hand on his face but couldn't make anything happen. The black veins didn't emerge, nor did my skin warm with the pull of magic.

He lurched backward and attempted to pull my arms from around him, but I was a thing possessed. I refused to be dislodged.

"I *hate* you," I growled in a voice I hardly recognized.

Ronan stumbled to a section of the room with a bare wall and flung himself backward, ramming me into the sheetrock.

Once.

Twice.

Three times.

My head slammed against the wall. The impact dazed me enough to loosen my grip, and I slid to the ground.

"You brought this on yourself. You should have picked *me*," he sneered menacingly. "I was everything you should have wanted. I did *everything* right. I played the perfect boyfriend—even saved you from the Red Caps when that imbecile led you straight to the trap that was meant for him. *I* saved you! Not *him*!"

He was psychotic.

How could I not have seen it? How many times had we talked? How could I not have detected that he was utterly insane?

Still on the floor, I gawked up at him in confusion and disbelief. "Who are you?"

His features fell blank as if someone had drained him of emotion. From barely contained violence to mechanical indifference at the snap of a finger. "Where is the necklace?" he asked tonelessly.

"What do you want with it?"

A glimmer entered his eyes. "It was convenient of you to take it off. I could hardly believe my luck when I saw you in the street this morning. I came to the museum to verify that you were worthless without it, and I was right. Everything lined up perfectly. Not only would I get the necklace but I also got *you*. Ruined you for him." His full lips curved back in an evil grin. The dimples and warm brown eyes I'd thought so handsome were nothing but a meticulous mask, hiding the depravity beneath.

Tears burned my eyes, but there was no way in hell I was going to let this Fae asshole see me cry. "Looks like all you get is me. Sorry to disappoint." I was pleased to foil at least one of his plans. "The necklace is gone. You're too late."

He reached down and grabbed me by the neck, hefting me to my feet with my back against the wall. His eyes glittered with madness. "Where is it?" he hissed, spittle dotting my face.

"Merlin took it. It's gone," I forced out painfully past his grip on my throat.

He screamed, a volcanic explosion of rage, then slammed my head against the wall. My vision narrowed as cobwebs filled my head. I was vaguely aware of him frantically tearing my room apart, scouring every nook and cranny for the necklace.

I wouldn't have time to retrieve it from the bathroom. All I could do was pray that he didn't find it and that his resulting anger didn't kill me.

As my head cleared, I rose to my feet, and the movement caught his attention. He charged over the clothes and debris piled on the floor, backhanding me across the face and sending me back to the ground in a heap.

Terror gripped me.

This man was crazy enough to kill me.

Lochlan's knife was in my purse downstairs, but even if I had it, I didn't think I had enough strength to defeat Ronan. I still wore Cat's bracelet, but it only seemed to defend against a single assault aimed at the bracelet.

I closed my eyes and searched for the feeling of power I'd conjured that morning when I'd removed the necklace. If there was any remnant of power left inside me, I couldn't find it. I was on my own.

"I know it's here. Where is it?" he growled savagely, still tearing apart my bedroom.

I had landed with my back to him, propped on my elbows with my hair pooling on the floor. Without warning, the little

Brownie appeared just inches from my face, hidden within the protective halo of my hair. He reached his hands forward and presented me with my necklace. He'd brought me a weapon. He was trying to save me.

My mind became laser-focused.

I took hold of the stone pendant, and the surge of power that rocketed through me was a shot of adrenaline straight to my heart.

The Brownie blinked away to safety the second he'd completed his task.

I inhaled a lungful of air, dropping my head back as I basked in the swell of energy. Without a care to my nudity, I rose to my feet and faced Ronan.

The air in the room began to swirl, carrying my hair in all directions. I didn't have to look in a mirror to know my eyes had gone jet black.

Magic thrummed in my veins, fueled by an unending supply of wrath.

I embraced what my necklace had to offer me. For the first time, its power felt like a gift.

Ronan turned, his eyes widening in shock.

"Get out." My voice echoed with layer after layer of magical malice.

His eyes darted briefly around the room. "Look what it's doing to you, Rebecca. You don't want this. Just give me the necklace, and you can have your life back." He held out his hand.

"If you don't get out right now, I'll grab that hand and drain the life from you one agonizing second at a time. Get. Out."

His jaw clenched in bitter defeat.

Any other day, he might have won in a battle against me, but not today. Not when he'd brought out the savage in me.

A snarl marred his pretty face an instant before he vanished. I didn't let down my guard for several long minutes. Eventually, the magical breeze died down, and my adrenaline ebbed. I sank to the floor, the necklace still clenched tightly in my hand. My gaze drifted over the chaos of my bedroom. Drawers pulled open, and their contents spilled on the floor. Picture frames shattered. The window blinds bent and broken.

My home had been vandalized. Violated. And I lay at its center, naked and alone.

For the second time in two days, I cried.

Sobs tore from my throat as reality caught up with me. As I processed the extreme betrayal I'd suffered and how close I'd come to dying.

Warring emotions ravaged what was left of my battered psyche.

Relief.

Hatred.

Gratitude.

Shame.

I snatched random articles of clothing from the floor around me, covering myself as I wept. I cried tears of frustration over being deceived. Tears of rage for my feelings of helplessness. Tears of relief that I wasn't dead. Tears of disappointment that the moment I thought I had shared with Lochlan had been a sham. And tears of acceptance that the necklace was a permanent part of my life moving forward.

Ronan's vile deception highlighted the ugly truth that I was a part of this Fae world, whether I wanted to be or not. The only thing I accomplished by removing my necklace was making myself vulnerable. If I had any chance of surviving—of overcoming the challenges around me—the answer lay in embracing my new existence. Mastering my abilities and facing the truth.

Crawling onto my bed, I sat with my legs to my chest and regarded the necklace that was both my savior and my curse.

Lochlan and the queen had said I was part Fae, but I obviously wasn't Fae enough to wield power without the magical amulet. I hadn't seen through Ronan's glamour or been able to use magic against him. The necklace either amplified or focused my abilities. I needed it to survive in the Fae world. I wouldn't be caught helpless again.

I couldn't dwell on whether the power in the necklace was malevolent because there wasn't another option. Without it, I would be dead.

My hands shook when I opened the clasp, but I didn't let it stop me. I brought the chain around my neck, and the necklace closed of its own accord.

A sense of calm and rightness settled over me.

I would never let myself feel so powerless again.

The images of him above me—of us kissing and touching—ran on an endless loop in my head. One particular moment caught my attention. When his head had been between my legs, and my hand fisted in his thick curls. I had been too lost in the moment to notice the discrepancy—Lochlan didn't have curls. Ronan did. His glamour worked to an extent, but when I stopped relying on my eyes, my other senses saw through the illusion.

My emotions tried to turn against me. Anger that should have been directed at Ronan turned inward—both for removing the necklace and for not picking up on the fact that it hadn't been Lochlan.

I slammed the door on those thoughts.

I refused to let Ronan win by waging war against myself. He was the perpetrator of the crime, and he was the only one getting the blame. I would not blame myself, but what I *would* do was learn from the experience.

Lying back in bed and pulling the covers up to my chin, I decided that it was time to learn to fight—both with magic and my fists. I would learn anything I could to arm myself.

If I couldn't run from the Fae world, I would master it.

No more vulnerability.

Ronan had been plotting against the Hunt from the inside, and no one had any idea. I would not forget the lesson that enemies were everywhere. I would learn everything that I could, gain every advantage available, and I would accept my fate head-on. If that meant stopping a war, so be it. If I got the opportunity to kill Ronan in the process, even better.

I would overcome my fear of the dark side of my magic.

I would embrace it, own it, control it.

Black eyes, black necklace, black clothes, black heart—black may have been just a color, but what it represented was my power. My power to take control of my circumstances and deny fear the chance to rule over me. Lochlan had said not to fear the transition to being Fae, and I wouldn't. I would wrap myself in the change, revel in my metamorphosis, and emerge stronger and more ferocious than ever.

TWENTY-THREE

"That spell you used on the bracelet—could you use something like that to ward a house? Some kind of spell to keep out intruders?" I asked Cat upon entering the museum the following morning. Her eyebrows shot up, and she looked around the room for the presence of others.

"I'm not supposed to share our knowledge, Rebecca, and you know that. My mom would skin me alive if she found out," she responded in a harsh whisper, hand anxiously twisting at one of her red curls.

"I know how important secrecy is to you and your family, trust me. I'm not asking you to tell me how you see the Fae or why you all are so deathly afraid of them. But this is my life we're talking about here—someone got in my apartment last night and attacked me. Please, will you help me?"

"Oh, Rebecca. I'm so sorry. Are you okay?" Her kind eyes rounded with worry.

"I am, but I'd rather not go through it again."

"Of course. When do you want me to come by? What my mam doesn't know won't hurt her."

"Thank you, Cat. I need all the help I can get right now. I have somewhere to be after work. Could you come by around eight, or is that too late?"

"Eight works just fine." She looked left and right before continuing. "Was it one of them? A Fae?"

"Yes, but it wasn't exactly your standard attack."

"Will you tell me what happened? You don't have to if it makes you uncomfortable," she quickly added before chewing on her fingernails.

"I let Ronan in my house, and it turns out he's not a good guy. I want to make sure he can't get back in, and if it's possible, I'd like to protect my place from anyone entering who intends me any harm."

"We have a couple of options we can discuss. Are you truly okay?" she whispered, her hand reaching for mine.

"I am, I promise. It wasn't anything I can't get over, but I don't want anything like that to happen again if I can help it." I gave her my address before heading up to my office with the intent of burying myself in work to keep my mind occupied. I was willing to accept that I was becoming Fae and that I couldn't escape my fate, but that didn't mean I wanted to spend time dwelling on the catalytic event that spurred on my change of attitude.

I was also actively avoiding thoughts of the visit I would make to Lochlan after work. I would need to tell him that Ronan was a traitor, but explaining how I'd learned that information would be tricky. He'd told me over and over to stay away from Ronan, and while I knew what Ronan had done wasn't my fault—that I shouldn't feel shame or guilt over his actions—I couldn't shake a degree of embarrassment.

The conversation would be endlessly awkward.

How do you know he's working with the enemy?

He told me the Red Cap attack was a trap meant for you.

Why would he tell you that?

Because I figured out that he'd tricked me into having sex with him.

You had sex with him?

Only because he was glamoured to look like you.

How is it you didn't see through the glamour?

I had taken off my necklace that morning in the hopes that I could go home and pretend the Fae didn't exist.

I didn't want him to know I'd been so stupid as to take off the necklace. That I'd been so damn naïve to think the necklace was the sole source of my problems. Lochlan was a warrior and a leader. I wanted him to respect me. I wasn't sure why, but I did, and because of that, I was desperate to avoid telling him what had happened.

DRAWING out my inevitable talk with Lochlan, I set out to walk to the Huntsman from work instead of taking a cab. The crisp evening air did wonders to clear my head. I practiced what I wanted to say for the hundredth time and gathered my courage.

The Do Not Walk sign was displayed as I came to the first major intersection on my route. I stood at the corner along with several other commuting pedestrians. Normally, I was an avid people watcher, but my chaotic thoughts were focused elsewhere until my eyes drifted to the car stopped next to me, first in line at the intersection. Inside the white base-model Toyota Corolla sat an older woman, both hands on the steering wheel, eyes diligently focused on the red light. What caught my attention was the gruesome Unseelie creature sitting in the passenger seat beside her.

He was the size of a small adult human and had brown skin with very large, pointed ears—what I might have thought Faerie ears looked like before moving to Ireland. His bulging yellow eyes peered over at me as he grinned mischievously next to the woman. She glanced over at her companion and smiled, no doubt seeing a glamour the creature was projecting. She had no idea of the danger she'd invited into her car with her.

Before I could process what I'd seen, the light turned green. The line of cars moved forward along with the river of pedestrians, but I stood rooted to the ground watching the white vehicle speed faster and faster down the busy city street. Without warning, the car sideswiped the vehicle next to it, causing a chain-reaction accident that resulted in one car flipping onto its side and a dozen other wrecks.

Witnesses shrieked and rushed over to aid the motorists, and within seconds, sirens sounded in the background. I let out a breath I hadn't realized I'd been holding and hesitantly stepped toward the chaos. I walked past car after crumpled car as I neared the cause of the catastrophe.

The older woman sat on the curb, sobbing as she explained to another woman that she had no idea what had happened. I can't claim to know exactly what had happened, but I knew who was responsible. Not far away, huddled beside a postal drop box, were not one but two of the vile creatures cackling with delight. They both glanced my way before darting down a nearby alley, no doubt in search of more trouble.

Why were these creatures being unleashed on Earth? What would happen if they infiltrated our cities on a massive scale as Merlin predicted? One of them alone could cause tremendous damage, but hordes of them? The Hunt wouldn't be able to stop them in time before they devastated city after city. Even if every country banded together in all-out warfare against the Fae invaders, it might take years to gain the upper hand over a magic race of evil creatures.

As much as I wanted to focus my efforts on my personal vendetta against Ronan, stopping whoever was opening the portals was of critical importance. They had to be stopped. I couldn't fathom what role I might play in that, but I wasn't going to run away from it. If I truly was needed, I'd do my part.

Once emergency crews began to arrive, I resumed my walk to the Huntsman with renewed determination. When I entered the building, I held my head high and walked with confidence, but my stomach clenched with nerves. The place was still empty. The only sound was the echoing clacks from my heels resounding throughout the silent lobby.

Upstairs, Lochlan stood talking with two other men in the main club. While I had painted on my confidence like a child in a Halloween costume, Lochlan was the real deal. He radiated an air of authority without any effort. A lion at ease in the Serengeti, he had embraced his place at the top of the food chain.

I wanted to know that feeling. The prospect alone was intoxicating.

Once the men ended their conversation, Lochlan motioned me over.

"Did you need something?"

"I do, but first, I saw a couple of Unseelie cause a twelve-car pileup on my way over."

He nodded to the two men, who immediately turned for the elevator. "Come to my office. We can talk there." He held open the office door, closing it behind me and causing us to pass within inches of one another. When his rich masculine scent wrapped itself around me, memories from the night before assaulted me. Ronan's cologne should have been a dead giveaway, but I'd been too blind to see—both literally and figuratively.

Taking a cleansing breath, I squashed my frustrations and self-doubt. Breaking free of my mental shackles, I realized that Lochlan hadn't moved from his spot near the door. Not only that, but his arms were crossed, and his glacial stare was shredding me to ribbons.

What the hell did I do now?

The last I had seen him, the *real* him, we'd been more than civil. He'd even kissed me. Why would he suddenly be upset with me?

"Why are you looking at me like that?" I asked warily.

"I would think it's obvious I'm not a man who likes to share. The next time you fuck Ronan, don't come waltzing in here reeking of him." His voice was deadly calm, and his words were a brutal blow to my gut.

Oh, God. He knows.

He'd smelled Ronan on me, despite my shower and endless scrubbing. He smelled Ronan and thought I'd intentionally had sex with him. If I hadn't felt dirty already from what had happened, my skin positively crawled at that point.

Lochlan's hateful words dug a spike straight into my heart. I'd wanted him to respect me, and now he thought the very worst of me. My downcast eyes blinked rapidly to hold back the moisture quickly threatening to spill over.

It's better this way. I'm better off not developing feelings for him or any of them. If you think this is bad, how much worse would it be if you cared for him?

Through sheer force of will, I regained control and masked my features. "I wanted to let you know that Ronan was the leak. He knew about the setup with the Red Caps. He was involved somehow. Their intent was to kill you in the trap." My voice was firm but hollow.

Lochlan's predatory gaze scrutinized me. "That doesn't make sense. Why would you fuck him, then rat him out?"

"Believe me or don't. That's your decision. The only thing I want to ask of you is whether you'd be willing to teach me how to fight. I've decided to stay and accept my fate, but I'll need to arm myself, and my options are limited." There. I asked. Now he could either tell me yes or no, and I could get the hell out of there.

The temperature in the room dropped a solid ten degrees.

Lochlan took one small step, then two, until he was a mere breath away. His hand gripped my jaw, forcing my eyes to his before asking in a lethal voice, "Did he hurt you?"

My breathing shuddered. "No."

He tilted my head to one side, and his gaze lowered to the base of my neck. The bite mark. I'd been so consumed about what I'd say that I'd forgotten to check if the mark had fully healed. A telltale circular pattern of teeth was easy to recognize, even when only a trace remained.

I slapped my hand over the area and pulled from his grip.

"*What the fuck did he do to you?*" Lochlan roared. His fury echoed off the walls.

I channeled my own rage, screaming back, "*None of your goddamn business!*"

And it wasn't. I didn't want to tell him what had happened, and I wouldn't. That was my secret to keep as long as I felt like it.

His nostrils flared, and jaw flexed so tightly I thought he'd crack a tooth. I glared back at him, my breath heaving through parted lips, lungs ready for a fight.

"Will you teach me or not?" I finally asked, bringing us back to the point.

He must have recognized my conviction and realized arguing would be pointless. It took several endless seconds, but he finally gave me a curt nod. "First thing next week. You come by each day after work."

It was my turn to nod.

"I'll kill him for this." His words were a murmured promise. He was talking about the undisclosed harm Ronan had caused me. Lochlan would kill him for it. Not the betrayal of the Hunt. He'd kill his fellow huntsman for me.

"He deserves it. He's betrayed all of us," I responded coolly, then redirected our conversation to escape further scrutiny. "Have you made any progress in locating the Sword of Light?" If they could use it on Ronan, maybe they could find out who was behind the portals.

Lochlan considered refusing me the reprieve of a subject change before thinking better of it. He walked to his desk chair and finally sat down. "It's taken us some time to follow the trail of custody. The last known location, as far as we have been able to track, was in the hands of humans in Scotland. That was centuries ago, and we haven't found any evidence of its whereabouts after that point."

I nodded, wishing there was more I could do to help. At least I had been able to help pinpoint who the traitor had been, although we still didn't know if any other Huntsmen were working with him. "Do you think Ronan could be working alone? Maybe he's the mastermind behind it all, and once we catch him, the portals will no longer be an issue."

"No, he's not nearly powerful or knowledgeable enough to be circumventing the queen's wards."

"I figured that was too much to hope for," I muttered.

"Someone powerful is orchestrating this rebellion, and who knows how many others are involved. I can't imagine that we would have more than one traitor in our ranks, but I would never have believed Ronan would betray us either." He was quiet for a moment, focusing his eyes far off, before turning back to me and continuing. "He was an asshole who did some terrible things in his past, but I hadn't thought him capable of treachery. What you're accusing him of, if true, is unforgivable. The Hunt was formed when Arthur and Guin had a falling out —Arthur was essentially one of Guin's generals. When he left the Court, his most loyal soldiers went with him, and they formed a brotherhood that became The Wild Hunt. We have no lands to call our own, so our freedom and commitment to one another are what we hold most sacred."

"King Arthur formed the Hunt? As in King Arthur and his knights of the round table?"

"He wasn't a king exactly, but he was the first Erlking, and the men who were loyal to him could be called knights. They were the most elite soldiers in the Seelie kingdom, and that expectation has been upheld through the centuries. New members are only accepted into our ranks with the highest degree of skill and cunning."

"That's fascinating," I said earnestly. "I'm still amazed at how Fae history evolved into human legends. Was the falling out between Arthur and Guin over Lancelot like the stories suggest?"

"I was never privy to the full details, but I know Lancelot played a part. However, it should be noted that the Fae don't marry like humans do. Lancelot was Arthur's right hand, and his relationship with Guin betrayed his leader. The Fae may not have marital relationships the same as humans, but that doesn't mean we don't value monogamy and expect fidelity. Arthur not only walked away from Guin but he also walked away from the Seelie Court. To his surprise, his loyal soldiers wouldn't allow him to go alone. Since then, the brotherhood has existed as an autonomous unit, and not once has there been disloyalty from within, until now."

"What else can you tell me about the sword?"

"The Sword of Light is an ancient Fae relic from the Faery city of Findias. It's had many names. Originally, it was called Caledfwlch, but it was also called Fragarach or The Answerer. Although more commonly, it's been known as Caliburn or Excalibur."

My jaw dropped. "I'm seriously going to have to do some research into the Arthurian legends. Of course, the great Fae Sword of Light and Excalibur are one and the same. Tell me about it. I can't remember much about what I read back in school."

"It's a magnificent weapon, or so the legends say. I've never seen it myself, but supposedly, the blade was artfully constructed of iron, and the hilt made of wood so the bearer wouldn't have to touch the iron. As you know, iron dampens magic. Its construction of iron is, in part, what makes it such a wonder. It's infused with a form of light magic able to exist despite the presence of iron. It was forged by the earliest Fae, and the knowledge of whatever method was used to create the weapon has been long lost."

"What about the sword's abilities?" I asked reverently, totally absorbed in Lochlan's words.

"Our best source of information outside of the legends would be Merlin if you can find him. He had access to the sword at one point, although it was created long before even his time."

As he finished, the door to his office opened. I looked up to discover the man who had helped me through the Faery queen's dinner standing in Lochlan's doorway. He was no longer wearing the Fae formal attire and was now the spitting image of a *GQ* model in well-tailored slacks and a pale blue dress shirt perfectly cut to his fit torso. His wavy light-brown hair was sculpted backward, and when his warm coppery eyes landed on me, I could feel my cheeks heat.

"Rebecca, I see you made it back home safely." His lips hinted at a smile.

"Yes, and thank you for your help. I was rather out of my element."

"It was my pleasure." He bowed his head.

Lochlan cut in somewhat tersely. "I didn't realize you two had become acquainted at the palace."

Was he upset that I had met this man?

The man in question lifted his chin as his eyes met Lochlan's. "Not formally. As you know, I happened to be at the palace the night Rebecca joined the queen for dinner, so I tried to guide her through the evening."

Lochlan held eyes with the man for an uncomfortable second before cutting his glance in my direction. "I suppose introductions are in order. Rebecca Peterson, this is the Erlking of The Wild Hunt, but you may call him Alberich."

Pronounced like *all-brick,* the name sounded vaguely familiar. I smiled and started to give a Faery bow of greeting but froze as bits and pieces of my prior internet research came back to me.

"I know that name!" My voice came out almost reverently. "Alberich is another name for Oberon! After we learned about the Fae, I researched Titania and Oberon to see what I could learn, and one of the names for Oberon was Alberich. Am I right?" I asked excitedly.

Alberich flashed a dimpled grin and bowed deeply. "It is a pleasure to make your acquaintance."

My eyes rounded, and I turned to Lochlan. "So that's how you knew I had been in Faery!" I was stunned that the man who had so gallantly given me guidance while I was in Faery had been the leader of The Wild Hunt—not that I had expected him to be brutish or anything. I was simply amazed that the mythological giant had been so seemingly ordinary and approachable. The legendary Oberon, or Alberich as he was called, stood just feet from me, eyes laughing as I gawked at him.

"I think you may have broken her." Lochlan groused.

"Wouldn't be the first time, son." Alberich laughed as Lochlan shook his head.

"Wait, is he your father? Your father is Oberon?" I gaped at Lochlan. They didn't look much alike—Alberich had a darker complexion and was altogether smaller, whereas Lochlan was blond, blue-eyed, and solid with muscle.

"Not exactly. He's not my biological father. If you'll recall, I mentioned being raised in the Hunt. Alberich took me in as a boy. He's my adoptive father, but we display a professional relationship unless behind closed doors."

I recalled Ronan telling me about Oberon, aka Alberich, with palpable disgust. If Ronan hated Lochlan and Alberich was essentially Lochlan's father, that would explain his agitation toward Alberich. Ronan had intimated at his own blatant disloyalty, but I didn't have the background to put the pieces together. Had I known that the man we had discussed was his leader, perhaps I would have caught on to his betrayal and could have stopped him before he had attacked me or hurt anyone else.

The what-ifs were a slippery slope, and while they might help me see ways I could do better in the future, they were also a one-way ticket to the blame game. Ronan was drowning in hatred, and that cancer had eaten away at his soul. There was nothing I could have done about that.

"Is something wrong?" Alberich asked astutely.

"No, I was just reminded of something Ronan had said."

"Rebecca just informed me that Ronan was involved in the Red Cap attack and has likely abandoned the Hunt." Lochlan's tone became grave. He cut his eyes over to his leader, whose face iced over. He closed his eyes and went still.

After several long seconds, I whispered to Lochlan, "Is he okay?"

Lochlan's eyes stayed fixed on Alberich. "When a new Erlking is chosen, the members perform a rite that grants him the ability to sense us. It's not a way to communicate, just a generalized sense of where we might be. In times of great stress, sometimes emotions may be communicated through the bond."

After a tense moment of silence, the Erlking's eyes opened, and they were filled with something akin to regret. "He has severed the bond. I cannot sense him."

The two men shared a look, and while I may not have been part of the exchange, the meaning was clear. Ronan had gone from hunter to hunted, and these men were now out for blood.

An unexpected sense of relief fell over me, and exhaustion tugged at my mind. I wouldn't feel safe with Ronan out there, but knowing these men were hunting him went a long way toward calming my addled nerves.

"All right." As I spoke, their heads swiveled in my direction. "I think you have this covered, and it's been a long day for me. I'd like to head home. I turned to face Alberich. "It was a pleasure to meet you, although I wish it had been under better circumstances." I gave him a tight smile and turned back to Lochlan. "I'll see you after work on Monday."

He dropped his chin in confirmation, and I felt his eyes track my movements as I left the room. I breathed deeply once I reached the elevator. I'd survived. Lochlan was going to teach me, Ronan would be ruthlessly hunted until he was captured, and I hadn't been forced to explain what had happened between us. In all, it was a highly successful evening, but also exhausting. I wanted to get home and collapse in bed, but Cat was coming over. I had one more important task to complete before I could lose myself in sleep.

CHAPTER

TWENTY-FOUR

I took an Uber home—with Ronan out there, I wasn't going to wander around looking for a cab. By the time I got home, I had about thirty minutes before Cat was supposed to come by. I changed into comfortable clothes and threw together a sandwich for dinner. I hadn't seen my Brownie friend since my fight with Ronan, but I had no reason to believe he had left, so I fixed a small plate for him as well and left it on the counter.

When a knock sounded at my front door, I checked the peephole to make sure it was Cat. It was a precaution I'd rarely taken prior to Ronan's attack. He'd changed me in a lot of ways in a very short span of time.

"Thank you so much for coming." I offered Cat a warm hug.

"I'm glad to help. I love your place, and it's so close to work!"

"Thanks. It's nothing fancy, but it works great for me. Not much longer and you'll have a place of your own."

She set her coat over the back of the couch and looked around my small living area. "Hopefully, otherwise, someone might end up dead. I can't honestly say if it'd be my mam or me, but one of the two."

I snickered on a cough. "What did you bring?" I pointed toward the plastic sack she held dangling from her hands and encouraged her to have a seat on the couch with me.

"Well, I wasn't sure exactly what type of spells you were looking for, so I brought this as an option."

"Great, tell me about it."

"The first thing we do is ward the home against any Fae entering the building."

Oh, crap!

I didn't want to ward the apartment against myself, but I wasn't ready to tell her that I was well on my way to becoming Fae. Not to mention, I had a Brownie living in the place, and I didn't feel a need to kick him out of his home.

"I really hate to create such a broad spell. What if I want to have Lochlan in my house or something?" I asked nonchalantly, hoping my request wouldn't raise any red flags.

Her lips pursed. "I've got two different broad protection spells. One uses these ashes I brought, and the other will involve wards on the threshold."

"That sounds good. How exactly do they protect the house?"

"They should stop anyone who wishes you harm from entering your home. I'm hoping the ashes work all right. They're a bit old but should do the trick."

"That sounds perfect, Cat. That's exactly what I was hoping for."

We spent the next hour laying ashes, drawing protection runes, and saying charms over both to activate the magic. Even if my good senses failed me, and I tried to let in someone dangerous, I was hoping that the magic would act as a security net and repel anyone who wanted to hurt me.

As Cat was gathering her things, an idea occurred to me. "Hey, Cat, I was thinking about getting away this weekend. It's been one hell of a week, and I could use a chance to decompress. You interested in joining me? Just a little overnight sightseeing adventure." Something to distract me from all that had happened and give my poor brain a break.

"That sounds amazing! When do we leave?"

I let out a chuckle at her enthusiasm. "First thing Saturday morning. Give me your address, and I'll swing by and get you on my way out of town."

She whipped out her phone and began typing. "Address sent—I'll be ready bright and early!"

I made sure Cat knew how grateful I was for her help and told her to text me when she got home so I would know she arrived safely.

Once she was gone, I shot a quick text to Ashley to check in with her. I then spent an hour or so planning my first Irish road trip before crawling into bed. I knew my mind would try to dwell on the dark events of the past two days, so the trip was a perfect distraction. I focused all my thoughts on the new places I'd see and allowed my excitement to overshadow everything else.

Whether from the power of positive thinking or just sheer exhaustion, I was rewarded with a long, dreamless night.

"You Europeans and your clown cars. I'm five-four, but I feel like a giraffe squeezing into this thing," I grumbled as Cat situated herself in the passenger side.

"Well, good morning to you too, sunshine," she teased with a smile.

"I'm sorry. The last hour was hectic getting over here. You ready to hit the road?"

"More than you could know; get me out of here."

We chatted about ex-boyfriends, parents, and places we'd like to see during the hour and a half drive through the beautiful Irish countryside. Being on the road with her reminded me of all my childhood travels, and amid all the craziness of my life, it was exactly what I needed.

Stopping through Londonderry, we toured the Guildhall cathedral-like building and checked out the enormous seventh-century stone city walls. I made reservations for a tour of a stone circle in the afternoon, so we had lunch at a local pub before driving out to the megalithic ruins, which was out in the middle of nowhere.

The enormous ring of boulders held court in the middle of a grassy field, clear of any trees or obstructions. I parked on the side of the road, along with another carload of people who also appeared to be there for the tour. It was about a quarter-mile walk to the stones, and they were larger and more impressive with each step. On average, the stones, speckled with moss and age, were about my height—a few stood well taller, and several were crumbled and worn down to a much less impressive size. It wasn't quite the same as the one shown in the *Outlander* series, but similar enough. I couldn't come to Ireland and pass up seeing one of their iconic stone circles.

"Think about it, Cat. These things have been here since the Bronze Age. How cool is that?" I said with reverence as we approached the stones.

"Done your research, have you?" she asked teasingly.

"It's probably not as exciting for you since you've lived around them your whole life, but we don't have this kind of thing in the States."

"I've seen less of them than you might think. As paranoid as my mom is, we stayed far away from these things."

I turned to ask her what she meant when a man's voice called out from nearby.

"Hello, everyone! I'm so glad you made it out. I'm Riley, your tour guide." A young man with shaggy brown hair and a large goofy smile waved at us. "Although it's not so much a tour as it is informational, since this is the only site we'll be seeing. Anyway, it looks like we're all here, so I'll get started. Welcome to our beloved Beltany Stone Circle. Prevailing theories date the site back to between 2100 and 700 BC, and some say it dates back to the Stone Age." As he spoke, we all gathered around him.

"There are sixty-four stones now. However, the original count was eighty with a circumference of one hundred and fifty yards. The circle was part of the Beltane summer celebration near May first, marking the start of summer and the point halfway between the spring equinox and the summer solstice. The word itself means 'goodly fire' and was associated with lighting huge bonfires here on Tops Hill. All household fires would be doused in the surrounding villages and relit with Beltane fires. Smoke and ashes were believed to have protective powers. The people would walk through the smoke along with their livestock, and piles of ashes would be carried to homes and walked around the property."

My heart started to race at the similarity of the Beltane ritual to Cat's use of ashes to protect my apartment. "Those practices sound like what you did at my apartment," I whispered to Cat as Riley continued his talk. "Did the people learn that from your ancestors?"

"I suppose it's possible, but I don't really know."

I turned back to our guide, but my mind raced with questions. Had the ancient inhabitants of Ireland been familiar with the Fae? I knew the Fae roamed Earth freely back then, but I wasn't sure how much they interacted or shared with the human population. Where had the public learned these techniques, and why were they no longer practiced? Not wanting to miss more valuable information, I drew myself out of my thoughts to focus on his words.

"The people would host huge feasts to celebrate. Doors and windows of homes, and even the cattle themselves, would be decorated with yellow May flowers. This ceremonial event marked when the cattle were driven out to summer pastures. The ritual was performed to protect the cattle and encourage the growth of crops. If you'll follow me this way." He indicated outside the circle where a single triangular stone sat southeast of the others.

"This outlier stone is believed to be related to sunrise and sunset. It's marked with what appears to be replicated constellations, and at sunrise on Beltane, the stone aligns perfectly with the tallest pillar on the west-southwest portion of the circle. While there may have been an alignment for the winter solstice, the deterioration of the stones makes it impossible to say for sure. There's much we don't know about the stones, such as the cup marks on the stones, and the biggest mystery is who created the circle and how they got them here."

We all followed his lead back inside the large circle as he continued. "It's the common belief of the locals that the stones were put here by the Aos sí—the people of the mounds. They have many names—the fair folk, the Tuatha De Danann, and as they are more commonly called, Faeries. Legend says that they warred with the Milesians, another mythical race, and eventually agreed to retreat and dwell underground in the mounds." He lifted his arm to indicate the rolling hills around us.

So that was why Cat's mom stayed away from the circles. If

the Fae created them, she'd want nothing to do with them. How silly of me to think I could take a break, no matter how short, from my new Fae reality. Hopes of a distraction were lost as my eyes raked over the countryside, and I wondered just how much truth there was to these particular legends. I couldn't see Lochlan and the others living underground.

Movement in a distant cluster of trees caught my eye. A large white wolf-like dog sat back on his haunches and watched our group. There didn't appear to be any homes nearby, but there also weren't fences. If he belonged to someone, he'd strayed some distance. We were likely the most exciting thing to happen out here in the quiet countryside all week. He watched us as if we were as fascinating an attraction to him as the stones were to us. With a quiet chuckle to myself, I turned back to join Cat.

After Riley finished his explanatory tour, he answered questions, and we spent time examining the stones up close. On our way back to the car, I was amused to note that the dog was still watching us from afar. He was a beautiful beast. I'd always wanted a dog, but my dad had been allergic. Having a housemate might not be a bad idea at this point—a guard dog sounded especially appealing—but nothing as large as the white wolf. I couldn't imagine he'd even fit in my tiny place.

I chuckled at the thought and folded myself back into the car. We drove to the nearby town of Strabane, where we entertained ourselves sightseeing before checking into a hotel. I'd picked the place for its authentic atmosphere and quaint little pub on the lower level. It had been an excellent choice, and after a delicious Irish dinner and a day of travel, we were both exhausted. We waddled back to our room, watched a few minutes of television, then called it a night.

My body might have been exhausted from the busy day, but my mind had other ideas as it bounced from one odd dream to the next. Somewhere along the line, I passed through a doorway to find Lochlan standing in a small room. His deep blue eyes assessed me questioningly, and his short blond hair was tousled in a way that made me want to run my fingers through it.

I was aware that I was in a dream, which wasn't usual for me. I'd heard of people who could manipulate their dreams, knowing on some level that it was just a dream, but I'd never experienced that sort of freedom. Not until now.

Peering at the bedroom around us, I recognized that it belonged to a cabin I had stayed in years before with my boyfriend at the time. Wood paneling gave the room a rustic feel, while a fluffy white duvet softened the look. The place was warm and inviting and a world away from all my current troubles.

When my eyes turned back to Lochlan, he was no longer wearing a shirt. He looked down at his toned bare chest, almost in surprise. A nervous giggle slipped past my lips. The sound drew his deep-blue eyes back to mine, pinning me in place with their intensity. All levity disappeared, and the air emptied from my lungs.

This was my opportunity to overwrite the memory of Ronan's fake Lochlan. To create a scene in my mind that wasn't tarnished with betrayal and pain. This was my mind's way of healing.

"What is this, Rebecca?" dream Lochlan asked.

I shook my head. "No questions. No arguments. This is how it should have been." I stepped closer, my gaze slowly devouring the solid planes of his chest before dropping farther to the delicious V peeking from the waist of his faded jeans. It was too tempting. I had to reach out and trail my fingers along the ridges of his rippling muscles.

"*Fuck.*" The curse was a feral growl—my only warning

before he tugged me close, and his lips slammed down on mine.

Lochlan didn't just kiss; he possessed. The sensual roll of his tongue. The gentle nip of his teeth. The branding touch of his hands holding me tight. His perfect siege overwhelmed my senses and commanded compliance.

He lifted me in his arms and moved us to the bed, lowering us down to lay his large body over mine. I took a shallow breath and reveled in the woodsy scent that was all Lochlan. Nothing artificial would suit him. He was unabashedly himself in every way without desire to conceal or modify himself for anyone's benefit. He embodied the truest sense of confidence without slipping into arrogance or conceit.

I slid my pajama shirt over my head, wanting to be just as bare and honest as he was for me. His gaze raked over me, unabashedly taking in every curve and valley of my exposed body. One of his hands trailed over my ribs before cupping my breast. His deft fingers gently twisted one of my pebbled nipples, drawing an electric bolt of pleasure that zinged from my chest down to my core. I arched off the bed on a breathless gasp, not given time to recover when his mouth closed over the angry peak.

Every pass of his tongue and graze of his teeth was reverent. His focus was absolute. His attention devout. In the confines of this room—this perfect dream I'd created—I was his sole purpose in life, and he conveyed his devotion with every single touch.

I writhed mindlessly beneath him.

I was the embodiment of need, reduced to my most basic form of animal instinct. No pretense or civility to force unnatural inhibitions. I allowed sensation to own me and used my body to communicate, pleading with him for more with every moan and roll of my spine.

Lochlan lifted up off the bed, and my gaze snagged on the corded muscle of his arms. Slowly ... deliberately ... he slid his jeans down over his thighs. He was naked beneath, his thick cock bobbing free. The sight of him standing naked above me jogged my memory to flashes of Ronan just before he unveiled himself.

The butterflies in my stomach turned putrid.

No.

This was *not* Ronan.

This was *my* dream, and *I* was in control. I would not let Ronan steal this from me, too.

Before fear could get the better of me, I slipped my pajama shorts down over my hips, and Lochlan pulled them from my feet, discarding them on the floor. He then brought his hands to my last scrap of clothing, my pink silk panties, and he pulled them achingly slowly down my legs as his eyes devoured me. As the fabric glided down each inch of my legs, waves of arousal surged and crested in my belly.

Dragging his body along mine, Lochlan lowered on top of me, little by little, until we were aligned from head to toe. The head of his shaft pressed at my entrance. I lifted my knees up to spread wide for him, but he paused, his eyes locked on mine.

You're magnificent, he seemed to say from behind those cerulean depths.

Only for you, I gave back.

His chest vibrated with a rumbling growl of approval as he slowly, so slowly, rocked inside of me. He wasn't just fucking me; he was forging a connection. Linking us on a primal level.

This is how it should have been.

My heart fluttered uncontrollably while my body stretched with delicious fullness. I arched and squeezed my inner muscles as I adjusted, raw sounds of unbridled lust purring from the back of my throat.

"Eyes, Bec. Give me your eyes." Strain shredded his voice to the coarse scratch of gravel on a paved road. I did as he commanded, making sure to keep my gaze locked on his as his pace quickened and each thrust became more demanding. Soon, the quiet room was filled with the sound of his hard body pounding into my soft flesh.

I felt his touch in every molecule of my being. A fire singeing me on the inside, threatening to consume me, body and soul. I didn't care. I wanted whatever death he had to offer because a life without this chaotic energy wouldn't be worth living.

My body quivered with the promise of impending ecstasy, just as divine as it would be devastating. Sensation clambered and clawed to the surface. It was impossible to direct or contain, and when Lochlan's fingers twisted my nipple, the sharp sting was the kindling needed to ignite the final explosion.

Lightning burst from my belly into my veins until my blood is a river of fire. The orgasm raged through me, a current of electric pleasure altering the chemical makeup of my body. Only vaguely aware, I noted the violent roar signaling Lochlan's release deep inside me just before I gasped awake, lurching upward in my hotel bed next to Cat.

"What happened? Becca, you okay?" Cat asked groggily.

I looked around the dimly lit room, attempting to orient myself. The oppressive weight of disappointment tugged at my shoulders when I realized I'd woken up and lost the dream. Not totally lost. I could still remember every passionate detail, but I was no longer safe in Lochlan's arms, and that was enough of a loss to douse the heated remnants of our time together.

"Yeah, I'm fine." Technically, it wasn't a lie, but I realized as I spoke that the heightened emotions had brought my magic to the surface. My eyes were obsidian shards that I'd never be able to explain should Cat catch a glimpse. I squeezed my lids shut and slid off the bed. "Just need to use the restroom. You go back to sleep."

Once I was safely inside the confines of the small water closet, I took several deep cleansing breaths, and only once I had ensured that my eyes were back to brown did I rejoin Cat in the bedroom. She was already fast asleep again, softly snoring as I tucked myself back under the covers.

After the threat of being discovered had passed, memories of the dream flooded my mind. I'd just had the hottest sex dream ever while sleeping in a bed with my friend.

In the name of everything holy, please tell me I didn't moan out loud or do something equally embarrassing.

I hoped that since she was back asleep again so quickly, I hadn't done anything too terrible. Just the possibility was upsetting. I was in a dark room with the covers over my head, and I still buried my face in my hands with mortification.

Her knowing about the dream might have been embarrassing, but the dream itself had been epic. One I would not forget for a very long time. And just to be sure the memory didn't fade like mist through the trees, I ran through the scene over and over as I drifted back to sleep.

TWENTY-FIVE

Monday morning at the museum was busy, so I didn't see Cat until lunch when she joined me in the break room.

"I was hoping I'd find you here." She sat with me at the table, though she didn't have a lunch.

"You not eating?"

"No, I just needed to tell you that the elders got in touch while we were gone. They want to meet with you."

I sat up taller in my chair. "That's great news, I think. Do you have any idea what they want to talk to me about?"

"No, they don't tell me anything."

"I suppose there's only one way to find out. When and where do they want to meet?"

"Tonight, seven o'clock at the Central Library. The ground floor study room right off the main reading area."

"Will you be there?" Having a friendly face present would ease my anxiety significantly.

"No. Though I tried. Mam said the elders wouldn't allow it."

I shrugged. "Oh, well. Thank you, Cat. I really appreciate all your help."

"No, thank *you*. You're the most exciting thing to come to town in my lifetime." She ended with a teasing smile, and I couldn't help but laugh. Unlike her, I could have used a little less excitement in my life.

"I don't think recent events had anything to do with me, per se. The issues with the Fae would have happened regardless, but I'm glad to help bring some pizzazz to these dreary Belfast skies."

"Well, without you, I wouldn't have been privy to any of it."

"Just so long as you don't go getting more involved than necessary. I have enough to worry about already."

She held her right hand over her chest across her heart. "Don't you worry. I'm entirely too scared of my mam to do anything stupid. I'd never hear the end of it."

We discussed a few mundane work-related topics before she wished me luck and headed back to her desk, her red curls bouncing as she left the room.

I spent a good chunk of the afternoon thinking about the upcoming meeting. Wondering what information these secretive elders might offer and what questions I should ask. As if the meeting wouldn't be nerve-wracking enough, I was scheduled to have my first training session with Lochlan as well. I was anxious about that for half a dozen reasons. With both events looming over me, I found myself chewing away at my fingernails while my leg bounced restlessly under my desk. Needless to say, I got very little done.

With only an hour left in the workday, I left my desk and began to walk the halls of the museum. Losing myself in the artwork was just the distraction I needed. No matter how many times I had seen the same pieces, I could still appreciate new aspects and see new elements from different perspectives. I found myself lingering at *The Quarrel of Titania and Oberon.*

I hadn't visited the painting since my tour with Fergus. A radiant Titania stood with a child hiding behind her while arguing with the statuesque Oberon. He looked nothing like the Fae man who had been its muse, and Titania looked nothing like the Fae queen I had met. The piece depicted a scene from Shakespeare's *A Midsummer Night's Dream* in which the two argue over who would keep a young orphaned boy. According to Shakespeare, Oberon had won the argument and raised the boy as one of his knights.

Lochlan had been raised by Alberich. I wondered how that had come about. Had Guin fought Alberich for the rights to Lochlan? I would have to ask him when the time was appropriate, but who knew when that would be.

Every time I saw him, I left more confused than the last. The dream, while cathartic, had done nothing to help on that front. My desire for him was undeniable, but I was too emotionally unsteady with everything going on to keep from forming attachments, and growing attached to Lochlan would be a disastrous idea for so many reasons.

It was imperative I kept our relationship professional and my head clear of confusing thoughts. Lust had gotten me hurt once. I wouldn't fall victim again.

THE LIBRARY and the museum were both stately buildings, and while they were similar in style, the library was constructed in red brick instead of the museum's white stone. The library was also much smaller without any modern expansion efforts.

I walked into the dated building and found the stairwell

down to the basement. Cat had said the ground floor, but here in Ireland, I'd come to discover that meant the basement.

The reading room was spacious and accommodated several long wood tables, each outfitted with reading lamps. Two patrons occupied the otherwise empty space, and I scanned the area in search of the study room Cat had mentioned. I spotted a door off to my right and moved closer to investigate. As I approached, my brows narrowed in profound confusion.

Inside were two men and three women sitting around a table talking, and among them was Fergus. Cat had mentioned that he was a family friend, but I'd never considered he might be a part of her secret group. I felt like smacking myself in the head.

"Thank you for joining us, Rebecca," said a woman who looked like an aged carbon copy of Cat. "Why don't you come in so we can shut the door and have some privacy while we talk."

I nodded numbly and did as she suggested, too dumb-founded to argue. Fergus wore a wry grin, but the features of the other man sitting next to him were considerably more stern. Recognition tugged at my mind, but I couldn't place where I might have seen him. The Cat look-alike had a single brow arched coolly, and the other woman, unfamiliar to me, offered a friendly smile.

Clearing my throat, I addressed the group. "Thank you for meeting with me."

The kind-looking woman answered. "You know Fergus, and my name is Maura. While you may not remember me, I'm the police investigator who interviewed you after your friend was attacked. This is Cat's mother, Colleen. You may recognize Niall Burke." She motioned to the man with cold eyes and pinched lips. "He's one of the anchors on the local news, and this is Rian Collins. He's a doctor at the local hospital. I know you've got a lot of questions, and we've decided to offer you some information but know that we expect answers in return." She looked at me pointedly.

"Yes, I'm more than happy to tell you what I know. A lot is going on, and I think we all need to work together."

"You aren't wrong. Let me start by explaining that our group consists of the modern-day descendants of the Druids."

After researching the history of magic in Ireland, I had suspected as much, but it was good to get confirmation.

"Many centuries ago, our ancestors were taken to Faery to serve as the queen's handmaids because she didn't trust the Fae in her court. Human women posed little risk as they didn't stand to prosper from her death, and over time, a close relationship developed between her and the women. Over the many years they were together, she taught these women magic through runes and spells. They formed a sort of family bond. When the queen decided to withdraw the Fae from Earth and keep the races separate, she sent her handmaids back to Earth on seemingly peaceful terms. However, not long after, the women were sought out and slaughtered like animals by the Wild Hunt." She paused, allowing the information to sink in.

Six somber faces watched me intently. These people might not have known their ancestors personally, but it was clear that the stories and lessons had lived on in a way that was real to them. The fear was real, and they did not take the subject of the Fae lightly.

"Very few of the original handmaids survived. Those who did taught their children what they had learned, and each generation after continued to pass on the knowledge of the Fae, their magic, and the inherent dangers."

"Why would the queen send the women home, then order their deaths? If she wanted them killed, why not just kill them in Faery?" I asked, trying to understand.

"We only know what we were taught—that the queen wanted no knowledge of the Fae to exist on Earth. Perhaps she intended to free them, then changed her mind. Regardless, she ordered the Hunt to kill us. That is why, to this day, our secrecy is our number one priority."

I rubbed my arms to ease the prickle of goose bumps from her chilling tone. I wanted to assure them that Lochlan and the others were not a threat to them, but I had no grounds for such an assertion. The Hunt had not threatened me, but that very well could have been because I was no longer fully human.

I was a loophole in the queen's mandate that no humans learn of the Fae.

Would Cat and the others be in danger if the Hunt found out about their knowledge? When I met the queen, she didn't act bothered by rumors of their past. That might have been incongruous with what the detective was telling me, but this wasn't the time to argue.

"I promise you that I'll keep your secret. I would never endanger you." I met each of their grave expressions with conviction.

"Maura has told you enough about our background." Cat's mom spoke up in an icy tone. "You need to tell us how you can see the Fae."

I nodded, and my hand involuntarily came up to touch my necklace for reassurance. "When I was a child, my parents brought me to Ireland on vacation. I was given this necklace while we were there. We didn't know it at the time, but it gave me the power to see the Fae. I only figured it out after arriving here in Belfast."

Their obvious fear of the Fae meant even if I had wanted to, I wasn't going to share that I was becoming Fae. I didn't know these people enough to trust that they wouldn't kill me for their own protection.

The stern-looking TV anchorman, Niall, spoke up. "How do you know the necklace is what gives you that ability?"

"It took some time for me to figure it out, but I'm certain at this point. The necklace is even spelled to keep it from being removed."

"Who gave you the necklace and why?"

"My parents thought it was just a kind merchant at an outdoor market, but I've since figured out that it was Merlin who gave me the necklace." Tension thickened the air around me, but I continued. "I don't know why he did it. I know portals have been opened to let Unseelie and Shadow Fae onto Earth, and the Huntsmen have been attempting to figure out who's behind it. I also know there's a rumor that war is coming and that … that I'm supposed to play some role in preventing it." My eyes landed on Fergus as I thought about how my choices had been taken from me, and my stomach started to churn. "I've asked myself every day why this is happening to me. Each day, I find more ways that my life has been mapped out for me or toyed with in some way. Now that I sit here with you all, I find it interesting that I happened to end up working for a Druid. I couldn't believe my luck when this job fell into my lap, but now, I have to wonder if luck played any part at all."

He gave me a tight smile, and his eyes apologetic. "Rebecca, I would have wanted you working for the museum regardless of how we crossed paths. However—"

"*Fergus.*" Niall chided. "She doesn't need to know. She's friends with the Fae. Anything she hears could go straight back to them."

I tried to assuage his fears. "I won't tell them anything about you, I swear it." Despite my pleas, a lifetime of wariness would not be mollified by a few empty words from me.

Fergus turned to Niall, sitting taller in his chair. "She

already knows we exist. That train has left the station. If she's supposed to play a part in preventing the war, I would think we would want to do what we could to help her."

They glared at one another for a prolonged moment, the air in the room thick with tension until Fergus eventually turned back to me and continued.

"What I started to say is that one of our numbers is an oracle of sorts. She instructed me to reach out to the school and told us a woman was destined to arrive on our shores and bring about great changes. While it seemed reasonable to guess that this woman would be a friend to our people, the oracle's predictions are not always clear, and there was debate as to how forthcoming we should be when you arrived. I do apologize for the deception."

I had assumed luck had played a role in my new job, but finding out I hadn't earned anything based on merit stung a bit.

"Rebecca," Fergus prodded for my attention. "You've been a great asset to the museum. Regardless of how you got here, you've done a fine job, and you deserve the position."

I gave him a small smile, his words making me feel marginally better, though I chided myself to remember that trivial matters like my pride were irrelevant. "I appreciate that, Fergus. Did your oracle tell you anything else?"

"Aye, she mentioned the possibility of the world as we knew it ending. Taken together with the recent increase of Fae activity, we knew something bad was coming. Do you know who is behind it or what they are planning?"

"Not exactly. Ronan, who was a member of the Hunt, played some role. Unfortunately, we don't know who he was working with or what they hoped to achieve. He's now on the run, and we're still trying to gather information. One of the things that would help us most is locating the Sword of

Light. Is there any information you can give me that would help?"

Like guilty children being interrogated by a parent, they all shared a knowing look before the detective spoke up. "That sword cannot end up in the hands of the Fae. For our own protection, there is no information we can give you."

I held my frustration at bay and tried to school my features. "I'm not sure I understand, but I respect your choice."

"We appreciate that," offered the detective graciously. "I know it took courage to meet with us, and I hope you can understand why our secrecy is so vital. We'll help you where we can, but not at the risk of being discovered."

"Thank you. Just out of curiosity, how much of this did Cat know?" If she'd heard the prophecy, she was an impressive actress to pretend I was anything but an ordinary new hire.

Fergus leaned forward in his chair. "Cat is young, and to protect ourselves, we don't disclose sensitive information to any but the elected elders. She wasn't told anything about you outside of what the other museum employees were told."

I supposed that was a relief. Had she known, I might find it harder to trust her going forward. I nodded then let them know that I appreciated their honesty. After establishing that there was nothing further to discuss, we said our goodbyes, and I left the library to head to the club.

I had texted Lochlan to let him know I was on my way, so he was waiting in the lobby when I arrived. He wore sneakers, black track pants, and a gray T-shirt already marked with splotches of sweat. Seeing him in workout gear confirmed my suspicions that the man always looked delectable, no matter what he wore.

"You get started without me?" I asked.

"Went for a run," was all he said as he led us to the elevator. He wordlessly pressed the button for the basement before placing his hand on a plate to scan his fingerprints.

"What, no retina scanner?" I teased, my anxiety manifesting in humor.

He slid his eyes over to me. "The fingerprint scanner is not the only security measure we have in place."

His comment jogged my memory back to the time I had broken into the building. I'd felt a shock of pain crossing the threshold from the alley. "You use wards? Is that part of your security?"

"Yes, part of it."

"Well, whatever you use isn't terribly effective."

"They are for just about anyone but you. I don't suppose you care to tell me how you managed to walk through them."

"Can't tell what I don't know," I quipped.

He lifted his chin and then gave a slight shake of his head in exasperation.

Stepping off the elevator onto the basement brought back all the vivid details from that night I had broken in, and chills ran down my spine. I had seen a dead Fae man flayed open and nearly gotten myself banned from the Huntsman. It hadn't been one of my finest moments.

I came to a dead stop, hands on my hips. "Wait a minute. This is where all the interrogation rooms are. Where exactly are you taking me?"

He stopped to look back at me like I was being absurd. "To the gym. You wanted to train, right?"

"You sure this isn't some trick, and I'm not unwittingly walking to my own death?"

"If this was a trick, saying yes sure would kill the surprise." He flashed his teeth at me before continuing to a door with another handprint scanner.

I was about ninety percent sure he was joking. The other ten percent was busy calling out, "Dead man walking."

Lochlan opened a thick metal door to reveal a large modern training room. My clenched shoulders relaxed at the sight. The light wood floors were reminiscent of a school gymnasium, although the smell was thankfully much more Old Spice than sweaty teenager. One corner of the room was dedicated to free weights and had rubber matting covering the wood. There was an array of equipment—punching bag, speed bag, pullup bars, weight bench with a wall full of weights, treadmill and more. Lochlan walked over to a shelf and grabbed boxing pads and white tape.

"Give me your hand," he murmured.

I set down my gym bag and held my hand out, which he proceeded to systematically wrap with white fabric tape from wrist to knuckles. Once both hands were fully wrapped and I had warmed up with a five-minute jog, he began our lesson. He showed me how to hold a fist so that I wouldn't break my thumb when I punched something. We also went over foot stance, how to guard my face, the difference between a jab and a cross, and proper follow-through of my hips during a strike.

Flutters of awareness danced across my skin each time he touched me. When he stood behind me, his strong hands guiding my hips in a pivot, it was all I could do to focus on his words. His spicy masculine scent was even stronger after his run, and every minute that ticked by made me more achingly aware of how alone we were in the gym. I had to actively squelch memories of our dream sex together.

"Now that you have the basics, let's practice a few sequences." He slid round pads on each of his hands and held them up at chest height.

I stood with my knees slightly bent in ready position—my

left foot forward, my right foot behind me—and held my hands up to guard my face.

"Give me a jab-jab-cross combo, then repeat. Make sure to exhale on your strikes."

Slowly at first, I went through the motions. Jab-jab-cross, then repeat—over and over. Along with jabs and crosses, we worked on uppercuts and ducking until I started to feel like one of those inflatable floppy balloons at used car lots.

When he finally called the session to a close, I collapsed onto my back and stared vacantly at the ceiling, wondering if I would be able to move the next day. The hair on top of my head, once an attractive messy bun, now more closely resembled a bird's nest than a hairstyle. Sweat drenched my shirt, and I wasn't sure any deodorant had survived the training session.

Lochlan barely showed signs of breaking a sweat. He sat on the weight bench not far from me, leaning forward with his elbows on his knees. "Am I going to have to carry you home?"

His words, spoken in a low murmur, stirred the butterflies in my stomach to life. They'd fully rested during my workout and were ready to wreak havoc on my insides.

"I'll manage, thanks." After a moment of deep breathing, I sat up on the matted floor with my legs crossed. "This is kind of random, but I was wondering about something I read a while back. When I researched magic and Ireland, there were tons of references to Druids. Were they real?" I wanted to hear what he knew about the Druids, but I wouldn't say anything to hint at their modern-day existence.

"They were, but they haven't existed for a long time."

"What happened to them?"

"They were killed by the Hunt." His quick admission took me off guard.

In a whisper, I asked hesitantly, "Were you a part of that?"

As I waited for his answer, I realized just how much I wanted him to deny his involvement.

"That was before my time. The Erlking back then was Odin, and it was at his command that the women were killed. When Guin found out, she was livid. War broke out between the Court and the Hunt. Eventually, Guin killed Odin for his actions, although he claimed from the start that Guin herself had come to him and given her blessing to hunt the humans. They had been her trusted friends, and she wouldn't forgive the transgression. That time period was marked by such darkness and bloodshed that once Alberich became the Erlking, both he and Guin have always endeavored to stay on good terms."

"Guin killed the legendary Norse God, Odin?"

"Legend maybe, but he wasn't a god. The Hunt spent many years in Scandinavia during his leadership, and rumors spread."

"Guin must be really powerful."

"She is. I wouldn't want to get on her bad side," he said gravely.

I had to take a minute to process everything he had revealed. Guin hadn't ordered the death of her handmaidens. Instead, she had avenged them. Could I convey that information to the Druids and convince them that they were not in danger? They wouldn't be happy to know I was discussing their past with Lochlan, but it would mean those people could live without the constant fear of being discovered.

I didn't think I could pry into the subject much further without making him suspicious, so I changed topics. "Has there been any trace of Ronan?"

He swiftly rose and stalked across the room, his hand running through his hair harshly. "No. We searched his home but found nothing out of the ordinary. We've traced his credit cards and used the most advanced tracking platforms out there, but we haven't had a single hit."

"That sounds awfully human of you. I figured you all would be using magic and your super Fae senses to track him down." I rose to gather my things near where he stood.

"We use our spidey senses too. No reason not to use all techniques available," he shot back.

"The Faerie's got jokes? I'm shocked!" I poked him in the chest. It was a gesture I would have made with one of my close friends, and I blamed my exhaustion for acting in such a familiar manner with him when our relationship had not yet progressed to that level. We had known each other for several weeks, but we rarely joked or teased one another, and we certainly didn't make casual physical contact.

He pressed forward to back me into the doorframe, and my face lifted to peer into his inscrutable face. "Careful with that smart mouth, or I'll have to find a better use for it."

The towel I was holding dropped from my hands, and my breathing became shallow. We had managed to temporarily avoid the dizzying sexual energy between us, but eventually, we always came back to it. I could feel the warmth from his chest. Like a beacon, it called to me, tempting me to move just a little closer.

This is bad news, Rebecca. You need to get a grip.

"I need to get going," I mumbled, dropping my gaze to his chest and pulling away.

"This is his doing, isn't it?" Lochlan asked coolly.

"What?"

"The fear you'd begun to overcome. Ronan brought it back with whatever it is he's done."

I shook my head fervently. "No, this has nothing to do with him. I just think it's a bad idea. I don't want to complicate things between us."

"You're scared."

Anger licked at the skin on my neck, drawing a heated flush. "I'm not *scared*. I'm being smart. We're dealing with a potential war, so neither of us should risk distractions."

"It's only being smart if you think the risk of injury is too great to justify. In other words, you've given weight to your fears. And don't try to tell me you aren't just as desperate for another taste as I am because I was right there with you in that dream. I know exactly how much you liked what we did."

The blood drained from my face, and goose bumps rose along every inch of my skin.

He knew about the dream. What did that even mean? It couldn't be. I had to have misunderstood. "What dream?" I whispered.

"What dream?" he growled. "The only fucking dream you and I shared. The one where I made you come so hard the rafters shook in that little cabin. Didn't you realize ... did you not realize that was real?"

My head started to ache, and my eyes frantically searched the ground for answers. How could it have been real? How could he possibly know about something that happened in my head?

The first time I thought I had sex with Lochlan, it turned out to be someone else. The second time, I thought it wasn't him when it really was.

Oh my God.

Ronan's deception was definitely worse, but this newest snafu was still excruciatingly embarrassing. I felt like someone had taken my most private journal entry and published it on the nightly news for all to see. Sure, I'd enjoyed the sex when I thought it was a dream, but an actual encounter with him hadn't been my choice. For the second time in a handful of days, my body had been shared with someone unknowingly.

My stomach twisted with revulsion and frustration.

"I need to go," I mumbled. Without meeting his eyes, I grabbed my duffel bag.

"Don't do it, Rebecca. Don't run from this."

I whipped around, seizing the opportunity to lash out. "*Fuck you*, Lochlan. I'm doing my fucking best, and the last thing I need is your judgment." I stormed out of the room, not waiting for a reply.

CHAPTER

TWENTY-SIX

For the first time in months, I sat down and wrote in a journal before bed. I was struggling. Just when I thought I could manage the challenges I'd been presented, some new bump in the road sent me reeling. I needed a way to work through all the emotions. Normally, I'd talk to Ashley. She'd been my sounding board for years—the person I could count on to help me through any crisis—but I couldn't share these new problems with her. I had to find a way to cope on my own. Therefore, journaling was going to be my new best friend.

I was a dozen pages into my rambling thoughts when I heard a noise from downstairs. I wasn't in the practice of leaving on a TV or radio, so the place was usually quiet. My neighbors kept to themselves, and traffic was minimal on the road out front. My small apartment should have been silent, but there'd been a noticeable crash below me.

It could have been the Brownie—although he had never made a peep before, and I had yet to see him since he helped save me from Ronan. Looking around for a weapon, I kicked myself for having left my knife in my purse, which was down in the living room. I grabbed the next best thing I could find and crept silently down the stairs.

In a tank top and panties, a black patent stiletto gripped in my hands, I poked my head into the living room. I'd turned off the lights when I'd gone up to bed, leaving the room shrouded in darkness, but my new Fae eyes had no trouble verifying that the room was empty. The same was true of the kitchen. I had no idea where the sound had come from, but my home was empty.

I sucked in a deep breath and coaxed my shoulders to relax. Everything was fine. My anxiety was understandable, but on this particular occasion, it had been unnecessary. I grabbed the knife out of my purse before taking one more look around and heading back upstairs.

The remainder of my night passed without incident.

The following morning, I cornered Cat the first chance I had at work. "Imagine my surprise last night when I walked into that room and saw Fergus. You couldn't have given me a heads-up?" I playfully chided her.

"You know I couldn't. You saw how serious they are. If you hadn't been genuinely surprised, they would have hung me out to dry."

I rolled my eyes but softened the effect with a smirk. "The detective who interviewed me after the Draug attack was there —Maura O'Brien—and I suppose you know that your mom was there."

"Yeah, I did ask again if they'd let me go, but they wouldn't."

"They told me about the queen teaching your ancestors magic, but how is it exactly that you see the Fae if they're glamoured?"

Cat turned and lifted her thick mass of red curls to expose the pale skin of her neck. Near the hairline was a small symbol tattooed into her skin. "The rune is given to each child when they are old enough to understand what they see and not risk exposure. It's a sort of truth rune that ensures the Fae can't deceive us." She dropped her hair and turned back to face me, one corner of her mouth hitched up in a smirk.

"Just how many runes do you have tattooed on you?"

She gave a small chuckle before answering. "Just that one. If we need to use a rune for a particular circumstance, we can paint them on or use other methods of magic."

"You guys are amazing. Humans dabbling in Fae magic right under their noses."

Cat looked shyly down at her feet for a second before saying with a wry smile, "When you're brainwashed from infancy, it's not so much about bravery as it is being in a cult. Once you're in, there's no getting out."

I burst out laughing at her characterization of the Druids, but I knew that despite her teasing, she loved her family. After a moment, I sobered and looked at Cat. "The other night, I asked them for information on the Sword of Light, but they wouldn't help me. Cat, I have to find that sword."

Her green eyes looked up at me helplessly. "I don't know anything about it."

"If I at least knew what it looked like, maybe I'd have some chance of finding it. Do you all have any memoirs or information that have been written down that you could look at? If you could get a description or take a picture of a drawing—anything would help." I was begging, and I wasn't ashamed. I didn't want Cat to get in trouble, but if we didn't find a way to stop the coming war, more than just Cat and her family would be in danger.

She hung her head back and closed her eyes in defeat. "I'll see what I can find, but I'm not guaranteeing anything."

"Thank you, Cat!" I wrapped her in a tight hug, and she

laughed at my enthusiasm but continued to remind me that she doubted she'd find anything. I assured her that I'd be no worse off than I was already.

The following morning, I prepared to entertain hordes of elementary school students. One of the local school districts was having a field trip day, and scores of first, second, and third graders would be joining us at the museum throughout the day. I needed to make it to the office early to get ahead of the game, so I was in a rush when I opened my front door and had to stumble to a stop when something caught my eye on the ground beneath me.

I had to blink several times before making sense of what I saw. To understand how it could be real.

My breaths grew shallow and erratic. Horror cleaved my insides and sent a lancing pain clear through my chest.

I dropped my bags and knelt to where my tiny Brownie friend lay dead. Not just killed but mutilated. His head had been plucked from his body and set in the crook of his arm as if posed for some sadistic joke.

This hadn't been an accident or an animal mauling. The tiny docile creature to whom I owed my life had been senselessly murdered and left for me to find.

Vengeful tears blurred my vision. Bile rose in my throat.

Had Ronan known the Brownie had helped me? Whatever the excuse, I had no doubt the little man had been killed because of me. I closed my eyes and whispered a litany of apologies. Nothing I said or did would undo this horrific crime, but I had nothing else to give.

He had paid the ultimate price for his good deed, and I would never forget it.

I had no idea how Brownies honored their dead or if there were even other Brownies around to care for him, but I couldn't leave him on the front step. With trembling hands, I gingerly scooped up his limp body and brought him inside. I laid him on a thick pile of tissues on the kitchen table, then plucked a handful of leaves off the shrubs outside my living room window. I placed the leaves under and around him, making a shroud as respectfully as I could. When I got home from work, I would find a special place to bury him if he was still there.

Taking an unsteady breath, I said a final goodbye to my friend.

When I stepped back onto the sidewalk to leave, I looked up at my two-story row house. Someone had come here in the night. Someone who wanted to hurt me. I didn't know how the Brownie had been captured, but my wards had kept the intruder out, and that was at least a small relief. I thanked the heavens Ashley was safely hidden away and prayed today's loss would be the only casualty I faced. Deep down, I knew the chances were slim.

APPROXIMATELY SIX HUNDRED kids passed through our halls that day. I helped plan the event and had tried to mentally prepare for the onslaught of children, but it had been pointless. There was no preparing for hundreds of six-to-eight-year-olds. You just ride out the storm and hope you make it out alive.

By closing time, I had tied more than a dozen pairs of shoes, watched enough kids eat their boogers to make me nauseous for a week, and answered at least sixteen hundred questions.

I was beat.

I gathered my purse and work tote, but before I made it out of the office, Fergus came bustling back through the door. "Becca! I was just about to leave when someone came in to tell us a big dog is trapped in the graveyard. Cat's gone, and so is most everyone else. Could you be a dear and call animal services to get the bloody thing out of there? We can't just leave him. He could start digging up graves, and we can't have that."

"Of course," I offered with more energy than I felt.

"Thank you so much. Normally, I would do it myself, but I have plans, and I'm already late. Thanks again, see you tomorrow!" He hollered the last part as he tore off down the hallway.

I plopped back down at my desk and pulled up the number for animal services. A recorded message informed me that they were closed for the day.

Great. Just how I wanted to end my day.

Friar's Bush Graveyard was a beautiful old cemetery next to the museum. It dated back to the early 1800s and was surrounded by a thick wall with an iron gate facing the street. I had no idea how a dog would have gotten inside, but I agreed that he needed to be removed.

After gathering my things, I exited the museum and walked to the front gate of the graveyard. A heavy layer of clouds drowned out the moonlight and shrouded the tombstones in darkness. The area was spotted with old trees and thick shrubs, making it even more difficult to see. However, my rapidly developing Fae vision was enormously helpful, and I was able to navigate the landscape with minimal fumbling.

Had I been in heels, traipsing through the moist grass would have been a squishy nightmare. In anticipation of leading the student visitors on tours through the museum, I had worn flats that morning and was now doubly glad for my practical decision. I rubbed my bare hands together for warmth and called out for the dog, hoping to retrieve him before my hands were permanently frostbitten.

"Come on, buddy, it's freezing out here. Where are you?" I

walked around a large bush, muttering to myself, not expecting the answer that followed.

"I see you've returned to wearing the necklace."

I froze, instantly recognizing the voice I'd once thought rich and charismatic. Now, the cloying sound of Ronan's words chilled my bones with icy terror. I'd thwarted him at my apartment, but I'd caught him off guard, and I'd been savage with rage. Alone in the dark cemetery, I felt vulnerable and unprepared. I'd only had a single training session, and I still didn't know anything about my magic.

I slowly turned in his direction and attempted to calm my breathing. Adrenaline was flooding my bloodstream, making my heart pound in my chest.

"What do you want, Ronan?" I managed to force a degree of confidence into my voice.

"Me? Just out for an evening stroll. Imagine my surprise when you showed up. Not very smart for a girl like yourself to be wandering about after dark." He was now allowing his twisted nature to shine vividly through his eyes, and my feet took an involuntary step back.

My pride and anger insisted I stay put and not give Ronan the satisfaction of seeing me run, but my legs were on the verge of mutiny. I commanded myself to stand strong against him. This was the fucking monster who had played me, tricked me into having sex with him, then nearly killed me. He'd set a trap to kill Lochlan and was unleashing bloodthirsty Fae onto Earth. He was the root of all my pain and anger, and I wouldn't cower in his presence.

"Did you kill the Brownie?" I asked through gritted teeth.

"It wasn't very nice of him to interfere in our discussion the other night. Something like that can't go unpunished."

"You fucking *coward,*" I hissed. "You hurt those who are weaker than yourself and betray your closest friends. You're nothing but a pathetic traitor." My calm façade quickly slipped away as my temper got the better of me.

Ronan stepped forward, his cocky superiority melting into a puddle of noxious spite. "You walked into our world five minutes ago, and you think you know anything about me or the Hunt? Those bastards deserve everything they get and more."

"If anyone deserves anything, it's you. You deserve to die." More hate-filled words had never crossed my lips, and I felt zero remorse.

"That's probably true, but it's not going to happen. Not anytime soon." His lips curled up in a vicious snarl.

"The Hunt is after you. They'll find you, and when they do, you'll wish you had never even considered turning your back on them."

"It's not turning my back on them if I was never on their side."

"Then whose side are you on? Either tell us who you're working for or stop pretending to be some great martyr." If I could only learn who was behind the portals, our confrontation would be worth every harrowing minute, but Ronan wasn't interested in cooperating.

He flashed his dimples in a wicked grin. "Nice try, but I'm not giving you anything but pain." His hand shot forward, and a blast of energy slammed into me, throwing me back against a large tree.

The air wheezed from my chest upon impact. I fell to my hands and knees, struggling to breathe. As soon as air began to filter back into my screaming lungs, I scrambled for my purse, where I had stashed the knife Lochlan had given me. My fingers wrapped around the hilt, and I scuttled backward in a crouch to press against the trunk of the tree, knife brandished in my trembling hand.

Ronan's grin widened with sick delight as if the sight of the blade excited him.

My tremors turned violent.

I didn't know how to shoot energy like he'd done. I hardly knew how to do anything with my magic, and even the things I had accomplished had been achieved through sheer luck and force of will. Any control was well beyond my understanding, and without the aid of magic, there was no way I could defeat him. I'd have to get close enough to touch him to have any chance, and he'd never let that happen.

A feral growl from behind me interrupted my frantic thoughts. The sound was so deep and guttural that I felt it resonate all the way down to my bones.

My eyes cut to the right, wondering what new horror I had to face. I could hardly believe what I saw. The enormous white muzzle of a dog crept slowly into view.

Not a dog. A wolf.

His snarling lip curled back to display an arsenal of gleaming white teeth with saliva dripping from his jowls. His head was lowered in a threatening stance while his golden stare was trained on Ronan.

The beast stood not three feet from me. Close enough to feel the warm steam from his terrifying growl. He could have ripped my head clean from my body had he wanted to, but his focus lay squarely on Ronan. All two-hundred pounds of coiled muscle was poised and ready to attack.

I could hardly believe what I was seeing. Not only was Ronan backing away in fear but I also swore this wolf-like dog was the same one I'd seen at the Beltany Stone Circle. The coincidence would have seemed preposterous a month ago, but after everything I'd witnessed in recent weeks, I wouldn't discount anything.

"*Get out of here*," Ronan spat at the dog, sweat beading on his brow as he tried to assert his dominance over the animal.

It didn't work.

In fact, the beast snapped his teeth in Ronan's direction before growling even louder and positioning himself between my assailant and me.

Ronan's maniacal eyes flew back and forth between us, his face contorted in anger and frustration. "You think you've won, but this is only the beginning. A mutt and a human girl are powerless against what's coming."

He blinked out of sight, and as quickly as the confrontation had started, it was over. Except now I was alone with the ferocious wolf. He continued a low growl as he scanned our surroundings. I didn't move a muscle. If ever there was a time to be invisible, this was it.

I scrunched my eyes closed and begged the universe to hide me.

The only answer I received was in the form of a long, wet lick across my face. I gasped and sputtered, wiping the slobber from my eyes and mouth.

"Oh, thank *God*." I sank back against the tree, my body sagging with relief. When I looked over at my shaggy savior, tongue lolling happily to the side, a hysterical giggle bubbled up from my chest.

The dog sat back on his haunches and gave a small tilt of his head as if I intrigued him.

"Thank you. You're quite the knight in shining armor." I gathered my purse and tote, continuing to hold the knife in my sweaty palm. When I gingerly stood on my shaking legs, the dog stood too and looked at me expectantly.

"Come on, let's get out of here." I hurried back to the entrance with my giant white shadow in tow. "You can go home now." I waved my empty hand toward the sidewalk, attempting to convey my message.

He dropped to his haunches again and simply stared at me.

I released a defeated sigh. "Whatever, big guy. *I'm* going home." I started down the sidewalk, white shadow keeping pace. "Where do you think you're going? I appreciate your help, but it's all clear now. You don't need to follow me."

His silent footsteps continued.

When I reached the front door to my apartment, I cracked the door open and made one last attempt to shoo away my new friend. "Time for you to go. Thanks again."

The ornery beast pushed past me, nosed the door open, and proceeded to make himself at home on the couch.

"Wait one mother-loving second. I did *not* invite you in here. You can't just move in without being asked. I don't even know if dogs are allowed under my lease." My flailing arms dropped to my sides.

The furry intruder simply stared at me, huffed, and lay his doggy head on the arm of my sofa. What was I supposed to do —drag him out? There was literally no way. It wasn't physically possible. Not to mention the dude was more than a little scary, and I didn't want to piss him off.

"Okay, maybe you're hungry." I dropped my things and grabbed some lunch meat out of the fridge. Waving the slices of turkey in the air, I stepped back outside. "Come on, big guy. Come eat. Don't you want some yummy food?"

No response. Not even a whimper.

I had to laugh at the absurdity of my situation. "All right. I'm in no position to argue." I came back inside, and almost instantly, my smile disappeared when my eyes landed on the kitchen table.

The tissue box coffin lay empty.

If the Brownie's family had come for him, I hoped they

knew how heroic the little man had been. He'd saved my life, and I wouldn't forget his sacrifice.

I lumbered upstairs to change with a heavy heart. The physical and emotional toll of my day had worn me down. The upside was that I had no fucks to give about my sex dream with Lochlan. Somewhere deep down, it still bothered me, but I was too exhausted to worry about what he'd think. I had focused all my mental powers on simply finding the energy to train. Ronan's attack was evidence enough that I couldn't skip a single lesson.

By the time I was ready to leave for the Huntsman, the dog was out cold. "Here's the deal," I offered reluctantly. "If I let you stay inside, you had better mind yourself. If I come back and find so much as a cracker out of place or a single thing chewed up, your ass is gone." I looked at him as sternly as I could with my hands on my hips. He stared back as though he knew my threat was entirely empty.

Rolling my eyes, I let myself out and prayed the giant beast wouldn't destroy my apartment. I caught a cab instead of walking. My nighttime strolls were at an end with Ronan on the loose. And the next time a dog ended up in the graveyard, Fergus was on his own.

"How DID you feel after yesterday's practice?" Lochlan asked after I'd warmed up and begun my workout.

"Fine. I thought I might be at least a little sore, but I wasn't."

"As a Fae, your muscle recovery rate will be significantly faster."

"*Ow!*" I had failed to block one of his strikes, and he tagged me right in the cheek again. While my body was in prime condition, my mind was distracted from Ronan's attack, and my performance with Lochlan was less than stellar.

"Pay attention. Where's your head tonight?" he chided.

"I *am* paying attention. You're the one talking to me about muscle fatigue and distracting me." I forced as much energy as I could into my next series of punches, angry with myself for making unnecessary mistakes.

"You have to be able to focus better than that. I shouldn't be able to touch you, no matter what I say. Get your hands up to guard and pay attention."

My frustrations peaked, and my sloppy form left my right side open to attack. Not one to go easy on me, Lochlan took full advantage and knocked me onto my ass. Again. Instead of jumping back up as I had each time before, I lay still and stared at the ceiling.

"Want to tell me what's going on?" He eased himself onto the mat next to me.

I was quiet for a moment before explaining. "Ronan showed up tonight."

He sat so still he could have been chiseled granite. "What happened?"

"He appeared out of nowhere, threatened me, then a dog attacked, and Ronan disappeared. That's the gist of it."

"You make it sound like a walk in the park."

"Graveyard."

"What?" he asked, confused.

I turned my face to his. "It happened in a graveyard."

I watched as Lochlan's eyes carefully scanned up and down every square inch of my body, most likely checking for signs that Ronan had harmed me. "Did anything else happen? Did he say anything?"

"*This is only the beginning,* and he said we'd be powerless against what's coming." I sighed deeply, my gaze turning back to the tiled ceiling.

"Come with me." Lochlan stood and pulled me to my feet.

"Should I grab my gear?"

"Yeah, we're done here. Training isn't going to do you any good if your head isn't in it."

He led me upstairs to his office and opened a desk drawer, pulling out a set of keys. "Take these. If you're going to be out after dark, you need a vehicle."

I stared at the Audi key fob blankly.

"You're giving me a car?"

"Don't you need one?" he asked gruffly.

"Yeah, but—" I shook my head.

Whenever this kind of thing happened in books and movies, which was the only place it ever happened, the heroine always refused. She claimed the gift was too much or didn't want to rely on someone else. I never did understand those women.

I needed a car. He was offering one free of charge.

Yes, please.

"Thanks, that would be a big help." I offered what I hoped was a grateful smile before awkwardness set in. I snagged the key from his hand. "It's been an incredibly long day, sooo I'm going to head out. I'll see you tomorrow." I waved, ignoring the hungry look in his eyes, and rushed for the elevator.

The Audi sports car was a sleek black piece of automotive artwork parked directly in front of the building. I wasn't a car girl, but I wasn't ignorant either. The car cost a small fortune.

My lips pulled back in a shit-eating grin as I slid behind the wheel. The supple black leather still had that new car smell. The dash was brilliantly lit, and every surface was the defini-tion of luxury.

She was a thing of beauty.

I had learned to drive a stick shift, thanks to my dad and the ancient Honda he had given me when I turned sixteen. However, driving a stick using my left hand on the wrong side of the road was an entirely different matter. I didn't exactly grind the gears, but it wasn't my most graceful performance. I stopped at a pet store to get dog food, then carefully made my way home, smiling the entire way.

CHAPTER

TWENTY-SEVEN

W HEN I WALKED INTO THE MUSEUM LOBBY THE NEXT MORNING, C AT was stationed at her post behind the visitor's desk. She didn't have to come to work until closer to opening, but she often preferred to get out of her house and away from her overbearing mother. Today, she was in even earlier than usual.

Cat's eyes lit with excitement the second she saw me. "*I did it!*" she squealed, racing around to the front of the desk. "I got you a drawing of the sword. I was so worried Mom would find me digging in her chest. I'm not ever allowed in there, and she doesn't know that I know where she hides the key, but I happened to see her put it away one time, years ago, and I've never forgotten."

"Slow down, Cat. You're going to pass out if you don't breathe."

She ran back to the desk and dug through her bag before triumphantly pulling out her phone. She thrust the phone at me to display the picture she had taken of an old drawing.

The length of the sword blade was embellished with ornate carvings. In contrast, the grip was surprisingly simple, drawn

277

in brown tones that aligned with Lochlan's description of a wooden handle. There was no guard, simply a bone-shaped grip possibly adorned with a jewel on each of the four nodules of the grip.

"Cat, this is amazing. Thank you so much. Text it to me so I can use it for reference."

My sweet friend beamed at me as she took back her phone. I started to thank my lucky stars that Cat and I were thrown together but decided it might be more appropriate to thank my Faery godfather instead. Ever since I'd been told about the oracle forecasting my arrival, I'd wondered if Merlin had been involved. All he would have needed to do was provide the oracle with a *vision* to kick-start my return to Ireland.

It made sense, especially if he was as powerful and crafty as Lochlan seemed to think.

If that was the case, he would have known I'd been planted smack in the middle of a Druid stronghold. He might not have been physically present since I'd arrived, but his influence was everywhere. I shouldn't have been surprised. If he had the foresight to give me the necklace twenty years ago, what more might he be capable of? I didn't want to know the answer.

When I reached the administrative offices on the top floor, Fergus was already working in his office. I gave a gentle tap on the door to catch his attention and smiled as he ushered me inside.

"Rebecca, good morning. What can I do for you?" He sat back in his desk chair, clasping his finely manicured hands over his crossed legs.

"I want to keep you and the others informed, and last night something happened."

He sat forward, his face growing serious. "Are you all right?"

"Yes, but when I went out to the graveyard after work, Ronan tried to attack me."

His already pale complexion became ghostly. *"Jesus, Mary.* I'm so sorry. I had no idea he was out there." He spoke quietly, his Scottish brogue thicker than usual.

"I didn't think you had anything to do with it. I just wanted you all to know, in case anyone thought Ronan might have fled, that he hasn't. He's still here somewhere in the city."

"Of course, I'll make sure the others know."

I nodded gratefully. "Actually, there is one other favor I might ask." I offered a tentative smile. "Could you teach me how to search for a particular artifact? How to track an item via auctions and whatnot?" I held my breath, knowing he would disapprove of my reasons for the request. The Druids had been very clear that they did not want the sword to be found and end up in Fae hands.

He sat for some time, assessing me through squinted eyes. He knew I was after the sword, and while I hadn't told him that was my purpose, he had to have guessed. "If I teach you how to do this, it would be for work purposes, would it not?"

"Yes, of course," I said, following his lead. I wasn't sure why he would help me against his people's wishes, but I wasn't going to question it.

"I would have no need to know if there was anything ... extracurricular you were wanting to search for." He tilted his head down, brow arched with implication.

"I'm sure I would only need the knowledge for work purposes—finding new exhibits and all." I held his gaze for a long moment before his chin dipped down.

"How about you put your things at your desk, and I'll show you a few methods."

I looked at my amazing boss and gave him a heartfelt smile. "Thank you, Fergus." My words were just a whisper before I quickly ducked out of his office.

An hour later, I had taken enough notes to write a book about artifact identification and was excited to try my hand at searching for the sword. Before we wrapped up the tutorial, Fergus imparted one final warning about ensuring that the sword did not find its way into the hands of the Fae. My stomach knotted in guilt at not telling him I was becoming Fae. I bundled up the useless emotion and tossed it on the growing pile. Hopefully, the ends would justify the means ... eventually.

I rushed back to my desk and began pulling up the sites that Fergus had demonstrated. For the next three hours, I completely abandoned my museum work and searched for the sword. I sorted through hundreds of images of swords that had traded hands through auction houses and other means over the past number of years. Either the blades were not embellished, or the grip was not wood, or the sword was so tarnished and decayed it would not have been of use.

On a whim, I began to search for replica swords. My thought was perhaps if the Sword of Light had been in pristine condition, it could have been confused with a modern production of an antique sword. I knew how paintings were authenticated, but I wasn't sure how a collector would authenticate a sword, especially if that sword contained magic that kept it like new.

As the clock crept toward noon, I clicked on an entry at the British Museum in London for a sword stored in the archives. My heart began to pound as I grabbed my phone and pulled up the picture Cat had taken. The rendering was identical to the sword at the museum. I took a picture of the sword and all its information before jumping up and doing a silent happy dance.

For the rest of the afternoon, I was practically giddy in anticipation of showing Lochlan what I had found. I hunkered down to tackle the work that I had ignored all morning. Before I knew it, the museum was closing, and it was time to go home.

Stepping outside, I found my new furry protector lounging on the cool stone steps of the museum entrance. I'd let him out of the house each morning, and he'd followed me to work. I kept thinking he'd eventually disappear, but I should have known better.

Apparently, the dog had claimed me, so I figured he needed a name.

"For your bravery in the heat of battle, I hereby dub you Sir Knight, the Protector, but that's a mouthful, so we'll stick with Knight for short." I gave his head a rub before turning in the direction of home, knowing he wouldn't be far behind me. He stretched out his long body and slowly ambled after me.

Once we were home, I changed my clothes and offered him some dog food. "Come on, you goofball." I fussed at the pouting dog. "This is quality dog food. You'll like it. Just look at the happy dog on the bag—he's loving it."

Knight sat on his haunches, giving me the best puppy-dog eyes a wolf could muster.

"Fine! You win." I grimaced at the unsavory odor of the hard food and tossed it back into the bag. "Guess I wouldn't want to eat that stuff either."

He had steadfastly refused to take a single bite of the dog food since I had brought it home two days before. Instead, he devoured my leftovers and had a particular affinity for sand-wiches. I slapped together a peanut butter sandwich, and he downed it in one bite.

I figured he had saved my ass, so the least I could do was feed him what he liked to eat.

THE SECOND I saw Lochlan waiting for me in the Huntsman lobby, I grabbed my phone and opened it to the picture of the sword. "Take a look at what I found. It's at the British Museum —so close!" I wore a smug smile on my face, and I didn't care one bit. I had managed to locate what the mighty Hunt had not yet found, and I was going to revel in that accomplishment.

"Care to tell me how you knew what you were looking for?"

Oh, shit.

"Um ... no?"

His assessing gaze held my eyes for a long moment in the elevator before acquiescing with a single nod. "I'll look into it, make sure it's authentic."

I grinned.

When we approached the door to the basement, instead of pressing his hand to the scanner, Lochlan pressed a series of buttons. "Put your hand here and hold it until the beep."

"You're adding me to the security system?"

"I'd move you in if you'd let me."

I swallowed uncomfortably, unsure how to respond. I'd been actively avoiding thoughts of Lochlan since the discovery of the sex dream, which hadn't been hard, considering all the other crap that had happened. Now that the subject had resurfaced, it didn't feel quite so repugnant.

"I suppose it's not out of the question," I said softly. "Let me think about it, okay?"

"My offers don't come with expirations, Rebecca. Not where you're concerned." He walked into the gym, leaving me reeling at his words.

This man was going to be the death of me. Brutish and gruff one minute, tender and compassionate the next. He was sexy as hell and protective. Intelligent and courageous. And from everything I'd seen, he was honorable.

The only thing he wasn't was human, and I was starting to doubt that it mattered.

CHAPTER
TWENTY-EIGHT

THE NEXT AFTERNOON, I WAS AT WORK WHEN AN UNFAMILIAR DING sounded from inside my desk. I opened the bottom drawer and pulled my cell phone out of my purse but found no missed calls and no missed texts. I hadn't set any alarms and wondered where the sound had come from when I remembered the burner cell that Lochlan had given me. I flipped open the phone that had been buried at the bottom of my bag.

Lochlan: We leave for London on Saturday.

London. That must mean he believed the sword was authentic. He was going to retrieve it from the British Museum, and he was taking me with him.

I'd done it. I'd located the legendary sword Excalibur.

I shot out of my chair with excitement, then froze as a barrage of questions hit me. How the hell would we get it from the museum? Was he planning to steal it? He might not be scared of the human government, but I had no desire to end up in prison.

Images of the Fae glamours I'd seen since arriving filtered

through my mind, including the convincing glamour Ronan had used to trick me. Considering what Lochlan could probably do with his magic, why was I worried? He'd be long gone before museum officials had any idea the sword was missing. And besides, we needed the damn sword. A war was coming, right?

Exhilarated at the prospect of finally making progress, I tore off toward the elevator to share the news with Cat.

"*I found it!*" I whisper-yelled as I hurried toward her desk. "I wasn't sure at first, but Lochlan checked it out and says we're leaving Saturday for London to get it from the museum. It's there. It's really there!" I handed her my phone displaying the photo of the sword at the British Museum.

"Is this what I think it is?" Her eyes rounded as she examined the picture inches from her face.

"The Sword of Light—I found it." My excitement faltered when Cat raised her eyes to mine.

"You're going with Lochlan? Rebecca, you can't let them have the sword! Helping you is one thing but putting the sword in their hands is another. I can't even imagine what my family would do if they learned I had helped the Hunt get that sword." Panic swept over her features, and that nagging sense of guilt was back like a stray cat I couldn't escape.

"They won't hurt you or your family, Cat. I promise."

"You can't know that." Her cheeks grew flushed, and anger sharpened her voice.

I reached my hand out to touch hers and met her eyes earnestly. "Please don't be upset. There are bad people out there who need to be stopped. If we don't find a way to stop them, the whole world may be at risk. I know we haven't known each other long, but please try to trust that I won't put you in danger."

Her eyes searched mine for a long moment before she let out a reluctant sigh. "I better get back to work," she mumbled defeatedly.

As she walked back to the visitors' desk, I said a little prayer that my decisions didn't come back to bite me in the ass. If Cat or her family were hurt because of my actions, I would never forgive myself.

LOCHLAN SAT WAITING for me on my front steps when I arrived home that evening. His elbows rested on his knees with his hands clasped as if he'd been waiting a while. I was instantly reminded of Ronan.

A bolt of panic shot through my veins.

This could be Ronan playing tricks on me again. I was wearing my necklace, but what if he'd found a way to overcome my limited magic?

I froze in place and concentrated on the man before me. There was no double vision and no signs of deceit. Just Lochlan sitting with his brows drawn in confusion.

"There something I need to know?" he asked warily.

There was one surefire way to know if this was *really* Lochlan. I charged forward and leaned down, bringing my face a hair's breadth away from his neck and inhaling a lungful of forest and sky and man. Not a hint of cologne.

I stepped back unsteadily, somewhat dizzy from the heady rush of his scent. "No, everything's fine." I flashed an awkward grin.

"Right," he murmured, eyeing me skeptically. "And I suppose I should ignore the fact that something in your apartment is growling?"

"Oh! That's just my dog." The overgrown oaf had refused to

vacate my sofa when I left for work that morning, so he'd been stuck inside all day.

"Dog?" He crooked an eyebrow.

"Yeah, my dog."

He continued to study me. "The one from the graveyard?"

"That's the one." I nodded.

He shook his head and unfolded his long legs to stand. "You need to pack and be ready to leave for London in thirty minutes. I have to run to the club, but I'll be back to pick you up." He walked past me and started toward his car.

"I thought we were leaving tomorrow."

He never stopped or turned around, simply called over his shoulder, "I didn't want to broadcast my plans in the event there's still a leak. We get the sword tonight."

"What if I have plans tonight?" I asked, still a little freaked about going.

He finally looked back at me, eyes narrowed. "Cancel them." He lithely slipped into the driver's seat then pulled into traffic.

I stood dumbfounded until a whine on the other side of the door caught my attention.

"Oh, Knight! I'm so sorry!" I opened the door for the giant dog who bounded outside. "I bet you're starving. Go do your business, and I'll get you some dinner." Leaving the door open, I set my things on the kitchen table and threw together a turkey and cheese sandwich. I cut it diagonally, and with a piece in each hand, I returned to the front steps.

The mountain of white fur trotted to me and sat, eagerly awaiting his dinner. I lay my hand flat with half the sandwich on top. He downed it in a single swallow.

"And that's why I cut these things in half. Do you even have a chance to taste what you're eating?"

His concentration was entirely devoted to my other hand, which held the remaining half of his dinner.

"All right, here you go." I turned over the last of the sandwich, then brought out a bowl of water. My giant protector slurped down gulp after gulp, tail wagging.

"I have to head out of town. I'm not sure when I'll be back, so you're going to have to be on your own for a bit. I'll leave your water outside and put a bowl of dog food out for you. Not that you'll eat it, but it'll make me feel better."

He padded to the garden wall and plopped down against the brick with a loud sigh. I rubbed his head before hurrying inside to change and pack my things. I tore through the house and packed in record time because I wasn't sure when Lochlan would return. By the time I stepped back outside, Knight was gone.

I texted Ashley while I waited but got no response. When Lochlan pulled up to the curb, I threw my phone back in my bag and jogged to the passenger door of a fancy black Land Cruiser SUV.

"New car?" I asked after taking a deep breath of the new car smell.

"Not really."

"How many cars do you have?"

"A few."

"Must be nice," I mused wryly.

The corners of his lips twitched.

Neither of us spoke again on the short ride to the airport. Instead of driving us to the main entrance, he cut around to the back and pulled up next to a large metal building near a sleek white jet.

"We're taking a private jet?" I asked in astonishment.

He opened the driver's side door, but I sat motionless. He

peered back at the plane. "The Hunt has been around for centuries. Longevity affords you the ability to amass a number of assets."

"You didn't just charter the jet. You *own* it?" I gawked out the window while Lochlan exited the car and walked to greet a man in a pilot's uniform.

In the three weeks I had known about the Hunt, their wealth had never crossed my mind. Now that it had been brought to my attention, what Lochlan said made sense. They'd never been flashy with their money. I wondered if that was intentional or if money meant little once you'd had it for so long. And why bother operating a nightclub if they didn't need the money? Was it just a way to kill time? I loved working at the museum, but if I didn't have to work, there was a world of things I would rather do than sit at a desk.

I snapped to attention and hurried to Lochlan's side when he waved me over to get on the plane. The interior was all soft creams and warm wood tones. The understated elegance stole the breath from my lungs. A set of leather chairs faced one another with a glossy wood veneer table between them. Across the aisle was a full-sized leather couch fit into the curved wall of the cabin. Past that was another set of four leather chairs, the entrance to a bathroom, and a closed door to whatever was at the back of the plane.

We each took a leather chair across from one another while the pilot got to work in the cockpit. My fingers raked over the soft leather as my eyes continued to examine every square inch of the opulence.

I would never be able to fly commercial again without feeling like a cow in a cattle car.

"Is this your first time on a small craft?" Lochlan asked.

His words startled me out of my musings, and when my

eyes flew to his, the amusement in his gaze sent tingles swarming deep in my belly.

"Yeah, I've only ever flown commercial, and coach at that."

"But you've traveled before?"

"Oh, yeah. My parents, Mom especially, love to travel. Being away from home was easier for her than being reminded of things ... problems and responsibilities," I added hastily. I wasn't opposed to telling Lochlan about my family, but this didn't feel like the right time. "I thought her love for travel was what had inspired me to take the job here, but I guess I was wrong. I was wrong about a lot of things."

He paused before responding, his deep blue eyes intent and meaningful. "You're still you, you know. Becoming Fae doesn't mean you become a different person."

Damn, he was perceptive.

He'd picked up on one of my biggest fears. I appreciated his reassurance, but I still had doubts. The necklace had changed me in so many ways. "When I was a little girl, I had blond hair and hazel eyes. Not until I got this necklace did my coloring change. I've learned of so many subtle ways I've changed that I can't be sure how extensive its influence has been."

"Not removing a necklace and drawing you to Ireland is a far cry from changing your personality," he pointed out.

"That's true, but with so many changes and so much uncertainty, it's hard for me to feel confident about much of anything."

"Yet look at how far you've come." His softly spoken words filled my heart like hot apple cider on a cool winter day.

I couldn't respond past the lump in my throat, but I didn't have to. He took the newspaper off the table between us and flicked it open, allowing me a pass.

The flight only took about an hour. I spent most of that

time wondering what would happen at the museum and enjoying a companionable silence with Lochlan. Once we landed, a black sedan with heavily tinted windows waited for us at the small private airport in the outskirts of London. Lochlan spoke with the driver, then we were off.

"I still have no idea what the plan is. How exactly are you supposed to get the sword out of the museum?"

"*We* will go in and take it."

"We?"

"Yes, *we*."

"But how am I supposed to help save the world if I'm locked up in jail for breaking and entering?"

Lochlan shot me a look from the corner of his eyes. "I won't let you get arrested. Have a little faith."

"Faith isn't really my strong suit," I muttered.

"So I've gathered."

I found little assurance in his words, but there was no point in arguing with him. "Do you know where the sword is being kept?"

"We obtained the museum schematics, archive location, and the type of alarm system. Not that any of it is crucial, but we try to stir up as little trouble as possible."

"What happens if there's trouble?"

He assessed me for a long minute before twisting to face me. "Rebecca, I'm not going to abandon you. The sword is important, but *you* are my priority."

My heart took an enormous jump off the diving board and leaped straight into the deep end. If I didn't get control of myself, I would be in very, very big trouble.

I nodded, deciding it would be best to keep quiet from now on.

The closer we got to the museum, the more anxiety

churned my stomach. By the time we arrived at close to midnight, I had chewed my nails to the quick and was ready to heave on the sidewalk. I had seen Lochlan unlock a door with magic, so that wasn't a concern, but I had no idea how he planned to circumvent the museum alarm system, not to mention the cameras and security guards.

He instructed our driver to park a block from the building, then directed me around to the back by a loading dock. Swinging his black backpack around, he pulled out a small electronic device with several wires attached. Once he had his tools in hand and was ready, his eyes met mine.

Here goes everything.

I wiped my sweaty palms against my thighs and gave a single nod.

Lochlan opened the door, then quickly stepped inside, holding the device up to the alarm panel. The characteristic beeping that normally sounded when an armed door was opened never chirped. The light on the panel glowed green, and we were met with chilling silence.

"Was it a silent alarm?" I whispered at his back.

"It would have been had the alarm been armed."

"Could workers still be here?"

It wasn't impossible, but the chances were slim. Museums housed countless priceless works of art. Even if an employee had stayed late or there'd been an after-hours event, certain portions of the security system would have been armed.

The tension creeping into Lochlan's shoulders told me he understood the implications as well.

We walked silently toward a back stairwell, me following his lead down the dimly lit corridor. As we neared the bottom of the stairs, Lochlan froze. I wondered what had stopped him until I heard a barely audible shuffling noise, then caught sight of a light flash from the basement hallway.

Lochlan's form visibly relaxed before he continued around the corner, and we were met by a woman and two men in all black. Our appearance caught them off guard, but they quickly pulled out weapons and settled into defensive stances.

Holy crap.

What were the chances that someone else was robbing the museum the same night as us? It was absurd.

"You will turn around and go home, and you will not remember anything about this night." Lochlan's voice resonated in my ears and made the hairs on my neck stand at attention. Magic. He had infused his voice with a magical command.

"It's not gonna work on us, but it was a nice try," quipped one of the men in a self-satisfied tone.

Double crap.

They were Druids, and they were outing themselves in front of Lochlan! I didn't think they were in danger, but I didn't want Cat or any of the others to think I had anything to do with the Hunt learning that the Druids still existed.

"That's too bad. I don't think you'll like the alternative," Lochlan warned with an eerie calm.

Unaffected by his menacing words, the man started to whisper a chant but was cut off as the woman in their group grabbed his arm in alarm. "This was not the plan. You know we can't. Let's go, *now*," she pleaded in earnest, but her efforts were wasted.

The man's eyes were lusty for a fight, and there was no way he was going to back down. "Once we have the sword, we won't have to live in hiding anymore. We can defend ourselves against their filth." He spat the venomous words, the gleam in his eyes almost feral.

Unfazed, the woman continued. "You know that wasn't our purpose in retrieving the sword. It's for safety, not to wage war." Her face turned to mine briefly, and I could see panic and fear etched in her features.

These people were after the sword. There was only one way the Druids happened to come after the sword the same day I'd told Cat about its location. My friend had ratted me out.

I suppressed my disappointment and frustration. I needed to defuse the situation, and reckless emotions would only make things worse. I'd promised Cat my protection, and I wouldn't fail her, regardless of her transgressions.

I placed my hand on Lochlan's back and pulled myself close to his ear. "I need you to occupy them, but please don't hurt them. I'll get the sword."

He never took his eyes from the Druids. "It's in the archives room behind us, bin E25." A blast of energy erupted from his hands, but the Druid leader crossed his arms and somehow deflected the attack.

The second man, who had remained a silent observer throughout, lifted his arm to reveal a small pistol. I watched in horror as he pulled the trigger. Lochlan's shoulder flung back with the impact. I cried out and lurched forward, wanting to help him. I'd seen him take two arrows to the chest and knew he was tough, but he wasn't invincible. He'd told me himself.

"Go, Becca. *Now!*" he ordered harshly, murder in his eyes.

"Please, don't kill them," I pleaded.

"You had better bloody well hurry before my patience runs out."

He sent another vicious blast in their direction. The two men stood their ground, but the woman fell back and disappeared around the corner. I raced down the parallel hall, reading the labels on each door I passed until I came to the archive room. When I bounded inside, the woman screeched to a halt in the opposite doorway.

Our eyes locked in a moment of surprise.

The room was filled with floor-to-ceiling rows of metal shelving, each full of white plastic bins labeled with a combination of letters and numbers. In my peripheral vision, I could just see inside the lower bins containing unique artifacts or collections of similar pieces. I decided to ignore the woman. She wouldn't be an issue if I could get to the sword first.

We both darted for the shelves at the same time, and when we met in the middle at E25, the woman swung her fist at my face. I ducked just in time but wasn't quick enough to avoid her uppercut to my gut. Her strike must have been bolstered by magic because it sent me flying backward, gasping for breath.

I attempted to suck air into my burning lungs while the woman pulled down a large white bin from an upper shelf. She lifted the sword into her hands, her face alight with reverence.

I couldn't let her take it.

An angry growl echoed from down the hallway. Lochlan was struggling. Had I not asked him to go easy on the Druids, we'd already have the sword and be on our way to the car. I couldn't be the reason this mission failed. I was here to help, not hinder.

Rising to my feet, I began to chant in my head, desperately calling on whatever magic I could pull forth.

IneedtohideIneedtohideIneedtohide.

A tingling energy danced beneath my skin. When I looked for my reflection on the side of the metal shelving, there was nothing.

No arms, no legs, no body.

Nobody.

I was invisible.

"You're Fae, too," the woman breathed. She stared in shock, the sword held precariously in her hands.

Seizing the opportunity, I ripped the sword from her grip. It instantly disappeared from her sight, drawing a desperate cry from the woman. I tore past her into the hall and raced for Lochlan. She chased after me, but with no visible target, her pursuit was limited.

"She has the sword! Stop her!" she screamed from behind me.

I rushed to Lochlan's side. "Let's go!" I grabbed his arm to tug him away without thinking about my invisibility. He responded on instinct to the unexpected touch and nearly leveled me with his fist.

"*It's me!*" I cried. "Let's get out of here."

He turned back toward the Druids and sent one final blast their direction that leveled both to the floor. We took advantage of their brief incapacity and rushed up the stairs, down another hallway, and eventually ended up back out on the loading dock.

"This would be a lot easier if I could see you," Lochlan barked over his shoulder.

"I don't know how to control it yet. It should stop once I calm down." My words came out between pants as we raced down the sidewalk, trying to stay in the shadows. The Druids shouted at one another as they exited the museum, but they were too late. We barreled into the car and were back on the road before they figured out where we'd gone.

I sucked in deep breaths, working to slow my labored breathing, then inched closer to Lochlan to examine his ravaged shoulder. "The bullet's still in there."

"Yeah, and it's iron. Bastards shot me with an iron bullet." He appeared unaffected, but the tightness in his voice told me he was in more pain than he was letting on.

"Is there anything I can do?"

"There's a first-aid kit on the plane. That'll work until we get back to Belfast."

I glanced at the driver, who could hear everything we were saying. He didn't seem bothered about what we'd done or the fact that Lochlan was bleeding all over his back seat.

"He won't remember any of this," Lochlan explained without any prompting. "And don't worry, he'll be paid well for his trouble."

The remainder of the car ride was spent in silence. Not until we were on the plane and in the air did Lochlan speak again. "In the bathroom cabinet under the sink, there's a first-aid kit. Bring it to me." His breathing had become shallow and strained, scaring me more than I cared to admit.

I did as he instructed. When I returned, I found him lying on his back on the couch, shirt removed and wadded under his injured shoulder.

"Get out the alcohol and pour it on the wound."

I kneeled beside him and chewed on the inside of my cheek. "Are you sure you don't want to wait until we're back home where there are drugs? And maybe a professional?"

His gaze raked over my face, those blue depths turbulent and unstable. "Need to do it now. I don't want any traces of iron left in me when this is done." He brought his hand to my face and trailed the back of his fingers along my jaw in a caress that made me forget how to breathe.

You got the sword, his eyes said proudly.

My chin quivered. *Thank you for sparing them.*

The ever-present magnetic pull between us intensified, and I found myself lowering my lips to his. The kiss was lingering and full of reverence. Its emotional depth was so intense that I kept my eyes averted when I finally pulled away.

"Okay, let's get this cleaned out."

I schooled myself for what I had to do and lifted the bottle above his wound. When the clear liquid poured onto his marred flesh, his teeth gnashed together, and he let out a ragged hiss. I held a hand towel next to the wound, and he rolled himself just enough to pour the fluid back out of the hole, staining the towel red.

When he lay flat again, he released a shaky, exhausted breath and closed his eyes. He lay so still that I started to worry that something was wrong. I scooted closer and verified that he was still breathing and was most likely passed out. That was probably best. No reason to suffer through the pain if he didn't have to.

The sword lay on the ground not far from me. It was the most magnificent thing I had ever seen. I could understand why the museum staff had thought it a replica. Nothing as old as the Sword of Light could have been in such pristine condition as this masterpiece of craftsmanship was—not without the aid of magic. The blade gleamed between sections of swirled carvings, and the wooden handle was smooth with wear but still had a well-oiled shine. Even the two stones on either end of the grip glimmered brilliantly in the airplane lighting.

I slowly extended my hand to touch one of the red gems, each the size of a dime. From there, I took hold of the grip. My hand felt home there, but even more surprising was the discovery that I could feel the sword's presence. As though the sword had a sentience—a magical essence distinct unto itself.

When I had killed the Red Cap by pushing darkness into him, the magic almost felt tangible, like an extension of me that I had pushed inside the creature. In that instance, I had forced my magic inside another being, but in this case, I could feel the sword's magic calling out to connect with my own.

On a series of deep breaths, I relaxed myself both inside and out. I felt as if a shield I hadn't known I possessed slid to the side and allowed the two magics to connect. In the same instance, the sword pulsed with light.

My lungs emptied on a gasp, and my mouth dropped open from the wonder and delight of the sensation.

"You obviously have Seelie magic—the sword can be handled by anyone but would only glow like that when used by someone who possesses light magic. But you can do things the rest of us can't. Things connected with dark magic. Have you been able to learn anything more about what you might be?" Lochlan lay still, but he had cracked his eyes open a sliver.

I shook my head slowly. "You said yourself I was becoming Fae. What do you mean 'what you might be?'"

"Certain Seelie and Unseelie can trace, jumping from one location to another. Shadow Fae can dissolve into smoky shadow. You became invisible in a lighted room. I've never seen another Fae accomplish that feat." He eased himself upright until he was sitting.

I set the sword back on the floor, my eyes avoiding him. "I wasn't sure I could make it happen, but from what had happened in the past, I was fairly certain I had the ability to become invisible. I've only been able to do it when I'm really upset."

"That's not all that uncommon for young Fae when they're learning to use their magic. Can I see the necklace?" he asked quietly.

My protective instincts toward the necklace made me flinch at his question, but I overruled the urge to flee and slowly joined him on the couch. He lifted the stone pendant from my chest, and I wondered if he could see my pulse skyrocket at his touch.

When he turned the pendant over, his brows nearly met in the middle as he studied the carving inlaid on the back. "It's not possible." His words were little more than a murmur.

"What's not possible?" Unease pulled the strings tight in my belly.

"These three crescent moons symbolize the dark magic of the Shadow Fae, and the circle in the middle represents the sun and light magic. This design indicates that the two types of magic have been somehow woven together in this pendant, but that's impossible. Light and dark magic are repellant—they can't coexist." His words started out casual but became more assertive by the end of his explanation.

"What about the sword, though?" I asked in confusion.

"What about it?"

"You said it's made of iron yet infused with light magic even though that should be impossible."

He stared at the pendant intently for a long moment. "Indeed. It would seem our friend Merlin has found a way to accomplish what was thought to be impossible." He let the pendant fall back to my chest, warm from his touch.

His features blanked as he sat back against the couch. "Why didn't you tell me about the design on the back?" His words were not accusatory, but I felt scrutinized under his hard gaze.

"I hadn't really thought about it. And in the beginning, I was worried if you and the Huntsmen decided you wanted the necklace, I'd be in even more danger."

He leaned his head back, closing his eyes. "And the Druids? I assume that's who they are. How much do they know?"

"I didn't know those people!" I assured him urgently.

"Yet you happened to ask about Druids not long ago. I don't believe in coincidences, and that would be a big one."

"You think I would sabotage my own breaking and entering escapade by telling a bunch of crazy Druids what we had planned?" I knew I was manipulating the truth a bit, but the intent behind my question was valid. I had not intended the Druids to show up and attempt to stop us.

"I know you're trusting, despite your best efforts to the contrary."

I had a sudden urge to poke him in the ribs and would have if he wasn't in so much pain. "I'm doing the best I can." I sounded a bit petulant, even to my own ears. I took a slow, steady breath and moved the conversation away from me and my shortcomings. "Now that we have the sword, what will you do with it?"

Without opening his eyes, he spoke through his fatigue. "I'll make certain the Hunt has no more traitors in our midst. We'll interrogate Ronan the second we catch him—or any other traitor for that matter." His injury rapidly depleted his energy stores, so he needed to rest.

I held off asking more questions and moved to a chair across the way. Pulling my knees into my chest, I reflected on where the evening had left us. We'd gotten the sword, but at the expense of the Hunt learning about the Druids. Not only that, but Lochlan seemed more convinced than ever that I was some type of mutant Fae. Was it not enough that I was becoming Fae? I had to be some sort of Fae mule—a magical cross-breed. It was just my luck.

The night sky outside the small oval window twinkled with distant stars. I concentrated on the constellations to help quiet my mind during the rest of the flight home. I could have gone over questions and what-ifs for hours, but none of it would do me any good.

To my great relief, two of Lochlan's fellow Huntsmen, Casek and Liam, met us at the airport. Lochlan needed help, and they would know what to do. Liam took Lochlan back to the club for treatment while Casek escorted me home.

When I walked up to my front steps, I found Knight

lounging placidly behind the garden wall in almost the exact same place I'd last seen him.

"Come on, boy. Let's go to bed," I called softly.

He got to his feet and followed me inside. On my way up the stairs to my bedroom, I texted Ashley again. She had never responded to my previous text, but I was too tired to put much energy into worrying. I took a quick shower to rinse the blood and grime off me and fell into bed exhausted.

CHAPTER

TWENTY-NINE

SATURDAY CAME AND WENT IN A SERIES OF NAPS, ONLY TO BE BROKEN up with periodic raids on the refrigerator. My batteries were in desperate need of a recharge, and mindless television between bouts of sleep was exactly what the doctor ordered.

I texted Ashley yet received no reply again. She really should have gotten back to me by now. We rarely took more than a day to respond to one another, mostly because we texted just about every day anyway. I didn't want to jump to any conclusions, but I started to worry.

On Sunday, I decided a phone call to Ashley was in order. Her phone rang seven times before voicemail picked up. It felt like an eternity between each ring, my stomach growing more and more sour with each unanswered tone.

Neither of us had any family in New York. Aside from a few friends, we had been on our own. I texted the few people who might have seen her, but none of them had heard from her in the past several days. Her office was closed for the weekend, so I planned to call the following day in the hope that I could track her down and settle my overactive imagination. I hated to contact the police if she had simply broken her phone and not had a chance to buy a new one. I would see what Monday brought and go from there.

Unfortunately, I would have to wait a good chunk of the day because of the five-hour time difference. New York wouldn't get its day started until we were well into the lunch hour. I decided to bite the bullet and use that time confronting what had happened at the museum.

"Cat, is Fergus in yet?" I asked upon entering the museum Monday morning.

"Yeah, he's in his office, I believe. Is something wrong?" Her features were pinched with concern, and a frown marred her freckled face.

While I hated to accuse my friend of anything, I had to know what had happened at the London museum. "Can you please come up with me to the offices? I'd like to talk to you both."

She gave a slight nod and followed me toward the elevator. Endless seconds ticked by as we rode up to the top floor shrouded in silence. We found Fergus working at his desk, a fast-tempo piano piece playing softly on the radio.

"Good morning, ladies," he offered congenially as we entered the office. "What can I do for you this morning?"

I gave him a tight smile and closed the office door. Cat and I sat across from Fergus, the strain in the room palpable.

"This weekend, I made a trip to the British Museum in London and came across some trouble." My eyes met Cat's, and my friend dropped her gaze to her lap. "Three Druids attempted to beat us to the sword. Lochlan was shot with an iron bullet, and we almost didn't leave the place alive."

Cat's eyes flew back to mine, her face pale. "Rebecca, you have to believe that I had no idea any of that would happen! I told my mom that you were going to get the sword, just so they would know you had it—not to stop you from getting it."

Fergus cleared his throat before cutting in. "I didn't know anything about your trip to London prior to Saturday," he offered slowly, fingers steepled in front of him. "However, after the events at the museum unfolded, there was quite the stir. From what I was told, either that necklace of yours has more powers than simply allowing you to see the Fae, or you yourself ... are Fae." He leaned back in his desk chair, hands still pressed together in front of him. "Is there something you need to tell us, Rebecca?"

The dynamic in the room quickly shifted as Cat gasped, and Fergus assessed me with curious eyes. After everything that had happened that night, I had completely forgotten about outing myself to the Druids. When I turned to Cat, she looked at me like I had just kicked her new puppy.

"Has everything you've said been a lie?" she asked shakily.

"No, Cat. What I told you and the others is the truth—the necklace I was given as a child has magic. I'm human ... or at least, I was. I didn't find out until a few days ago that the power had changed me. It's been a lot to process, and I didn't know how to tell you. You all have so much fear and hatred for the Fae. I didn't want you to feel that way toward me. I'm still *me*, and I'm still trying to stop a war from coming. None of that has changed." I'd been so worried about the changes in me that my ardent defense took me by surprise. Deep down, I did believe I was the same person. That the magic wasn't making me evil. The revelation was a tiny silver lining from our difficult conversation.

"You're going to be like them?" Cat asked, crestfallen.

"I'm going to be like me. I'll learn how to use my magic, and I've been learning how to fight, but I'm still *me*. Even where my magic is concerned, I'm not exactly like them. My necklace somehow has both light and dark magic combined, so my powers are unlike any other Fae." I paused for a moment and looked at both of them earnestly. "I promised that I wouldn't put you and your families in danger, and I take that promise seriously. I won't let anyone hurt you. I'm on your side. *Please* believe me."

Fergus let out a long sigh. "I don't think any of it matters now. With that damn Daeglan O'Connor going off to steal the sword without the approval of the elders, our existence has been exposed. One idiot goes off half-cocked, and centuries of secrecy are washed down the toilet. We'll just have to see what happens."

"The elders didn't send those three to get the sword?" I asked in confusion.

"No. Daeglan and his followers have always hated that we hide our abilities, but until now, they have respected the elders' wishes and maintained our secrecy. At the first mention of the sword, he was off to London under the delusion that possessing it would make secrecy unnecessary."

Cat cut in. "Daeglan and my mom are friends, but I had no idea he would do something so stupid."

"I'm extremely confident that you aren't in danger. I didn't want to tell you because I knew you wouldn't be happy about me bringing attention to the Druids, but I had asked Lochlan about whether they still existed. I never gave any indication that I'd encountered any—I simply asked under the guise of curiosity. He said the order to kill the Druids wasn't given by Guin, and that when she found out what had been done, she murdered the Erkling Odin for his actions. Odin claimed she had ordered the deaths, but it seems she didn't. Regardless of what happened back then, I don't believe anyone wishes the Druids harm at this point."

We all sat quietly for a moment, each mulling over the new

information we'd received until the loud ring of Fergus's office phone startled all three of us. With a nervous laugh, Fergus answered, and Cat and I quietly dismissed ourselves from the office. Instead of turning toward the elevator, she paused, and I could tell she had something on her mind.

"You know," she started warily. "I joke about my family being a cult, but there's some truth to it. I've been told all my life to fear the Fae, that they were capable of terrible things." Her sad eyes met mine, her mouth pulling down in a frown. "But I'm not scared of you, and I won't quit being your friend just because this has happened to you."

I pulled Cat into a tight hug. "You can't know how much that means to me," I whispered.

When she eventually pulled back, her eyes were glassy with unshed tears. "I'm so sorry that I put you in danger."

"You couldn't have known it would happen. I'm sorry I didn't tell you the whole truth about me. It's been a lot to process in a very short amount of time."

"We'll figure it out together." She squeezed my hand. "No more secrets?"

I grinned. "No more secrets." And I genuinely hoped that would be the case.

I CALLED Ashley's office that afternoon, hoping to track her down. The receptionist answered and informed me that Ashley was working from home because of her broken arm and was not expected back in the office for another week.

Apprehension filled my insides like a thick smoke, making it hard to breathe. Something was wrong, but what? Was she angry with me? Had she been hurt in a car accident? I could blame her silence on a broken phone, but something told me it was more than that. Maybe I was being silly, but I'd rather be silly than find out I did nothing when she was in trouble.

I looked up the New York police department phone number and called. I explained that I needed someone to check on my friend, and they promised a car would be sent around in the next hour. Aside from the police, I didn't know what else I could do, and the helplessness gnawed at me.

Pulling out my burner phone, I texted Lochlan, telling him about Ashley. I received a surprisingly quick text back, considering he'd told me he hated texting.

Lochlan: I'll have someone look into it immediately.

While I hadn't specifically asked for his help, I had hoped he could do something. Knowing I had the Hunt's resources on the matter helped me relax, but only a little. Until I heard from Ashley, I'd be plagued with worry.

CHAPTER

THIRTY

"ALL RIGHT, BUDDY. TIME FOR YOU TO GO OUTSIDE FOR A BIT."

The giant lump of fur didn't budge. Instead, he blinked his sad doggy eyes at me from where he lay sprawled on the couch. He'd been a welcome distraction from my worries when I'd come home from work, but it was time to train and find out if Lochlan had any information on Ashley. The police had called back to tell me her apartment was empty. The super had let them in, but there were no signs of a struggle. They told me to give it another twenty-four hours, then file a missing person report. I prayed the huntsmen were able to find out more.

"I know you're used to being outside, so don't look at me like that," I groused at Knight.

He sighed and rolled farther onto his side in protest.

"You are such a lazy bum! What did you do before you found me to mooch off? Yeah, I'm talking to you, which is really just talking to myself. *Ugh!* Fine, but you better not tear anything up while I'm gone, or I'm going to make a dog-skin rug out of you." I slammed the front door and hurried to the car.

309

The street in front of the Huntsman building was lined with parked cars. Seeing as I was not hugely comfortable with parallel parking on the wrong side of the road, I had to go farther than I would have liked to find a sufficiently large parking place.

I hadn't expected such a long walk, so I had only grabbed a hoodie instead of a warmer coat. Pulling my sleeves down over my hands, I wrapped my arms around my body and began to jog toward the building.

Two buildings away from my destination, I heard a muffled wail. The sound startled me, slowing my pace as I peered around to see where it had come from. I wasn't planning to jump in the middle of anything dangerous, but it was human nature to be curious in such a situation.

I stood still for a solid minute listening to the sounds of the vibrant city, but nothing struck me as out of the ordinary. Assuming it had probably been a stray cat, I ducked my head against the cold and hurried down the sidewalk. I didn't make it far before the noise came again, just behind me this time. I lurched to a stuttering halt as the blood in my veins turned to ice—this time, the wail had been followed by my name.

Even more terrifying, I recognized the voice.

It was Ashley.

I would know her voice anywhere, and she was in distress. Without hesitation, I raced in the direction of her cry. When I rounded the corner to the nearest alley, I stumbled to a stop.

"*No!*" The word was wrenched from my throat on a horrified gasp.

Twenty feet away, in the shadows of the narrow alley, Ronan held Ashley with a knife to her throat. Tears streamed down her battered face. One of her eyes was swollen shut, and her busted lip quivered in fear. Her arm was still in its cast from when we were attacked by a Draug in yet another Belfast alley.

This was the exact situation I'd desperately tried to avoid, yet all the secrecy and lies had been for nothing. Ashley was back in danger, and it was all because of me.

A barrage of emotions battered my insides.

My internal chaos ignited my powers, the surge lighting my skin on fire and shifting my eyes to black. Leaves and debris lifted into the turbulent air stirred up by my magic. I wouldn't allow another person I loved to die because of me. Ronan was depraved enough to kill Ashley, but I was powerful enough to stop him. I had to be. I was her only hope.

Ashley's jaw dropped in astonishment as she took in my Fae eyes. I hated that she was seeing me like that for the first time without any warning, but there was nothing I could do about it.

"Look at how much you've learned since I last saw you," Ronan crooned. "That necklace is truly miraculous. I'm going to need you to hand it over."

"Let her go. She has nothing to do with this," I growled back.

"I'd be happy to. That's why she's here, after all. You give me the necklace, and I'll happily hand your little friend over."

Shit. Fucking shit.

He'd known Ashley would be the perfect leverage. I'd hoped her location would keep her safe. I'd told myself my problems were contained to Ireland, but that wasn't the case. Ronan and this impending invasion were so much bigger, and I'd failed to embrace the magnitude of his threat. This was my fault, and I had to fix it at any cost.

Death would be an acceptable price to pay for her life because I wouldn't want to survive knowing I'd failed her.

I allowed my fears to melt like rain onto the frigid pavement.

"Take the knife from her throat, and I'll undo the necklace," I ordered calmly but forcefully.

His eyes sparked with madness. "Try anything, and I gut her," he warned, lowering the knife to her middle.

I did my best to ignore the sight of my best friend. Her bloodied and broken body eroded my composure, and I desperately needed to stay focused. Raising my hands to the back of my neck, I worked at the clasp and begged it to open, but there was no sign that it would comply.

If I couldn't get the necklace off or find a way to stop him, Ronan was going to kill Ashley. My chest fluttered with the threat of sobs.

I had to think. I had to get us out of this mess.

The only form of attack I had used previously was pushing darkness into the Red Cap. If I could repeat the trick, maybe I could get us out of there alive, but it would require me to get close enough to touch him.

An idea sparked a ray of hope.

I gave permission for my tears to fall. I let my face crumple with desperation and choked on my shaky breaths. "I can't get it. I swear I would give it to you. Please, don't hurt her. I'll take her place, and you can use your magic to take off the necklace. Just please, don't hurt her." I turned my back to him and lifted my hair to reveal my neck.

I prayed he would see my vulnerability.

I prayed his prowess as a Fae warrior would convince him I wasn't a threat.

He cursed angrily. Needing to be aware, I peered back and watched in horror as he slammed his fist into Ashley's temple. The impact made a sickening crunch before her body fell limply to the ground.

A rage-filled wail burst from my throat.

"Stay where you are," Ronan commanded.

I looked down and realized I lunged forward without thought.

I know you're scared, but you have to keep your wits. Ashley needs you to be smart.

My best friend was unconscious on the ground. It was terrifying, but at least he'd let her go. I would have to focus on the positives. This was my one chance to kill Ronan, so I couldn't waste it.

Commanding my body to remain still, I waited as Ronan approached. When he was close enough, the heavy scent of his cologne assaulted me. It was the same one he'd worn the night he tricked me into having sex with him.

My stomach seized tight, causing me to dry heave. To help hide the movement, I raised my arms and lifted the hair from my neck, praying he didn't decide removing my head was the easiest solution.

Thankfully, he directed his attentions to the magical clasp at the back of my neck. I took several deep breaths to quell my shaking, encouraged by his frustrated grunts. He took the necklace in two hands and pulled with all his might, but the chain didn't budge. When he released the chain to contemplate his next steps, I spun around with lightning speed I hadn't known I possessed.

My hands clamped down on either side of his face.

Almost immediately, the tendrils of darkness extended under his skin. Relief and exhilaration coursed through my veins. I'd done it! I'd made the magic happen on command.

For a split second, he stood stunned. His brown eyes were startled wide into a look of innocence that hinted at the sweet boy-next-door I had initially believed him to be. I wasn't fooled any longer.

Instead, I forced as much magic as I could into my attack, but unlike the Red Caps, Ronan was powerful. He managed to cast enough magic to fling me away with a guttural roar. My back slammed into a brick wall, but I didn't collapse to the ground. Unnatural energy held my arms and legs immobilized in a prone position. I was trapped and defenseless.

The crushing weight of my failure compressed my chest until my ribs threatened to crack.

Ronan bent over, gasping for breath several feet away. He held his face with shaking hands, the black veins still visible beneath his fingers. "*Fucking bitch*! You have no idea who you're up against. Morgan of the Lake has been plotting her uprising for centuries. Do you really think she's going to let *Merlin* and a pathetic human get in her way? The necklace may be spelled to stay on your neck, but that won't be a problem when I cut off your head," he spat viciously.

His ragged breathing calmed, and he stood tall, his eyes drawn to where my purse had emptied across the wet pavers. Among the discarded clutter was the black switchblade Lochlan had given me.

A bitter, viscous terror coated my insides.

Did he truly plan to hack off my head with a switchblade? Looking at the soulless gleam in his eyes gave me my answer. There wasn't a word for this brand of depravity. The Shadow Fae might be vicious, but Ronan was pure evil.

"Did Lochlan ever tell you that I was the one who gave him that pretty scar on his eyebrow?" he asked, clicking open the blade. "I've always had an affinity for knives, and thinking of him finding you sliced open with his own blade ... I think I'm getting a hard-on."

"Was any of this ever about me and the necklace, or has it always just been about Lochlan?" I asked, hoping to buy myself some time. His words and my vulnerable position terrified me, but every time I started to panic, I reminded myself that crying and begging wouldn't help me.

"Of course, it had nothing to do with *you*. At least, not in the beginning. Lochlan told us there was a part-Fae woman in Belfast, and I was intrigued. The more I learned, the more certain I was that you were a threat to Morgan. That your necklace might have the power to stop her. I can't let that happen. I owe her too much." He spoke matter-of-factly as he stepped slowly toward me. "But then I saw how Lochlan looked at you. How much he wanted you. Stealing you from him was just a bonus. Had you made the right decision and chosen me, I would have made you a queen." He shrugged nonchalantly, but his words were tinged in spite. "But killing you will also achieve my goal."

"You're wrong about Lochlan. He doesn't care for me as much as you think."

He slowly closed the distance between us, raised the knife, then sliced across my exposed wrists. His eyes stayed locked on my face the entire time, absorbing my fear with unabashed delight.

I cried out in pain. Blood poured from my opened wrists, dripping onto the pavement below. The sight brought on a vicious wave of dizziness.

It's okay, Bec. You heal quickly, remember? Try not to freak out.

My attempts at rational thought did little to calm my chaotic emotions, and bile burned at the back of my throat.

"Please don't do this. You don't have to kill me. Give me another chance to take it off." I pleaded with him hoarsely.

"I'm afraid I do. We can't have Merlin getting in our way. Once Morgan has the necklace, she'll be unstoppable." His eyes danced with excitement as they dropped to my neck.

He brought the knife up between us and tilted his head as if fascinated by the sticky red remnants of my wounds. His eyes then drifted to my throat again.

I couldn't get enough air.

Shallow breaths puffed from my dry lips, but oxygen escaped me.

How was this happening? Why couldn't I use magic and get myself free? I frantically tried to summon the swell of power I'd felt before, but all I could do was struggle in vain against the invisible bonds holding me prisoner.

My eyes clenched shut, my nostrils flaring.

I'm so sorry, Mom and Dad. I tried so hard to protect you. I'm so sorry...

The blade was icy cold as it sliced into my flesh and pulled seamlessly across the front of my neck. My eyes flew open in shock that it was really happening. Ronan was killing me.

My lips parted, and pain seared every nerve in my body.

Then Ronan dropped the blade and screamed, gripping his head in both hands.

I watched dazedly as he collapsed to his knees. My magical bindings evaporated once he became incapacitated, and I fell forward, stumbling away from him as far as I could manage.

Pounding footsteps closed in on us. Lochlan.

He looks so angry. Why's he so angry?

My thoughts were murky, emotions drowning in a rising sea of numbness.

All I could do was watch the scene unfold before me and try to grasp what was happening. Ronan and Lochlan fighting. Lochlan flung backward. A thud on the ground. Then he was gone. No, wait. He was behind Ronan, arm around his neck. Hard bodies blinked in and out of focus, appearing and disappearing. Arms swung, and bones cracked. They pounded each other with merciless aggression.

"You should keep a better watch on your pet," Ronan

goaded Lochlan. "As soon as she took off that necklace, she couldn't even see through a simple glamour." He grinned a blood-streaked smile. "It was priceless watching her realize that she had fucked *me* instead of you."

That was me. He was talking about me. It was my secret, and now Lochlan knew.

No! No, no, no, no ... My eyes closed, but no tears fell—I had no energy to cry.

Lochlan had gone motionless, and in the brief instant when his eyes cut over to me, Ronan made his move. He lunged at Lochlan, taking him to the ground and pouncing on top of him. Ronan landed blow after blow to Lochlan's face until Lochlan caught his fists, and the men grappled for control.

I had to stop this. I had to find a way.

I lay in a heap on the filthy ground. At least it was no longer cold to the touch. My head began to feel excruciatingly heavy, and darkness threatened my vision, but I strained to focus my eyes.

I was looking for something. What was it?

Then I spotted the black blade just out of my reach. Using all the energy I had left, I rolled myself over toward the knife. I took it in my numb fingers, then looked up at the fighters.

Lochlan flipped Ronan over his body with a kick from his strong legs, and Ronan flew into the wall, where he landed in a heap. He was too disoriented to trace but quickly began to regain his bearings.

"*Lochlan,*" I rasped.

His eyes flew to mine. I slid the knife across the pavement, and in one motion, he grabbed the handle and swept the blade up into the middle of Ronan's chest three times in quick succession.

Ronan staggered backward, his face contorted in shock and horror. He fell back against the brick wall, sliding down to his bottom. When his eyes rose to Lochlan's, a bloody smirk tugged at his lips. "Morgan is going to kill you all."

Lochlan lifted his booted foot and kicked Ronan square in the jaw, his body slumping to the side. Lochlan then pulled out his phone and hurried over to me. "I need you and as many of the men as you can gather in the alley next to Murphy's, *now!*" He dropped the phone and sank to his knees, where I lay on the ground.

"Stay with me, little warrior. Help is coming."

I hadn't remembered lying down, but his worried face peered at me with the night sky above him. Even bruised and bloody, he was beautiful. If I was going to die, at least his face was the last thing I'd see.

Dying—I was dying, and Ashley was hurt.

"Ash ..." The name left my lips on an exhale.

"*No!* No, you don't. Stay with me—*fuck!*" I could tell he was yelling, but his words sounded far away.

What I could hear was the thud of my heart as it slowed to a hobble.

Lochlan swept me into his arms, and the jostling rush of his frantic steps was the last thing I knew before the darkness took me.

CHAPTER

THIRTY-ONE

I drifted in a place where there was no time or space, experiencing periods of vague consciousness followed by nothingness. During my brief moments of awareness, regardless of how hard I tried to lift my eyelids, nothing moved. I swam in a thick ocean of sticky lethargy. I tried to pull myself from its grasp, but it held me prisoner, suspended like a fly in a web.

When I finally managed to open my eyes, I was met with more darkness. As I blinked away the misty remnants of sleep, my eyes slowly focused, and I scanned my foreign surroundings. I was tucked beneath the blankets of a large bed in a spacious, modern bedroom.

"It's good to see you awake."

I started at the gravelly voice to my right but quickly calmed as recognition dawned. Lochlan sat in a chair by a window covered with heavy drapes. He looked tired, bent at his waist with his elbows resting on his knees, and his hair uncharacteristically ruffled. His face was lifted just enough to see me. For me to see him. The cuts and bruises. Crusted blood and smeared dirt.

He and Ronan.

Fists pounding each other mercilessly.

"Ashley," I croaked, sitting up, then coughing uncontrollably from the discomfort in my throat. My hand raised to trace along the soft bandages wrapped thickly around my neck. I cringed at the reminder of how close I'd come to death.

For a long moment, Lochlan was quiet. "Becca, I'm so sorry..." His deep voice trailed off, leaving me in confusion.

"What are you sorry for? You couldn't have known Ronan would do what he did. Where's Ashley? I need to see her and explain."

He leveled me with a look of such profound sadness I stopped breathing. "She's alive," he said. "But she's not doing well. We took her to the hospital as quickly as we could. She suffered a bad head injury. The doctors don't think she's going to make it." He spoke the words softly, but nothing could have eased the blow.

Tears streamed down my cheeks.

I'd done it again. I'd killed someone I loved.

How could I ever forgive myself?

"It's not your fault, Rebecca." Lochlan was trying to soothe me, but his words had the opposite effect.

"Not my fault? How else could it be anyone else's fault?" I hissed. "The only reason she came to Belfast was *me*. The only reason Ronan took her was because of *me*." I threw off the covers and flung myself from the bed. "No matter how many times you or my mother try to tell me it wasn't my fault, I won't believe it because if it weren't for me, they'd both be alive. Don't you understand that? Ashley would be safely back in New York, and Callum would be—" My words snagged on a hitched breath. "Callum would be finishing college. He'd be a teacher or a doctor ... he'd be *alive*. My brother would be alive, and Ashley would be alive if it weren't for my *fucking* stupidity." I thumped my fist against my chest, tears and snot running down my face. As my rage ebbed, heaving sobs began to wrack my body.

My legs wobbled, but before my knees could hit the floor, Lochlan swept me into his arms. He sat us on the bed, cradling me in his lap. He didn't hush me or try to talk. He simply held me while I hiccupped and sobbed and wept until a cavernous emptiness filled my chest.

"I know you probably thought I was just scared all this time," I started in a hollow, rasping voice. "But it was more than that. I killed my infant brother when I was little. It was an accident, but that doesn't change anything. I caused my parents the ultimate grief, and I promised myself I'd never hurt them again. All I've ever wanted was to protect the people I love. There aren't many, but Ashley is one of them. And now, I have her blood on my hands as well." I lifted my head off his chest and searched the depths of his azure eyes. "Is there nothing you can do?"

His lips pressed tightly together. "Fae healers specialize in herbal treatments and the limited magic suited to mending injuries beyond our own powers to heal, but none are here on Earth. It would take time to retrieve someone, and in that time..." His lips thinned.

The implication was clear. Ashley didn't have that long.

"I need to see her," I rasped. "I don't want her to go through this alone."

"She's in intensive care, and the visiting hours are limited. I'll take you over there as soon you're allowed to see her."

Of course. Why should anything at this point be easy? I lifted my wrists and pulled one of the bandages up my arm. The skin beneath was nearly healed. "How long was I out?"

"It's two o'clock on Tuesday, so about fifteen hours."

"And Ronan ... is he dead?"

"We have him contained in the basement waiting to be interrogated." His voice was laced with a fury that simmered beneath the surface.

I nodded but couldn't seem to muster anything more. My heart was void of anything but pain—gratitude, relief, worry, fear—everything else was absent. In their place was a lake of pain, its water seeping into my nose and filling my lungs as I watched the surface fall farther and farther from my reach. Cold numbness was all that was left.

"I'm so sorry I didn't get to you sooner." His words were whispered into my hair as his arms gripped me tighter.

"How did you find us?"

"You're usually on time for training, so when seven came and went, I knew something was off. I checked our security cameras and saw your car parked on the street, so I went looking for you."

I could hear the sincere remorse in his voice, but no words came out to assure him it wasn't his fault. Nothing I said would change the fact that Ashley was dying. It didn't matter if we felt guilty or sad, or if we screamed until our vocal cords gave out. She was dying because I didn't do enough to keep her safe.

I deserved every ounce of my pain.

I deserved to live a long life and be reminded every day of the devastation I'd caused.

Aside from that, the best penance I could offer was to dedicate myself to stopping the Fae invasion. To protect as many other innocent lives as I could. Ronan might be contained, but this Morgan was still on the loose. I couldn't allow her to wage her war and bring about more death to the people around me.

I would not let Ashley's death be in vain.

I would dedicate myself to becoming a weapon—to doing whatever was necessary to stop these evil people.

I pulled back, scooting out of Lochlan's lap. "I'll move into the Huntsman."

He stilled, surprised at my shift in focus. Once he nodded that he understood, I took a folded pair of joggers off the dresser and slid them on, followed by a thick pair of athletic socks. It was time to see my best friend, visiting hours or not.

Walking into Ashley's room and seeing her hooked up to a ventilator, machines beeping, and her skin ashen shattered the icy shell restraining my emotions. My shaky legs carried me to the chair beside her bed, and I lowered myself with a shuttering sob. Heart-wrenching, guttural wails tore from my chest as I held her chilly, lifeless hand. I cried until my eyes were swollen, and my throat felt like it was bleeding, inside and out. I begged, and I pleaded, apologized, and swore—and none of it made any difference.

When I finally sat back in the chair, feeling hollow and numb, Lochlan stepped inside and stood against the far wall. "Her parents have been contacted and are on their way."

I sat motionless, eyes frozen on my best friend. Her straight blond hair, usually golden and shining, was straw-like and ratted. Her chest rose and fell in even intervals as the machine pumped oxygen into her lungs—the swelling in her brain prevented her from performing even the most basic life functions. She would never again tell me about a new book she had read or ask me what was for dinner because she was a terrible cook and couldn't make anything herself. No more rummaging through thrift shops or exchanging late-night texts. No more pedicures or movie nights.

"Visiting hours end in thirty minutes. I'll come get you then." Lochlan slipped from the room soundlessly.

I wasn't going anywhere unless they dragged me out kicking and screaming. Ashley was here because of me, and the least I could do was not leave her alone.

Time ticked on, yet it stood still in that small, sterile room. I kept her hand in mine.

Eventually, the air on the other side of the bed shimmered with magic as a man materialized. Merlin stood opposite me, his features wrought with sympathy. His white-blond hair was neatly styled, and the cutting edge of his ice-blue eyes was softened by a few wrinkles in the corners. He looked like any ordinary man, but I knew he was so much more.

He was the grand composer of the tragedy we'd been living.

Our eyes held each other for a long pregnant moment, long enough to further thaw my ravaged emotions. I had thought I would have nothing to say to this man who had set the events in motion that led me to the absolute lowest point in my life. However, seeing him stand before me, I had questions that needed answering.

"Why have you done this? Why me?" My voice was no more than a whisper.

"I spent years in that market, watching and interacting, knowing I had to find just the right child. Someone receptive to the magic. Someone who lived far away where Morgan wouldn't find them. Someone very special. When you approached my booth and were drawn instantly to the necklace, I knew you were the one."

"Did you know it would make me Fae?"

"I wasn't entirely sure, but I had my suspicions," he said evasively.

"Did you think about the other impacts on my life? The effect all this would have on my loved ones?"

"Nothing I say or do will ever ease the burden of what I have forced upon you. Some of us bear a disproportionate degree of hardship in life, whether owed to the circumstances of our birth or a course of events during our lifetime. There is never a reason adequate enough to justify our struggles. No explanation is sufficient to ease the burden. The only balm that will help you is that which comes from acceptance. The ability to embrace your circumstances and move forward. Once you let go of how you got to your current situation and look toward how you can improve your future station, then you will be enlightened in a way that is truly empowering.

"When I discovered what Morgan had planned and realized that I would be unable to stop her if I went about it alone, I knew that whoever was appointed to the task would bear a great weight upon their shoulders. That consideration was an important factor in my selection process. You possess the strength and constitution required to endure the necessary loss and strife that accompanies any great task. You have shouldered it before, and you will do so again." He motioned down at Ashley.

"I'm not so sure," I rasped past my constricted throat. "I feel like I'm being crushed under the weight of it all."

"The pressure and adversity are precisely what will mold you into the spectacular diamond you are becoming. Don't give up, Rebecca."

"You say I'll become a diamond, but what does that mean? Lochlan said the combination of dark and light powers is impossible, yet that's what I have. What am I becoming?"

"What I accomplished wasn't easy. Few are alive that could have even attempted it." Another evasive non-answer.

"That's what I hear, that you are exceptionally powerful.

Yet, for some reason, you need my help. You have this task you need me to perform—something you set in motion decades ago. And I have accepted that responsibility, more or less, without question. But now, I have one request in return. Try to heal my friend. I'll continue to fight against Morgan, learn my powers and continue to walk this new path that you have dictated for me, but I need to know that everything possible was done to save her. If you're so powerful, and you recognize all that I'm sacrificing, you will do this one thing for me." My words grew in strength as my convictions solidified.

Lochlan had said the Fae couldn't heal, but Merlin had already proven himself capable of miraculous feats. Why should healing Ashley be any different?

"Something so great cannot be done without a cost." His voice dropped low in warning.

"What would be worse than death? I'm pretty that's the ultimate cost, so whatever it is you're considering, do it, *please*." I urged.

He tipped his head once in my direction and then vanished for no more than thirty seconds before reappearing with a small dark vial in his hand.

I narrowed my eyes at him. "You can trace a whole lot farther than the others, can't you?"

His only response was the hint of a smile before he became somber again. "Are you sure you want to do this? It has never been tested, and I am not certain it will work."

"Is it going to make her a zombie or something?" I shook my head. "Forget it—anything is better than her dying. Just do it."

I wrung my hands nervously and watched as he uncorked the vial and removed Ashley's breathing tube, making one of the machines beep angrily. Merlin waved a hand, and the machine went silent. He then poured the clear, viscous contents into Ashley's open mouth.

I could feel my pulse thudding behind my eyeballs in the oppressive silence of her room. Activity from the hallway filtered in but felt miles away from our small bubble in time where I prayed a miracle would happen.

The stillness felt interminable. What if nothing happened? What if Ashley was well and truly lost?

I couldn't think like that. I had to hold out hope.

The warring thoughts in my head waged on until the heart-rate monitor that had been silently keeping time to Ashley's steady heartbeats began to accelerate. The line jumped up and down faster and faster on the monitor, and Ashley's limbs began to shake as if she was having a seizure. I looked up in question at Merlin, but he was gone.

That's when a single steady wail sounded from the machine. Ashley had flatlined.

Despair like I've never known clamped its vise-like grip around my heart.

Nurses tore into the room, one climbing on top of Ashley and starting chest compressions while others shouted words that didn't make sense to me. I stared at them helplessly, unsure what to do.

Was this supposed to happen? Was the elixir working, or was my best friend dying right in front of me?

My chest heaved for air that wouldn't fill my lungs. One of the nurses took my arm and pulled me outside the room. She went back in and closed the door, but I could still hear the chaos. I stood with my back against the wall in a haze as I listened to the frantic voices.

After about ten agonizing minutes, the room started to quiet before a man's voice called out, "Okay, we can stop resuscitations. Time?"

"Time of death 16:27," offered a female voice.

Slowly, the staff exited the room with faces drawn and shoulders drooping. The charge nurse stopped next to me on her way out of the room and wrapped her arm around my shoulders. "I'm so sorry, sweet girl. Would you like to go in and say goodbye?"

I opened my mouth, but no words came out.

On the second attempt, I managed a single breathy word. "Please."

The sterile room was heartbreakingly quiet. The machines had been turned off, and not even the harsh fluorescent lights dared to buzz as I sat down next to Ashley. I wove my trembling fingers with hers and held her lifeless hand.

She was gone.

It hadn't worked.

My chin quivered, and tears streaked down my face. "I'm so sorry, Ashley. I never meant for you to get pulled into this. I tried so hard to keep you safe." I trailed off with a sob.

Just as the pain dragged me under to a place deeper than I could manage, I felt a squeeze of my fingers.

My head shot up, eyes wide. I didn't blink or breathe or move a single muscle. When Ashley's eyelids started to flutter, I lunged for the nurse call button but was pulled up short at the sight of glowing blue eyes.

"*Ashley*," I gasped.

She blinked rapidly as she looked around the room in confusion, the glow in her eyes fading to her natural blue. "What's going on? Am I in a hospital?"

I shot forward and wrapped her in a tight hug, never wanting to let her go again. "Ashley, you're alive."

"Good grief, Becca. What's going on?" She pulled herself from my grasp and stared at me like I'd grown a third arm.

I sat on the bed, holding her hand in mine. "Do you remember anything about what happened?"

She scrunched her face in thought, and I could see the moment the memories resurfaced. Fear flashed in her eyes, and her jaw fell slightly open on a silent gasp. "Ronan ... he kidnapped me. I remember you and the alley, but that's about it."

"He hit you over the head, and Lochlan's men brought you here. The doctors said the swelling was too much. You weren't going to make it."

"But I feel fine." Her brow pinched with confusion.

"That's where things get a little crazy. You were dying, so I did the only thing I could do. I asked Merlin to save you."

"Merlin, as in the wizard? Honey, did you hit your head, too?"

"I didn't tell you about him. There's so much I didn't tell you, and I'm so sorry. I was trying to keep you safe, but it didn't work. Merlin is an ancient Fae—he's the one who gave me the necklace, and he was also the odd man I talked to in the museum my first day on the job." I paused, gathering my courage to tell her what I had done. "Ash, I told him to save you, and in order to do that, I think he made you Fae."

Her head tilted to the side. "What are you talking about? How would he make me Fae?"

"I don't know exactly. He made you drink something, and then the machines went crazy. The doctors tried to save you, but you died. I didn't know it had worked, but then you woke up, and when you opened your eyes ... they glowed."

"Are you shitting me?" she exclaimed, sitting tall in the bed.

"I wish I was. Do you remember how you got back to Ireland?"

She swallowed hard. "I had dinner and drinks with a friend

from work. The restaurant wasn't far from home, so I walked. It wasn't particularly late, just around nine o'clock. A block from our place, someone called my name out. When I turned to see who it was, Ronan stood by a building not far from me. I was surprised to see him, and my first thought was that something had happened to you, so I hurried over to him to find out what was wrong. Before I even got a word out, he was behind me with his hand over my mouth. He tugged me down into a basement stairwell and said such awful things." Her eyes filled with tears as they met mine. "I woke up to him kicking me and discovered I had been brought back to Ireland. I had no idea what was happening. Why would he do those things?"

I reached over and put my hand on hers. "He was an awful man, but he won't hurt either of us again. I want to tell you everything that's happened, but we have to get out of here first."

"If they think I'm dead, how are we supposed to do that?" She swung her legs over the edge of the bed.

"I think we're going to need help with this." I pulled out my phone and texted Lochlan.

When he entered the room, he froze. "Fucking *Christ*, she's Fae. What the fuck happened in here?"

"We don't have time to explain it all. Essentially, Merlin showed up, and I begged him to help. He gave her something to drink, and she died, the doctors left me to say goodbye, but then she woke up. Now we need to get out of here, so we need you to do your Jedi mind trick thing on them."

His head moved slowly side to side in bewilderment. "Every day is a fucking trip with you around."

First, Lochlan used his magical powers of persuasion to convince the staff of Ashley's miraculous recovery. On our way out, we stopped in orthopedics and had a nurse remove the cast from Ashley's arm. Then we were free. Lochlan drove us back to my apartment while Ashley called her parents to inform them of her returned health. I could hear her mother sob through the phone. Fortunately, they hadn't made it out of the country, and Ash convinced them to hold off on flying over. She made up an elaborate story to explain how she'd ended up back in Ireland and how the hospital had mistakenly called the wrong patient's family. Ash didn't get along with her mom, so she'd had years of practice being evasive.

"Should I pack a bag and go with you to the Huntsman?" I asked Lochlan quietly.

"Ronan's contained, so the threat is neutralized for the moment. I think you two can have one night to catch up before we tackle a move."

I grinned, grateful for his understanding and relieved that he thought we'd be safe.

At the apartment, Ashley changed out of her hospital gown, and we both curled up on the bed while I delved into a detailed explanation of everything that had happened to me. I told her about the necklace and my transformation. About Merlin and Ronan, the Red Cap attack, and my trip to Faery. As much as I hated to relive it, I told her about Ronan tricking me into sleeping with him, and she cried along with me. I told her about light and dark magic, the Shadow Court, and the war being waged by the woman named Morgan.

We spent hours catching up.

"This is crazy, Becca. We're both Fae. And I don't feel any different. My eyes glowed, but maybe that was just his magic leaving me. How can I know for sure?" Ashley asked once we had circled back around to discussing our transformation.

"I guess that's something we'll have to talk to the guys about. As soon as Lochlan came into your hospital room, he could sense that you were Fae, though. And I trust him. He knew the moment he saw me on the street that I was Fae."

"Trust, huh? A lot *has* changed." She grinned coyly.

I rolled my eyes. "With everything that's happened, *that's* what you choose to focus on?"

"Oh, I'm curious about all of it. Like my powers. If I'm Fae, shouldn't I have powers?"

"I would think so, but our transformations are unprecedented. Who knows how your powers will manifest or how long it will take."

"Awesome, nothing like being a living science experiment. You know how patient I am."

I bumped my shoulder against hers. "Yeah, but there's no one I'd rather be a science experiment with than you."

"Aw, Becca. You say the sweetest things."

We both giggled, and my heart fluttered with happiness at having my best friend back.

"All joking aside," I said, studying her. "How are you handling all of this?"

Ashley's fingers toyed with the blanket thrown over her legs as she thought. "You know I was a little jealous of you when I left. This kind of thing was sort of a dream of mine, but I know it's impossible to fully grasp all the implications. Clearly, there's an element of danger involved in the magical world. We'll just have to see how it all plays out."

"No kidding. At least you aren't being asked to stop a Fae invasion," I muttered.

"You don't think I went through all this just to let you fight this alone, do you? Because that's absurd. You and I are a package deal. Your fight is my fight."

"Ashley, I don't want you getting hurt."

"And how did that work out for you the last time? It didn't. I got sucked back in. Not to say it's your fault, just that I'm involved, no matter how much you hate it. I'm helping you any way I can, so don't try to fight me."

I gave her a tight smile. "It *is* my fault, and I'm sorry. But I'll admit it's really great to be able to talk to you about it all. Being secretive really sucked."

"You better not pull that shit again. My powers come in, and I will zap your ass if I catch you keeping secrets."

"You can try, but don't forget, I have powers of my own." I arched a brow at her in challenge, and we both collapsed in a fit of giggles.

What I said had been true. If I had to walk this road, there was no one I'd rather have at my side.

THIRTY-TWO

When the next morning rolled around, I felt better than I'd expected. It was hard to wrap my brain around how quickly I healed. And with Ashley alive and well, I was in a much better mental space than I'd been in weeks.

Today, we'd get ourselves moved into the Huntsman, and Ronan was going to be interrogated with the sword. We were making progress, and it felt great.

I texted Fergus, telling him that I needed to take the afternoon off and explained the move. After that, I texted Lochlan to let him know we'd be by sometime around three or four after I'd had a chance to pack. My morning at the museum passed quickly, consisting primarily of talking with Cat and Fergus. They insisted on breaking down every detail of Ronan's attack and Ashley's transformation. Now that they knew I was becoming Fae, there was no reason not to tell them everything. I didn't want them to have any doubt in their minds that we were on the same side.

Halfway through the morning, I had a surprise visit from Lochlan. He had never come to the museum before—Ronan had stopped by pretending to be Lochlan, but Lochlan himself had only ever appeared unannounced at my house. Despite knowing Ronan was no longer a threat, any deviation from the normal sounded my internal alarms. I tried to squelch the anxiety as best as I could.

"Is everything okay?" I asked, joining him in the museum atrium.

"I wanted you to know that it's over. Ronan won't ever hurt you or anyone again," he said softly. He'd asked after Ashley's recovery if I wanted to be part of the interrogation, but I'd declined. I trusted him to pass on whatever information he gathered, and I preferred to never set eyes on Ronan again.

"Did the sword work?"

"Yes. There are no other traitors in the Hunt, which is a relief. And he confirmed that he's been helping Morgan La Fey overthrow Queen Guinevere."

"Do you know anything else about Morgan?" I knew of her through legend, but we needed more than hearsay.

"She was Merlin's apprentice, and for centuries, we thought she was dead."

I thought back to the first time I talked with Merlin and realized I needed to reexamine that conversation. "I'd like to show you something if you have a minute." I led him upstairs to the painting of Morgan La Fey. The woman depicted was wearing silk robes and had curly dark hair flowing down her back. She appeared lost in the throes of casting a spell over a small cauldron filled with flames.

"The first time I talked to Merlin after coming to Belfast was here at the museum. He studied this painting for a long time and said something about the timing. Something about how the artist got that right. Does that mean anything to you?"

We both peered at the colorful canvas.

"No, I'm afraid not, but there's no telling with a man like Merlin."

I sighed heavily. "I don't understand why he didn't come out and tell me all this from the beginning. If he wanted to stop her, why keep us in the dark about who she was?"

"Merlin is a master of manipulation but not in a villainous way, per se. He's an expert at influencing people and events with the smallest touches. For whatever reason, he saw fit to simply lay hints for us to uncover rather than hand over a dossier."

"I'd say he's a pain in the ass," I muttered, turning back to the painting. "So Merlin is trying to stop his own apprentice? What happened? She get too powerful?"

"I don't know the full story, but their relationship is more complicated than that," he explained. "Morgan was the daughter of Merlin's longtime lover, Viviene, the original Lady of the Lake. She was a water nymph, and the two were madly in love. Merlin's twin sister, Mab, grew insanely jealous of Merlin's relationship with Viviene. She abducted Viviene and tortured the woman for years. By the time Merlin figured out who had taken Viviene and attempted to rescue her, it was too late. At the time, Morgan was still a child. Merlin raised her as his own, and she became his apprentice."

"And Merlin killed Mab, his own sister, because of Viviene, right?"

"Yes."

"So why does Morgan want to start a war? Is she just power hungry?"

"I don't believe so. Morgan's history with Guin goes back to when Arthur was the Erlking around 500 A.D. Merlin brought Morgan to the Seelie Court as a teen. While she was at the palace, she became infatuated with Lancelot, who was having an affair with Guin. When Guin's relationship with Lancelot was discovered, Arthur was enraged and exiled Lancelot from the Hunt. In an attempt to placate Arthur, Guin also snubbed Lancelot. He was forced to leave Faery and wander Earth. Morgan was devastated that Lancelot left and blamed both Arthur and Guin. My understanding from Alberich was that she'd become a recluse and had hidden herself away."

"Her anger toward Guin has been festering for centuries, and I'm supposed to stop her?"

His hand lifted to guide a wayward strand of my hair back behind my ear. "As crazy as it may sound, Merlin knows what he's doing. I believe that if anyone can do this, it's you."

I was speechless, both at his touch and his confidence. Lochlan was an incredible warrior. The fact that he believed in me was beyond humbling.

Before I regained use of my brain, Lochlan leaned in and placed a kiss on my forehead. "I have to go," he whispered against my skin. My eyes drifted shut, mesmerized by the feel of his soft touch, and when they reopened, Lochlan was gone.

I took a shaky breath and fought back a giddy grin.

"I thought he'd never leave," came a voice behind me.

"*Jesus!*" I gasped and spun around.

"No, although I have been called a god before." Merlin eyed me with a wry grin.

I crooked an eyebrow. "A god with a rogue apprentice."

"For reasons that Lochlan just explained, I owe Morgan in ways that I cannot describe. Plus, it goes against the nature of a parent to harm their child. Even if I had been able to overcome those obstacles, Morgan would have seen me coming and run. I'm more powerful than her, but she knows enough to keep well away from me. Our best chance is you, and I have done what I could to equip you for that challenge," he offered sagely.

"You say that, but I don't know what I'm doing. I don't have any idea how I'm supposed to stop her."

"Some things take time in order to unfold properly. Had I told you as a teen, before you had ever come here, that you were destined to fight a Faery sorceress, your life would not have unfolded as it did. Just because you explain complicated mathematics to a child doesn't mean they have the maturity or ability to use that knowledge. There is a natural timeline of events that must unfold, and even I cannot rush that continuum. As it so happens, you are ready for the next stage in your journey. Do you recall what I said about the painting?"

My gaze followed his back to the rendering of Morgan La Fey. "You said the painter got her passion correct and the timing, but we don't know what that means. There's a window with a sunset or sunrise in the background. Is that what you were referencing?"

His chest swelled with pride, and he tipped his head in a bow. "What you need to know is that between worlds, there is a little-known place called the Twilight Realm. Morgan is using that realm to open the portals and circumvent Guin's wards. As you have learned, there are two types of power, light and dark. The two cannot coexist in most circumstances. However, after many years of trial and error, I found a way to imbue your amulet with the essence of both a Light Fae and a Shadow Fae. They are woven together yet separate, allowing them to function together," he explained with a touch of self-satisfaction.

"That's why my powers are different from other Fae," I offered what we had already deduced.

"Yes. Morgan possesses light magic and uses a dark magic amulet and blood magic spells to combine the powers, but at a high cost. In theory, your combined powers should enable you to open a portal to the realm without the use of blood magic. But first, you must learn to wield those powers. Only then will you be able to access the Twilight Realm and face Morgan."

"What does that mean? We'll have an epic battle of magic, or are we talking hand-to-hand type fight?"

"As hard as it is to believe, I am not all-knowing," he said with a wry grin. "I've done what I can to get you access to Morgan. The rest will unfold however it must."

He started to turn away, but I reached out and took hold of his arm.

"Wait! No one knows how to teach me since my powers aren't the same as theirs. How am I supposed to learn without a teacher?" I asked in exasperation.

"Lochlan is working on that," he assured me.

"One more thing!" I called out as he again started to turn away. "What did you give Ashley?" She would have questions once she could wrap her mind around what had happened, and I wanted to get as many answers for her as I could.

His lips pursed together momentarily before he began to explain. "In order to gather the essence of a light and a dark Fae, I had to learn how to extract and store Fae essence, or magical energy. Seeing as the experiment was not something I cared to broadcast, I practiced on myself." His eyes were soft, and the edges of his mouth tipped down just slightly. "What I gave her was a dose of my magic—a pure source of my power. Ashley is now, in a way, my daughter."

"So she's not like me?"

"No, her magic is all light-based. *You* are one of a kind."

A direct from the source dose of magic from one of the most powerful Fae ever. Ashley was going to wet herself.

I smiled. "Thank you for saving her."

He tipped his head in a bow, then disappeared from sight.

～

I WENT BACK to the apartment at lunch and discovered that Ashley had packed for me. Granted, there wasn't a lot involved, but I hadn't expected her to do that.

"I had nothing better to do while you were at work," she explained. "I have no money here or books or ... anything really, and I was restless."

"Yeah, you're going to need to get your things from New York if you're planning to stay. I assume, after all that 'your fight is my fight' talk, you're now a permanent resident of Belfast?"

"You bet I am. How else would I learn to use all my badass Fae powers?" She wiggled her eyebrows, making me laugh. "We can work on getting me a ticket home after we move your stuff to the Huntsman. So long as we stop at a pharmacy on the way over, I can just wear your stuff for a few days."

"Sounds like a plan. I was going to change, but I'm guessing that's not an option now." I peered at the pair of suitcases and three boxes sitting at the bottom of the stairs.

"Not unless you want to pop these suckers open and dig."

"No way. Let's get them in the car and head out."

"Car?" Her eyes lit up.

"Didn't I tell you?" I grinned wickedly. "I've got a sweet new ride." I showed her to the black Audi, laughing hysterically at her giddy squeals.

AFTER A QUICK LUNCH and a not-so-quick stop at a pharmacy for toiletries, we drove to the Huntsman. Midday parking options were much better than in the evening. I was able to snag a front-row spot right away. We decided to leave the bags we could squeeze into the trunk until after Lochlan had shown us to our new apartment. The move would take a few trips since not much fit in the car, but we had nothing else to do for the rest of the day except settle in.

Inside the main club, we found Casek sitting at a table with a cigarette in hand and papers splayed out before him. "You're early," he murmured.

"That a problem?" I teased, not letting Casek's perpetual bad humor get to me.

"I suppose it depends on who you ask."

Such a sweetheart.

I rolled my eyes. "Whatever. We're going to look for Lochlan."

"I'll wait here," Ash shot back.

"Careful sitting with that one. His surliness might be contagious." I couldn't fathom why she'd want to sit around with Mr. Grump Pants, but that was her call.

"I'll take my chances." She smirked.

Casek's head slowly swiveled in her direction, and the two exchanged a contentious look that I wasn't even going to try to decipher.

I shrugged and started for the back hallway where the offices were located. His office was empty, so I moved farther down the hall toward the conference room when I heard a murmur of voices. As I neared the door, I realized that what I had heard was actually a woman moaning.

How awkward.

Was somebody getting freaky in the conference room with the door wide open? Despite knowing I should do the polite thing and walk away, my curiosity got the better of me. I peeked around the doorframe just enough to verify that my suspicions had been correct.

I'd been wrong. I'd been so horribly wrong.

My heart crumpled like a wadded-up piece of paper destined for the wastebasket.

Each breath I tried to take made my lungs feel like they were lined with shards of glass. The pain didn't spare a single nerve in my body. It devoured all thought and gouged permanent scars deep into my soul.

A woman lay on the conference table, naked from the waist down, her knees spread wide with her fingers sliding in and out of her pink folds. Her face was drawn in a look of pure ecstasy, mouth parted on a gasp and eyes closed in concentration. While she performed this intimate act, Lochlan stood over her, his face lifted to the ceiling and one hand clamped firmly around her thigh. It didn't matter that he was fully dressed with his eyes averted. He was clearly a part of this scene. That truth was unavoidable, and so was my pain.

How could I have been so incredibly wrong about him?

I'd thought we'd been developing a connection. Something substantive and real, not to mention crippling attraction to one another. No, we hadn't made anything official or vocalized any level of commitment, but the understanding was there. Wasn't it? Had I just imagined the bond we'd been forging? I'd trusted him. Opened myself to him and handed over parts of myself I hadn't given anyone else before. He had to know these weeks we'd spent together meant something to me.

Or was this just a demonstration of Fae nature? Had I handed over my heart to a man who was incapable of reciprocating my feelings? They didn't do marriage like we did. Maybe they had different rules for loyalty and fidelity as well.

How foolish I'd been to assume anything about him.

To think anything about my life would ever be normal again.

The cavernous hole in my chest filled with acid. A radioactive substance that mutated my pain into a scaly, slithering thing with venomous fangs primed for attack.

My shallow breaths settled.

Antifreeze flooded my veins until my fiery anger cooled to a frost-covered bitterness.

I gave two raps with my knuckles on the door, face void of emotion. "I hate to interrupt, but Ashley and I are ready to get the keys to our new apartment. Whenever you have a minute."

The moment I started to speak, Lochlan's back went ramrod straight. I didn't wait for a response.

"*Rebecca*! Get the fuck back here." He barreled out of the room and clamped down on my arm, denying me a hasty retreat.

I yanked violently against his hold, not wanting him to touch me ever again, but he wouldn't release me. "Let me go. I have nothing to say to you."

"Maybe not, but you can at least listen to me explain."

"Explain what? That was pretty fucking self-explanatory."

"Oh, yeah? Then you know I was just feeding my magic? Then you'll understand that meant no more to me than eating a steak or brushing my fucking teeth?"

"Feeding your magic?" I stilled, my thoughts recalling him explain that some Fae feed on sexual release. "But that can't be."

"What can't be?"

"Those things you said—that was about the Unseelie, the Fae who feed off humans, like the vampire woman and the other vicious creatures." My head slowly slid back and forth, unable to comprehend what he was saying.

"No, Rebecca. All Fae have to feed their magic, and most of us do that through sexual energy." He paused, gingerly releasing me. "I suspected you didn't realize, but I've been hesitant to explain because you've struggled to accept our existence as it is. I knew this might push you away even more."

"You're right. It's much easier to just keep me ignorant and unaware while you fuck whoever you want."

"I haven't touched another woman since you waltzed into my world—not like that. Feeding only. What happened in there meant *nothing* to me." His eyes began to glow as his anger shredded his control.

God, it was the most stereotypical cheater rhetoric in the book. A part of me wanted to smash my fist into his face for being *that* man. The one who can't keep his hands to himself but finds every excuse to explain away his wandering eyes.

But that wasn't exactly what was happening here. From a human man, the explanation would reek of deception, but Lochlan wasn't human. He was Fae—a man with magical powers that, according to him, required a specific energy source.

I wrestled with my emotions to gain control of my thoughts, taking a slow step back. "You feed off sex?"

"The energy created from a sexual release," he offered cautiously.

"But I haven't needed to do that."

"I can only assume the necklace is currently serving as your power source. But even without it, you're different from the rest of us."

Lochlan and all the others have to use sex in order to have magic. Like he said, the act was just a part of their daily routine. It meant nothing to them.

I didn't like that prospect any more than I liked seeing him with that woman. How was I supposed to trust a man to be loyal to me when our views on sex were so vastly different? Sex was intimate and personal to me. While I wasn't virginal, I'd also never been one for flings. I needed to develop a degree of trust in order to make myself vulnerable enough to allow someone inside my body.

Sex for Lochlan was a bodily function. How many times had he *charged his magic* over the past weeks?

I swayed with a particularly crippling wave of nausea. "I need you to let us into the apartment," I said without looking at him. It was all more than I could process at the moment. I needed time to think.

"You have to understand that this is a part of who we are—who *you* are."

My insides recoiled in response to his accusation. That I was anything like him or Ronan or any of the others. That I could toy with another person so callously as they had.

"Who *you* are—not me. I'm nothing like you," I hissed. "I don't have sex with other people because it's easier than telling the truth, and I certainly don't *trick* people into having sex with me." Bitter tears burned the back of my eyes. "I may be Fae, but I'm *nothing* like any of you."

A fierce blue glow shone from Lochlan's eyes. "I made him pay for what he did," he said through clenched teeth, the air around him shimmering with violence. "We aren't all like that."

"No, you coaxed me to trust you before you revealed your true nature." My breath hitched as pain took hold of me, all pretense of rational thought trampled to dust. "Don't worry about the key. I'll get it from Casek. You finish what you were doing." I motioned to behind him to where the black-haired beauty peeked at us from the doorway.

Lochlan roared as I walked away, but I didn't turn around, even when his fist crashed through the sheetrock behind me.

ASHLEY'S EYES rounded when I rejoined her and Casek, but she didn't push for an explanation in front of him. He showed us to the apartment we'd be sharing, then begrudgingly helped us get the first carload of stuff brought up. The place was incredible. Twice the size of my rental with two bedrooms and fully furnished with modern, upscale furniture and décor. If I wasn't so utterly devastated, I would have been thrilled. Instead, I struggled to share in Ashley's delight as we checked the place out.

Once we were alone, she stopped me from my task of sorting through the contents of a suitcase and peered at me with worried blue eyes. "You want to tell me what happened?"

I burst into tears.

Ashley wrapped her arms around me and held me while I let out all the emotions that had ravaged me since peering into the conference room. When I was able to talk, I told her everything that had happened.

"I can't even imagine, Bec. I'm so sorry, honey."

I wiped at my eyes for the twentieth time. "I just need to make him off-limits and focus on what's important. Learning my magic. Learning to fight. Saving the world. That's the only stuff that should matter."

"Yes and no. We do need to learn how we fit into this Fae world, but there's no immediate rush." She trailed her fingers over the plush bedding beneath us. "Do you think ... we'll have to use sex to make our magic work?"

"So far, I haven't needed to, but I have my necklace. I have no idea how things will work for you. Do you feel like you need sex?" My brows knitted together.

Ash's lips scrunched as her eyes danced around in thought. "I mean ... no more than usual," she said playfully, finally drawing a reluctant chuckle from me. "Come on, let's get this shit unpacked, then watch a movie."

"Ugh, I am supposed to train tonight with Lochlan, in theory." That was the absolute *last* thing I wanted to do.

"That's easy. Don't go."

"I have to, Ash," I said softly. "This threat I'm facing is too dangerous for me to take a day off. I have to be ready when the time comes."

She smiled sadly. "That's very responsible of you. Just go in there and be firm from the beginning that you aren't interested in any funny business. He'll get the hint."

Yeah, but seeing him—touching him—was going to be torture.

I nodded and scooted from the bed, done dwelling. We spent the next three hours getting everything moved and unloaded. When it came time to train, I discovered that being angry with Lochlan was a surprisingly effective training technique, not to mention therapeutic. He didn't push me to talk, I kept things professional at all times, and we both did our best to ignore the lumbering elephant hanging out in the room with us.

It was awkward at best, but I preferred that feeling to the heartache that set in once I was alone in bed that night. The anger only lasted so long, and once it dissipated, I was left feeling empty and alone. But maybe that was best. Not everyone was meant for an epic love.

With that depressing thought, I closed my burning eyes and surrendered myself to sleep.

DECEMBER

JANUARY

FEBRUARY

MARCH

THIRTY-THREE

My back slammed onto the mat. Lochlan was using more sophisticated techniques every day, but the impact that would have knocked me breathless months ago did little to slow me down. Three long months I'd been training, and I'd made vast improvements in my fighting skills. Three months of ignoring the blistering sexual tension between Lochlan and me. Three months of missing Knight, who I had to leave behind when we moved to the Huntsman. Three months without word from Merlin or any signs of Morgan. Three months of uncertainty. Three months of dedication, consistency, and focus.

I no longer even resembled the same girl who showed up in Belfast with a canister of pepper spray and the American Airlines webpage bookmarked should I need an emergency ticket home. My body was now resilient and fortified with lean muscle. My mind was centered and fixed with purpose. And my heart was safely protected beneath coils of barbed wire and a steadfast conviction that I was better off alone.

Magic was my one weakness. I couldn't master abilities I didn't know I had, and my magic was reluctant to show itself.

Each time Lochlan attempted to teach me to trace or manipulate memories or even do a simple glamour, nothing happened. The only real progress I'd shown was in learning I could manipulate smoke. Not just air, it had to be smoke. As far as I could figure, it had to do with the element of darkness in the particulate.

I had tried to burn some birch wood in the fireplace in our apartment after Cat had told me about the protective qualities of ash. Apparently, the chimney hadn't been updated with the rest of the building, and smoke filled the place. I funneled it out a window—the sensation was somewhat similar to the darkness I injected under the skin. It felt like the smoke was an extension of me, and I simply pushed it out the window.

It was a handy skill to have, considering Ashley's cooking abilities.

Ash had taken to her new life in Belfast with gusto. She didn't have a great relationship with her parents, so leaving them behind to move here hadn't fazed her. She took a quick trip to New York and settled her affairs, arranging with her boss to work remotely. Her one main struggle was the fact that her magic had yet to develop. While my powers had been tricky, hers had been nonexistent. She wasn't a happy camper. But in typical Ashley style, she didn't let that get her down. She made friends with all the guys—all but Casek, who didn't seem to be friends with anyone except Lochlan. Casek had been in Faery for the past three weeks, but I'd hardly noticed since he kept entirely to himself.

Outside of Ashley, I spent the most time with Lochlan. We sparred every day for hours, day after day, month after month. I'd become a master of self-control in that time. The leash I kept on my emotions was made of military-grade Kevlar. Lochlan was my instructor, and I wasn't going to allow him to be anything more. His rigorous training regimine reminded me daily of how dangerous distractions could be.

I learned to use my size to my advantage and accepted the necessity of fighting dirty. The Fae might be hard to kill, but they felt pain just like humans. That meant a good kick to the balls or a finger in an eye socket were effective techniques no matter the race of my attacker. I learned to throw knives with pinpoint accuracy and how to fight with a knife without stabbing myself, hopefully. We also trained with other weapons, but our primary focus was knives.

Our sessions were respectful. Professional. He treated me as he would any student ... at least, at first. I felt his patience at the barriers between us erode more with each passing day. He started to press me with small gestures. A heated stare when he pinned me to the floor or an extra touch when correcting my form. I did my best to ignore him. To ignore the swoop deep in my belly when his touch lingered or the way my nipples ached when his gravelly voice scraped across my skin.

I'd come to crave and dread our training sessions in equal measure.

Today was no different.

Once I was back on my feet, Lochlan snuck in a lightning-fast grab at my wrist and pulled me toward him. I immediately went limp and dropped to the ground, punching up at his unprotected junk but missing as he stealthily jumped backward. He hadn't released my hand, so I was tugged along with him and used the momentum to swing my legs around and wipe his feet out from under him. Still not relenting his hold on me, I was flung on top of him as he went crashing to the ground on his back.

I should have scrambled off him.

I should have averted my eyes and held firm to my convictions.

Instead, I lay immobilized. Our chests heaved as we both fought for air, eyes locked in a battle of their own. It was the intensity of his stare that finally coaxed me to pull away. He had a way of challenging me with just a look, and I wasn't ready to take that bait.

We both lay on our backs for a moment, our labored breaths filling the quiet room. We had been at it for hours and were both exhausted.

"We're done for today. You need to pack a bag. We leave for Faery in the morning." Fatigue wore at Lochlan's voice.

I jerked upright. "What?"

"Casek returned earlier today. He's found someone who could help teach you. Someone who is familiar with Shadow magic."

"So that's where Casek's been. Was there a reason you hadn't told me?"

"I didn't want to get your hopes up. I'm still not certain this will work." His reasoning was sound. If I'd known what Casek was off doing, I would have thought about it incessantly.

"I'll have to tell him how much I appreciate what he's done," I offered softly, hoping Lochlan understood that I was also thanking him. Casek wouldn't have gone searching if Lochlan hadn't ordered him to.

He rolled his head in my direction, and our eyes met. The air around us thickened with the weight of unsaid words. Every day I wondered if he'd break his silence and push me to reconsider. Plead with me to understand or demand I give him a chance. Every day we stewed in the oppressive tension, and every day we both toed the lines we'd drawn in the sand.

"We'll have to stop at Guin's palace when we first arrive in Faery."

I nodded, not crazy about the idea but unable to do anything about it. "How long do you think we'll be gone?"

"I'm guessing a month or so."

"Is that Earth time or Faery time?" The last time I'd been in Faery, a full day in Faery had only been half a day back on Earth. Either way, I'd have to hope Fergus was understanding and allowed me to keep my job despite my absence.

"It's hard to say, Rebecca. I think we should keep our minds open. I can explain things to your boss—your job won't be a problem."

If Lochlan tried to alter Fergus's memories, the magic wouldn't work, and Lochlan would know Fergus was a Druid. That was unacceptable. If I told Lochlan not to worry about it, he would be suspicious why my boss would allow me to leave for weeks at a time. The only way I could see through the issue was to tell Fergus what Lochlan had planned and have Fergus fake it.

Oh, the webs we weave...

THAT NIGHT, I lay on the couch thinking about the trip when Ashley strolled into the apartment.

"Did you hear that Casek's back?" she asked with a note of curiosity.

"I did. Apparently, he was off looking for a teacher to help with my magic. He found someone, and now Lochlan is taking me to Faery first thing tomorrow."

"What?" She gaped at me. "For how long?"

I shrugged. "Maybe a month."

"No way! That's too long."

"You're telling me. I want to learn my magic, but I have no idea how I'm supposed to manage traveling with Lochlan for a month. Training with him a couple of hours a day is hard enough."

"I've been thinking about that. I know you don't want to hear this, but are you sure you shouldn't give him a chance?" she asked warily. "He can't help that his magic needs sex. Seems wrong to punish him for it."

"I'm not punishing him," I shot back. I didn't want to lash out defensively, but I was already stressed, and she'd hit a nerve.

She didn't respond. She didn't need to. Her expression conveyed plenty of doubt on its own.

"Look, I just don't think any kind of relationship is a good idea right now. We both have too much going on to let that distract us."

"Too much? There's been no sign of Morgan or this invasion for three months. For all we know, she could have given up, and all this training is for nothing." Ashley's voice grew sharper.

My temper sparked in response. "You weren't there at the portals, Ash. You didn't fight off a dozen Red Caps or see the man who'd been gutted as a sacrifice. Merlin didn't spend twenty-odd years planning to take down Morgan for nothing. People have died. I watched *you* die, and I'm not taking anything for granted anymore." I marched into my room and grabbed my backpack out of the closet, figuring I'd rather pack than fight.

I had been instructed to limit myself to a single backpack. A single *backpack*. I'd have to find a way to get everything I would need to go to an unknown place with an unknown climate for an unknown duration into a *single backpack*.

Was he nuts? It was hard enough for me to pack for a trip without taking double the clothes I needed. Was I supposed to re-wear the same outfit for days at a time?

I shuddered.

It was an impossible task. No matter what I chose, I'd end

up wishing I had something else. I was blankly staring into my underwear drawer when Ashley's arms wrapped around me from behind.

"I'm sorry, Bec. I don't want you to leave for your trip upset with me."

I clasped my hand on her forearm and squeezed. "I'm sorry, too," I whispered, then turned to give her a hug. "I'm scared, Ash."

"I know, honey. I am, too. But if there's anyone who can handle this, it's you." She pulled back and grinned at me with glassy eyes.

I nodded, my throat tight with emotion. "Okay, help me figure out what to pack. I'm at a complete loss."

"I can totally help you pack. I'll get your suitcase."

"No, Ash." I held up the backpack helplessly before me.

We both stared in silence.

"A month?" she asked.

I nodded.

"In a backpack?"

Another nod.

"Oh, shit," she breathed.

Yeah. Tell me about it.

CHAPTER

THIRTY-FOUR

I DIDN'T SLEEP WELL THAT NIGHT DESPITE MY BEST EFFORTS. ASHLEY'S words haunted me. My withdrawal from Lochlan hadn't felt like punishment. I was protecting myself. Keeping myself focused. Not punishing him. This was about me and what I needed, not him. But when I considered why pushing him away from better for me, I realized it came down to trust. And if I didn't trust him because of a genetic trait all Fae possessed, wasn't that in a way punishing him for being Fae?

I argued with myself for hours until exhaustion finally took me under. By morning, I was no closer to an answer. If anything, I was only more confused. Lucky for me, I was about to have loads of time on my hands to overthink any number of subjects.

Super.

I met Lochlan in the lobby once I was ready, and we made a quick stop at the museum to talk with Fergus. Lochlan did his magic voice to alter Fergus's memories, and Fergus did a masterful job of pretending it had worked. Once that task was finished, Lochlan drove us to a nearby church.

St. George's Church was built in the early 1800s and was the oldest Church of Ireland sanctuary in Belfast. Although not nearly as large as the museum, the building was constructed of the same white sandstone, stately columns, and large, multi-paned windows.

"There's a portal inside the church?" I asked with surprise.

"The church was built on the site where the original portal was located. Portals are only opened in specific geographic locations, which were originally marked with stone circles. They became known as holy sites, so some had churches placed in those locations. This is the only one inside the city. Most are more remotely located."

"Back in November, I visited the Beltany Stone Circle. The guide said the site was used during the Beltane celebrations at the start of summer to help protect the cattle and crops."

"I'm sure the locals developed their own beliefs about the stones, but they were first used to mark sites for the portals. Beltane, along with the equinoxes and solstices, is when the veil between the worlds is the thinnest. That's why Morgan plans to attack on Beltane."

I stalled on the steps of the church, mouth gaping at Lochlan. "How do you know that?"

"Ronan told us when we interrogated him." He led the way into the church as if oblivious to my shock.

"You've known this whole time when Morgan would attack, and you're only telling me now?" My booming voice echoed off the cathedral ceilings, making me scrunch up my shoulders with a grimace.

In a soft tone, Lochlan replied. "You get stressed. I didn't want you to waste time worrying."

"I'm a big girl, Lochlan. I think I could have handled it. Don't you think it would be important for the person who is supposed to fight Morgan to know when the crazy hag was planning on making her move?"

I could have done little differently over the past months, but that didn't mean he had any right to keep the information from me—especially something as crucial as when Morgan planned to attack.

"You getting upset isn't helping to support your position."

My jaw clamped shut, fighting words perched on the tip of my tongue. "When exactly is Beltane?" I clipped.

"This year, it's on May third. That's why we left on this journey so quickly."

Shit. That was just over a month away.

All of a sudden, this mission I'd been tasked with felt all too real. I fell quietly into step behind Lochlan as he continued inside the main chapel.

The room contained rows of pews separated from the raised dais by a partial wall of columns. Colorful murals and vibrant stained-glass windows that captivated the eye covered the back walls surrounding the dais. I would have loved to have spent more time appreciating the intricate elements of the church, but as Lochlan had just informed me, we were running out of time.

We closed ourselves inside a small study room just off to the side of the chapel. The room had a small desk against one wall and a set of bookshelves but was otherwise empty. Lochlan pulled out what appeared to be sidewalk chalk and drew out a complex symbol on the old stone floor. He stepped back and softly murmured a series of words I couldn't make out. The air before us shimmered and blurred until we no longer looked at the opposite wall. Instead, a circle about the height of a man showed a window into what looked like a stone mausoleum.

Looking through the spatial distortion was disorienting. It

was like looking at a high-definition television screen displaying an image of another room, and my brain fought to accept that the image was real and not just a 2D projection.

Lochlan stepped through the portal, one foot at a time, then peered back at me expectantly. My heart pounded in my chest, and my eyes widened with uncertainty. I had been through a portal before, but I had been unconscious. This was essentially an all-new experience. I took a steadying breath and stepped over the barrier from one side of the portal to the other. Walking through itself didn't feel like anything, but once I stepped fully into Faery, energy and power swelled inside me. The air felt electric, making my skin tingle and my muscles buzz with the need to move. As I absorbed the sensation, my eyes fell shut.

"The natural occurrence of magic is much higher in Faery. We don't have to feed as often to sustain our magic here, and more powerful spells can be performed," Lochlan commented as I opened my eyes and watched the portal close behind us.

"Won't the people at the church notice your markings?"

"Part of the rune that I drew makes the markings essentially burn up after the portal closes."

Any follow-up question I might have asked was silenced at the sight of the two Fae warrior women standing guard at the door of the tomb-like room. They were exceptionally tall for women and had golden blond hair with hard blue eyes staring fixedly at the opposite wall. While their eyes never strayed to us, I was confident they were clocking our every movement. Both were solid with muscle and wore fitted hunter-green uniforms that were not bulky or armored but still looked battle-ready. In their hands, each held long staffs with gleaming spearheads on the tips.

Lochlan paid them no attention, walking past without so

much as a hello. I followed him but had trouble taking my eyes off the fascinating women.

"I assume they're some kind of guards?" I asked after we had exited the stone building and began walking through tall green grass.

"They're Valkyrie."

"As in the warrior women from Norse mythology?" Why did I continue to be surprised when legends became real? Was there any subset of mythology that wasn't rooted in fact?

"As in the Seelie Queen's Fae warriors who guard the city. There are always two Valkyrie on guard at the portal to make sure no one attempts to open it and leave Faery."

"What if someone tries to open the portal from Earth? There were no guards on that end."

"There shouldn't be any Fae on that side of the portal to open it, aside from members of the Hunt. Anyone who is on that side of the Portal got there against the queen's command and certainly isn't going to come back."

"I suppose that makes sense."

As we emerged from a cluster of trees, a city skyline could be seen in the distance. Like Dorothy approaching the Emerald City, lost in the splendor of the shimmering buildings, I was in awe of the sight before me. On my prior visit to the Faery, I'd only seen the inside of the palace and its gardens, so I had no idea what the rest of Faery looked like.

There were no billboards, highways, or any signs of civilization, just sprawling trees and greenery, aside from the single cluster of buildings surrounded by a solid wall. As we grew closer, I realized that most of the buildings tall enough to be seen over the wall appeared to be part of a single structure —the queen's palace. It reminded me of a sandcastle with turrets and spires, all built of a material that glittered in the sun.

"Is that Avalon?" I asked as we trekked through the gently rolling hills.

Lochlan glanced over at me questioningly. "How did you know?"

"When the queen abducted me, she told me I was in her palace in Avalon. You said we were going to stop by the palace, so it only made sense." It was a surprising change of pace to actually know what was going on, and I gave myself a mental pat on the back for paying attention.

We walked a mile or so to the city gates, where we were offered a mount by the city guards to ride to the palace in the center of the city. Not anticipating visitors, they only had one spare horse at the gate. We would have to ride together.

Of course, we would.

I took a deep breath and joined Lochlan near the majestic black beast. The horse began to whinny anxiously and prance in place, his brown eyes bulging wide. I was no horse expert, but it was plain that the horse was uncomfortable with my presence.

"Stop upsetting the horse," Lochlan said as he walked up to the agitated creature and took the reins, stroking the behemoth's neck while cooing softly at him.

"I'm not doing anything!" I replied indignantly.

Lochlan grunted, then swung me onto the saddle without warning. I squealed like a five-year-old girl.

"Stop your screaming. You'll upset the horse more than he already is."

"I couldn't help it. You startled me. Next time, let me know before you throw me onto the back of an angry animal." *Boorish, impossible man.*

Lochlan lifted himself onto the saddle behind me, one arm snaking around my middle. His lips lowered to my ear. "Keep up with the attitude and see where it gets you."

His words sent an avalanche of shivers down my spine.

Before I could recover, he gave the reins a tug. The horse surged forward, forcing me to cling to Lochlan's arm at my waist.

We leisurely wound our way through the cobbled city streets. Consistent with what I'd seen in the palace, the Fae lifestyle was similar to Western Europe in the 1800s. In the palace, that meant corseted gowns and chamber pots. The general population lived in cottages with simple glass-paned windows and flower boxes in bloom. Clothes were made from something akin to linen and were restricted to a basic color palette. The occasional carriage clanked down the street, but most people were on foot. It looked like a simple life, and while not my personal ideal, those around us looked happy with their station.

My back pressed firmly against Lochlan the entire trip through the winding streets. I fit perfectly against him. With him at my back, I felt unusually calm about my uncertain surroundings, especially when whiffs of his masculine scent enveloped me. I found myself leaning back into his chest when I should have been doing the opposite.

In response, a satisfied rumble crossed from his chest into mine, sending a zing of desire down to my core, which was already pulsing warmly. I wiggled in an attempt to relieve the ache.

Lochlan's lips lowered to the shell of my ear. "Do that again, and I won't be held responsible for my actions."

That was twice now he'd made suggestive comments. Twice in one day when he had kept himself in check for months. That did not bode well for me.

Had he been biding his time all these months, waiting for my resolve to wane? Most men would have moved on by now.

Lochlan isn't most men.

Yeah, I was in trouble.

Within the city wall was a separate wall encircling the Seelie palace. As we were escorted through the gates, I became entranced with the grandeur of the royal residence. The enormous structure was smooth with curved facades and numerous spires—straight out of a Disney movie. Rows of guards stood at attention in green livery on the cobbled road as we approached the large double doors of the front entrance.

Inside the great hall, I was reminded of the old-world opulence I saw in the palace on my first visit. Two guards led us back to the throne room, where Lochlan had explained we would need to greet the queen. Courtiers in formal gowns and suits were clustered throughout the room murmuring. We walked side by side down the length of the long room to the throne, garnering little attention as we passed.

The last time I had been there, I had been impressed with the queen's dining chair, going so far as to think of it as a demi-throne. However, the glorious work of art she called a throne made me realize that calling the dining chair a demi-throne was like comparing a Swarovski crystal to a diamond—the crystal was lovely, but it wasn't the real deal.

Stationed tall upon a dais, the official throne was a masterpiece of silver metal molded into intricate vines making up the body of the throne with tendrils curling in all directions off the top like a living crown. Queen Guinevere sat regally atop her throne, conversing with several men nearby. Her ethereal beauty was just as breathtaking as it had been before. Long red hair fell in waves down her lithe torso, and her pale skin was highlighted with a scattering of freckles. But her most enchanting feature was her penetrating green eyes. In contrast to her delicate frame, she carried herself with a commanding strength.

As soon as her eyes caught sight of us, she lifted her hand

slowly to halt the conversation. "We will finish this discussion later."

Each man swiftly bowed his head and scuttled off the raised platform. Lochlan dropped to a low bow. I followed suit with a curtsy, hoping I had performed the task adequately.

"Lochlan, it's been quite some time since I've had the pleasure of having you here." Guin's seductive voice was breathy with innuendo.

Surely, not. Please, God. Not her.

Bile rose in my throat at the image of them together. I ground my teeth together and attempted to calm myself since I had no grounds to be upset.

"Guin, I believe the pleasure has been all mine."

His tone might have been neutral, but his words fanned the flame of my fiery temper.

Are you jealous? Because you can't reject him, then be jealous when he's with someone else.

Was I jealous?

Yeah. Yeah, I was. But look at her! She was a freaking queen and ridiculously gorgeous. How could I compare to someone like that?

My pulse began to thrum in my neck. Out of nowhere, Lochlan's hand clasped mine and squeezed as if he'd sensed my discomfort. Then I realized I'd gotten so lost in my head that I hadn't noticed the subtle shift of my eyes turning black. Magic lifted the hairs along my arms and warmed my skin to the touch.

Lochlan had been right. Faery did make magic easier.

"Rebecca, I see you've made progress with your powers," Guin crooned.

"I suppose a little."

"You still believe there's a war brewing?" she asked, sounding genuinely curious.

I looked at Lochlan, but he kept his eyes trained forward. Clearly, I had to answer on my own. "Yes, and I'm doing everything I can to prepare. I hope you're doing the same."

Lochlan stiffened.

Her head tilted as she eyed me appraisingly. "I am always prepared, but I'm still not convinced of this war. I hear that young Morgan has resurfaced and claims some vendetta against me, but her tantrum is of no concern. She cannot get inside my realm," she said with a haughty lift of her chin.

I wasn't sure what I should and shouldn't reveal, so I kept my mouth shut.

Lochlan took the opportunity to cut in. "We must leave for the Wilds in the morning, but we'd be grateful if you would allow us the honor of staying in your home for the night."

Her eyes stayed trained on me as though debating whether she was through with me. Eventually, her gaze shifted to my companion. "Of course, you are always welcome here. Your company at dinner will be a welcome reprieve." She glanced at the men she'd been talking to when we arrived and crooked her fingers in a summons.

They rushed forward, and Lochlan tugged me backward away from the dais.

We'd been dismissed.

THIRTY-FIVE

"Come this way, I'll show you to your rooms," mumbled a man in servant's formal attire with downcast eyes.

"Was something upsetting you?" Lochlan asked as we followed the man.

"No," I said quickly.

Lochlan merely slid his eyes in my direction with a curious look.

We wound our way to the staircase I had descended before my first dinner at the palace. Not far from where I'd stayed the last time, we were shown adjacent rooms. The extravagance of the bedroom was similar to the one I had been given before, but the layout was different. This room held a bed, chest, and a small sitting area, along with bathing facilities. Unlike the last room, this one contained an extra door. It seemed unlikely that it would be a closet, but who knew what might be in a Faery queen's castle?

My curiosity got the better of me. I slowly turned the metal knob and cracked open the door. When I peeked inside, I was treated to a delicious view of Lochlan's naked back.

Definitely not a closet.

The servant had given us adjoining rooms. Perhaps we'd seemed like a couple. It didn't matter. I should close the door and pretend it didn't exist.

I should...

Lochlan ran his hands through his short hair, offering up his rippling back muscles on display. I couldn't even make myself blink, let alone close the door. He was the statue of David, and I was helpless but to appreciate the fine contours of his sculpted physique. His shoulders bunched powerfully. His lats pulled outward like wings. He even had two perfect indentations at the base of his spine that marked the mouthwatering curve of his firm backside. Even his smooth skin was flawless—not too pale or overly tan, just the right golden shade to make a girl want to lick every square inch.

Damn him. Why did he have to be so gorgeous?

I never allowed myself to ogle him when we trained, so this moment of indulgence was a treat. A dangerous temptation.

"You do realize that I know you're there." He turned, his eyes glinting with amusement.

I was so mesmerized that I didn't immediately slam the door shut, which is what I would have done had I been in control of all my faculties. Instead, my lips parted, and I stood transfixed like a child in awe of the tricks of a magician.

In the span of a heartbeat, he'd blinked across the room and was opening the door, pushing me back into my room along with him. His hands lifted my face to his, bringing our lips together. And for the first time in months, I felt like I could breathe. I couldn't break away from the kiss if my life depended on it. I'd been starved for his touch, and this small taste of him had spiked my hunger beyond my control.

"You don't get to look at me like that without getting

kissed." His words caressed my skin, warming me from the inside out.

One of his hands found my lower back and pulled me against his firm body while my hands were busy roving over the muscled planes of his chest. My head tipped to the side, and he kissed down the column of my neck, sending goose bumps down my arms. His hands found the bottom of my shirt and lifted it over my head, tossing it aside. When he brought his lips back to mine, the brush of his bare chest teased my nipples, abrading the tips then soothing my skin with the searing heat of his own.

Just when I felt the last of my restraint give way, Lochlan pulled back, his hands on either side of my face, hypnotic eyes boring into mine. Penetrating. Demanding.

"Tell me you've finally accepted this. Accepted who I am. Because as much as I want to fuck you, I won't do it just so you can hate me after."

I opened my mouth, then closed it when thoughts and emotions became a tangled mess in the misty haze of lust. "I do ... I do accept that Fae view sex differently. That it's not necessarily personal." I knew my words were a mistake the second they left my lips.

An iron gate slammed shut behind his eyes, locking me out. "Does anything about what's happening right now not feel personal to you?" he growled.

"No, that's not what I mean. I'm trying to say that I know it's part of Fae biology, and sometimes it's needed and doesn't have to entail intimacy."

His hands fell away from me as he drifted back, and I felt his loss like a blast of arctic wind.

"That's not acceptance. Those are excuses. You've found a way to explain your distrust of me. A reason to see me as less than I am." He took another step back, retrieved my shirt from the floor, and handed it to me. "If you truly saw me, you'd know there would never be anyone else." With his parting blow, he retreated to his room, the door closing behind him with resounding finality.

What had I done? I felt like I'd held liquid sunshine in my hands, then watched helplessly as it slipped between my fingers and was lost forever.

I numbly slipped my shirt back on, then buried myself under the covers of my enormous bed. Curled into a protective ball, I closed my eyes and did my best not to think because the fear was just too much. I was engulfed in a sense of impending loss, and I felt helpless to prevent it.

An hour or so before dinner, a woman came to help me prepare. I had hoped to see Cyrene so that I could hear how she'd been, but I'd been assigned a different palace maid. I wasn't interested in talking with anyone else, so our time together was quiet. My hairstyle was simple but elegant, and I felt lovely in the ivory gown I had been given.

When the bell tolled, I stepped into the hall at the same time as Lochlan. He looked incredible in the suit he'd been provided, like a real, live Mr. Darcy—tall, handsome, proud, and completely closed off. If I hadn't seen the passion he was capable of myself, I would have said he was the most heartless, callous-looking man I'd ever met.

I did that to him.

It was my fault, and I hated myself for it.

My gaze dropped as I fought back emotion. Lochlan stepped silently forward and extended his elbow to escort me. He didn't look at me. The chill he cast was still unbearably cold, but he wouldn't send me into battle alone, even when he felt hurt and betrayed.

I gladly hooked my arm in his, feeling a tiny spark of hope

that we could somehow navigate this mountain that stood between us.

Dinner at Court was a production performed each evening, and the actors had perfected their roles with years of practice. The scene unfolded exactly as it had the first time I had dined with the queen. I could only imagine how tedious it would be to go through the motions nightly. Not that the courtiers seemed bothered by the affair. In fact, they all chatted animatedly, alight with nightly gossip and intrigue.

Lochlan sat between the queen and me and managed to field all of her questions. The conversation remained on superficial topics ranging from a new theater production being performed at the palace to a recent bountiful harvest of misha fruit, whatever that was. Matters of politics were not discussed at the table. I didn't know the reason for her rule, but it was strictly enforced.

After the meal concluded, the ladies separated into a drawing room for tea and the men to a parlor for after-dinner drinks. I wasn't thrilled to leave Lochlan but had little choice. Guin summoned me to sit with her on a royal-blue, velvet-tufted settee. Women clustered throughout the room, absorbed in discussions as they daintily sipped from crystal glasses. Everything about the scene before me felt surreal like I'd been sucked into a historical television drama and had to pretend I belonged.

"Has Lochlan told you where you will be traveling?" Guin asked quietly, her eyes roaming the crowd.

I was terribly anxious about saying the wrong thing. Unlike at dinner, Lochlan wasn't available to answer on my behalf. "Not exactly, just that we're going to the Shadow Lands," I replied cautiously.

"What could Lochlan possibly want in the Shadow Lands?" she scoffed.

I tensed, worried I'd said something I shouldn't have. "He seemed to think he'd find something there that would help us stop Morgan." If he hadn't told her what we were up to, I wasn't going to either.

Calculating green eyes assessed me. "And for some reason, he saw fit to bring you along?"

"I suppose so. He doesn't usually explain himself to me."

That seemed to ring true enough for her to ease her scrutiny.

"And you know that not even the Unseelie dare to venture into those lands? Your encounter with the Draug will look like child's play should you encounter a Fachan or a band of Sluagh. There are a host of other possibilities, each more terrifying than the last."

I wasn't sure how she knew about my encounter with the Draug, and I probably didn't want to know. I had enough to worry about already.

"I know very little about what I'm walking into, but it's my understanding that we have little choice in the matter."

"Ah, so easy to be brave when bolstered by ignorance. There are always choices," she pressed, smirking condescendingly.

"I suppose you're right. I could choose to ignore the threat." I blanched after the words were out, wondering if I'd overstepped, but the queen merely shrugged one shoulder.

"In that scenario, you have already chosen to accept that there is a threat."

"Yes," I said with a confident lift of my chin. "There is a threat. I've seen its effect and nearly been killed by the Unseelie entering Earth." An idea struck me suddenly. I wasn't sure if it was brilliant or utterly insane, but swept up in the moment, I decided to give it a shot. Taking a deep breath, I continued. "Morgan is after your throne, and I would propose that should I eliminate that threat, you allow me to remain on Earth if and when I become fully Fae."

My heart pounded out a frantic staccato. Guin's head tipped back, and she laughed heartily. The chatter in the room quieted as the other ladies curiously gazed in our direction.

Abruptly, Guin's laughter stopped, and her eyes narrowed on me. "You seem to suffer from the delusion that you are doing me a favor. There is no war. You have no leverage over me. My decree states that all Fae must live on Faery, save only for the members of the Hunt. There are no exceptions. The only reason I have allowed you to stay on Earth is my desire to be civil with Merlin. The moment he is done with you, I expect your obedience."

Adrenaline-induced panic raced through my veins, making my hands sweat and my heart pound against my rib cage. She wasn't going to let me stay on Earth. My parents, everything I'd ever known, would have to be left behind.

I'd tried to forget her original assertion that I'd have to move because I simply couldn't accept that eventuality, but I might have no choice. Guin had zero intention of granting me any leniency.

Frustration, anger, and a swell of emotions surged inside me. The air gusted all around me, extinguishing the candles and sinking the room into a stunned darkness. The ladies of court gasped and twittered about the uncontrolled burst of magic, but the queen's eyes stayed glued to me unwaveringly. She slowly lifted her hand, and a ball of light began to glow from her palm. It then broke apart and scattered tiny flames to each unlit candle, bringing the wicks back to life.

"And you're Merlin's best hope?" She chuckled condescendingly.

Embarrassed and overwhelmed, I hurried from the room and raced up the curving staircase. I had to get away from these people. From Guin and all the prying eyes that chipped away at every ounce of confidence I'd worked so hard to collect and nurture.

My long strides stalled as I approached my room and heard my name called out in warning. I spun around and had to feign to the side just as a man with a knife slashed at me from behind. He snarled his disappointment at missing me, then bent his knees in preparation for a second attack.

In my peripheral vision, I could see Cyrene down the hall, hands covering her mouth in fright. Though I never took my eyes from him, the distraction was enough to draw a second lunge in my direction. He jabbed the knife straight at my belly.

The motion felt familiar, and I moved on instinct. Employing techniques I'd been learning for months, I circled him in a defensive stance—something that was somewhat more difficult in a gown and heels.

Sweat beaded on the man's forehead, and his jaw clenched in desperate urgency. This time, he swung at me with his fist before swiping with the knife in his other hand. I was able to block the punch and grab the wrist of his hand holding the blade. We grappled for control of the weapon, both grunting and straining with the effort.

Wanting to help me, Cyrene snuck up behind the man and brought a vase down upon his head, but her kindhearted nature kept her from swinging hard enough to knock him out. Instead, he roared in fury. With a quick swipe, he plunged the knife into her stomach.

A guttural cry tore from my chest, and I whipped my leg out in a round-house kick to his head. Taking advantage of his disoriented spin, I grabbed his fist holding the knife and plunged the blade into his throat. He stilled in shock, his own hand still holding the knife protruding from his neck. Blood oozed from the wound and spilled out from his parted lips before his eyes glazed over. He dropped to his knees, falling face-down on the intricate hall rug.

I tore my gaze from the gruesome scene at my feet and raced over to Cyrene. She sat gasping for air, the wound up near her ribs leaking blood at a rapid rate.

"Cyrene, you stay there. I'm going to get help," I assured her before racing back toward the stairs.

Before I could descend, I spotted Lochlan below me. His eyes flew up to where I stood, and when he saw the blood on my white gown, he traced in next to me.

"What's happened? Are you all right?" he growled, his eyes scanning me for injuries.

"I'm fine, but my friend's been hurt. She needs help." I took hold of his hand and raced back to where she sat. After Lochlan quickly assessed her, he disappeared, returning seconds later with a host of other men and several of the queen's Valkyrie guards.

Some men gently lifted Cyrene and carried her to the stairs as I looked on nervously.

"She's going to be fine," Lochlan assured me. "They're taking her to a healer. A wound like that won't be deadly." His eyes turned to the man bleeding out on the ground.

The Valkyrie soldiers placed iron cuffs on his hands and lifted him unceremoniously before dragging him off as well. I had thought I'd killed him, but it seemed they thought he might live. I hoped they might get information out of him, and I was relieved to know, despite his attack, that I wouldn't be the one to end his life.

One of the guards stayed to question me about what had happened. I told her what I could, then Lochlan and I were allowed to return to our rooms. Still stunned over the attack, my brain struggled to catch up.

Someone tried to kill me in the safety of the palace.

How had this happened? Was Morgan's influence that expansive? How many more spies and assassins might she have hidden away? How far would she go to stop us from getting in her way?

I shivered.

"Let's get you cleaned up." Lochlan took my hand and led me to my room.

Once we were inside with the door closed, he magically filled the tub with steaming water and instructed me to turn around. I did as I was told, relieved to have him there with me. His strength and compassion.

He unbuttoned the back of my sullied gown with agile fingers. When it fell to the ground, there was no awkwardness between us. He was there to care for me, and I was desperately in need of his support.

I eased myself into the water, closing my eyes as tension left my body.

Lochlan pulled over one of the wing-back chairs from the window and sat. "I'd like to hear what happened," he said softly.

Giving as much detail as I could, I walked him through the attack. It had only lasted a matter of minutes, and no words had been exchanged, so I had little information to share. The most important thing I'd learned was that I'd been foolish to assume my safety here or anywhere. I hadn't even had my knife holstered to my thigh like I should have. I wouldn't make that mistake again.

"You took out your assailant, keeping your cool and not hesitating to strike a killing blow. I'd say your training has paid off. There has to be at least some reward in knowing how far you've come," he assured me.

He raised his long body out of the chair and closed the distance between us. Placing a towel next to the tub, he leaned down and gently kissed my forehead, his lips lingering just briefly. Without another word, he exited to his room and allowed me the privacy to finish bathing.

Even after I'd hurt him, he was still encouraging me—protecting and caring for me. Guilt and shame made me want to sink beneath the water's surface and hide from myself. I was trying my hardest to be the person I needed to become, yet I continued to feel as though I were falling short.

Fear of failure was holding me back. Fear that I wouldn't be enough.

If I was bound to fail because of my fear, perhaps the only thing I could do was embrace my failure. Accept that I was giving all I could and own that it might or might not be enough. I only had control over my own efforts and responses. As long as I was true to myself—proud of my choices and what I'd given—that was a success in its own right. Without fear, I at least had a *chance* of winning. With the venomous under-tones of fear sabotaging my efforts, I was almost guaranteed to lose at least one battle—my fight with Morgan or the war I was waging in my heart.

CHAPTER

THIRTY-SIX

Early the following morning, Lochlan and I strapped on our backpacks and walked in companionable silence to the stables. My designated horse was a reasonably sized golden beauty named Penway. Despite living in Texas throughout my child-hood, I wasn't familiar with horses. Lochlan groomed and tacked her up for me. His mount was another enormous black beast like the horse we rode in on from the palace gates. When both horses were ready for our journey, Lochlan led them outside and handed me Penway's reins. The moment I neared her, the horse reared up, front legs dancing with agitation.

"*Shhhh*, it's okay girl," I cooed at the horse, trying to imitate what Lochlan had done to calm the horse from the day before.

He had mounted his steed without issue, but this mare wanted nothing to do with me. Her anxiety was palpable as I slowly inched forward, hands out placatingly. I could almost feel the bristle of her tumultuous emotions.

When I was able to get close enough to touch her, I placed my hand on her neck soothingly and realized that her fear had an almost tangible feel that called to my magic. I took a slow

380

mental pull on her stress and fear, similar to how I manipulated smoke, and the response was instantaneous. Her bunched muscles relaxed, and she stopped her strutting hooves, settling into an easy stance.

On the other hand, I now had energy coursing through my veins from the thrill of the exchange. With a full grin on my face, I lifted myself into the saddle and gave a pat to my new friend.

"What just happened there?" Lochlan asked, his brows pinched.

"I don't know. I just calmed her down," I offered simply and gave a gentle tap of my heels to start Penway in an easy cantor.

Lochlan caught up, and we rode for some time before he broke the silence. "I take it you're feeling better after last night?"

"Seeing Cyrene on the mend this morning helped. But I'm still worried about everything else. Aside from this mess with Morgan, Guin's not going to let me stay on Earth when this is done. She was adamant that there are no exceptions to Fae living in Faery, aside from the Hunt."

"It's been the law for many centuries now, so I doubt she'll deviate for you. As for the Hunt, there have never been women allowed in the Hunt. Not that I could tell you why. It's just always been that way. Women run the Court, and men run the Hunt," Lochlan explained.

"I didn't mean to imply I wanted in," I hurried to explain, not wanting to ask more of him than I already had. "She's not pushing the issue for now, so I'm trying not to worry about it. I just wanted to tell you what was on my mind. You know ... to share where I'm at."

To show you I'm trying.

He met my eyes briefly but said nothing.

For miles, we rode at an easy pace, not wanting to push the horses too hard. The lush scenery was almost too perfect to be real—vines crawling over bushes, thick trees waving in a gentle breeze, and the occasional pixie flying by. Several hours in, we neared a crystal-clear stream where Lochlan dismounted.

"We can stop here to eat and let the horses rest," he said as he removed some food from the saddle bags.

I hefted myself off the horse with a groan. After a few hours riding, my crotch was already sore, along with almost every other muscle in my body. "How much longer is the ride?" I asked, half afraid of the answer.

"We won't reach the edge of the Seelie Lands until almost dark," he responded.

After months of agonizing training to mold my body into a fighting machine, it was going to be a horse that did me in. Several more hours on Penway's back, and I wasn't sure I'd be able to sit for a week. I tried not to waddle as I walked over to the edge of the creek to admire the clear water tumbling between the smooth river rocks.

"Guin asked me last night about the purpose of our journey. I didn't tell her anything."

"That's probably best," he murmured.

"You said Casek had found a teacher for me, but I don't know more than that. Is there anything more you can share before we meet this person?"

He strolled to where I sat and lowered himself to the ground next to me. "I suppose that would be wise. Many centuries ago, a Fae man named Fenodree lived on Earth and fell in love with a human woman. It hadn't been long after Guin had taken the throne, and she exercised her power strictly to ensure the people would know she was not to be crossed. A mandate was in place that forbade Fae to form romantic relationships with humans while the Fae were allowed to roam Earth. Sex had to be permitted for feeding purposes, but Guin didn't want the cultures entangled in any way. Somehow, word got back to Guin that Fenodree had fallen in love and had taken a human wife. The queen had his wife killed and banished Fenodree to the Shadow Lands to make an example of him."

"That's awful," I gasped, shocked at the atrocity Guin had committed.

Lochlan gave a solemn nod. "It took time for Casek to track him down, and I'm not certain Fenodree will help, but as far as I know, he's our only hope. He's spent centuries with the Shadow Fae and will know their powers better than anyone."

"But you don't even know if he'll help us? Did Casek not talk to Fenodree when he tracked him down?" Our finite number of days were quickly slipping away. We didn't have time to waste gallivanting across Faery just to be turned away.

"He asked, but Fenodree wasn't exactly receptive. I had no other ideas than to bring you here and hope we could convince Fenodree ourselves."

My lips pursed with worry. But I had no other solutions either, so I had to trust that this was our best course of action. "Tell me about how you ended up with Alberich."

Gathering his thoughts, Lochlan finished peeling an orange-like fruit before he spoke. "My mother had been one of Guin's few Fae female companions. She lived with Guin in the palace while I lived with my grandmother at her cottage inside the city. On one of my mother's visits home, she and my grandmother had ventured outside the city walls to gather berries for dying fabric. They never came home that night. I was only five, so I had no idea what to do. The next day, Guin showed up at the house asking why my mother had not arrived back at the palace for their evening meal. I was a sniveling little thing, crying and scared. Guin had her guard search for my mother and grandmother. Their bodies were found by a creek, thought to have been killed by a Phooka—a nasty Unseelie that had snuck onto Seelie Lands. Guin brought me back to the palace and had decided to claim me as her own. My family had all been killed, and Guin had been very close to my mother. Alberich happened to be at the palace and demanded I be turned over to him. The two fought unlike they ever had before. No one wanted a repeat of the war between Guin and Odin, so the conflict garnered much attention."

"I take it Alberich won the fight?" I asked in awed fascination.

"Yes. He's never discussed why they fought over me or how the conflict was resolved. I just know that the next morning, he strapped me to his horse, and we set off for his hunting lodge." His voice was distant as he recalled events from centuries before.

"Are you aware that your story was memorialized by the famous human playwright William Shakespeare?" I asked with a smirk.

His eyes cut over to me, humor clearly written on his face. "A donkey's head? The son of an Indian chief? I'd say he took substantial artistic liberty with the tale."

I laughed at his response. "Are you saying *A Midsummer Night's Dream* was rubbish?"

"I'm just saying it was creative. I wouldn't know how to turn a man's head into a donkey's head if my life depended upon it. Magic is much more elemental, more about manipulating energy than transforming objects."

I was quiet for a moment, thinking about energy and recharging Fae magic, which led me to thoughts of Ashley and how she was getting along.

"I hope Ashley's magic kicks in while we're gone. That's really been bothering her."

"I'm sure the transition is just taking time. I would imagine the development of her magic is hindered somewhat by being on Earth. Most new Faeries have the natural wealth of Faery magic to help draw forth their own powers." Lochlan sounded confident, so I tried not to worry. "I think it's time we get back on our way." He stretched out his long body as he stood, and my mouth went dry.

The many years spent on Earth had caused the men of the Hunt to assimilate to human culture. They talked like an ordinary Irishman would, used technology with ease, and seemed to prefer human clothing. Despite his countrymen wearing an entirely different style, Lochlan hadn't changed to Faery attire. He sported dark-wash jeans over his motorcycle boots and a long-sleeved cotton shirt. His body would have been drool-worthy regardless of his clothing choice, but I was particularly partial to his current look and had to force my eyes back to Penway.

Not until nearly dusk did we reach the edge of the Seelie Lands. The border was a visible barrier where everything beyond it blurred as if we were inside an enormous opaque bubble.

"We'll camp here for the night. On the other side of the wall are the Wilds, and I have no desire to sleep there unguard-ed." He dismounted in a single graceful movement, and I followed suit, although notably less gracefully.

He untied the cinched bag he had brought from the palace and set it on the ground before reaching both arms inside, far deeper than the bag should have allowed. I watched in awe as he extracted blankets and what appeared to be a folded-up tent.

"Dear God! Can you imagine what human women would

carry around if they had access to one of those?" I gawked at the fascinating accessory.

He chuckled as he began to set up camp, which consisted of a single pup tent and a small campfire. He explained how the bag contained a portal where things could be stored in an in-between to be pulled out when needed.

Over dinner, we talked about magic and the Fae people who lived outside of Avalon. The Seelie Lands were generally protected from intruders, but there were instances when something nasty made its way across the border. Some chose to live a more rural life outside of the cities at the risk of less protection from the occasional Unseelie. The conversation was enlightening, and I thoroughly enjoyed Lochlan's company as we relaxed by our small fire.

The day had been exhausting, and as the night air grew chilly, we retreated to the tent. There was no way that thing had ever been intended to house two people at once. I hesitated awkwardly once I had wriggled inside. Unbothered, Lochlan took hold of my waist and pulled me gently to my side, settling my back to his chest.

"Don't overthink it, Bec, just rest." His gravelly voice near my ear teased my insides, but it was his tender use of my nickname that warmed me from the inside out.

Despite the hard ground and cool temperatures, I slept better than I had in weeks.

THIRTY-SEVEN

In a manner similar to opening the portal to Faery, Lochlan traced a rune symbol on the barrier the next morning. Instead of the air blurring where the passage appeared, the already opaque wall became clear in a space just large enough for us to squeeze through.

The Wilds resembled Seelie Lands but were not as lush and didn't seem to thrive as thoroughly. The most noticeable difference was the quiet. The ambient noise in Seelie Lands had been unremarkable until we had taken several steps into the Wilds, and the absence of sound was glaringly obvious. There was a slight breeze, but other than that, nothing. No buzzing of insects or flapping of bird wings—none of those normal forest sounds were present. The stillness that gripped the wilderness when a predator is on the prowl seemed to encase the Wilds in a permanent standoff.

The change was unsettling.

Each of my senses pricked with alertness.

I wished we had been able to take our horses with us, but Lochlan had explained that it was too dangerous for them. The

Wilds, though not nearly as vast as the Seelie Lands, were inhabited by violent Unseelie who would tear apart anything they thought weaker than themselves. Our best bet to make it through the Wilds without conflict was to avoid detection, and that would be immensely easier without the heavy hoofbeats of the horses. We released Penway and the stallion before leaving the Seelie Lands, and Lochlan assured me that they would find their way home safely.

We spoke only when necessary, and when we did, we kept to a whisper. While I had no idea how Lochlan knew where he was going, he walked with purpose, directing us around a hillside or through a grove of trees. We stepped carefully through grasses to limit our noise, keeping out of clearings to minimize our visibility. Our lunch was consumed on the move. We stopped only for restroom breaks, which were monumentally awkward—both because of the company, but also because no one had mentioned packing toilet paper. It would be just my luck to pick a poisonous leaf for my personal use and end up with a rash on my nether regions.

As we ventured farther from Seelie Lands, we didn't see a single animal. Lesser creatures of the Wilds had perfected the art of remaining undetectable. By midafternoon, fatigue and our uninterrupted progress had relaxed my sense of readiness. My thoughts wandered as we walked, though I tried to remain alert. When we neared a large lake, I admired its glassy surface as we skirted the shoreline until a line of gentle ripples gliding unsettlingly fast caught my attention. Something was gliding just under the serene water.

I clasped my hand on Lochlan's arm. He followed my gaze and stiffened.

Whatever creature lurked beneath the surface moved parallel along the shore, precisely where we had walked. It was fast and much larger than I'd first imagined.

"Run."

The urgent command was too late. A fountain of water exploded outward as the creature burst through the surface and into the air. It was large—the size of an elephant or an orca whale, though it looked nothing like either. The red-ish blur arced over the water and landed on four short legs about twenty feet away from us. The scales and shape resembled a giant lizard, or perhaps a dragon, since it had shimmering wings spreading wide from its back. A barbed tail whipped from side to side as the animal shook excess water from its scales then puffed angrily in our direction.

Lochlan angled himself between me and this new threat.

"It's a Lambton Worm—a kind of Unseelie water dragon. I shouldn't have a problem with it, but you need to stay behind me." He then bowed his head, and to my shock, he addressed the creature. "I'm Lochlan of the Wild Hunt, and we seek passage through the Wilds. Let us pass." His rumbling voice was impressively commanding and would have made any normal creature cower. But the Lambton Worm threw its head back and roared so loudly that I reflexively covered my ears.

Lochlan sent a warning blast of energy in its direction. The rippling magic reverberated harmlessly off its scales. Rising to the challenge, the Lambton Worm shot blue flames from its mouth directly at us. Lochlan cast an energy shield, redirecting the flames around us. The searing heat of the dragon's flames was unrelenting, even through the protective shield.

While Lochlan had said he could manage the creature, panic gripped me in its clutches. I hadn't witnessed him take on such a powerful threat. Even if I wanted to help him, I would have no idea how.

The instant the flames retreated, the creature swept its long tail toward us and managed to catch Lochlan's ankle, sending him flying ruthlessly into a nearby tree. In the seconds it took Lochlan to recover, the dragon surged forward with me in its golden sights before suddenly pulling up short and going eerily still.

Every molecule in my body begged me to run, but I wrestled myself into stillness. Knees slightly bent, muscles coiled, I stood ready to face my opponent. But an attack never came. Instead, the beast cocked its head as if studying me.

Lochlan started to step toward me but was forced to halt when the dragon growled in his direction. I lifted my hand just toward Lochlan to keep him from coming any closer. He could trace to me, but I got the feeling that the movement would enrage the beast. At that moment, it seemed more intrigued than anything.

The dragon sniffed heavily through its large nostrils, then a terrifying rattling sound emanated from its chest. The aggressive sound could only be perceived as a threat. My magic came bounding to life, stirring up the air around me into the start of a cyclone.

The beast's gaze met my black eyes and stared. Again, it sniffed at the air, but this time, the dragon huffed, lowering its large head in an unmistakable bow.

I could hardly believe what I was seeing. Before I could grasp his response, the beast leaped with astonishing grace back into the sky, diving back beneath the dark surface of its watery home.

The air I'd been holding in my burning lungs whooshed out in relief. "Oh my God, that was terrifying."

Lochlan had yet to relax. His hunter's gaze was still trained on the water's edge. He grabbed my hand and hauled me back into the cover of the trees.

"Slow down, Lochlan. What's wrong?" I stumbled behind him, trying to keep up with his punishing pace.

He slowed to a stop, releasing me, then spat a quiet strain

of curses. I gave him a moment to collect himself, hoping for an explanation. When he finally turned his azure eyes on me, I rocked backward at the fear on display in those stormy depths. Not once in all the time I'd spent with him had I seen him give way to that insidious emotion.

"I don't know how you did it, but I was certain I had failed you," Lochlan said, his voice ragged and strained. "I've never seen a Lambton Worm give such deference to any other creature. I was so relieved, but also..." His eyes raked over me. "It makes me realize the enormity of what Merlin has done to you. The danger he's put you in. I don't like it."

I crossed over to him and wrapped my arms around his middle. We held each other for countless seconds in the unnatural silence of the Wilds, the assurance of touch fortifying us both.

When I pulled back, I drew upon all my courage when I looked at him. "We'll get through this. He wouldn't have set me up to fail."

The muscles in Lochlan's jaw flexed and bulged. "You are fucking incredible," he breathed, filling me with enough confidence to walk on water, should I need to.

"Come on, let's keep moving." I smiled softly. Neither of us spoke again until we reached the edge of the Wilds.

If the Wilds were withered compared to the Seelie Lands, the Shadow Lands were positively desolate. Looking through the magical barrier, it appeared as though I was looking through a black and white filter on a camera. The desolate landscape was painted in shades of gray as though life had been leached from the very fabric of the land.

I breathed in through my nose and out through my mouth, calming my nerves before stepping through to the other side.

Where multiple suns shone in the Wilds, the Shadow Lands bore only a series of moons casting a luminescent glow over the land. The sparse trees seemed to produce leaves already dried up and cracking. The grasses were brown and brittle, and the dirt beneath eroded and hard. I thought of the old western movies my dad used to watch. I could hear the classic showdown melody in my head and pictured a tumbleweed rolling through an empty ghost town.

"How are these two places next to each other yet so different?" I asked in amazement.

"The legends say that millions of years ago, Faery and the Shadow Lands were separate. The two collided such that they were inextricably joined. Like the fabric of two dimensions sewn together—the time and space around each remained separate, but the inhabitants could pass between the two worlds. Eventually, those who lived in the Shadow Lands became known as the Shadow Fae, although they were not originally Fae. The two races rarely mingle. Only the very daring Fae venture into Shadow Lands, and few Shadow creatures will risk the exposure to sunlight elsewhere."

Lochlan pulled out his knife and tipped his head toward a cluster of trees before walking in that direction. Once we reached them, I could see a small ramshackle structure on the other side. It appeared sturdier than a hut but calling it a cabin would have been generous.

As we approached, Lochlan sheathed his knife and called out, "Fenodree, we've come for your help."

Silence followed—no birds chirping, no rustling leaves, just silence.

Lochlan was unfazed. He stood patiently waiting.

"You have wasted your time," came a low voice, void of emotion.

"Morgan of the Lake is threatening war against the Seelie Court. We need your help, or thousands may be killed." Lochlan tried again to plead with the disembodied voice.

I closed my eyes and listened to the shadows. In this new dark land, I discovered a virtual map of my entire surroundings in my head. Like a bat using sonar to guide it in flight, my shadow voices outlined the terrain. Turning as I opened my eyes, I found where the man stood back to our right behind a tree.

When my eyes found his, he cocked his head and stepped forward. "Your man already made your arguments, and they mean nothing to me," he spat out, his anger spiking. "Why would I want to help a queen who killed my wife and exiled me to this wasteland?"

I stepped toward him and hoped that I wasn't making a massive mistake by jumping in. "You aren't helping her, you're helping me and all the humans who would be killed if Morgan succeeds in releasing the Unseelie onto Earth," I offered softly. "I am ... I *was* a human, like your wife. I only recently was transitioned into a Fae for the sole purpose of avoiding this war, but I need help. I need someone with knowledge of the Shadow Fae to help me learn my powers. Please, help me." I pleaded plaintively. If he didn't agree to teach me, I didn't know how else I would learn my magic. Our time was quickly running out.

One slow step at a time, he advanced toward me until he stood directly in front of me. His clothes were nothing but dirty rags, and long dirty black hair hung down his back. Everything in this wretched place looked somewhat anemic, but his dark eyes bore an edge that spoke to his internal strength. His wife had been killed, and he had been cast out of his home, made to live in this miserable land. Yet he had found the will to keep going.

"What do you mean you transitioned into a Fae?" he asked with a cautious curiosity.

"When I was a little girl, I was given this necklace." I pulled out the pendant from beneath my shirt and turned it over to show him the back. "It contains the combined essence of both a dark and a light Fae. Wearing the necklace for twenty years has changed my fundamental makeup—I now possess magic. However, this combination of powers has never been achieved before, so my abilities are different from other Fae. We think they may be more similar to the Shadow Fae than the Seelie, and I need someone familiar with their powers to help me master my own abilities."

"How did you come into the possession of this amulet?" His curiosity morphed into open skepticism.

"Merlin," I said simply.

Fenodree lifted his head in understanding. He then glanced over at Lochlan before briefly touching the pendant. He drew his hand back and met my eyes for a long moment before he spoke softly. "If I do this, it would only be to help keep you alive. Not for Guin. Not for anyone else." His eyes roamed over my face, and I could hear a hint of a rumble come from Lochlan's chest. In my mind, I begged him to contain his sudden possessiveness.

I beamed at my new teacher, beyond grateful for his help. Maybe, just maybe, I would be able to do what Merlin had asked of me. "Thank you, Fenodree." I was not normally a hugger, but I was so relieved that I had to refrain from throwing my arms around him. I didn't, mostly because I didn't know the man, but also because he stunk to high heaven. He also didn't strike me as the touchy-feely type.

"What powers have you exhibited so far?" Fenodree asked gruffly, seemingly uncomfortable with my show of gratitude. His accent sounded Old English, and he spoke formally, without the use of slang or contractions. Altogether, the effect was very aristocratic. The juxtaposition of his courtly dialect and his impoverished conditions was bizarre.

"Some common powers like unlocking a door, but I've also been able to become invisible in daylight. I can control smoke, and I've put darkness into a Red Cap and killed him."

He remained still, a study in stoicism. "These powers are definitely unusual, but the magic of the Shadow Fae is quite varied. You say Merlin used the essence of a Shadow Fae as the source of your magic—it would help immensely if we knew exactly what creature was used. First, let us get you both settled inside. The cabin was not built to hold three, but it will have to do."

The wood structure he called home was comprised of a single room that appeared to be exclusively used for sleeping and storing his supplies. We set our bags down in a corner opposite Fenodree's straw mattress, and Lochlan extracted our blankets.

Fenodree squinted toward me, eyes on my necklace. "I believe that I know what we can do to learn the source of your dark magic. Come with me." He led us to the remains of a small cooking fire. "Take off the necklace," he ordered.

"I can't—it doesn't come off," I said apologetically.

He looked up from where he had been searching in a small pouch and grunted. "Of course, you cannot remove it. I believe I am going to regret agreeing to this."

I didn't respond to his comment. Instead, my eyes sought out Lochlan, who looked like he was holding in a laugh. My eyes narrowed at him, and a single corner of his mouth raised as he leaned back on his hands. I rolled my eyes at my two companions as Fenodree lifted a pinch of ash from the fire.

"Around here, it can be essential to know who and what is out hunting. I developed a spell to show me what creatures might be near. I think that the same spell should work to detect the source magic of your amulet."

He stirred his concoction with a mortar and pestle while

whispering words over the mixture. His finger swiped up a dollop, and his other hand lifted my necklace. He rubbed his finger down the stone pendant in a single line and then waited. I could barely see the pendant down below my chin, but I was able to see when sparks started bursting from the stone. The substance he had wiped on the necklace burned up into a thick smoke that rose above us, taking the form of a horned creature.

Fenodree inhaled a deep breath and stared intently at the shape. "The Nuckalavee," he said gravely.

"Are you sure this is accurate?" asked Lochlan in a hard tone.

"How do you think I have survived out here all these years?" snapped Fenodree.

"What's a *nooka-lavee*?" I asked the men.

Fenodree cast his harsh gaze my way. "It is a being so malevolent and dangerous that it is believed that even the mention of its name brings bad luck. There are tales of its immense dark magic—just sensing its presence would be enough to frighten away a lesser creature," he explained as he began to clean out the mortar.

My eyes caught Lochlan's as I thought of our encounter with the Lambton Worm. Had it sensed the Nuckalavee and given us a wide berth? Was that why it had left us alone?

"What powers does the Nuckalavee have?" I asked.

"I can only tell you what is rumored, as I have never had the misfortune to cross paths with one, nor do I know anyone who has. I would dare not ask what Merlin did to acquire the essence of such a creature." He noted darkly. "The Nuckalavee is renowned for its rare ability to create hellfire. It also manipulates dreams, giving its prey nightmares to feed upon fear and turmoil. The creature is rumored to enslave its victims in their own nightmares indefinitely, feeding off them until they die."

My gaze returned again to Lochlan at the mention of

manipulating dreams. Heat flared in his gaze as we were both taken back to the brief window of pleasure we had shared when I had pulled him into my dream.

I cleared my throat and turned back to Fenodree. "I have nightmares of a shadow man who haunts me in my sleep. Could that be a byproduct of the Nuckalavee sending me those dreams?"

He cocked his head in thought, eyes narrowed. "They are not exactly shaped like men, but that does not necessarily rule it out. It would not surprise me if his essence is powerful enough to have a sentience. That essence may be tiny, but it sounds like perhaps it is still trying to feed itself from your fear."

"Is there a way to stop it?" I asked, hope swelling in my chest.

Fenodree shook his head. "You could perhaps learn to keep it contained, but not disable it entirely. Not as long as you wear the necklace. The two of you are connected. There is no getting around that until the bond is severed."

I nodded gravely.

The queen had talked about my transition to becoming Fae as if it were a process with a clear beginning and end. Hopefully, I would get to a point when the necklace was no longer necessary, and I could be free of my haunting shadow man.

We spent the few remaining daylight hours showing Fenodree what little we knew about my powers then shared a little about our backgrounds over dinner. Lochlan offered to start hunting while Fenodree trained me, and we laid out a plan for the coming days.

When the dim light of day began to wane, Fenodree stood. "We need to get inside. This place is not safe in the darkness of night."

Unease pricked along my skin as I followed his lead, scanning the horizon for unwanted visitors. "Will the walls of the cabin be enough to keep us safe?"

"While I am not proud to admit it, I have utilized blood magic to craft wards around the premise. It was the only way to keep out all that might come after me. Only inside my ward will we be protected from the creatures that stir in the dark."

I told myself that if Fenodree had lasted this long, we were most likely safe, but it was hard to override my internal alarm system. Had it not been for an exhausting day of travel and running for our lives, I doubted I would have slept at all. But as it were, Lochlan pulled me into his chest as he had the night before, and I quickly relaxed into his warmth.

"Why didn't you tell me you had nightmares?" His words next to my ear were hardly a whisper, but their gentle caress was felt down my entire body.

Not wanting to bother Fenodree, I turned around to face Lochlan and realized too late just how intimate the position was. "I had them when I was little and had always assumed they were just a part of growing up. Then they stared up again when I arrived in Belfast."

"I suppose there was nothing I could have done, but I would have liked to have known." His words were gruff but surprisingly sweet.

"If it's any consolation, the dreams haven't bothered me when I'm in your arms."

He grunted and tucked my head into his chest, pulling me snuggly against him. Cocooned in his woodsy scent, I settled into a deep and dreamless sleep.

CHAPTER

THIRTY-EIGHT

Over the next two weeks, I worked relentlessly with my magic while also training with Lochlan twice daily to keep my combat skills sharp. Lochlan would hunt during the day while I worked on my magic with Fenodree. He was a fan of repetition, so I practiced skills over and over with varying degrees of success until I began to flinch at the word "again."

We started my education by learning to locate my power within me and pull it to the surface on command. I came to discover that I could differentiate between the two distinct types of power within me. When Lochlan had tried back on Earth to teach me, he had explained that the magic was like an energy buzzing in my body, just waiting for me to channel it, and that was the case for the light magic. However, the dark magic was less responsive to my requests and more reactionary. I almost had to unlock it from where it hid within me before I could gather its menacing energy.

Once I learned to identify the magic, I had to learn how to call it forth. When I had tried to unsuccessfully to make myself invisible in the safety of my apartment, I had only envisioned the results and had not summoned the power. Focusing my intentions was an important element, but without the power, there was no magic.

There wasn't one specific muscle to flex—it was more like gathering the energy throughout my body and focusing it on whatever task I needed. However, there was a complicating factor to my magic. The two forces acted like Italian dressing— I could shake it up as much as I wanted, but the oil would always ball up and keep itself separate from the vinegar. Similarly, my dark and light magic felt like they had protective coatings, keeping them from ever fully uniting into one substance. Instead of simply summoning the magic, I also had to determine how much of each power was necessary and coax the proper proportions.

Once I could summon the power inside me, I had to learn to direct the magic to do my bidding. We started by working with the elements since they were the most basic form of magic. My power was linked to air, which was why the air around me would swirl and come to life every time I powered up. I practiced moving the air with intent, then tried to gather my power without moving the air at all, which turned out to be substantially harder.

Along the same lines, I was able to master my ability to control smoke. The process was essentially the same as moving air, but the particulate in the air gave me more to work with. I discovered that I could compact the smoke into a shield, similar to what I had seen Lochlan use against the Lambton Worm.

Oddly enough, once I learned the basics, making myself invisible was fairly simple. The best part of the process was showing off to Lochlan when he would return from an afternoon of hunting. Although, I quickly learned that surprising him with my invisibility was not the best idea. The first time I tried, he came close to taking off my head. But smaller tricks delighted me to no end. I would make the wind blow leaves onto his head or make my arm invisible to steal food off his plate. I was endlessly tickled with my antics, and I gave credit to Lochlan for enduring my pranks good-naturedly ... mostly.

While the Seelie could manipulate memories, the Shadow Fae could send images to a person's subconscious, often using the ability to create nightmares. We discussed my ability to pull Lochlan into a dream and dubbed the power "dream walking"—a sort of telepathic FaceTime. The best part was that I could do this even when awake, a form of active daydream.

After much trial and error, we discovered the power had a couple of limitations. It required an element of proximity—either an intimacy with the other person or geographic proximity. I couldn't simply pull someone into a dream that I hadn't met or a friend who was far away. However, the closer my ties to the person, the farther I could be from them geographically and still pull them into a dream.

Between my sparring sessions with Lochlan and the mental strain of using my magic all day, I was utterly exhausted by nighttime. I hardly said a word before I passed out cold each night in Lochlan's arms. I had wondered if being so near the heart of dark magic would trigger my nightmares but was surprised to find I didn't have a single one. I mentioned the fact to Fenodree and explained that it was most likely the wards around his cabin and my own powers growing that were keeping the Nuckalavee from exerting itself. It wasn't a guarantee that I wouldn't have any more nightmares, but it was a step in the right direction.

About a week or so into my training, Fenodree and Lochlan began arguing over something they discussed privately after dinner. When I curled up with Lochlan later that night, I could still feel the tension radiating off him in waves. I hated to see him upset and had the urge to pull his frustrations into me. It was similar to how I had felt when I had calmed Penway, so I reached my magic toward him and pulled the tension into me.

Lochlan stiffened. "What did you just do?" he whispered with a note of awe.

Fenodree grumbled, "This place is not exactly spacious, and I haven't had a woman in centuries. Can you save that for later?"

"Fen, you said Shadow Fae feed on negative emotions. I think Rebecca may do the same," said Lochlan. "Becca, what did it feel like to you?"

I sat up and explained what I had done and how I had done the same with the horse. "You think that's how I feed my magic? Instead of sexual energy, I feed on … tension?"

"That's exactly what I'm saying."

I supposed that was better than needing to have sex to feed my magic, and it was a relief to figure out what my energy source would be. "Why haven't I needed to feed before now? At least, I don't think I've needed to feed."

Lochlan pulled me back down to our pallet to talk softly while Fenodree's breathing slowed with sleep. Apparently, he wasn't as riveted with our new discovery. "I can only assume the necklace acts as a power source, and since up until now you haven't performed much magic, you haven't needed an additional source."

"This could be really handy," I said sleepily.

"How's that?" he murmured softly in my ear.

"Whenever you're all broody and intense, I can use that to make you happy."

"I'm not broody," he grumbled.

I stifled a small giggle. "You are, but that's okay. It's a part of your charm."

"Now I'm charming?"

"I wouldn't go that far," I teased sleepily.

Lochlan huffed out a laugh, pulling me snugly to his chest before we both drifted to sleep.

As I learned more and more of my magic, I was also able to control the change of my eyes to black and back again. In the perpetual dim lighting of the Shadow Lands, I discovered that when my eyes went black, I could see in the darkness almost as well as in daylight. It was important to control the change because any bright light was extremely painful when my eyes were black. I understood why the Shadow Fae were hesitant to travel outside the Shadow Lands.

One of the things I was most anxious to learn was how to defend against someone using immobilizing magic against me like Ronan had done when he captured me in the alley. As it turned out, for better or worse, a defense against that type of attack was relatively easy. Magic was a manipulation of energy, and immobilizing someone was a matter of restricting their use of their own energy—like holding their energy hostage. When a person couldn't access their own energy, it allowed the other person to take control as a puppeteer would a marionette. The trick could only be used against individuals who couldn't control their own power or who had no magic.

Once Lochlan had explained how it worked and walked me through a simulated attack, I could easily detect how his magic bound mine. When I threw off the constraints, he no longer held me prisoner. I had dreaded the helplessness I experienced when Ronan pinned me to that alley wall, and I was relieved to know I wouldn't be so easily controlled in the future.

The most difficult challenge I faced was manipulating darkness. After I had worked with Fenodree extensively for two weeks and had become relatively comfortable with my powers, he suggested we try to duplicate how I had killed the Red Cap. My best guess was that I had pushed dark magic into him, and it acted as a kind of poison, but I wasn't entirely sure. I hated even thinking about the terrifying experience, let alone voluntarily recreating it. I had also briefly managed to use the power when Ronan was attacking me. Both incidents had been life-threatening situations, and I wasn't sure what I had done to make it happen.

As much as I wanted to avoid using that power, I knew that I needed to master all possible uses of my magic. Not only did I hate thinking I might need to use such a gruesome ability but I was also scared of its effects on me. When I had performed the magic, I reveled in the killing, and I was terrified of that feeling. As if the Nuckalavee's dark desires had taken over, and I had ceased to be me.

We practiced various drills for a couple of hours when Fen walked off abruptly and returned holding a five-foot-long, two-headed snake tightly behind the heads. "Show me what you did to the Red Cap," he commanded.

My stomach clenched, and a nauseating surge of panic shot from my head down to my now-sweaty palms. The snake looked like any other ordinary snake, aside from the extra head. I wasn't a big fan of snakes, but I also hated the idea of killing anything without provocation.

"I can't just kill it!"

Fenodree's face contorted in anger. "What do you think we are doing here? We are not training for tea with the queen," he spat with disgust. "When you came to me, you talked of war. In war, you have to kill. It is not pretty, or kind, or just. War is strategy and death and requires absolute ruthlessness. If you cannot overcome your sensitive upbringing, then we are wasting our time."

He said the brutal truth I needed to hear, but it was as easy to swallow as a mouthful of nails. Killing Ronan or the Red Caps who had attacked me was substantially easier than hurting an innocent bystander. Just because there were casualties in war didn't mean I wanted the loss to be at my hands. Whether it was people, dogs, or snakes—my mind violently rebelled at senseless killing. However, if I didn't suck it up and do what was needed, the losses could be infinitely worse.

Fenodree's dark eyes bore into me until I acquiesced and stepped forward. He held the snake out, and this time, I reached forward and tentatively took its brown-scaled body into my hands.

"Don't let it bite me," I fussed at him. I might have agreed to kill the snake, but I wasn't happy about it.

Just as I had been practicing for the last two weeks, I concentrated on the low-level hum of the dark energy inside me. The snake had its own energy frequency, and I pressed my energy forward until I could feel it seep into the snake. I couldn't see any evidence that I was putting darkness into it. Instead, the snake went limp and stopped moving entirely. "Did I kill it?" I asked in confusion.

Fenodree lifted the lifeless snake to his face. "No, you relaxed it to sleep. The thing is out cold," he quipped.

I sputtered a laugh but received a glare from Fen.

"Come on, Rebecca. You can do better than that. All you did was essentially feed on it. You need to know exactly how to kill with a touch. Not many Fae have an ability like yours, so you need to master it. If only so that you do not accidentally kill without intending to do so." He gave me a meaningful look, and I was sufficiently chided by his warning.

I exhaled and took hold of the snake again, using thoughts of Morgan's war and innocent children being killed to bolster my determination. I imagined my parents, helpless to defend themselves, and the devastation that would occur if creatures like the Lambton Worm, the Red Caps, or even the Nuckalavee ended up on Earth.

Crackling power sizzled in my veins, and I isolated the dark, malevolent part of that magic. Stoking it like a fire inside me, I drew the thick power toward the tips of my fingers and pushed it inside the snake. Both of the snake's heads reared backward against Fenodree's hold, and its body started to seize as its scales around my hand grew darker. Once the circle of black emanating from my hand extended about three inches in all directions, the snake went limp.

My relief that I had accomplished the task was quickly squashed by an oppressive sense of guilt that I could celebrate my actions. After a brief glance at a satisfied Fen, I spent the next hour by myself in the nearby grove of trees, attempting to come to terms with the ease with which I could end a life.

"I brought you some lunch." Fen lowered himself to join me under the shriveled trees. "You can't afford to be skipping meals."

"Thanks," was all I said as I opened the small leather satchel of food and began to munch on some jerky. We sat for some time in the eerie quiet where no breeze ever blew, and the sun never rose. I couldn't imagine living multiple lifetimes in solitude. "Have you ever tried to leave here?" I asked, finally caving to my curiosity.

"There is nothing I want to go back to," he replied as he looked away. "Plus, it is not so bad here."

"Seriously?" I scoffed with wide eyes.

"I have lived here for many lifetimes now. It is hard to remember what life was like before."

"You lived on Earth with your wife?"

He gazed off in the distance, unfocussed. "I had been nomadic for many years when I first saw her. She was a proud

Viking woman, chopping wood near the water's edge of the northern sea. I was captivated by her strength and independence—no law could have kept us apart. I do not regret one minute of our time together."

I was deeply touched by his devotion to his dead wife, especially considering the harsh consequences of that love. "Fen, can I ask you something personal?"

"You can ask. It does not mean I will answer."

I gave him a small eye roll before asking, "If your magic requires sexual energy, how has it survived in your isolation?"

He lowered his head just a fraction but spoke without shame. "My magic faded long ago."

"But you used magic. I've seen you."

"I used spells and runes—that is not the same as magic born within someone."

As I looked at the resilient man I had come to know and respect in a short amount of time, my heart ached for him. "One of these days, I'm going to get you out of here, Fen. I'm not sure how yet, but I'll do it," I said with conviction.

He offered me a small conciliatory smile. I could only imagine that getting out would seem like a pipe dream after so long in the vapid wasteland.

I vowed to myself that I would find a way.

Making a quick grab for his knife, Fen jumped to his feet, eyes trained intently on the distant trees. I brought forth my Fae eyes to see what had alerted him and was shocked at the figure coming toward me. Placing my hand on Fen's arm to assure him it was safe, I stepped out of the tree cover.

"Knight! Come here, boy," I called out to the giant white fur ball who lopped in our direction.

"Rebecca, do you know who that is?" Fen asked with surprise.

"That's my dog, Knight. He saved me from Ronan, and he

has a tendency to follow me—although this was unexpected." I bent over and hugged the furry beast as he bounded over. "I knew you weren't a normal dog, but this was an awfully long journey, even for you. How did you find me?" I said playfully as I rubbed his head.

In an awed voice, Fenodree placed a cautious hand on Knight. "That is Gally Trot. He is Merlin's watchdog. You truly are here to stop a war."

"What the hell, Fen! Did you think I was making all that up?" I balked as I stood back up to look at my mentor.

He stiffened. "Not exactly—perhaps embellished slightly?"

I shoved him lightheartedly with a laugh, and the three of us made our way back to the cabin.

THIRTY-NINE

Thump, thump, thump.

My eyes opened blearily in confusion at what had woken me. Lochlan's arms were steel beams holding me in place, his body inhumanly still.

Thump, thump, thump.

I became fully awake and alert.

"Hello, old friend," came a familiar voice outside the cabin. "You need to be quiet, or we'll wake everyone."

My body relaxed back into Lochlan just as his arms released me. We rose from our pallet, and Fen gave us a questioning look?

"It's Merlin," I offered as I opened the door to find the man himself sitting on a nearby stump, rubbing Knight's head. Regardless of what Fen had called him, he had been my knight in shining armor, and I would call him Knight accordingly.

The dog was lounging outside, his tail thumping happily against the cabin wall. I had argued that he needed to stay the night inside with us, but both men had adamantly refused. They claimed that there was not enough room and that Knight would be just fine outside. While I had conceded my defeat, I had done so begrudgingly.

"I apologize for my early arrival," Merlin said with a smile.

I shook my head at the mysterious Fae man. "We would have been up soon anyway. Merlin, this is Fenodree." I motioned to the raven-haired man eyeing Merlin warily.

"It's good to meet you, Fenodree. I believe we all owe you a great deal for helping our Rebecca with her magic."

Fen dropped his head in a small bow but said nothing.

"I won't be staying long," continued Merlin. "I have one more thing I must teach Rebecca before she will be ready to face Morgan." His smile thinned. "As I have mentioned to Rebecca, the reason no one has been able to uncover how Morgan is circumventing Guin's wards is because she is using a little-known place called the Twilight Realm. I had discovered its existence when Morgan was still a young apprentice, and while I had not taken her there, I told her of my discovery. It seems she spent her years in seclusion learning how to access the realm. I believe it is time to test your abilities to open such a portal, now that your magic has progressed. Though, I think breakfast would be a good idea before we get started. You'll need your energy."

Merlin hadn't seen me do anything with my magic, though Knight had been around during my afternoon practice session the day before. The two must have communicated somehow. Not only had Merlin sent someone to help keep me safe since my arrival in Belfast but he'd also been keeping apprised of my progress the whole time. I wondered what other ways he'd been involved without our knowledge. Asking would likely be an exercise in futility, so I stashed the question away for later analysis.

We ate a quick meal, and I attempted to wash my face and brush my teeth. Weeks had gone by without bathing, and I was worried the dirt would be so caked on that I would never get clean again. I couldn't even imagine how Fenodree had lived so long in that state.

When we were all ready, Merlin explained that a portal to the Twilight Realm absolutely had to be opened from outside. That was one way this portal was different from the ones between Earth and Faery. He gave some explanation about being one with nature and energy fields. I did my best to understand, but his words went over my head.

"As its name implies, the Twilight Realm is a place of both light and darkness—not fully light, nor fully dark. Therefore, a combination of both light and dark magic must be used to reach it. As you all know, the two forms of magic repel each other and are not easily combined." Merlin raised a brow in my direction to emphasize my importance.

"Morgan uses ancient magic spells to combine her own light magic with a medallion infused with dark magic. Her method is much more tenuous than ours, making it difficult for her to maintain a portal. That is why she has not been able to open one long enough to allow many Fae to pass through. On Beltane, when the veil is thinnest, she will have the opportunity to open a portal on a massive scale."

He led us to an open area not far from the cabin, giving us a moment to visualize the horrifying possibilities of Morgan's actions. Lochlan and Fenodree sat on the ground while I stood with Merlin, scanning my surroundings anxiously. We had gone farther from the safety of Fen's wards than I'd yet to go, and the vulnerability was making me tense.

"You will need to concentrate to open a portal. Trust that I won't let anything harm you here." Merlin's tone reminded me of my dad when I had put off homework and needed to get busy working—not exactly chiding me, but a fatherly reminder.

I gave him a tight smile and wiped my sweaty palms on my jeans. "I'm ready. What do I need to do?"

"First, I'm going to open a portal myself so that you can get a feel for it. Once you see how its done and get a sense of the realm, you should be able to lead yourself there. You haven't been able to trace, but if you had, you would have learned that the magic takes you where you envision yourself." He closed his eyes and held up his hands, reminding me of a video I had seen of people in an evangelical church raising their hands in prayer. As he chanted under his breath, the air before him sparked and blurred.

Lochlan and Fen both shot to their feet, and I stepped back cautiously.

As the circular portal solidified, Merlin stepped through, then turned to usher us in after him. My mind couldn't comprehend what I saw on the other side. A vast star-lit sky surrounded us in all directions, including beneath our feet, as if the ground was a perfect reflection of the sky. Galaxies of stars could be seen, and there was just enough light to hint at a sunrise or sunset, but no sun or moon was visible. There were no signs of life, as if the place only existed as a stopover between worlds.

"What is this place?" I asked in awe.

"That is a good question. I stumbled upon it quite by accident," replied Merlin whimsically.

"I have no magic here," Lochlan grumbled with a snarl on his face.

"That is the odd thing about the Twilight Realm. Only a combination of light and dark seems to work here. Your light magic alone is of no use."

Lochlan narrowed his eyes at Merlin. "How exactly did you open the portal?"

Merlin merely gave Lochlan a knowing smile and otherwise ignored the question. "Once Morgan arrives here, she can open a portal to Earth or Faery from here. The queen's wards are only effective against opening portals between Faery and Earth. The Twilight Realm is a loophole in the magic."

"What I don't understand is why she's opening portals to Earth instead of Faery. If she hates Guin so much and wants to end her reign, why not just send the Unseelie and Shadow Fae to the Seelie Lands?" I wondered aloud.

"The reason is twofold: first, she wants humans to learn of the Fae so that Guin can no longer keep them a secret. Second, she knows that Guin is arrogant, and without direct evidence of Unseelie entering her lands, she will not believe the threat is real until too late."

"If that's the case, her plans are unfolding nicely," I groused.

Merlin's lips thinned at the reminder of Guin's reticence to acknowledge Morgan as a threat. "On that note, let's see if you can get us back from where we came," he suggested.

I raised my hands and closed my eyes, summoning the power within me and visualizing the grassy clearing. The magic swelled and then ebbed, but no portal appeared. "How much of each magic am I supposed to use?"

"That is something you will have to discover for yourself. My methods are not the same as yours, and I have no experience as a Twilight Fae from which to guide you."

"How do you know I can even open one of these portals then?"

"I don't," he said casually as I stared at him wide-eyed.

"Well, super," I muttered.

My forehead beaded with sweat as I repeatedly tried to open a portal with no success. I had no idea how much time we had actually spent there, or how the time there compared to the time in Faery or on Earth. The uncertainty weighed on me.

Eventually, Merlin applauded my efforts and suggested we head back. He held open a portal as each of us stepped back through to the Shadow Lands. Once his turn came to pass through, Merlin simply smiled at me affectionately from the other side of the portal. "Don't get discouraged. You will master this ability as you have done all the others. I have other matters to attend to, but I will see you again soon." With that said, he dropped his hands, and the portal opening collapsed.

My mouth opened and closed twice before I turned to the others. Lochlan shrugged then led us back to camp in silence.

I was mentally drained after my efforts and emotionally overwhelmed. In the past, I would have crawled into bed and lost myself in lethargy as I struggled to cope with such a monumental morning. But the new Rebecca had learned to find comfort in training—sweat and strain and physical exertion. When I asked Lochlan if he wanted to spar, he jumped at the suggestion. I wasn't the only one needing to work through some tension. We spent the next hour sparring until my body was limp with exhaustion.

It wasn't until I sat down for our evening meal that I realized Knight had also disappeared along with Merlin. Perhaps it was the day catching up with me, but his absence weighed heavily on my heart. Having Knight there had been like having a piece of home. He had given me a sense of normalcy in an unexpected way, and losing that made me realize how homesick I'd been.

I was torn between being desperate for more time to prepare and hoping we'd made enough progress to return home soon.

My melancholy soon brought me to thoughts of Ashley. Had anything happened with her magic? Was she staying safe, or had she encountered any of Morgan's minions?

Days earlier, I had tried to reach her by dream walking but

had been unsuccessful. With nothing better to do, I decided to try again. If I learned anything at all during my time in the Shadow Lands, it was the importance of not giving up.

I closed my eyes and drew my powers to the surface. Dream walking was a predominantly dark magic tool and required me to pull those powers from deep inside me. I visualized Ashley with her long blond hair and vibrant blue eyes. In my mind's eye, she wore one of her sultry clubbing dresses and was smirking at me as though she was about to rope me into going out. I concentrated on every tiny detail about my best friend—the small mole on her left cheek and the coral color she loved to paint her nails. The image in my mind slowly became the image before me. I was standing with Ashley in the living room of our apartment in the Huntsman building.

Her eyes narrowed at me, and she crossed her arms over her chest. "I'm not happy with you."

"What did I do?" I asked, taken aback.

"You left me here while you went gallivanting in Faery. I hate sitting here helplessly, not knowing what's going on."

"Well, don't hold back. Tell me exactly how you feel."

She dropped down onto the couch with exasperation. "Why shouldn't I? You're just a figment of my imagination."

"I'm not a figment of your imagination. We're dream walking. It's one of my powers. I came to check on you!"

Ashley paused, her head tipping to the side as she assessed me. "How would I know you were really you and not just a dream? If I give you a question to answer, I'd know the answer, so you would too. I would have to ask a question that I don't know the answer to, but then I couldn't verify the answer was correct."

"Good Lord, Ashley, I have no idea. Can you just talk to me regardless of whether I'm real or not?" I dropped down on the couch next to her.

"Whatever, it's not like there's anything to say anyway," she groused.

"No magic?"

She lay her head back on the couch cushions, eyes drawn up to the ceiling. "None. Nada. Zilch."

"I'm sorry, Ash. I wish I could help. Maybe next time I see Merlin I can ask him about your magic."

Then Ash shot upright. "Do you think he could help?"

"I'd say he's our best bet, but I don't exactly have his phone number. I'm not sure when I'll get a chance to ask him."

"I'll take any hope I can get." She grinned and stood, closing the distance between us, then booping me on the nose with her finger. "Real or not, I'm glad to see you, Bec."

I wrapped her in a tight embrace. "Same here. You be safe, Ash, and I'll see you soon." I pulled back and met her fading gaze. One blink later, and I was back by the campfire in the chilly evening air.

A throat cleared beside me, making me jump.

Lochlan sat just inches away, staring into the dying flames. "Dream walking?" he asked softly.

"Yeah, I wanted to check on Ashley and use the opportunity to test my skills."

My eyes lifted up to the clear sky above. Three moons, all in some phase of waxing or waning, glowed softly on the landscape below. The etching on my necklace bore the three crescent moons representative of the Shadow Lands and its dark magic. As bleak and frightening as that place could be, it was also beautiful. My magic was a product of that land—entrenched in mystery and deceit but also glorious in its own right. What a gift that I'd been able to visit my best friend. The magic itself wasn't intrinsically evil, just as light magic wasn't necessarily benevolent. Learning my own powers was helping me to understand that the Fae weren't as simple as Seelie versus Unseelie or light versus dark. They were just as complex as humans and shouldn't be judged on their brand of magic—or the fact that they had magic at all.

"Lochlan?" I said hesitantly.

He lifted his chin in answer.

"Did you know that Fen lost his magic because he can't feed here?" I asked quietly, not wanting Fen to overhear me talking about him.

"I hadn't discussed it with him, but I assumed it was likely."

I looked at the stoic Fae warrior who sat beside me. We had been there for two long weeks, and he had told me previously that he needed to feed every two to four weeks, depending on how much magic he used. Was his magic growing weak? How quickly did the Fae's powers fade? The thought of Lochlan being rendered powerless to perform the simplest of his natural Fae abilities tore at my heart.

"Do you need to feed?" I asked him, avoiding looking in his direction.

His head slowly turned toward me, and when I met his eyes, they were frighteningly intense. "I can survive until we get back home," he said gruffly.

"What if ... I didn't want you to just survive? What if I volunteered to help?"

"Why would you do that?"

"Because I want to." I kept it simple, but there was so much more I felt. I didn't want him to suffer. I didn't want him to feel weak. And I wanted to see for myself what it would be like to share the experience.

The modest campfire flames glinted in his eyes as his expression turned from wariness to something heady and seductive. He stood and extended a hand, leading me to the patch of trees at the edge of Fenodree's protected enclosure.

My mentor had already gone to bed for the night. So long as we were quiet, we'd have the next thirty minutes alone before nightfall would force us inside.

We stopped, hidden among the trees. Lochlan's hand raised, his hand at my chin and thumb caressing, then tugging at my bottom lip.

"You have two options," he rasped. "You can touch yourself, or you can allow me. It can be as intimate or as clinical as you prefer."

"I know you want to show me that side of things—that feeding doesn't have to be personal—but that's not what I want. With you, it *is* personal. I don't want to remove that."

He huffed out a guttural growl of approval before his hand reached around to clutch my hair and bring our foreheads together. In a voice splintered with strain, he whispered, "Lie down."

The rocky ground wasn't comfortable, but that didn't matter. As I lay back and looked up into Lochlan's eyes where he settled himself beside me, the thrill of connecting with him so intimately washed away any pesky discomforts.

I unbuttoned my pants while Lochlan's hand drifted beneath my shirt. He cupped my breast over the thin lace of my bra then teased at my nipple with a pinch. I gasped and arched against the sudden burn that made my core weep. Simply knowing I'd be the focus of Lochlan's attentions had stoked a simmering heat in my lower belly, but now that I had him touching me, teasing me, my body was brimming with sensation.

"Remember ... be quiet," he murmured before lifting my shirt, releasing my breast from its lace confines, then devouring my flesh with his mouth.

The warning had been prudent. I had to fight back the need

to cry out. So much pleasure. So much need. My body ached with desire.

Lochlan worked my breasts devotedly, occasionally kissing and nipping at my neck, before his hand drifted down and slid beneath my panties. He glided two fingers on either side of my clit, careful not to overwhelm the sensitive bundle of nerves. Coating his fingers in my arousal before he started his ministrations, Lochlan commanded my body with the perfect touch. I felt as though he knew my body better than I knew it myself.

My mouth dropped open on a silent cry at the intense pleasure flooding the highways and byways of my body. I rocked my hips, encouraging hit touch and pleading for more. On occasion, he dipped his fingers into my body, curling them deep to roll over that special spot within. The alternating sensations gave my body time to settle so that each touch felt like the first, driving me mindless with pleasure.

"I could see you like this every fucking day and never tire of the sight," he rumbled in my ear before nipping at my lobe.

A tsunami of pleasure rose up and crashed over me, drowning my body in overwhelming bliss. Lochlan's mouth slammed down on mine to muffle my scream as wave after wave of sensation electrified my body.

Afterward, I was ruined. Lifeless and limp and perfectly content.

I had to force my brain back to reality when Lochlan began to right my clothing. "Did you feed? I never felt anything," I murmured dazedly.

"You didn't feel anything?" he teased.

"Well, you know what I mean. I couldn't feel you feed."

"I did. What exactly did you think you would feel?"

"I don't know. I just figured I'd be able to tell."

His eyes drifted over my face. "If a Fae was greedy when they fed, their partner's orgasm might seem stunted because all the energy would have been siphoned out. I didn't need to do that, but more importantly, that wasn't really our purpose anyway, was it?" His words weren't spoken like a question. They were confident and backed by the wisdom of a man who'd lived a number of lifetimes.

"Thank you," I whispered, hoping he'd understand that I was talking about so much more than an orgasm.

His eyes blazed possessively. "Come, let's get inside. Night will be here soon."

CHAPTER
FORTY

It took me three long, frustrating days of failed attempts before I was finally able to figure out how to open a portal to the Twilight Realm. Granted, it was another two full days until I actually opened one sufficient to walk through. Still, I learned the balance of power needed and had been able to create the start of a swirling portal door before I lost concentration and it dissipated.

The first time I opened a portal large enough to walk through, I lost my head and began screaming ecstatically. Lochlan came tearing through the trees, bow aimed for possible threats, and found me jumping up and down like a lunatic. After I had received a thorough chastising, I reopened a portal, and we were both able to walk through.

I continued to work tirelessly, training with Lochlan in the mornings and evenings. During the middle of the day, I would rotate practice on various magic skills, focusing on opening portals. If I couldn't open a portal to the Twilight Realm, none of the other stuff mattered.

On the morning of our twenty-eighth day in the Shadow

Lands, Fenodree and Lochlan informed me that it was time for a test. As much as I was terrified of what kind of test I would face, our time was running out. I grew more anxious each day to get back to Earth. Unless Lochlan had some type of telepathy or secret carrier pigeons that I was unaware of, we had no way of communicating with anyone. The only person outside of Lochlan and Fen that I had been able to dream walk with was Ashley, and I had been unable to duplicate my visit with her. There was no telling what had transpired in our absence, not to mention, I was ready to get home and take the longest, hottest shower on record.

We skipped my morning hand-to-hand session and instead followed Fenodree to a clearing several miles from the cabin. The farther we strayed from the safety of our little homestead, the more on edge I became. By the time we reached the grassy stretch about fifty meters across, I was jumping at every sound and had chewed the inside of my cheeks raw.

It was still early, and a low-level fog blanketed the dry grasses. When we reached the middle of the clearing, I started to notice a foul odor and scanned the area for its source. "What the hell is that smell?" I asked with a hand over my nose and mouth.

Lochlan froze mid-stride, and his head drew back to search the skies beyond the tops of the paltry trees surrounding us. "Fenodree, we discussed this. It's too much," he said in a hushed tone.

"It is not too much. It is a test, and she will succeed," Fen replied harshly. "Her skills need to be tried in a situation of duress."

I grabbed Lochlan's arm to snag his attention. "You guys are freaking me out. What is this test?"

Fen turned his attention to me, his face a mask. "What you

smell is the Sluagh. They are the Unforgiving Dead—a swarm of malevolent souls of evil Fae. They seek to slaughter and destroy all they come into contact with. You will need to think quickly and use all your resources."

"*Jesus*, a swarm?" I shot at him in horror. "One evil Fae soul isn't enough. You want to sic a swarm of them on me? I can't do this, Fen. We need to get out of here *now*." I looked frantically back at the tree line, searching for the host of Sluagh. While I couldn't see anything, the smell became more putrid by the second. When I turned back to Fen and Lochlan, they were gone. I spun around in a circle and found myself alone.

I was going to fucking kill them when this was over.

I had to get a grip on myself. Taking a cleansing breath, I pulled out my knife and stood in a defensive posture. A terrifying whining sound emanated from the distance—almost like pinching the neck of a balloon and letting the air out slowly. The shrieking noise was painful to my ears the louder it became.

My breathing stalled into shallow puffs, struggling to keep pace with my racing heart.

I had thought I'd experienced terror before when I'd defended myself against the Red Caps, Ronan, and the Lambton Worm—they had all been frightening experiences. But the lengthy anticipation of knowing something horrible was approaching was infinitely worse. With a sudden assault, there was no time to dwell on the danger. As I stood in the clearing waiting for the arrival of the host of undead Fae, crippling panic gripped my mind. Instead of strategizing my defense, I stood rooted to the ground, paralyzed with fear.

Not moving particularly fast, a mob of amorphous beings with a gray, cloudy aura around them floated over the treetops just before me. They were packed together tightly in a group of about thirty opaque spirits wailing as they drifted through the sky. They were still some distance away, but I could make out their contorted, malformed faces.

Unexpectedly, seeing them helped me shake off my panic-induced trance. My mind raced for ways to combat the nebulous cloud of angry souls. First and most logical, I became invisible. If they couldn't see me, perhaps I could avoid them entirely.

The Sluagh continued purposefully in my direction.

Next, I pulled the misty fog from the clearing and formed a protective shield between the mob and me.

The closer the phantoms came, the faster they moved in my direction. Somehow, they could see me despite my invisibility and weren't at all deterred by the mist. Rage and fury rolled off them in waves.

I decided that maybe if they weren't so angry, they wouldn't feel the need to come after me. I reached out with my power and attempted to calm them, pulling the negative energy toward me as best as I could from a distance. My actions only seemed to enrage them, their wailing growing more intense and chaotic.

There was no way I could put darkness into them since I needed touch to perform that trick. The Sluagh wasn't corporeal—and besides, I wasn't willing to get close enough to try.

My breathing became ragged as the screeching ghosts closed in on me. I had no idea how to stop them, and terror was impeding any rational plan I might have concocted.

Drawing from some innate instinct to rely on intimidating, I screamed "*Stop!*" and summoned the air around me to swirl. I was shocked when the word came out multilayered, as though fortified with magic.

To my utter astonishment, the swarm pulled up short. They moaned and vibrated with energy, but before long, individuals shook off their confusion, and the wailing picked up louder than ever. The mob began to make a beeline to where I stood.

I took in a deep breath, concentrated all my power into my words, and screamed, "*LEAVE!*"

Hissing and whining, the host of malevolent spirits scattered in all directions, disbanding in their hurry to flee from my command. They dispersed beyond the trees, leaving only their rank odor behind them.

I wasn't exactly sure what I had done, but it had saved me, and that was all that mattered. My adrenaline surge morphed into an ecstatic high.

"*I did it!*" I hissed quietly at the guys, not sure where they were and not wanting to draw the Sluagh back to us.

"Well done, Rebecca," congratulated Fen behind me.

I whipped around with a giant grin to see both men smiling at me. My own smile dropped, and I lunged forward, shoving each of them with one of my hands. "How *dare* you leave me to face them alone! What if I couldn't do it? What if they'd *killed* me?"

Lochlan managed to grab my flailing hands. He spun me around, pulling my back against his front and pinning my arms firmly across my chest.

His body resonated with a chuckle. "Calm down, little warrior. I would have traced in to help you if needed. I didn't know exactly what Fen had planned, but we had discussed the test weeks ago." He placed his cheek against mine and offered in a gravelly whisper, "I'd never allow you to be hurt on my watch."

His words assuaged my anger until my heart rate calmed, and I relaxed back into his arms.

Once he released me, I turned to Fen. "The Sluagh saw through my invisibility. How could they still see me?"

"They are the undead—they see souls, not physical forms.

They zero in on energy, so it is known that one cannot hide from the Sluagh. Aside from their stench, that is their most well-known characteristic," Fen offered in explanation.

"How was I able to make them leave?"

"Because they are pure energy, they are susceptible to magical commands when issued with sufficient strength. Their most effective weapon is simple intimidation. When their victim becomes immobilized with fear, the Sluagh surround the individual and entrap them in a world of mind-bending horror."

"I could see how someone could be easily overwhelmed by them—they were terrifying."

"You did well, Rebecca, but now, we must get back to the cabin. The Sluagh could return, or something else might chance upon us. The undead are not the only thing to fear in these parts." Fen spoke with an eye turned to the trees.

I quickly fell into step behind Fen, with Lochlan taking the rear as we hurried back to camp. I took the remainder of the day off, which was the first chance I'd had to spend time at length thinking about my situation. One would think that without television or work, or any of the multitude of distractions available on Earth, I would have had loads of time to let my mind wander. However, in a place like the Shadow Lands, Maslow's hierarchy of needs came into play, and my mind was focused on survival rather than more superficial concerns. Staying alive, finding food for the day, not letting Lochlan ring my bell as we sparred, and mastering my magic had been all-consuming.

Now that my window for learning was quickly closing, I would soon face the ultimate test—one infinitely more critical than my confrontation with the Sluagh. If I lost, it wouldn't be just my life at stake. The Sluagh, the Lambton Worm, and all the other bloodthirsty creatures in Faery would be free to terrorize Earth.

The pressure resting on my shoulders was crippling. However, I was proud of the progress I'd made. I had advanced far beyond the naïve girl who had arrived in Belfast months earlier. Yet there was no way to know if it was enough until I faced Morgan on Beltane. There was no safety net or stunt doubles, no retakes or backup plans. I would face trial by fire, and I had to win at all costs.

By evening, I had withdrawn into myself under the weight of knowing so many lives were in my hands. Lochlan drew me from my thoughts as he sat down beside me.

"I don't think I've ever seen anything so beautiful as you are when you wield your magic."

His unexpected admission stole the breath from me. He thought I was beautiful. The swell of warm emotions his words had evoked clashed against the wall of dark clouds my brooding had stirred up. Together, they brewed a storm inside me.

I offered Lochlan a shaky smile, attempting to tamp down my swelling emotions. "Thank you."

"Want to tell me what's wrong? You haven't been yourself all day."

"I'm worried I won't know what to do to stop Morgan," I confessed, dropping my eyes to the sandy ground.

"You've spent countless hours training and have taken every opportunity to improve yourself. You've evolved from a timid mouse to a mighty lion. Have confidence in those abilities." Lochlan's confidence in me was absolute. Like a deep network of roots anchoring a tree, his belief in me gave me the support I needed to remain strong.

"If you cry," Lochlan warned with a quirk to his lips. "I will take back every word of what I said."

As intended, his teasing comment drew a chuckle from me. "Can't take a few tears, you big baby?" I shot back playfully.

His eyebrows rose in challenge, and I bolted from where I sat with him hot on my trail. When he caught up with me, he pulled me back against his chest, lifting me off the ground and spinning me around in circles as I squealed and laughed. He had successfully cast away the stormy skies and brought a ray of sunshine back into my world, if only briefly.

When he set me back on my feet, I turned to face him, and his full lips lowered down to close over mine. His kiss was a thing of legends—it made my problems feel manageable and the future seem brighter. It was the touch of warm sun on a chilly morning and the bliss of cold water on a parched throat —refreshing, comforting, and right in every way.

We pulled back from one another slowly, reluctantly, and in a land where there was no breeze and no nocturnal bugs chittering, the only sound in the night air was our labored breathing. He took my hand and led me to the cabin to rest for the night, tightly wrapped in each other's arms.

It's DISORIENTING to wake in the morning to nothingness—no birds chirping, no police sirens or passing traffic, no air-conditioning hum or upstairs neighbor thumping around above you. The first week we spent in the cabin, I would come awake to a racing heart, sure that we were about to be attacked or some tragedy was about to befall us. After an entire month in the Shadow Lands, I could wake and appreciate the stillness. Inevitably, Lochlan would already be awake. Once I stirred, we would both get up for the day.

On the morning following my test, I started to sit up but was softly pulled back into Lochlan's warm arms.

"It's time to go back." His voice was throaty from sleep, and his proximity to my ear made the fine hairs on my neck stand tall.

"Go back home?" I asked in surprise.

"Yes. We need to get back, and I think you've learned what you needed from Fenodree."

I turned back to face Lochlan and gave him a cautious smile. His full lips lifted in response as he gave me a squeeze, and we both got up to prepare for the trip home.

DESPITE OUR VAST age difference and our short time together, I felt profoundly connected to Fenodree. At times, I'd wanted to strangle him, but the thought of saying goodbye and leaving him to struggle alone in the wastelands felt heartbreakingly wrong.

The stoic Fae man wore a straight face, but in his ancient dark eyes was a world of longing. His years in exile were hard enough, but now, he'd had a reminder of the comforts of companionship, and it was clear to me that we would be dearly missed.

I would do everything in my power to help get my new friend out of the Shadow Lands, regardless of Guin's mandated exile. However, without a specific plan of action to offer, I kept my convictions to myself. I encouraged him to stay strong and promised that I would come back to see him.

To myself, I swore to find a way to save him.

FORTY-ONE

Our trip back home was blessedly uneventful, although it took almost twice as long as our trip there without the advantage of horses to carry us. I was so ready for a shower and a soft bed that I was prepared to sprint the distance if necessary.

We arrived at the palace late and were thus relieved of the obligation to attend dinner. To my surprise, we were dismissed to return to Earth immediately, no doubt owed to our rank odor and filthy appearance.

We had left Faery late into the night and found it was equally as dark outside the church back on Earth as it had been in Faery. It turned out to be evening in Belfast, rather than early morning as it was in Faery. People were still crowding sidewalks as they walked to and from dinner and other evening obligations. The sight of something so normal was immensely reassuring. And I was certain I'd never seen anything more beautiful than the picture-box windows of the Huntsman building when Lochlan parked out front.

I could hardly get out of the car fast enough.

When I bounded into the lobby, I found Liam and another

Huntsman standing at the elevators in front of a long line of people hoping to get into the club. I threw myself at Liam for a hug, and he laughed heartily in surprise.

"Darlin', it's great to see you, too, but you positively reek," he said as he gingerly untangled himself from my arms.

I turned a big smile to the other man, who shook his head in warning. "Don't even think about it. I can smell you from here."

I stuck my tongue out at both of them and followed Lochlan into the elevator. As we stepped inside, Liam informed us that we had been gone three weeks Earth time—longer than I'd expected. That meant we were down to the final week before Morgan planned to make her move. I tried not to let that information steal my joy at returning home.

When the elevator opened on my floor, I abandoned Lochlan and tore down the hall to my apartment. I pounded on the door, too excited to dig out my keys, but Ashley didn't answer. With a huff of frustration, I dug through my backpack for the key and managed to steady my hands sufficiently to unlock the door. My grin as I walked in could have brightened even the most dreary of Belfast skies.

I was Julie Andrews in the Swiss Alps spinning in circles and singing "The Hills are Alive"—never had I been so happy to be somewhere in my life.

Dropping my bag, I walked directly to my bathroom and stripped out of my clothes. I cast them in a pile with plans to burn them at the earliest opportunity.

I had never been an overly emotional person, and I couldn't remember a time when I cried from pure, unadulterated joy. But as the warm shower pelted my skin, tears pricked my eyes, and I began to sob with relief. For a solid half an hour, I scrubbed, shaved, washed, conditioned, and buffed my neglected body. I let the stress and uncertainty flow down the drain along with a month of greasy dirt. By the time I stepped out of the shower, I was ready to take on the world.

Not long after I had dressed and brushed the extensive tangles out of my hair, Ashley came into the apartment and launched herself into my arms.

"I was so worried about you," she whispered, still clinging to me tightly.

"I know, honey, and I was worried about you."

We pulled back and took a long look at one another. I was surprised to detect a slight difference in her—something intangible I couldn't quite put my finger on. I wondered if I seemed different to her as well. I felt different.

"Without you here to cook," she teased, "I'm afraid there's no food in the place."

"You have some wine and cheese?" I asked, knowing the answer already.

"Of course, what do you think I've been living on?"

She made a cheese platter while I poured the wine, and then we curled up on the couch to eat and catch up. The first taste of wine burst on my tongue with a tang so intense that my jaw ached. For a solid month, I had consumed a bland assortment of root vegetables and the rare bit of salty game. My palate had grown accustomed to the bland cuisine more than I'd realized.

I set my glass down, recognizing that I'd have to go easy on the wine. "Tell me what's been going on while I've been gone."

"I assume you know it's been three weeks, but let me tell you, it's been a long-ass three weeks. Morgan must have opened another portal at some point because there's been a load of Unseelie causing trouble. Violent crimes in the city have skyrocketed, and the news channels have been looking into the source. Alberich has been trying to contain the damage as best as he can. The men even talked about shutting down the club for a while."

I hated to hear that things had gotten worse while I was away, but it strengthened my resolve to put an end to Morgan's campaign of terror. "I've learned a lifetime of skills while I was away, which was almost five weeks for me, by the way."

"*Five weeks?*" she gawked.

"Yes, and it's totally disorienting, and not just because of the time difference. The Shadow Lands are in perpetual darkness, so even the overhead lights in here seem blindingly bright. The vegetation there is brittle and withered, and you have to be constantly on guard for predators."

"Oh my God, that's awful! Tell me *everything*," she insisted, inching closer.

Over the next hour, I detailed my month in Faery and answered her onslaught of questions, including questions about our dream-walking session.

"You are telling me that was *real*? That's like telepathy or something. Can you read my thoughts?" She grasped my hand excitedly.

I laughed from deep in my belly. It was such a relief to be back with my best friend and see her happy. "It was definitely real, but it's not exactly telepathy. I can pull a person into a dream—it's like FaceTiming in our minds. We can talk, but I don't hear thoughts or anything."

"That's crazy cool," she said wistfully.

My smile wilted. "You'll get there, Ash. Although it might be best if you don't."

"Why would you say that?"

"On top of everything else, I may get stuck living in Faery when this is all over. If you essentially stay human, you'll avoid that fate."

Her eyes rounded. "What the hell are you talking about?"

"Queen Guin mandated centuries ago that all Fae must live in Faery. I talked to her while I was there, and she refused to allow me an exception. I didn't mention you, so your involvement is still secret. But if you gain powers and word gets out, you would have to move to Faery, too."

"Oh, shit," she breathed.

I nodded. "Exactly."

"Could she really make you leave?" Worry creased her forehead.

Not wanting her to be upset, I lay my hand on hers and reached out with my magic, gently pulling her tension into me. "I'll be okay, Ash. Promise."

She swayed a little, and her eyelids fluttered before she met my eyes with a dreamy, stunned expression. "What the hell was that?" she asked reverently.

"That was me feeding on your stress. Feel better?" I asked with a smirk.

"Feeding? You figured out how you feed your magic?"

I nodded. "I feed on fear and negative emotions rather than sex."

"I'm so freaking jealous that you can do that. Coolest. Trick. Ever. And so much less complicated than sex."

I laughed at my dazed friend, and her lips lifted in a smile. It was nice to know that after causing so much trouble, I at least had a temporary means to soothe the trauma.

Not long after, Ashley called it a night, claiming I had relaxed her into a coma. I curled up in bed, enjoying the warmth of my cotton duvet and the supportive cushion of my pillow-top queen mattress. However, despite the late hour in Belfast, I couldn't convince my mind to shut off and sleep. I lay in bed tossing and turning when the familiar sensation of being watched lifted the hairs on the back of my neck. Sitting up, I turned to face the shadow man who had haunted my dreams for too long.

As a child, I'd been terrified of going to bed for fear that the amorphous shadow man would be there when I closed my eyes. Now, I knew it was the essence of a Nuckalavee that had tormented me, and somehow the knowledge was empowering.

The thick, inky cloud in the shape of a man hovered next to the bed menacingly. It began to vibrate with energy, but before it could rush at me, I lifted my hand.

"*No.*" I threw as much power as I could into the command, and the smoky form twisted and writhed in agitation. "I know you're powerless except to haunt my dreams, but I refuse to allow this to continue."

I closed my eyes and sought the place where my dark magic resided, pulling it to the surface and forming a protective barrier around me. As I did, I met resistance, but I forced the Nuckalavee presence from my mind. It didn't go easily, but I didn't quit until the barrier between us was solid and impenetrable. Brick by brick, layer by layer, I mentally reconstructed the Great Wall of China.

When I opened my eyes in the dream, the room was empty.

Three weeks' worth of text messages and missed phone calls sat waiting for me the next morning. Most were unimportant, but my mom had started to get worried when she hadn't heard from me, so I called to let her know that I was alive.

I also had thirty-five texts from Cat, starting off casual and growing more concerned each day until she was yelling in all caps. As soon as I hung up with my mom, I rang Cat and assured her I was still alive. Apparently, she'd assumed I wouldn't be gone long and had panicked when I didn't return right away. I told her all about my trip, and she updated me on the Druid situation. I explained that while I was back in the city, I wouldn't be able to return to work until after Morgan was dealt with. Every hour we had to prepare was precious. She offered to help however she could, and I hung up pleased that all my relationships seemed back in good sorts.

I debated about checking in with Lochlan but figured he had plenty to manage after being gone for so long. He knew where to find me when he was ready. When I heard a knock on the door just after lunch, I fully expected to find him on the other side, but it was Alberich who stood somberly in the hallway.

"Oh, hello. Can I help you?"

The Erlking's mahogany eyes were shadowed with concern. "I know you've only just gotten back, but I'd like for you to begin testing your magic here on Earth. It won't be the same as it was in Faery, and you'll need time to adjust."

"Of course. Merlin said I'd need to be outdoors to open a portal. Do you have somewhere in mind for me to practice?"

"There's a park not far from here. Lochlan and I will accompany you if you can be ready in fifteen minutes. We'll meet you downstairs."

I nodded readily. "That's not a problem. I'll see you down there."

Lochlan was leaning against a wall in the lobby when I arrived. I smiled at the sight of him only to receive the sobering stare of a man ready for battle. Combined with the sight of the Sword of Light strapped to Alberich's back, my anticipated practice session suddenly felt entirely too real.

Our days of leniency and levity were gone. From now on, there was no room for anything but absolute dedication and unerring focus.

Only a sparse word or two were spoken on our way to the

park, which consisted of a playground and a large open area for sports and recreation. Beyond that was a forested area lined with giant trees covered in spring leaves. The park was especially lovely on such a beautiful day, an odd juxtaposition to the serious nature of our situation.

We set off on one of the paths winding through the wooded area until we got to a small clearing. Not nearly as large as the one where I had faced the Sluagh, the space was filled with lush green grasses and a sprinkling of wildflowers.

Alberich continued on to the far side of the clearing and disappeared behind the thick tree trunks while Lochlan and I remained in the middle of the clearing. The sun was blindingly bright to my sensitive eyes, and now that I knew more about my powers, I could feel my energy drain from the sun. I walked back to a patch of shade near the tree line, but Lochlan remained out in the open, his eyes trained off in the distance.

I closed my eyes and reached out for the two distinct energies deep within me. The push and pull of light and dark felt more remote than they had in the Shadow Lands. I had to coax the energy forth, and coiling them together for a portal proved even more difficult. Despite the consistency I'd obtained in Faery, I could barely create a spark now that I was on Earth. I'd been warned the magic would behave differently, but I hadn't expected it to be so challenging. The reality of my situation was enormously disheartening.

I tried two more times before I sat down in the grass in exasperation. I only had a handful of days left. How could I master this in time? What if I didn't? Would Merlin show up and give me guidance?

Lochlan came crashing to his knees next to me, startling me from my inner crisis. He clasped my hands, and his wide eyes bore into me intently. "Rebecca, listen to me carefully.

Morgan is here. Alberich is distracting her in the trees, but I need to help him. You have to go invisible now."

Morgan? She was here? I knew I'd have to face her, but I hadn't expected my time to come so soon.

"I thought we had until Beltane?"

"You do," he assured me. "She's not here for you. This isn't your time."

"But what if it is? What do a few days matter? Either I'm ready or not. Maybe I can catch her off guard now." The more I thought about it, the stronger I felt that this might be a perfect opportunity to get this whole damn thing over with.

Lochlan's iron grip clamped down on my arms angrily. "Listen to me. This is not the time. Do you truly believe Merlin would have set everything in motion for you to battle her in the Twilight Realm if it wasn't necessary? Promise me you'll stay invisible no matter what. *Promise me.*"

His argument made sense, though I hated to admit it. I didn't want them to have to face Morgan while I cowered meekly in the shadows.

"*Now*, Becca," he urged fiercely. "I have to go."

He stood and rushed for the trees, disappearing as he traced away. I drew my magic around me like a protective cloak and became invisible. Sticking to the shade beneath the trees to protect my eyes, I raced after him. I would stay invisible, but I needed to see what was happening.

Once I broke the barrier of the trees, the faint sound of voices guided me in the right direction. I slowed my pace when the three came into view beyond a cluster of trees. A blond woman with striking blue eyes stood opposite Lochlan and Alberich. Like Merlin had said, she looked nothing like the painting that bore her namesake. This woman was stunning, with a long thin neck and high cheekbones, equally as regal as the queen. However, she wore skintight black pants with a dark gray scoop-neck top falling off one shoulder and stylish black heeled booties. This woman was more than comfortable with human culture. I had envisioned a half-mad woman scraggly from years of isolation and festering hatred. I couldn't have been more wrong.

"I'm glad you're here, Lochlan," Morgan crooned. "You should know the truth about the man who raised you."

"Tell me whatever you like, then leave. Nothing you say means anything to me." Lochlan was cool as tempered steel.

"You wouldn't want to know that the precious leader of your brotherhood was nothing more than Guin's pathetic lapdog? You wouldn't want to know how he took children from their mothers at her command and carried out unconscionable deeds without so much as blinking?" Her rage was palpable. A clawed thing with scales and a hunger for blood.

Lochlan wasn't impressed. "You condemn him when you plan to unleash death and destruction on Earth? How many will have to die for your own ambitions?"

She bared her teeth at him before tracing in behind him, a blade held tightly to his throat. "You're nothing but a spoiled child with no understanding of history. You may think I'm cruel and deranged, but you're just one of the deluded masses. How could I expect anything different when you were raised by that spineless bitch of a man?"

Undeterred by the threat, Lochlan snarled. "I'm deluded? You're the one who's concocted some convoluted story in your head to justify ending countless lives."

I wasn't far from where they stood. With my training and invisibility, I knew I could distract her enough for Lochlan to free himself.

Blood began to trickle down his neck, and adrenaline-laced panic coursed through my veins.

I couldn't lose him.

Before I could make a move, his hand fisted nearest me extended its pointer finger, and slowly waved back and forth. He was telling me no, reminding me of my promise.

My heart lurched in rebellion.

How could I stand by and watch? If I didn't attempt to stop her, I might as well have plunged the knife in him myself. I couldn't live with that.

"*Enough!*" Alberich barked, stepping in before I had a chance. "Morgan, I'm the reason you're here. Don't take your grievances out on him when I'm the one you want to punish." Alberich unsheathed the sword and tossed it to the ground.

We all stood stunned as the breeze blew peacefully around us.

"You would do that? You would give your life for his?"

"You know I would."

"*No*, Alberich!" yelled Lochlan, and then his body stilled so completely that he appeared to be petrified in stone. For all intents and purposes, he had been. Morgan had used magic to paralyze him. I hadn't thought someone as skilled as Lochlan could be immobilized so thoroughly, but Morgan's powers were exceptional.

The next moments would haunt me for the rest of my life. I would forever wonder if there was more I could have done. Had it been the right thing to do nothing? How had the situation gone so wrong? Why wasn't Alberich fighting back?

Morgan traced in behind the Erlking of the Wild Hunt, and though she never picked up the sword, it appeared in her hands, its ancient carvings glowing brightly. She swung the blade at lightning speed.

Alberich never even flinched.

He dropped to his knees, and when his body fell forward, his head rolled off and bounced on the ground. Blood began to spurt from the gaping opening at his neck.

Cupping trembling fingers over my mouth, I trap the vomit and horror that's clawing its way out.

Lochlan roared with fury. He'd been freed from her magical hold the second she'd traced away, but he'd had no time to stop her.

"I don't care what you think of me," she said in a hollow voice, eerily devoid of emotion. "I *will* bring down Guin's walls and her reign, and there is nothing you can do to stop me."

And then she was gone.

Lochlan raced to Alberich but stopped cold, his eyes bouncing between head and body. He tipped back his head and released an agonized scream, arms held wide and fists clenched with helplessness. For the first time since I'd met him, I saw the depth of his emotions. The air was saturated with his grief, the earth soaked in his sorrow.

A searing pressure filled my throat and burned the backs of my eyes. My heart constricted so painfully I had to clutch at my chest to prevent my ribs from collapsing under the pressure. I was desperate to help, but there was nothing I could do.

Lochlan removed his shirt and wrapped it gently around Alberich's head, holding the bundle gingerly to his chest. I approached slowly and looked into Lochlan's devastated eyes as I wordlessly offered to hold the bundle. We would need to get the body back to the car, and he couldn't do it alone. Together, we carried the late Erlking out of the park and drove in heart-wrenching silence back to the Huntsman.

CHAPTER

FORTY-TWO

Casek met us at the front of the building. He and Lochlan carried their fallen leader inside. I left them to their grief, knowing they needed each other more than anything, and went to shower back at my apartment.

After I rinsed the blood from my body, I sat under the spray and cried for a man I had come to respect despite our short acquaintance. I cried for the unbearable pain Lochlan was enduring and for my feelings of helplessness to prevent any of it.

Once my eyes burned, and I was certain there were no more tears to cry, I toweled off and curled up in my bed. It was still late afternoon, but I had no energy for anything beyond sleep. I'd failed to open a portal, then watched as the man I'd grown to care deeply for lost his father in the most gruesome way possible. And to top it all off, we'd lost possession of the Sword.

How could we possibly recover from such horrendous setbacks?

Morgan had marched in and disabled Lochlan as though he were a mere human. How could I possibly conquer that kind of power?

I couldn't face the reality of it all. I needed to lick my wounds before mustering the strength to resume my fight. Within minutes, I was asleep and didn't stir until the early hours of the morning.

The sun had not yet peeked over the horizon, but my mind would not allow me to go back to sleep. I bundled up in warm clothes and a blanket before quietly going to the roof of the building, where I could watch the sunrise. Lochlan had been the one to show me how to access the roof, so I wasn't overly surprised when I found him standing along the railing, eyes fixed on the horizon. I joined him without a word, and we watched as a sliver of light slowly blossomed into breathtaking swaths of pinks and oranges.

"My first memory is of Alberich teaching me how to use a bow," Lochlan shared quietly. "Throughout the majority of my youth, we lived at his lodge in the woods and spent our days tracking and hunting. Despite being Erlking, he devoted those years to raising me. When I was strong enough to hold back a bow, he made me one of my own, along with a set of arrows. The first time I made a kill, he carried me on his shoulders all the way back home." His eyes were distant as he smiled softly at the memory.

"I hadn't known him well, but from what I witnessed, he was a good man. I'm so sorry, Lochlan." I wished there was more that I could do or say to ease his pain, but some things couldn't be fixed.

"I just wish I knew why he did it. Why he just handed himself over. With the two of us there, we could have fought her off." Remnants of his desperation hung on his words.

"We can't know what he was thinking, but he was clearly committed to his decision. There was nothing you could have done." I knew what it was like to blame yourself for losing a loved one, and I didn't want Lochlan to suffer that fate.

He looked at me with the hint of a sneer on his lips. "That's a pretty sentiment, but it's a lie. I could have done any number of things differently. I could have traced in and attacked without warning. I could have argued or fought. I could have done *something*. My inaction was a choice, and that choice got him killed. Nothing you or anyone else can say will change that."

I clasped his forearms and forced his eyes to mine. "Morgan is the only one to blame here. She swung that sword. You are not responsible for her actions."

"Is that what you tell yourself when you think of your brother?" he shot back.

I recoiled, the force of his words winding me.

He continued before I could recover. "Don't tell me about blame when you still blame yourself for his death even though you were nothing but a baby yourself. I wasn't a child. I was a grown man who stood there and let my father get *slaughtered*." He shoved away from the railing and stormed back inside, leaving me breathless and rattled.

Tears I'd thought all dried up forged warm trails down my chilled cheeks. I started to walk back to my room but found myself in the elevator to the ground floor. I needed to be alone. I didn't even want myself for company. At that moment, I would have given anything to be someone else—anyone else— so long as I escaped the debilitating pressures of my life. I wanted to be someone who wasn't responsible for the survival of the human race. Someone who didn't hurt everyone they loved. Someone who saved lives instead of ending them.

I walked the early-morning streets aimlessly with my head lowered and hands tucked deep in my pockets. My steps were slow, weighed down by my leaden thoughts. My need to flee had been so great that I'd thought distance would make me feel better, but with each step, the vise around my chest pulled tighter.

After half an hour, my feet slowed to a stop, and my eyes lifted to the tangerine skies of a sunrise teasing me with the illusion of possibilities. Like clickbait, the brightly painted clouds promised a wealth of happiness and hope, when in reality, the brilliant strokes of color were simply camouflage that hid pelting rain and eminent catastrophe just beyond the horizon.

The tar-like grip of despair coated my insides, holding me trapped until the sounds of a scuffle drew my attention. Some fifty yards away, near a couple of trees in a small city park, a man was yelling to scare away two large dogs. The angry animals flanked either side of him, heads lowered menacingly. Together, they both lunged, bringing the man to the ground with a terrifying scream of agony.

Without thought, I pulled my knife from its sheath in my boot and ran toward them.

"Get out of here," I yelled, waving my arms to scare them off.

The two beasts were thick, barrel-chested animals that had to weigh over a hundred pounds each—not as large as Knight, but still plenty intimidating. Their glossy black coats molded over rippling muscle, and ferocious growls warned of their feral intent.

The man cried out helplessly, his arms curled protectively around his head, but the two dogs were relentless in their assault.

I slowed when I finally approached close enough to draw

their attention. The two dogs finally released their victim to train red, glowing eyes in my direction. I stopped breathing entirely. An ancient instinct still alive in my muscles screamed for me to run, but I held my ground as I reassessed my situation. This wasn't any ordinary dog attack. These were Unseelie creatures, savage and thirsty for blood.

While I frantically tried to regroup, the man on the ground was lost to his fear. Incapable of logical thought that would have urged him to remain still, he attempted to scuttle backward away from the beasts.

Eager for any hint at a chase, the animals both turned and descended upon the man like rabid wolves starved for flesh. One grabbed the man's leg while the other clamped vicious jaws around the man's throat and tore out muscle and tissue with one merciless pull.

The man's body jerked violently. Silently.

He never had a chance against these powerful monsters.

With blood running down their jowls, the creatures peered back at me as if in debate. Eat their kill or go after a second?

I wasn't going to give them an option.

The second they ended the man's life, I'd begun to back away. There was nothing I could do for him. I cloaked myself with invisibility and made a careful retreat. The dogs looked around in confusion, sniffing the air for me, but decided I wasn't worth the chase. I kept my eyes on them until they turned to continue feeding.

I started to walk away when my conscience hooked me with sharp claws and pulled me up short. Putting myself at risk right before Beltane would be reckless. But how could I allow those creatures to continue killing? Wasn't I just wishing I could save people rather than hurt them? I might not be able to save everyone, but I could choose to try.

I could choose courage instead of fear. Hope over despair.

Lochlan was right. Everything was a choice. I might feel overwhelmed, but my response to that feeling was *my choice*. If I knew I'd done everything I could, guilt was a choice. If I knew logically that my brother's death was a horrible accident, blaming myself was a choice. I could feel remorse and grief, but punishing myself above and beyond those emotions was a decision I'd made long ago. A decision I could unmake.

It might take time, but I could do it. Learn to give myself grace. To be true to myself without living in constant fear of falling short. Because in the end, all I could do was be myself. Not every decision will be right, but I had to trust myself to do the best I could.

And at that moment, leaving those creatures alive to terrorize other people wasn't an option.

Still invisible to their bloodred eyes, I crept back toward the dogs, where they feasted side by side on the man's corpse. To keep the nausea at bay, I told myself the scene was nothing but movie magic—fake intestines and red food coloring. I employed the stealth training Fenodree had imparted, approaching without making a single sound and staying downwind. As I moved, I tugged at my dark magic, allowing it to flood my veins with crackling power.

I placed a hand on each of the beasts' backs and commanded the darkness into them.

I had no room for uncertainty. Though I'd never tried to subdue two creatures at once with my darkness, I attacked with the confidence of a woman who was absolutely sure of her power.

Both dogs seized in surprise, but I held my hands firmly to them as they stumbled to the ground and collapsed in convulsions. My magic flowed into them without resistance, bringing their lives to a quick end.

Once they were both still, I stepped back and assessed the

site with a newfound certainty. A sense of acceptance and surety.

I couldn't be sure of the future or my success, but I could give this life my all, and that meant no more fear. No more holding back, and no more doubts.

A sense of absolution wiped the grime from my eyes and gave me an entirely new perspective. A purpose revolved around carving out a future rather than running from the past. I was ready to move forward.

Pulling out my phone, I texted Lochlan about the need for a cleanup before getting back on my way. This time, I knew exactly where I was going. I needed to talk to Merlin, and there was one place I could count on finding him.

The museum would not open for a couple of hours. Fortunately, I had a set of keys and was able to open a side door and silence the alarm. When occupied by visitors, the museum was stately but alive. Walking through the dark corridors without another soul around made it feel almost sacred—like a shroud honoring the artists and their works. Each piece was a memorial, and the building was a mausoleum to the creative process.

I wound my way upstairs to the mighty bronze stallion, where I first spoke with Merlin after moving to Belfast. The sculpture was breathtaking. Aside from capturing the coiled energy of the horse's motion, the artist had perfectly captured the ferocity of emotion as well. He faced his unseen enemy with dauntless courage and determination.

"I wasn't able to open a portal here on Earth," I said aloud when I sensed from the darkness that I wasn't alone. Glancing over my shoulder, I confirmed that Merlin had traced into the room and stood silently behind me in the shadows.

"Opening portals is a tricky business." Merlin strolled closer, eyes lifting to the stallion. "You'll need to tap into the magic of one of the ancient portal locations. Lochlan and

Alberich should have known that," he explained with a hint of remorse.

"You know then, that Alberich is dead?"

"I do. His passing will be a profound loss for the Hunt. He was an admirable Erlking. While I have never been a part of the Hunt, I respected his leadership of the brotherhood."

"She's powerful."

His chin dipped low. "That she is."

"I'll do everything I can to stop her." I held his pale eyes unwaveringly.

"What a difference six months has made," he said with no small amount of pride. "I have absolute confidence in you, Rebecca. Though you may not have approved of my choice of altering your life course, you have embraced your new fate admirably. You are the product of my life's work, and your mere existence gives me pride beyond imagination."

I hadn't expected a pep talk, but it was appreciated, nonetheless. To have someone as impressive as Merlin believe in me was humbling.

"I wasn't terribly pleased with you for a while, but I've come to see things differently. I'm glad I have this opportunity to help people. I would much rather take this on my shoulders than see the world as I know it fall to darkness."

Merlin's eyes glinted with mirth. "I may not be omniscient —I can't say with absolute certainty how this will play out— but I do have an uncommon ability to see things others can't. I told you already that I knew you were the one the moment I laid eyes on you, and that is one thing that has not changed. You have lived up to every one of my expectations and then some."

I had to get out of there before he reduced me to a puddle of emotions.

"Thank you," I whispered.

He gave my chin a gentle touch, then vanished into thin air.

~

EACH OF MY steps grew more urgent as I neared the Huntsman. By the time I reached Lochlan's door, I was out of breath and sure my hair was a knotted mess. I didn't care about any of it. All that mattered was getting to him and telling him how I felt.

I pounded on the door with more force than I'd intended, drawing Lochlan's quick response. The second his stony features came into view, the dam lifted on all the words and emotions bottled up inside me.

"You were right," I blurted before even saying hello. "I've lived my entire life in the shadow of guilt and regret. I've been living in fear of making bad choices, and I can't let that continue to haunt me. I won't allow it anymore. I respect myself enough to trust that I'm doing the best I can. You and I, we're both doing the best we can, and that's all we can ask of ourselves. You've taken in a Fae-human mutant, upended your brotherhood, and put your life at risk because you know it's the right thing to do. You've made the absolute best choices you could. You're honorable and courageous, and I love ... I love you ... so damn much. I can't stand to see you hurting like this. Please, don't blame yourself for what happened. *Please.*" I ended on a whispered plea, my heart wrung clean after my outpouring.

Shadowed beneath his severe brow, Lochlan's volatile blue gaze was unrelenting as I bared my soul to him. He listened intently to each and every word with no hint of response until my last word was out. Upon my final plea, he pulled me into a crushing embrace, his lips crashing down on mine.

Our kiss was a carnal confession.

A pledge sealed with a tangle of tongues and breathless murmurs.

"I'm sorry I snapped at you," Lochlan said before dropping delicate kisses along my cheeks. He eased us into his apartment and used a foot to sweep the door shut behind him.

"Don't be. I needed to hear it. I've been so damn blind."

He stripped my hoodie off along with the T-shirt beneath in one quick motion. "You've had to face more in the past six months than most people face in a lifetime. Your strength has astounded me every step of the way."

One article of clothing at a time, we removed every physical barrier between us until our bodies were just as bared as our souls.

I brought my body flush against his, my lips pressing reverent kisses to the hard planes of his chest. "I want you, Lochlan. I want you exactly the way you are. No caveats. No doubts."

He lifted me into his arms and walked us to the bedroom, lowering us onto the rumpled covers of his bed. At first, he didn't speak, not audibly. He let his eyes communicate the depth of his raw emotion as he pressed his hard length slowly, tenderly inside me.

Then with our bodies were joined, he welded our souls together with a litany of perfect words.

"Love doesn't begin to describe what I feel for you. You're the reason this world is worth saving. The reason I'd burn it all down. There is no line I wouldn't cross for you. For me, you exist in a place without rules or limitations. You are my everything." Softly spoken yet ardent with conviction, Lochlan's words imprinted themselves across the surface of my heart. Just beneath, his signature, laying claim to what would always be his.

Joy seeped from the corners of my eyes, leaving salty trails down to the pillow beneath me.

A vein now pulsing in his neck, Lochlan began to move inside me. Our eye contact never wavered. Even when his thrusts were frenzied with need and my body writhed with pleasure, our blue and black gazes remained locked on one another.

I began to feel a chorus of hands caressing, teasing, squeezing my body in all the most perfect places. The overload of sensations was too much to comprehend. My brain couldn't concentrate on any one touch. I had to give myself over and simply feel.

He was using his magic to seduce, and it was incredible.

This wasn't something to be afraid of. This was a gift—a cacophonous, exultant gift of pure ecstasy.

"*Yesss*," I encouraged on a breathy moan.

Lochlan's eyes sparked with hunger, and a wolfish grin teased the corners of his mouth. He toyed with me, drawing out my release until I thought my mind would shatter. Then he gave me what I begged for and more—a cataclysmic release that sent my inner muscles spasming and flooded the highways and byways of my bloodstream with electric waves of bliss. One after another, the rolling pulses of chemical elation singed my insides in the very best way possible.

While I drifted on a swiftly flowing river of sensation, Lochlan found his own release deep inside me. His arms clutched me tightly as his breathing hitched with each shudder of relief.

We lay entwined in one another for long minutes as we recovered. He rolled onto his side, keeping me held snug against his chest.

"I could get used to this," I murmured sleepily.

"If you get used to it, then I'm not doing it right." The

gruffness in his voice was softened with amusement. "I look forward to keeping things interesting. With you, that never seems to be a problem."

I smiled at his teasing, too content to even fake offense. "I do my best."

His hand cupped the back of my head, and he kissed me on my crown. "Best or not, you're incredible just as you are."

CHAPTER

FORTY-THREE

WE PUT ALL OUR PROBLEMS ON HOLD AND DIDN'T LEAVE HIS apartment for the next two days. He told me about his early days in the Hunt, and I told him all about my family. I learned that Alberich's body had been taken back to Faery, where a ceremony would be held to honor his passing. Lochlan refused to go back to Faery for the ritual, insisting that he remain on Earth with the others to prepare for Morgan. He claimed it was what Alberich would have wanted, and I was apt to agree.

We listened to the rain beat against the windows and lounged in bed while we ate whatever food we could throw together. We learned about each other in a vacuum of time where there was no war, no death, and no deceit.

Our exploration was equally carnal as it was intellectual. We indulged in our primal natures without the hindrance of societal norms or preconceived expectations. I cooked us eggs in the morning, and he fucked me on the kitchen counters. He ran us a bath, and then I rode him until there was little water left in the tub. I didn't have to wonder if I was expected to leave, and he didn't have to ask for my number.

We just were.

The simplicity of accepting what was between us without question was liberating.

I was his, and he was mine.

We didn't check our phones, and no one intruded on our hiatus. There was no television or radio, nothing to distract us from one another. After half a year spent training to save the world, this was our moment of selfishness. A window of time in which nothing mattered but us.

My deadline was fast approaching, and I was prepared to accept whatever my fate would be. Beltane would come, and I would pour all of my strength into stopping Morgan. Hopefully, it would be enough. In the meantime, I would celebrate everything I was grateful for in life.

When we finally emerged from our self-imposed isolation, we had three days before Beltane. Our first priority was to ensure I could open a portal. Lochlan took me to one of the smaller ancient portal sites just outside the city, and I was able to briefly open a portal to the Twilight Realm. My relief was overwhelming. I would need to keep the portal open for a longer period, but I had faith I could muster that in a few days. Once I figured out the magic, mastering it would only be a matter of time.

We decided it would be best to relocate to the site where the barrier between worlds was the thinnest. As it turned out, that was the Beltany Stone Circle. I packed a bag and gave Ashley a teary goodbye before leaving for the Irish countryside. We went directly to the ancient stones and confirmed it was that much easier for me to hold open a portal at that location. Everything was in place. All we had to do now was wait.

～

THAT EVENING, I leaned back against the headboard of our hotel bed and called my mom.

"Becca, baby. What are you up to?" Mom's voice was warm with a twinge of longing.

It had been eighteen months since we'd seen one another—the longest I'd ever gone without one of her hugs. I'd had to discourage her from visiting several times over the past six months. She'd been hurt by my rejection, but I'd had no other choice. As much as I hated to take on Morgan without seeing her one last time, I would have hated myself more if something had happened to my mother while she was here.

Tears burned the backs of my eyes at just the sound of her voice.

"Not much. I had a few minutes and thought I'd see how you were doing."

"That's sweet of you. It's been pretty quiet around here. I have the garden ready to plant now that we're out of freeze danger."

"Did you secure the fence?" At the end of the last growing season, Mom's small backyard garden had been terrorized by bunnies. They found even the smallest of gaps between boards to squeeze through the fence and get at her strawberries and tomatoes. Once they found a way through, Mom and Dad would have to go around the perimeter of the yard blocking any openings with stones or old bricks.

"I did, but who knows if it'll keep them out. You know how wily they can be."

I grinned, recalling Mom's unending battle with the neighborhood rabbits. "Good luck with that."

She huffed playfully. "How's work been?"

"Quiet but good." *I haven't gone in weeks because I'm preparing to save the world.* "I miss you, Mama. Maybe it's time we plan a visit."

"I'd love that, baby girl." Her voice softened with the endless warmth of a mother's love.

"I love you, Mama, with all my heart." I didn't want to freak her out, but I needed to ensure she knew how much she meant to me. I wanted to face Morgan, knowing my affairs were in order.

"Love you more," she said back like she had when I was little.

I grinned. "Start thinking about dates, and I'll plan some fun stuff to do. Tell Dad he's not allowed to bring work with him."

She scoffed affectionately. "Fat chance, but I'll do my best."

We talked for several more minutes about nothing of great importance aside from the connection it forged between us. When we finally hung up, I felt a sense of calm settle over me.

Two more days and the wait would be over.

My fate and that of the world would be decided, one way or another.

CHAPTER

FORTY-FOUR

The morning of May third crested the foggy Irish horizon with the crisp newness of any other day. Children went to school, and adults prepared for work with the expectation that the sun would set on their day the same as it had hundreds of times before. I woke to face the challenge of making their expectations a reality.

My greatest victory would be ensuring that no one outside of my newfound family in Belfast would ever know how close their lives had come to disaster. No one would cheer for me or offer praise. No one would race home to their loved ones for a final hug. No one would ever feel the sting of loss owed to Morgan's tyrannical ambitions or even know she'd existed.

Victory would be another quiet sunrise over the rocky Irish coast.

Lochlan and I spent the morning with his men. I wasn't exactly a member of the brotherhood, but I'd been accepted as a part of the team—in this endeavor, at least. We managed to keep the mood from growing oppressively heavy. It helped to be surrounded by experienced warriors who weren't daunted

458

by the threat of loss. As far as many of them were concerned, an Unseelie invasion would provide decades of entertainment. They were prepared to fight, but a loss wouldn't devastate them the way it would me.

Therefore, the men were able to joke quietly as they readied their weapons and discussed possible scenarios, and their relaxed demeanor helped keep me distracted. After lunch, Lochlan did his best to distract me for an hour or so. His efforts were remarkably successful, though tension crept back into my coiled muscles as the afternoon hours progressed.

When the evening sun finally listed wanly back out of sight, our party relocated to center stage of the Beltane Circle. All traces of easy levity had disappeared with the light. Each Huntsman performed his job with clinical professionalism. The ice in their veins was a stark contrast to the jet fuel burning in mine. My body was so overrun with adrenaline that I could feel my pulse thrumming from the tips of my fingers to the backs of my eyeballs.

Once everyone was prepared, I stood with Lochlan at my side and summoned my magic to the surface. The world around me became eerily quiet as I envisioned the Twilight Realm and focused on creating a passage to its perpetually starry skies. The iridescent waves of a portal rippled and swirled before me—a gateway far larger than I'd been able to conjure even the day before. The magic of Beltane was nearing its peak. The veil between worlds would be at its thinnest, and Morgan would be on the cusp of ruination.

Lochlan ushered his men through first, then stepped through himself with his hand firmly clasped in mine. He'd been adamant through our planning that he would remain at my side at all times and appeared to be sticking to that proclamation.

I wasn't sure what exactly I had expected, but the vast emptiness wasn't it.

Just stars and silence. Nothing else.

The eleven men stood in varying degrees of awe as they took in their surroundings. I had no idea how large the Twilight Realm was and hadn't even considered that we might have to find her once we arrived, assuming she was even there. Was it possible we had made some epic miscalculation about Morgan's plans?

Staring blankly at Lochlan, I raised my shoulders in question, then closed my eyes. I concentrated on connecting with the perpetual darkness and was bombarded with a mass of whispers. "Over there." I pointed, my voice lodging in my throat. "There are thousands of them."

We all turned our gazes toward the distance, and with hardened resolve, we began our march into war. Not one of us said a word, and before long, an audible hum confirmed that we were headed in the right direction. A great swarm of creatures slowly took shape on what would have been the horizon had such a thing existed in this place. The gathering extended as far as the eye could see—hordes of beasts, both large and small, huddled together in waiting.

My rational mind screamed at me to turn back and run. At one point, my steps even faltered. But I'd come too far to give in to fear.

When we drew near enough to be seen, one by one, the creatures turned in our direction and began to hiss and growl with contempt. A tall ogre-like beast with tusks and scaly gray skin spat in our direction, and others gnashed their sharp teeth at us.

Lochlan pulled two canisters from his pockets and twisted the tops before tossing them onto the ground between the crowd and us. Thick gray smoke spewed from the metal cans, and the Fae mob began to grumble and holler as they backed farther into themselves. Drawing the smoke to me, I formed it into a solid barrier around our group, compacting the molecules until they were nearly impenetrable.

Once we were fully encompassed on all sides, we began to make our way through the crowd. The vicious Unseelie lashed out at the wall of smoke, slicing with razor-sharp claws and pounding to test its strength. While a magical attack might have proven challenging, their paltry physical assaults were no problem. My shield withstood their abuse, and I formed a plow at the front to slice our way through the group. Despite the tightly packed density of the creatures, they squeezed out of our way as we pushed toward the middle of the mass.

The nucleus of the horde was a space about one-hundred feet in diameter and was nearly empty, save for Morgan and two large Fae standing guard. Her terrible beauty was almost mesmerizing, and her regal confidence commanded attention. It was deeply unsettling to think that a woman who appeared so delicate could be capable of such destruction and death.

As our group entered the open circle, Morgan lifted her chin and smirked. "I was wondering when you'd arrive."

"If you knew I was coming, then you must know I can't let you do this."

"What I know is that you are just a pawn, the same as I was once. Our lives have been toyed with and destroyed without care. The only difference between us is that I have chosen to fight back." She believed what she said, and it disgusted me.

"You and I are *nothing* alike. I'm attempting to save lives while you're here to end them." I spat back at her.

"I suppose it's all a matter of perspective." She shrugged.

"Killing innocent people is never a matter of *perspective*."

Morgan sauntered closer, dressed in black leather armor similar to the Avalon Valkyries. "Your black and white ideology exposes your immaturity. What about the lives of these citizens of Faery?" She motioned to the mass of creatures surrounding us. "What about their rights and those of the Seelie caste who've been repressed by precious Queen Guinevere? Should no one stand up for them as well?"

The crowd raised their fists and bellowed in support of her speech, and my heart raced when I was reminded just how outnumbered we were. "Call them off," I demanded. "If you have a problem with Guin, take it up with her and leave the people of Earth out of it."

"The problem with uprisings is that the oppressor always criticizes them as unwarranted or inconvenient or inappropriate. Tell me, how should I successfully go about ending a queen's rule if not by force?"

My patience grew thin with her games. "This is your last chance, Morgan. End this now or face the consequences," I demanded.

Her spine stiffened. "Tell me, Rebecca, are you familiar with the Bergresar?" When she said the name, the crowd behind her parted, and a hooded figure about seven or eight feet in height stepped forward. "They are Shadow Fae and among the oldest creatures known to still exist. With such a long lifespan, it's easy to understand why they thrive on chaos—what a boring existence it would be otherwise. My friend here is a Bergresar, and his proclivities made it remarkably easy to align him to my cause. A small touch of his essence in my amulet, similar to the one you wear, and I was able to bring us all here." She raised her arms like a child standing in the rain for the first time before continuing. "Unfortunately for you, I don't have any more time to waste on this conversation. Take care of them," she commanded tonelessly.

The huntsmen surrounded me in an instant. From between

their bodies, I could see the Bergresar step out into the open, away from Morgan.

"I need you all to hold him and the others off while I deal with Morgan," I ordered in a hushed tone as I released the smoke barrier around us.

Lochlan's eyes held mine. For a moment, I thought he would argue, but instead, he peeled away from my side. He barked a soft command to the others, and all but two pulled away to face the Bergresar, leaving me to address Morgan with him and another at my back.

The Bergresar unsheathed the Sword of Light, and the nine members of the Hunt arced around him menacingly. What would have been a battle fought entirely with magic was instead a physical fight of nine against one. I would have thought our men had the clear advantage in numbers, but the Shadow Fae creature leaped and parried with dizzying speed. He struck out at the men between moves so quickly that he could hardly be seen. Their advantage in numbers was nullified by the Bergresar's skill and physical abilities.

Forcing my attention back to Morgan, I reached out and summoned the smoke that still lingered in the air. I wrapped it behind my guards and me to help keep any ambitious creatures from trying to interfere. Before I could take a step toward Morgan, she issued a sharp whistle and unleashed a blindingly bright light that scalded my sensitive eyes. Along with myself, hundreds of Shadow Fae screeched in pain and covered their eyes to protect themselves. As my eyes struggled to recover, my mind grappled with how she could have accomplished light magic when Lochlan and the others had not been able to do the same.

"What ... *how*...?" I stuttered.

"You assumed I would have no magic here?" Her voice was dripping with disdain.

With my hands still pressed to my eyes, I was caught off guard yet again when her hand took hold of my necklace. I squinted open my eyes and wrenched myself backward to free myself from her grasp. However, my attempt was in vain. She stood rooted to the ground, the pendant of my necklace firmly clutched in her white-knuckled grip. Her blue eyes began to glow, and she murmured a chant in a foreign tongue.

"*Stop!*" I yelled using the magical command that had worked so well with the Sluagh.

Morgan merely shook her head with a smirk. "I assure you, one of the first things I learned when I made it to this realm was how to use my magic when here." She lifted her chin haughtily and resumed her chant.

A horrific wave of nausea nearly took me to my knees and would have if it hadn't been for Morgan's death grip on my necklace. Glancing behind me, I could see my two guards pounding on what appeared to be an invisible wall separating Morgan and me from everyone else. Behind them, the horde of Fae were no longer spectators in the Hunt's fight with the Bergresar. One by one, they entered the melee, causing the Huntsmen to fight back-to-back for protection.

Summoning all my dark power, I slapped my hands over hers and prepared to press darkness into her, but nothing happened. Again, she began to laugh. That was when I realized she wore fine leather gloves. I hadn't noticed because they were a flesh tone, but it was just enough of a barrier to prevent my magic from working.

My killing touch required skin-to-skin contact.

Altering my attack, I reached for her face, but I was too late. My thwarted first effort had given her all the time she needed. The second I made contact with her skin, my necklace disintegrated into dust and scattered like ash on the wind.

My mouth gaped open, and I stumbled backward in horror.

The loss of the amulet was a devastating blow. I felt stripped naked, bare, and helpless.

As I struggled to process what had happened, two amorphic clouds rose from the dust—one dark and ominous, the other shimmering and ethereal. They lifted into the twinkling twilight sky, free of their prison.

You knew this wouldn't be easy, Rebecca. Panic will only make things worse.

I summoned every ounce of confidence and composure I could muster and squared my shoulders. When I pulled for my magic, I found that while it wasn't entirely gone, it was greatly reduced. A powerful showdown was no longer an option, and we were gravely outnumbered. If I had any chance at stopping her, I would have to find a way to outwit her. It was our only hope.

Morgan stepped back a few feet and relished my distress. I could practically feel the anger and spite radiating off her in waves. In fact, without the interference of my necklace, I realized I could feel a vast sea of negative energy from the hordes of Unseelie and Shadow Fae. The emotion crackled and buzzed around me. There was such a plentiful supply that I didn't even have to touch anyone to feed on the sea of turbulent emotions. The sheer magnitude of negativity pulsing around me allowed me to simply reel it in like a fisherman pulling in his nets.

I gasped as the power surged in my system, making my skin tingle and the hair on my arms stand on end. When I focused my attention back on Morgan, her brows were creased with uncertainty. She knew something had happened but couldn't decipher what that was.

"Your hatred has blinded you for too long, Morgan," I said in an even tone as I regained my composure. "You have wallowed in misery, oblivious to anything but your plans of vengeance, and your weakness has warped your reality. You thought you could take down Guin, but you never had a chance." My tone was intentionally condescending, and I stood tall with my arms down at my sides.

Morgan's eyes narrowed, and she bared her teeth at me. "How dare you pretend to know anything about me? You who are nothing but a child playing in the affairs of being centuries older than yourself."

I shut out the Huntsmen fighting, the thousands of Fae seething around us, and the weight of the consequences I would face if I failed. Instead, I narrowed the focus of all my concentration on Morgan.

"Yes, I'm newer to all this than you, but I've been given guidance by someone even more knowledgeable than yourself."

"If Merlin had been able to stop me, why isn't he the one standing in your place?"

"He isn't here because you would have run from him. You wouldn't have had a chance against him, and you know it."

She sneered at me, and when she spoke again, her tone had dropped to a low, menacing growl. "Has he told you how he killed my mother? He didn't just kill her. He allowed her to be driven mad over *years* before he attempted to save her. But it was too late, just like it will be for you," she ground out, her otherwise pristine features screwed up with hatred.

She lifted her hand and lashed out to send a hailstorm of energy blasting my way, but nothing happened. Her head tilted slightly, eyes wide with confusion. Again, she flung her arm toward me with no results, this time with her teeth bared in a snarl.

"What's happening?" she hissed, hand clutching the amulet around her neck to assure herself of its safety.

I pulled back my magic, releasing her mind from my hold. No longer trapped in my dream walk setting, she could clearly see her two guards pounding on the wall of smoke I'd created to shield us from distractions. Her hand again returned to her chest, only to find it bare.

Extending my hand, I dangled her broken amulet before her, cracked down the center.

"*No!*" she hissed, eyes blazing at me. "What have you done?"

I turned to where the Hunt still fought for their lives and infused my voice with power as I yelled out over the cacophony of sound, "*Stop your fighting.*"

Like a well-orchestrated dance, fists froze in midair, and bodies lurched to a halt. Without their magic, every single being was subject to my magical command. Now that I didn't have to worry about Lochlan and the others, I turned to address a bewildered Morgan.

"It's called dream walking. I pulled your consciousness into my dream, where we talked so I could distract you while I removed and disabled your amulet. It's over, Morgan. Only Twilight magic works in this realm. Without your amulet, you have no power here, nor can you return home." Concentrating on two realities at once hadn't been easy, but it was the only way. I *had* to make it work. I'd completely disabled Morgan, and I hadn't even had to kill her.

Her chin quivered. "I have no home to go to." The despondency in her voice almost made me feel bad for her. Almost.

"My dear Morgan," a deep voice said through the crowd.

We both gasped as Merlin approached. Had he been present to witness the entire exchange? How had he known the precise moment to appear?

"I did everything in my power to keep you from this fate, knowing how challenging it was when you lost your mother. You were the only one who could comprehend the depravity of the loss we suffered, so I have tried to be kind throughout the years. But this cannot go on. I want to help you find your way back."

"You don't want to help me. You want to stop me." Defeat leached all emotion from her voice.

"You're very wrong. You may think me the monster responsible for your mother's death, and while I was responsible for her capture, her death is not on my conscience. After I killed Mab, I located your mother, who had suffered dearly at the hands of my sister. She was not the same woman, lost in her mind where the torture could not reach her. I did not have the heart to end the life of someone I cherished so dearly, even out of mercy. You and everyone else were under the impression that she had been killed, but that was the case."

Morgan stood unmoving, her eyes wide with disbelief. "It's not so," she said, her voice just a whisper. "Had she been alive, you would have told me. I would have known."

Merlin's lips thinned, and he dropped his gaze to his feet before looking back at Morgan. "She was not well, and I had no idea if she would ever recover, so I did not wish to offer false hope. You had already lost so much."

"*Lies!*" she screamed and surged toward Merlin. He lifted his hand, and instantly Morgan's eyes rolled back into her head as she dropped to the ground in a heap. Merlin bent down with a sigh and placed a set of iron cuffs around her wrists.

I looked at Merlin in horror. "You're not going to kill her?" I was relieved to have avoided killing her myself, but I felt she was too dangerous a threat to continue breathing.

"She is lost in pain and grief. That should not condemn her to death."

"Not alone, but think of all those deaths that have resulted from her actions," I argued.

"None of us are perfect, Rebecca. One of these days, perhaps you will have a child of your own. Maybe then, you will understand the lengths to which we will go to protect them, even when it means protecting them from themselves." His voice was heavy with sadness.

"What happens when she gets out and tries to incite another war?" I continued to push.

"Where I am taking her, she will not get out. Please try not to worry." He smiled softly. "I could not do on my own what you have accomplished here today, and I will always be in your debt." His head dipped in a bow, and I bit my tongue, holding in the flippant response I wanted to give.

Merlin turned toward the hordes of Fae, who were watching with uncertainty. The woman who had brought them there and offered promises of absolute freedom had been defeated. Not only had her promises not been fulfilled but she had also left them without a way home.

"I should leave you all here to suffer the consequences of participating in this rebellion." He spoke in a commanding voice, his words magically amplified to the mass of Fae. "But I am not heartless, like some of you who would kill on a whim. We will open a portal to the Shadow Lands, and you will return to Faery peaceably, or you will be left here to rot," he said with finality.

Murmurs spread across the crowd, along with distinct grumbling, but Merlin ignored the chatter and turned to me. "Together, we should be able to open a portal large enough to get these cretins back where they belong."

I followed his instruction, and eventually, the mob of vicious Fae were gone. The threat of a slow death in the desolate Twilight Realm was enough to earn their begrudging cooperation. The Bergresar attempted to sneak past our notice with the Sword of Light hidden beneath his robes, but Lochlan forcibly regained the sword.

Once the horde had been disposed of, Merlin lifted Morgan in his arms and began to open a portal for his own use.

"You're lucky I didn't kill her myself," I called to him. "I could have, you know."

His eyes glinted when he peered back at me. "You could have, but I knew you wouldn't if you didn't have to." That was why he'd chosen me. He didn't have to say it. I could read between the lines.

"Will I see you again?" I wasn't sure what I wanted his answer to be, but I needed to know either way.

"Of course, though, I'll have my hands full for a while. Until then, you take care, Rebecca." And then the great Merlin flashed a brilliant smile and winked before disappearing home to wherever he came from.

I sighed heavily, a sense of relief only now starting to set in. Turning back to my companions, I took in their weary state. The men of the Hunt were alive but worse for wear. Several had been badly injured. I'd already raked my eyes over Lochlan's form, searching for injuries on several occasions. Each time I found him whole, my heart did a little dance.

We'd done it. We were both alive and going home.

I could hardly grasp the truth of it after so many months of worry and uncertainty. Using the last of my power stores, I opened a portal back to the stone circle and helped the men step through. Once we were back on Irish soil, some whooped and hollered. I found my eyes glued to the man I'd come to adore, my smile reflecting in the brilliant gleam of his eyes. He was lending his weight to help one of his brothers stand, so I couldn't leap into his arms as I'd wanted, but there'd be time for that.

"I knew you could do it," he said softly as we made our way to the cars.

"I wasn't so sure when I realized she still had use of her

magic." I should have planned for that, but it took me by surprise. I'd thought her methods only enabled her to open a portal, not use magic once she was there.

"And even with her magic, she was no match for you." His eyes caught mine, then traveled down to my neck. "Your necklace is gone."

"While you were keeping the creatures at bay, she crushed my necklace. I'd started to panic for a minute, thinking I was helpless, but my power was still there, though weaker. Do you think that means the transition is complete? Am I fully Fae now?"

"I'd say so. You certainly didn't seem any weaker to me." His voice was a touch more guttural than it had been moments before, and I had to clear my throat before I could continue.

"Without the necklace, I could feel the negative energy of the creatures calling to me. It was massive—I almost couldn't help but feed from it. After that, my entire being was alive with power. And I needed that too because Ronan had told her about my killing touch. She had come prepared with gloves and clothes covering everything but her face. Lucky for me, she didn't know about my dream walking. I wasn't sure I'd be able to focus both inside the dream and outside. It was like having double vision, but I managed to fool her while I destroyed her amulet."

"And once she couldn't use the dark magic of the amulet, her light magic was useless in the Twilight Realm," he concluded.

"Exactly. But the moment she left this realm, she could regain her power. My abilities wouldn't be a secret the second time around."

"If she causes trouble again, Merlin's daughter or not, I'll kill her myself," he swore on a vicious growl. "It fucking gutted me to see you go up against her alone. I'm not doing that shit again."

I grinned, appreciating his desire to protect me. "I'm safe, for now. I'd say a celebration is in order."

He shot me a look with such smoldering heat that my insides melted with need.

Two hours later, Lochlan bolted us inside his apartment and celebrated every square inch of my body. We gave thanks for one another, worshipping in the most natural, primal way imaginable. For hours. Then we succumbed to sleep—a deeper, more peaceful-type sleep than I'd ever known possible.

CHAPTER

FORTY-FIVE

The next morning, I lay cocooned in Lochlan's body, listening to his even breathing behind me while I thought about my situation. I couldn't fully enjoy my victory over Morgan when I still had Guin's threats hanging over my head. If she found out my transition was complete, would she try to forcibly remove me from Earth? How long could I stay here until she learned my necklace had been destroyed?

The uncertainty was almost as bad as the prospect of living in Faery.

I had to find a solution.

I lay silent in Lochlan's arms, but my mind was a frenzy of activity. I ran through everything I knew about Guin and Fae life until an idea struck me. I wasn't sure it would work, but the longer I considered my limited options, it seemed my best bet.

Lochlan eventually made a rumbling sound in his chest and pressed his lips to the back of my neck.

"Morning, sunshine," I said softly. "Sleep well?"

"Like the dead." The sleepy gruffness of his voice made my inner feline purr with satisfaction.

"That's good to hear because I have a favor to ask," I went on tentatively. "I need you to take me to speak with Guin."

He was still, and I started to wonder if he had fallen asleep again until he finally responded, fully awake. "Why would you want to do that?"

I rolled onto my back so that I could see his face, and he leaned up on his elbow, head resting in his hand. I wouldn't have thought it possible, but he was even more stunning first thing in the morning with his ruffled hair and beard scruff. "I need to settle things with her. I can't leave it hanging over my head."

He huffed. "I think it's a bad idea. You need to wait and see if she even makes the move to force you to Faery before you go instigating a fight."

"I've been living for months with the uncertainty of Morgan's attack weighing on me. I'm not going to escape that problem just to live in the shadow of another. I want it all done—no, I don't just *want* it done. I *need* it done. This isn't negotiable. I have to do it."

His fingers ran lightly along my hairline from my forehead down behind my ear, and his eyes roved adoringly over my face. "No matter what she says, I'll be at your side. Whether we live in Faery or on Earth, we're together. That's all that matters."

My heart spun drunkenly in my chest with pure happiness. What had I done to deserve this man? He was everything I could have asked for, and he was all mine.

I brought my lips up to his hungrily. Who needed breakfast when I had Lochlan to fill me?

∼

WITHOUT A STASH OF Elizabethan gowns in my closet, I did what I could to select a respectful dress to wear to the palace. I chose a black sheath dress with an asymmetric neckline and black heels. I did my hair and makeup as though I were going out on a date in order to bolster my confidence. Guin was all about power plays, and I needed to come armed with absolute authority while still showing deference so as not to piss her off.

I would need to perform the dance of a lifetime.

My palms sweat, and my stomach churned the whole way to the palace, which took forever. I hadn't considered the walk when I decided to wear heels. By the time we made it to the grandiose throne room, I was more than ready to get the show over with.

Word must have gotten around about who I was because this time, the room when silent upon our entrance. Clusters of curious courtiers studied me, no doubt picking apart every subtle nuance of my dress and demeanor. I ignored their greedy gazes, my entire being focused on the regal woman sitting atop the throne.

I offered a deep bow in greeting as I approached the dais. "Your Majesty, thank you for receiving us. I'm pleased to come with the wonderful news that we have apprehended Morgan and ended her rebellion. Tens of thousands of Unseelie and Shadow Fae were set to be transported onto Earth through a place called the Twilight Realm, which is a barren vastness that exists between our worlds. She was using the realm to circumvent your wards. That is why you were unable to detect her uprising. The only way to reach this realm is through the combination of light and dark magic used together."

The queen raised a single brow as she lifted her chin. "That is impossible. The two forms of magic cannot be used together."

"It seems that Merlin found a way."

A flood of whispers swept through the room.

"*Silence.*" The booming command resounded more forcefully than seemed possible from the dainty woman. She turned her attention back to me. "I take it since you have defeated Morgan that Merlin has seen fit to gift you with this knowledge as well?"

This was the part I'd been most concerned about. Guin was savvy, and I knew she wouldn't like the idea of someone having powers beyond her own.

I swallowed hard.

"As you know, the powers from my amulet transformed me. What I didn't realize at the time was that the power imbued in the necklace was derived from both light and dark magic. While I'm able to open a portal to this realm because of the unique nature of my powers, I don't know how Merlin accomplished what he did. I am simply a product of his making."

"That sounds more like the Merlin I know," she said sarcastically. "So what powers is it that you possess?" Her critical gaze was more than enough to know I was treading on very thin ice.

I had to show her that I was different while convincing her I wasn't a threat.

I allowed my eyes to darken, and I slowly made myself disappear, ensuring she would understand that I had not simply traced.

Guin's Valkyrie guards moved in close to protect their queen.

"I can't trace like the rest of you, but I have the power of invisibility. I can wield smoke and am able to see in almost absolute darkness. Outside of those specific mutations, my powers are similar to other Fae." I hoped giving her a few unique powers would be enough to keep my killing touch and dream walking a secret. The less I told her, the better.

Guin's eyes locked on mine once I returned to visibility. She motioned for her guard to stand down, but a seething green glare told me that she'd judged me to be a valid threat.

"Why exactly have you come here to share this with me?" She was cunning. I had to give her that. She didn't overreact or lash out. Instead, she assessed her opponent and gathered all the information she could before making her move.

"I've come in goodwill to assert my independence as a Twilight Fae. While your mandate to keep the Seelie in Faery was made clear to me, as you can see, I am not Seelie. I've spent my life on Earth and want to continue doing so, though I also wish to maintain good relations with you. I'm hoping that in light of the circumstances, you will agree with me that my situation is unique and won't see fit to challenge the independence of a simple girl."

"A simple girl," she mused icily. "Somehow, I get the impression you're being modest, Rebecca."

"Regardless of my powers, all I want is to live the life I'd originally been given—a simple life."

She tipped back her head in contemplation. I could almost see her run through the possible implications of each outcome, and once she had made her decision, her lips pursed tightly. "Very well. But know this, if you are not Seelie, you are no longer welcome on Seelie lands without express invitation," she ordered in a biting tone.

I bowed, more than willing to pet her ego if it meant getting what I wanted.

"Guin, I'm so pleased to see I'm not too late." Merlin's voice rolled over the crowd from the back of the long room.

I turned quickly, shocked to see his suited form approach with Ashley at his side.

"Clearly, you've been busy," Guin deadpanned, her patience running thin.

He tipped his head with a smile. "Indeed. But the advancements I've made have proven advantageous to us all, so one can hardly argue." He placed a hand on Ashley's back and slowed to a stop. "I find that now would be a fitting time to introduce Miss Ashley Moore. She is another product of my extensive efforts of late."

"Another mutant Fae?" Guin's eyes flashed a glowing green.

Merlin waved a hand of assurance. "No, no. Ashley is Seelie—her magic derived from my own." He paused, holding Guin's now curious gaze. "Now that I find myself relieved of certain pursuits, I believe it is time that I take on a new apprentice, and I have decided that Ashley would be a perfect fit." He smiled over at my best friend, whose eyes rounded. In Merlin fashion, it appeared he hadn't done any explaining before bringing Ashley before the queen.

The crowd around us burst into a cacophony of chatter.

"*Silence!*" Guin barked, and the room instantly quieted again. "You mean to include her in our ... arrangement, is that it?" she clipped bitterly.

Merlin offered a small smile and tilt of his head. "She would not be in this circumstance if it were not for me, so in that regard, she is my responsibility to guide and to teach. The work of someone such as myself requires a good deal of freedom. As my apprentice, Ashley would need to have the same flexibility in her movements as myself."

Guin pursed her lips before asking, "Should I expect any more 'children' of yours to come crawling out of the woodwork?"

"None of which I am aware," he said with a coy smile, amused at Guin's irritation.

The Faery queen looked from Merlin to Ashley with disdain.

My heart tripped and stumbled over its frantic beat as I waited for her decision.

"So long as our bargain remains"—she looked at Merlin pointedly—"she is free to *accompany* you." She rose swiftly and looked around the room at her subjects. "Let it be understood to those of you who will go forth and spread the word of what has been said here today that there are no exceptions to my laws, and those who defy me will be punished severely. My arrangement with the sorcerer Merlin is unique. Do not act under the misconception that I will be lenient with anyone else who thinks they can circumvent my mandates." With that said, she spun in a twirl of wrath and gossamer fabric, then disappeared behind a curtain.

Ashley was safe!

My heart stuttered in relief that everything had gone better than I'd even dared to hope. I looked back at Ashley with an enormous grin. The second our eyes met, we rushed to hug one another.

"Becca, that was almost as terrifying as being attacked by Ronan. Oh my *God*, I can't even believe this place and that woman! Merlin showed up unannounced, and then we were in Faery. I didn't know what was happening, and I was scared shitless, but he swore everything would be fine." Ashley unloaded all her fears in a rush of words as her body shook in my arms.

"It's okay now, Ash. Everything is going to be okay."

"Ladies," Merlin cut in with a hand on each of our backs. "I believe it would be best if we left the palace and gave Guin some time to cool down."

We readily agreed and hurried from the room. As we made the walk to the portal and discussed everything that had happened, I realized I needed to do one more thing, and I needed to do it before Guin had the chance to raise wards and alarms against my presence.

I pulled Lochlan aside, encouraging Ashley and Merlin to continue home. "There's one more thing I need to do before we go." I struggled to meet his gaze, squirming beneath the weight of his questioning stare.

"What exactly is it you need to do?"

I stepped back away from him, leaving several feet between us before I whispered, "I can't tell you that." I blinked into invisibility and stealthily darted away before shouting, "Wait there, I'll be right back." I knew he wouldn't leave Faery without me. It was easiest to let him wait where he was, then go back home together.

I ran for some distance until I was hidden by a copse of trees, then opened a portal to the Twilight Realm and hurried through. Now that I knew how to open the portals, I was able to quickly open one directly to the Shadow Lands not far from a familiar hut.

"Fenodree?" I called out his name several times softly, not wanting to scare the man and get myself killed. "It's me, Rebecca. I'm here to get you out of Faery."

For countless seconds, there was no response, and I began to worry that something had happened to him.

"What you offer is a dangerous prospect."

I whipped my head around to search the trees behind me. Fen stepped forward, and I couldn't help the grin that spread across my face. "Dangerous for whom?" I teased playfully.

"For you. Helping me would be directly disobeying the queen." He clearly did not see it as a joking matter.

"I'm not her subject. As of today, I am officially an

autonomous nation of my own. I am the queen of the Twilight Realm. I'm also my only subject. Guin's mandates don't apply to me, so if you're willing to risk fleeing to Earth, I'm willing to take you there." My eyebrows lifted in challenge.

He considered the options for a moment, but only briefly. "When do we leave?" he asked as a new light sparked in his eyes.

I did my best to explain the modern world to Fen in a few brief moments, which was grossly inadequate, but it was all I could give him at the time. I instructed him where to hide out until I could come help him. Before I sent him through the portal to the Beltany Stone Circle, I gave him the small amount of cash I had on me. I worried about him, but he assured me that Earth should be no problem if he could survive in the hellish Shadow Lands. Had so much not changed since he'd been there last, I would have agreed.

"Be safe, Fen, and I'll see you soon." I gathered the Fae man into a hug, and after a moment, he awkwardly returned the gesture.

"Thank you, Rebecca. This kindness you are doing for me will not be forgotten." He bowed his head deeply then stepped through the portal to Earth.

I'd done it. I'd given Fenodree a second chance at life.

After everything he had suffered, I desperately hoped he would find happiness.

When I returned to Lochlan, he was leaning against a tree with his arms folded across his broad chest. "Do I want to know what you were just up to?"

"Definitely not."

The corners of his lips turned down, but his head gave a single nod. He held out his hand for mine in a show of trust and support. "I suppose it's time to go home then."

My cheeks ached from smiling with such elated joy. All my

loved ones were safe, and I was going home. Life truly didn't get any better.

~

"Oʜ, my God. I thought you'd never come home." Ashley came charging at me the second I opened the door to our apartment the next morning. I'd spent the night with Lochlan celebrating the outcome of my little chat with the queen and hadn't seen Ashley since we parted ways in Faery.

"Why? What's going on?"

"After Merlin brought me back here last night, I asked him why my powers still hadn't shown up. He said something about a guidewire and how unique I am. Bec, he held my hands and did some magic summoning spell that helped draw my magic to the surface! I could feel it—like an electric buzz just under my skin—and now I can sort of sense my power. I can't even believe it!" Ashley's eyes began to glow as she spoke. It was the first time since her transition in the hospital that I'd seen any sign of her magic.

I could hardly contain my excitement for her. She'd been stuck in limbo for months, wondering if she'd ever manifest any powers. Without magic, she wasn't entirely Fae but also wasn't human. Now, she could finally move forward and figure out her new path in life.

I clasped her hands in mine, and we both began jumping up and down.

"Oh, *Ash*! That's so exciting! I can't wait to see what powers you have. It's like Christmas but even better."

"Best. Christmas. Ever."

We both burst out laughing and fell into a hug.

"Okay, I need to shower, but let's have a girls' day after

that," I suggested. "We can do lunch, then some shopping. I'll even hit the club with you tonight if you'd like."

Her eyes rounded. "Oh, *hell* yeah. We can shop for dresses to wear out tonight!"

My heart was so full that it pressed against my lungs and made it hard to breathe. I would never have imagined when I took the job in Belfast that six months later, I'd have developed magical powers, fallen madly in love, and saved the world from disaster—and keeping my best friend close was the cherry on top that made it all that much sweeter.

My life was unrecognizable now, and I couldn't have been happier. I'd finally come to understand that new and unexpected wasn't always a bad thing. In fact, sometimes change could be a very, *very* good thing. While I missed my parents, my future in Belfast looked more brilliant by the day. I would treasure each precious moment because, six months from now, who knew what the future might bring?

"Oh! Here comes Lochlan, and he's got Casek with him." I grinned at them, setting down my pomegranate martini. We'd had the perfect day of shopping and were decked out in our new purchases, huddled around a table at the club with Cat and Liam. After spending most of the day escorting us around town, Lochlan had spent the last few hours attending to business. Seeing him walk across the club, eyes locked hungrily on me, made my stomach dip and swirl in the most delicious way.

"Liam," Lochlan smirked. "It's good to see you've been generous enough to keep the ladies company tonight."

Liam cut in from across the table. "Ashley here was just telling us about her chat with Merlin the other day. I, for one, am eager to see what she's capable of."

Ashley beamed, but it was Lochlan who spoke next. "Regardless of the nature of her powers, she'll need someone to guide her learning. After watching Rebecca go through the process, I've realized how much more difficult this is for someone who wasn't raised around magic." He paused, looking back toward Casek. "Now that things have settled down, Caz, I think you'd be a perfect candidate."

The intensity of Casek's stare was so corrosive that I thought he might bore a hole straight between Lochlan's eyes. Eventually, his gaze cut to Ashely, his nostrils flared, then he was gone. He'd traced in a club full of people.

My jaw fell open. Performing magic in front of humans was strictly forbidden. Granted, the people in the club were mostly drunk off their asses, but his blatant disregard for the rules was shocking.

"Oh, shit," Ashley whispered.

I met her wide-eyed stare in confusion. "What was all that about?"

"Well, you remember how we all celebrated at the club the night after Beltane while you and Lochlan were doing your own thing?"

"Yeah?" I asked warily.

She shrugged sheepishly. "Casek and I … might have … gotten a little carried away."

"*You had sex with Casek?*" I hissed. "And you didn't *tell* me?"

"It was nothing! Just too much alcohol. And besides, he's avoided me like the plague for the past few days. I figured it was a one-and-done. But now…" Her head dropped back in exasperation.

I looked over at Lochlan on my other side. The bastard had a knowing smirk on his face.

"I hope you know what you're doing here," I shot at him.

He shrugged. "We'll see soon enough."

"I think it's time for that drink now," I muttered.

"Make it a double," Ashley added.

It looked like I wouldn't have to wait long for the next adventure to begin. With Ashley's stubborn exuberance and Casek's brooding surliness, their time together was bound to be cataclysmic—one way or another.

Heaven help us.

EPILOGUE

It took me two agonizing days until I could sneak away to check on Fenodree. I raced to Strabane the second I had a chance and breathed an enormous sigh of relief when I found him at the hotel where I'd instructed him to go. This time, I came prepared with a wad of cash and some supplies. My visit was short, but I felt so much better after seeing him. Once he acclimated to modern Earth society, we'd have to figure out a new plan for him, but there wasn't an immediate rush.

I was simply relieved to see him free.

The next major change in our lives occurred just a week after the showdown with Morgan. Lochlan was named the new Erlking of the Wild Hunt. The ceremony took him and all the other huntsmen to Faery for a couple of days, giving Ashley and me the run of the building. We invited Cat and had a full twenty-four hours of girl time—facial masks, nails, wine, chocolate, chick flicks, and every other stereotypical female activity you could conjure. Ashley and Cat hadn't spent all that much time together, but they hit it off like long-lost sisters.

Knight even partook in the festivities. After Merlin named

Ashley his apprentice, the furry beast had become her constant companion. She'd taken to his intrusion remarkably well, considering she wasn't a fan of pets. His quirky independence suited her well. The two quickly formed a sort of understanding that bordered on friendship.

I was just glad to have him around again. Seeing him in the Shadow Lands had made me realize how much I missed his playful presence.

Once the men were back, they planned an epic event. It was billed as an anniversary celebration to the public, but we all knew it was really an event to honor Lochlan—the newest Erlking of the Wild Hunt. We covered the club in black and gold decorations and roped off the entire VIP seating area for ourselves. They used hired staff to work so that all the men could be off for the night. The atmosphere was electric. We toasted to the future, danced like no one was watching, and I laughed until my belly ached. I wasn't sure I'd ever had so much fun in my life.

When I finally slipped away for the bathroom, my smile lingered as though my happiness had imprinted on my face. It wasn't until I stepped back into the hall that the grin melted into surprise as I just barely stopped myself from careening into a broad chest.

"Oh!" I startled, stepping back to steady myself. "It's you." I peered up into tempestuous blue eyes, softly glowing in the dark hallway. "Are you following me?" I asked coyly, remembering the first encounter we'd had in this very spot just months earlier.

Lochlan took a step forward, and I responded by retreating a step back. Once. Twice. Three times. He walked me slowly back until he'd caged me against the office door.

He leaned close and sniffed the skin at my neck. "Always. There's not a minute that goes by that I don't know *exactly* where you are." The raw need in his voice scraped over my skin.

I swallowed, playful flirtation quickly transforming into something far more urgent. Something dark and chaotic and delicious.

Lochlan opened the door and pushed us inside, not bothering to turn on the light. In two seconds, I was up against the wall, my legs around his waist, and the crotch of my panties ripped away beneath my short dress.

"I never thought I'd get you alone." He devoured my mouth with an ardent kiss while his hands freed himself from his pants. "You were so fucking radiant out there."

I clung to his shoulders, relishing the feel of his lips on mine. My core pulsed and ached for him, the only relief coming when he fisted his hard length and pressed inside me one mind-blowing inch at a time. I shuddered and moaned at the fullness.

He didn't give me time to settle into the feeling. Like a man possessed, he began to pump ruthlessly inside me as though lost in the hunt for the holy grail of orgasms. I had no choice but to accompany him on his quest—muscles squeezing, heart pounding, and nerves alight with sensation. I allowed him to drive us with maddening speed to the cliff's edge then launch us over into the abyss below.

I cried out as a wall of pleasure slammed into me. White lights dotted my vision, despite the velvety darkness of the room around us. I basked in the waves of perfect contentment, aware on some level that Lochlan had found his release and was slowing his movements.

"I take it you've changed your mind on whether I belong here." My words were soft and lazy, just barely audible over the music pulsing in the air around us.

"You belong with *me*, wherever that might take us," he returned with an unexpected degree of sincerity.

My chest clenched. "You can't say stuff like that, or I'll cry, and Ash will yell at me for ruining my makeup she worked so hard on."

I felt his cheeks lift against mine with a smile. He lowered my feet to the ground and patted my ass. "Okay, little warrior. Let's get back to the party, then."

I nodded and wriggled out of the remains of my shredded panties. "Guess it's commando for the rest of the night."

"*Fuck*," he growled. "I didn't think that through."

"Too late now," I goaded him with a grin, opening the door and leading us back to the party.

Thank you so much for reading *Curse & Craving*!
Curious about Ashley and her new mentor? What about
Fenodree or Knight or the fate of our heartless villain, Morgan?
While Rebecca and Lochlan's story is complete, so many others
have yet to be told!

In book 2, Venom & Vice, Ashley's stuck working with Casek to
learn her new powers—*unique* magical powers that have
painted a target on her back. What she doesn't know is, Casek
isn't just her teacher, he's also her new bodyguard, and he's
grown very protective of his newest charge.

In book 3, Blood & Breath, Cat finds herself deep in the clutches of
a forbidden love affair. Fate has brought them together in a way
neither expected, but forbidden love comes with a price. Will the
two find a way to overcome or be lost to one another forever?

In book 4, Siege & Seduction, Morgan Le Fay teams up with a sworn enemy to help her achieve a life-long desire, uncovering truths about the villainess that will change everything. Siege & Seduction ties together the four previous books in a romantic adventure full of jaw-dropping twists and heart-stopping heroics you won't want to miss!

Make sure to join my Facebook reader group and keep in touch! Jill's Ravenous Readers!

Acknowledgments

Everyone needs to have at least one person in their lives that they know without fail will be by their side—whether on an impromptu road trip, holding your hair back after a night out, or helping to hide the body. I have been blessed in life to have two of those people by my side. My soul sister, Sarah, who told me I needed to write a book and then held my hand through the entire process. And my husband, Jason, who jumped on the bandwagon with a smile and helped pick up the slack when I was buried deep in creating this book. A special thank you to these two from the depths of my heart, for everything you do and all that you are.

About the Author

Jill Ramsower is a life-long Texan—born in Houston, raised in Austin, and currently residing in West Texas. She attended Baylor University and subsequently Baylor Law School to obtain her BA and JD degrees. She spent the next fourteen years practicing law and raising her three children until one fateful day, she strayed from the well-trod path she had been walking and sat down to write a book. An addict with a pen, she set to writing like a woman possessed and discovered that telling stories is her passion in life.

SOCIAL MEDIA & WEBSITE

Release Day Alerts, Sneak Peak, and Newsletter
To be the first to know about upcoming releases, please join
Jill's Newsletter. (No spam or frequent pointless emails.)
Jill's Newsletter

Official Website: www.jillramsower.com
Jill's Facebook Page: www.facebook.com/jillramsowerauthor
Reader Group: Jill's Ravenous Readers
Follow Jill on Instagram: @jillramsowerauthor
Follow Jill on Twitter: @JRamsower

GLOSSARY OF TERMS

Below are a number of the important terms and characters from *Curse & Craving*. I have included pronunciations as I would say the word, not pronunciations as the dictionary would offer because I have no idea how that works.

Arthur—Powerful Fae General who broke away from Queen Guin and formed the Wild Hunt.

Beltane—The day halfway between the spring equinox and the summer solstice (early May). One of the naturally occurring days when the veil between worlds is the thinnest and the availability of magic is greatest. The Druids celebrated the day with bonfires and used ashes to ensure the protection of their crops and livestock.

Bergresar—Ancient, evil Shadow Fae.

Blood Magic—An ancient, dark magic that requires the use of sacrificial blood. Used too many times, blood magic eventually creates a bloodlust in the user so intense he or she is reduced to a state of mindlessness in the search of blood. This condition is considered a flagrant violation of the laws of nature by most Fae, and thus the use of blood magic is often punishable by death.

Brownie—Small green-skinned Fae that lives peacefully in homes, often known to clean and sometimes steal items for itself.

Draug (*drog*)—Shadow Fae creature that can dissolve into shadow and is drawn to finding jewels and other treasure.

Druid (*drew-id*)—Descendants of the people who were taught the use of rune magic by the Fae.

Elders—Druid leadership council made up of 11 district members, one of which is elected as the chief elder who presides over council meetings.

Erlking (*earl-king*)—The elected leader of the Wild Hunt.

Faery—A world with latent magic that can be accessed from Earth via portals.

Fae—The inhabitants of Faery, also known as Faeries.

Fenodree (*Fen-oh-dree*)—The Fae man exiled to live in the Shadow Lands because he broke Seelie law by marrying a human woman.

Gally Trot—(aka Knight) The name given to Merlin's canine companion.

Glamour—The use of magic to change one's appearance.

Guinevere—Queen of the Seelie Fae.

Hellfire—Unnatural green fire that burns through anything it encounters. One of the only know beings to wield the substance is the Nuckalavee.

Hell Hound—Unseelie creatures usually found in pairs. They are roughly the size and look of a large Earthen dog but have red glowing eyes and violent temperaments.

Lambton Worm—Dragon-like aggressive Unseelie Fae who lives primarily in water but can survive on land as well.

Leannan-Sidhe (*Lee-an-an shee*)—Vampire-like Unseelie

that uses glamour to lure Fae or human prey. They feed their magic through the draining of their victim's blood.

Mab—Extremely powerful Queen of the Unseelie killed by her twin brother Merlin.

Merlin—Eccentric Fae sorcerer.

Nukalavee—Shadow Fae that is so ancient and malevolent that it is believed even the mention of its name brings bad luck. It is known for its unique ability to create Hell Fire, and can manipulate dreams among its numerous dark powers.

Oberon— (aka Alberich) The leader of the Wild Hunt and foster father to Lochlan.

Phooka (*poo-kah*)—Small Unseelie about the size of a young child usually found near large bodies of water.

Portal—Magical doorway between worlds.

Red Cap—Vicious Unseelie known for cannibalism and wearing caps soaked in the blood of their victims.

Rune—Magical symbol used in spells.

Seelie (*See-lee*)—The Fae who live peaceably under the Seelie Queen's rule; most of the Seelie possess light magic.

Shadow Fae—The inhabitants of the Shadow Lands. Not technically Fae, but became known as such after their world became joined with Faery.

Shadow Lands—A dark and dangerous place believed to have been joined with Faery in an ancient cataclysm of worlds. The landscape steeped in perpetual darkness appears barren, and its inhabitants are a vicious face of beings who possess dark magic.

Sight—The ability to see through a Fae glamour.

Sluagh—(aka The Unforgiving Dead) A host of malevolent souls of deceased evil Fae.

Sword of Light—(aka Excalibur) A sword crafted by an ancient species able to imbue iron with magic. The sword is also known as "The Answerer" for its ability to force any at its blade to tell the truth.

Trace—The ability to transport instantly from one place to another.

Twilight Realm—A temporal plane between worlds that can only be accessed with a combination of light and shadow magic.

Unseelie (*Un-see-lee*)—The Fae who refused to be governed by the Seelie Queen and are thus forced to live in the Wilds of Faery. They tend to be vicious and solitary creatures.

Wild Hunt—The group of Fae men who separated from the Seelie kingdom when the Erlking Arthur had a falling out with the Seelie Queen Guinevere. They are self-governed warriors with no lands of their own and who choose to roam in search of prey to hunt.

Wilds—The uncivilized parts of Faery outside of the Seelie kingdom inhabited by the animalistic Unseelie.